Something I never knew still existed, something too deadly to exist, was emerging from the darkness of the freight compartment into the light of the passageway. A metallic horror moving on metal tentacles, armored sensors glinting. All of us crowded around the viewing console jerked back, as if the image were the thing itself. "What's that?"

The Battle-Captain knew. "A boarding machine." My ancestor was speaking with cold authority, masking his excitement, his fear.

"A fighting machine that's programmed to kill every living being it meets, to force its way to the flightdeck, to hold the flightdeck against all attacks until its masters arrive to take over the ship. If there are no masters to arrive—then it will hold the flightdeck forever. And we will all be dead."

EDWARD LLEWELLYN
has also written:

The Douglas Convolution
The Bright Companion
Prelude To Chaos

SALVAGE
AND
DESTROY

Edward Llewellyn

DAW BOOKS, INC.
DONALD A. WOLLHEIM, PUBLISHER

1633 Broadway, New York, NY 10019

First Printing, January 1984

1 2 3 4 5 6 7 8 9

DAW TRADEMARK REGISTERED
U.S. PAT. OFP. MARCA
REGISTRADA. HECHO EN U.S.A.

PRINTED IN U.S.A.

PART ONE

I

**Extract from Commander's Report, First Sol Mission
(Terran 1680 AD)**

(Machine-Translated into English from the original Ara)

*(Earth). . . . the only oxygen planet in the Sol System is
violent in both environment and inhabitants. The diurnal and
annual cycles are similar to those of many worlds in the Cluster,
but the climatic changes are extreme. Surface temperatures range
from negative sixty to positive seventy and winds reach velocities
of two hundred. Two-thirds of the surface is covered by corro-
sive saline seas. Every mobile life-form preys on some other
life-form.*

*Because of these harsh conditions the only intelligent beings,
the Humans, are belligerents. They are typical ultoids, unusual
only in that they are larger than most other ultoid races and are
divided into two sexes. On Earth their intelligence appears to be
directed primarily toward plundering each other's property and
destroying each other's persons. Their technology is protobar-
barian with large populations living in savagery. They have no
self-powered machines and their ships are wind-driven. During
the last ten of their generations however they have developed
explosives which they use in war.*

*Our Ara compulsion to rescue fellow-intelligents in imminent
danger had already forced my survey teams into saving some
fifty varicolored Humans whom I was holding in stasis while
looking for a safe place to release. Not wishing to add to that
number I selected an underpopulated continent for the collection
of plage data (later I learned it was called Newengland,
Northamerica). Despite my caution the lander, skimming low
above the edge of the sea, lifted over a headland and suddenly
came upon a group of Humans isolated on a sand-spit by the
rising tide. Their situation did not speak well for their intelligence,
but the pilot reacted to instinct rather than hesitating to reason.
He immobilized them and, as most of the specimens were small,
his team was able to load them into the lander before the
sand-spit was swept clear, and as they could only be revived on
the Ship he had to lift them to the Ship. The Ethic forced me to*

add them to those already in stasis, and as I could not identify any surface release-site which my conscience would accept as safe, I still had them aboard when we started the return voyage to Edrin.

By then only half my crew were fit for duty. It occurred to me that the Humans might be able to grasp the rudiments of watch-keeping, so I revived the one nearest my own size and, after her initial shock, she proved able, willing, and affectionate. She quickly became sufficiently fluent in Ara to tell me that her name was Mary Knox, that she was twelve years old, and was grateful to us for her rescue. After she had been shown how to use the autoinstructors she learned the elements of ship-handling, and was able to take over a watch on Main Drive.

Her physical and mental similarities to us outweighed her differences and, most important, she seemed immune to space-sickness. I therefore explained our need and asked her to select from her fellows those most likely to make adequate watch-keepers.

She chose individuals smaller than herself, supervised their revival, calmed their fears, showed them how to use the autoinstructors, and aided them in learning the duties of the various stations. The number of Humans in my crew increased as the voyage progressed. They also increased in size, and it was only then that I realized they were immature specimens.

Against Mary's advice I revived one of the largest adults, thinking it would also be the wisest. The result was disaster, and after shocking it back into stasis I thenceforth revived only those whom she selected. Despite the fact that several grew taller than Mary during the remaining four years of the return voyage she retained her authority and emphasized it by being the first to produce young.

None of the Humans who had been revived wished to return to the oblivion of stasis, so I could increase the rest-periods of my Ara cohort thus lengthening their life-span and reducing their sick-time. When we arrived in orbit around Edrin I had fifty-eight trained Humans in my crew plus thirty human infants, the young of a race who seem physiologically and psychologically suited to space, immune to space-sickness, and not excessively pugnacious outside their Terran habitat.

They can make a valuable contribution toward meeting the shortage of spacers. Apart from a few plants (''char,'' kohi,'' ''tabac'' etc.) they are the only positive outcome of the Mission. The planets in all the other starfields explored are too widely dispersed for useful inclusion in Cluster civilization. We have buoyed the interstarfield vortices and left a radiomonitor in Sol orbit to measure cosmic variables in that section of the Spiral Arm. It should continue to transmit data back via the buoy-repeaters for millennia.

In view of our heavy casualties and meager returns I cannot recommend further exploratory voyages among the outer starfields of the Cluster. I do recommend that the Ship be placed in care and preservation and left in orbit around Edrin. Mary Knox not only taught it to speak her language but, during her initial watches while she still thought the Ship alive, she talked to it a great deal. She was an "orphan girl," a term whose import I did not then appreciate, and had apparently met little kindness and suffered much abuse during her twelve years. She addressed the Ship as "Hyperion," the name of an animal (horse) she had had to tend and which she was convinced had been the only living creature on Earth to love her and to listen to her. As a result of its conversations with Mary Knox the Ship now assumes that its sex is female, and that its name is Hyperion. It only acknowledges orders prefixed by that name, which is not a word easily pronounced by an Ara.

> Akar of the Scar Clan
> Commander, Sol Mission.

Classified Addendum:
A low-level survey of the entire world showed no traces of Drin. This confirms that all starfields explored are now clean.

Akar's report contains most of what I knew about Humans prior to my arrival on Clur. Since then I have become suffi-ciently fluent in their language to appreciate both its absurdities and subtleties, and sufficiently anthropoid to mimic a human male. I remain however what I was: Lucian (the English approxi-mation of L'cien), Ultron of the Ult, Extron of the Fringe, Enforcer of the Will (titles which inspire awe in Ult but sound faintly absurd in English). I went to Clur at the request of the Prime Ultron, and it is with our meeting on the terrace of his villa that this account commences.

"Welcome L'cien!" The Primate, slim and exquisite in ex-tended youth, rose to greet me with the courtesy due an equal, a ceremonial relic of the distant days when all Ultrons had indeed been equal.

"Greetings S'en Sart'r!" I bowed to avoid overtopping him by a head, and sat down when he waved me to a couch.

He inspected me with large limpid eyes, then spoke with a

flatness which left me uncertain whether he was voicing a question, a statement, or an accusation. "You know about Humans."

"I know of them. I was Extron of the Edrin Sector when Akar brought back the originals."

"You have studied them?"

"Only to the extent of reading Akar's report and evaluating their potential as spacers. I have traveled in human-crewed ships but have had no other contact with them."

"Until recently you were the only Ultron to have ever heard of them." The Primate keyed the terminal beside his couch. "Here is an updated report. Give me your opinion of it."

Interaction between Human and Ara Colonies on Edrin.

At last census Humans numbered about one hundred thousand, but as most of them are spacers, the count is inaccurate. They are the smallest group on Edrin, whose total population is over ten million, drawn from fifty-one races (Edrin is a trading world), including three million Ara. Only Ara and Humans are now willing to serve in space, and have formed an alliance stronger than is usual between civilized peoples (Ara are simple-minded benevolents and Humans quasibarbarian).

The outstanding Ara characteristic is a concern for the well-being of fellow-intelligents. It is this concern which keeps them crewing spaceships after all other spacefaring races have given up such an uncomfortable life-style. Ships are still the only means of transportation between worlds outside the Teleport Net, and if ship transportation were to fail many Fringe planets would be isolated, allowing their peoples to slide back into barbarism.

This continuing need for crews stimulates the sense of service stamped deep into the genetic structure of every Ara. Unfortunately their inherited altruism is not associated with immunity to space-sickness. Civilization's outward drive faded with increasing casualties and decreased returns. The First Sol Mission was the last exploratory voyage, and, as can be seen from the Commander's report, the only inhabited planet discovered was savage in all respects.

Opinions differ as to whether the Mission justified itself by bringing back the founders of the present human Colony. Those worlds dependent on shipping consider that the existence of human spacers has been important to their economies. Those worlds for whom shipping is not essential but who have had some contact with Humans consider them likely to be a source of disturbance in the future. Both groups agree that Humans are unusually well-suited for service in space. And space, both groups also agree, is the best place for Humans. On other people's planets they tend to be intolerant, arrogant, and avaricious.

Nevertheless, the combination of human talents and Ara education has produced crews of a caliber unmatched since the Exploration Era. The two races complement each other, for while Humans do not share Ara altruism they have a drive almost as effective; an instinctual sense of relative values and a fascination with trade. A fascination which lures them onto worlds at which even the Ara balk. They land on planets which have dropped out of civilization, trading with the neobarbarians and sometimes fighting with them. And they make their voyages to take a profit rather than to provide a service; behavior offensive to the traditional merchant-peoples of the Cluster.

The last characters faded from the screen. "Your comments, Luc'n?"

"That carries the claw marks of a Societist! The Ara are a steadfast people. They have served civilization well. Their naïveté is their strength. They still believe in the rightness of good. And basically they are Ult. To call them simple-minded benevolents is to insult the memory of our common ancestors!"

"I am not seeking your opinion of our devout but declining relatives. I am asking whether you agree with that description of Humans?"

"I hardly know enough to comment. The facts are probably accurate. But a race cannot be both venturesome and placid. Humans have talents which they do not display when grounded."

"I note that they are divided into two sexes." The Primate's serene expression approached the smug. "Such sexual bimorphism generates internal turmoil and external hostility. Those unfortunate races with the brains to control energy and the rutting habits of the schanorn usually destroy themselves, sooner or later." He spoke with that infallibility which allowed neither contradiction nor question. "All reproduction involves emotion, even among hermaphrodites such as ourselves. To mature is to regress from logical thought to irrational action. I hope that metamorphosis is still far in the future for both of us, L'cien!" A reminder that while the Primate himself was close to immortal I had only interim status. That I could still be relieved of my rank; released to mature, to breed, to age and to die. He let the lure of extended longevity dangle before me for a moment. "Why did Humans excite your interest?"

My irritation at being questioned overcame my usual caution.

"Why was I interested in Humans? Why am I still interested in them? Because of their immunity to space-sickness. Because of their natural ability as spacers. Most of all because they volunteer to serve in space! Council does not seem concerned about the shortage of crews. Those of us who enforce the Council's edicts along the Fringe see that shortage becoming critical."

The Primate must have noted my imperfect emotional control and filed the fact in his own perfect memory. "What do you know about the situation on Terra?"

"What has been happening on Earth?" For over two centuries the Monitor left by Akar had retransmitted only geophysical and cosmic data back along the string of beacons linking vortex to vortex. Then, less than a century ago, signals from Earth had started to break through on every band. Signal restoration is an art in a Cluster where the distances are vast, signals can travel at only the speed of light between repeaters, and the Galaxy itself fills the background with its private mutterings. An art which our experts had mastered and it was on their restoration of Terran broadcasts that knowledge of events on Terra were based. "The situation on Earth?" I repeated. "The last I heard they were fighting each other with metal ships, high explosives, and aircraft. I am interested in human spacers within civilization. Not human barbarians outside it!"

"At the time of Akar's visit they had no self-powered machines and had only just attained firearms. An advance to even the stage you describe is unprecedented, and their technology has expanded exponentially since then. They now have nuclear power. More significantly—they have fusion weapons!"

"What?" I forgot protocol and stared directly at the Primate. "It took our ancestors many generations—" I broke off, embarrassed by my vehemence and silenced by a sudden sadness. Internal war and fusion weapons could not coexist for long; the combination would soon terminate all Terran culture, if not Terra itself.

The Primate must have noted this second exhibition of emotion. "The current forecasts, based on Monitor information, predict the survival time for Terran culture as between fifteen and fifty Terran years."

"So soon?"

"That is what the forecasters estimate." The Primate hitched his gown higher over his thin shoulders. "When the human Colony intercepted the first signals from the Monitor they requested Council that contact be made with their home world."

"Intercepted? They have a listening-station for Monitor signals?"

"Apparently they have. They were only able to pick up scattered words and phrases, but they claimed meanings were unimportant. The existence of a signal was the real message. It showed their kin had achieved a telecommunications technology, proving they had risen above barbarism and should be considered for contact."

"That is, I suppose, not illogical." I was trying to anticipate the Primate's attitude.

"They went further. They asked for permission to send a second mission to Earth. They were prepared to pay the expenses and to provide the crew. Your Humans must have prospered greatly, L'cien!"

They were not "my Humans," but the Primate was in no mood to be corrected on details, so I only said, "I presume Council refused?"

"The request never reached Council. It was dealt with by Junior Executives, as is usual when dealing with microminorities. They replied in the Council's name, congratulating the Humans on the speed of their Terran kin's technological advance. When the culture emerged from the technological-belligerent phase Earth would certainly be considered for inclusion in civilization. Until then contact was inadvisable."

"And the news that Terrans have fusion has changed that policy?"

"It brought Terra to the attention of Senior Executives. They told the Planners to prepare a report for Council." The Primate lay back on his couch and outlined the sequence which had followed.

The leap demonstrated by nuclear fusion had both disturbed and reassured the Planners. A barbarian people advancing from gunpowder to atomics in three generations could be dangerous if loose, but analysis had satisfied them that Terra was now a self-solving problem. The millennial forecasters were consulted by the eon forecasters and both groups of specialists agreed that Terra was unlikely to become an irritant in the immediate or distant future. They had advised Council that "vigilant inaction" would be the wisest policy.

The news that the Terrans had placed artificial satellites in orbit and were dispatching probes to neighboring planets changed the Planners' advice to "Immediate Action." The merest possibility that these barbarians, so rapidly becoming technologically sophisticated, would detect the Monitor, use it to vector on a vortex, and at some time in the future come bursting into civilization, raised ancient fears. That was how we Ult had originally invaded and finally conquered the Cluster. After discussion the Council had decided that a mission must be despatched to destroy the Monitor and suggested to the Ara that they mount it.

For the first time in recorded history the Ara had refused a Council suggestion. Their casualties on such a long voyage could not be justified now that there were Humans able to make it in less time and without major losses. Ara logic was too clear for Council to strengthen the suggestion to a request and so a message had been sent to the Colony stating that Council had reconsidered the Colony's offer to crew a Second Sol Mission and was now prepared to approve.

The Humans on Edrin had responded by offering to make a trade. Their kin on Earth had risen to technobarbarism at an unprecedented rate and were now accelerating toward autodestruction. The hectic flowering of a great barbarian culture was approaching its climax and civilization could do nothing to prevent its end. But if Humans were to be responsible for crewing the mission and deactivating the Monitor they wanted a salvage component included in the program so they could rescue something from the wreckage of their parent world.

I had been listening with growing incredulity. "Surely Council did not accept that!"

"The Council, who knew little about your Humans, did consider it. I, who had learned about them, would normally have vetoed such a dangerous proposal." He paused for me to appreciate where the real authority lay. "But danger must sometimes be accepted to divert a greater danger and to achieve a greater good. The probability is high that Terra will autodestruct before Terrans achieve inertial drive, but the converse probability, though small, is real. Their scientists seem to be on the verge of inertia theory."

"They would have to make such immense strides—" I stopped. It was not my place to point out to the Primate the generations of engineering genius needed to go from inertia theory to inertial drive. "This sudden technological explosion on Terra—could it have been initiated by Drin survivors?"

The Primate's face reflected his displeasure at my reference to our Old Enemy, but he answered me directly enough. "My Executives assure me that all traces of the Drin had been eradicated from the Cluster long before the Sol Mission discovered Earth. And Akar's report shows all starfields explored were clean."

"Of course! Please forgive my precipitate suggestion."

The Primate excused me with a gesture. "It is to deal with the slight threat presented by the Terrans themselves that I have approved acceptance of the Colony's offer. We have said that they can send down salvage parties to Earth, but only under certain conditions. The crew must be made up of the most experienced and trustworthy of the human captains. The Governor of Edrin must supervise the selection. All Humans aboard must be under psychic lock."

"How did the Colony respond?"

"They have agreed. Their message of thanks assumed that as Council had revived the project, then Council would pay for it."

I laughed.

"Council accepted the Colony's terms, but stipulated that an Ultron Adviser must accompany the mission."

I froze. The Primate did not need to say anything further. My passing interest in Humans, my physical resemblance to them, this meeting, all showed that I was the Ultron already named for a task which, in addition to being dangerous, promised to be uncomfortable, undignified, and unnecessary. I had undertaken more than my share of expeditions to enforce the Council's will, returning to be congratulated on my success, criticized for my methods, and resented for my recommendations. I knew a great deal more about the realities of space than either the Primate or his advisers, none of whom ventured outside the Teleport Net. But the fact that he had left his capital on Ladrin and come to Clur in person showed he took the remote threat from Terra seriously. If I refused his challenge I was likely to lose my status and my extended future.

For a moment I considered that alternative; a prospect not as unpleasant as it had once been. I would be appointed Governor of some Fringe world, make my last metamorphosis, and become a mature Ult. I would discover the joy of breeding, about which I had heard so much. I would also pay the price of maturation—I would age and die. Age slowly, for we Ult are a long-lived race, but age inevitably. I decided I was not yet ready to surrender continuing youth.

"If you wish, S'en Sart'r, I will go as Adviser."

"I had hoped you would, Luc'n. You are one of the few Ultrons of your class to have my complete trust. When you return you can expect to be raised to permanent rank and Council membership." The Primate paused to let me appreciate that reward. "How long before you will be ready for the journey?"

"I will have to learn the human language and metamorphose into human form."

"You will imitate a Human?" The Primate allowed himself to show surprise, and keyed his terminal. A solidium of a human male and a human female appeared, turning slowly to display their bodies. "Gross—but ultoid!" He looked at me. "You already resemble a perfected image of the male."

"The differences are too obvious for me to pass as one. And I will need a Human's size and strength."

"If you think it necessary to take on the appearance of a savage, then make the change!" The Primate's face showed his distaste. "Your villa terminal can access Central Information so you can call up whatever data you need on these barbarians while you are making yourself look like one. My Executives will supply you with anything else you consider you require." He stood up. The interview was over. He was free to turn his mind toward the major problems of maintaining tranquility on the thousands of civilized worlds in the Cluster; he had dealt with the problem of one microminority within it and one barbarian world outside it. "Inform my Chief Executive when you are ready to leave. The task of the mission is to silence the Monitor. Yours is to make certain the task is completed and that any threat of a future Terran incursion into civilization is removed." He took from his sleeve a small transparent cube, and laid it on the table between us. "This contains my imagon. Consult it during your journey."

I stared at the cube, then at the Primate. "But the equipment to reconstruct—?"

"I understand the Explorer-class vessel in which you will be traveling is equipped to produce imagons from recoes. Activate mine regularly, whether or not you need my advice. Then, upon your return, it will be able to tell me of the mission's achievements." He raised his hand. "May the Light shine upon you, L'cien!"

"May the Light illuminate you, S'en Sart'r!" I bowed as he left the terrace, then picked up the cube and rolled it on my palm; the convoluted threads embedded within flashed in the sunlight. He had assured me of his complete trust; giving me his imagon showed he doubted my wisdom.

I shrugged and put the thing in my belt-pouch. At least it would protect me against future charges of ill-advised actions. Then I walked across the terrace and stood watching the sunset shadows spreading across the well-ordered landscape of Clur. Straight from the turbulence of the Fringe, smarting from the Primate's subtle contempt, I was irritated rather than calmed by the tranquility before me.

Clur is the epitome of a teleport world. Its planning is complete—even the weather is programmed. A cool night to follow a warm day, an evening breeze to ripple the surface of its lakes, a dawn shower to water its manicured countryside. A planet cleared of distractions and landscaped into a bland background for scholarly thought. A world free from the scars of manufacture and trade, the giant systems which serve the intellectual life on its surface buried underground. An information center where reports from all over the Cluster are collected, classified, abstracted, and stored. A library world run by librarians for librarians, generously supported by those who need access to its data-banks. Scholars from every culture in the Cluster come to Clur to extract wisdom from its catalogued knowledge and members of many races to collect facts they can use to their advantage.

The tranquility of Clur irritated me because the systems which allowed that tranquility were hidden away beneath its beautified surface. It typified our whole Cluster civilization; a Teleport Net of tranquil worlds with the energetic societies of the Fringe out of the public eye and far from the Council's mind.

A civilization burdened with impedimenta from the past. Customs, courtesies, clothing, philosophies—all ornamented with items which had once been important but were now symbolic or meaningless. The need for a function fades but the symbol endures, gaining prestige as it loses relevance. Savages are the least likely to perpetuate the pointless, for their race-memories are short and empirical. They discard the ineffective so their current customs reflect aspects of reality, even when hidden. Barbarians keep few records, apart from genealogies, so they forget easily and do not wear the outworn for long. It is only within civilization that superficial fashions change while antique futilities remain.

We Ultrons, we High Intellects, are ruled more strictly by the tyranny of the past than any other group in the Cluster. Only those few among us who go out from the Net to enforce the Council's will among the less structured worlds of the Fringe realize how firmly we are held captive by our own congealed customs. And now I was about to go farther than any Ult had been for millennia, in a ship crewed by a people whose actions were less predictable than those of any race I knew.

II

Some ultoid races, Humans for example, develop by gradual growth from infancy to adulthood. Others advance in a stepwise fashion through a series of metamorphoses. We Ult are unique in that we can delay our final step into maturity, and can also mimic most other ultoid races through controlled metamorphosis.

The relationship between the ultoid body and the rational brain is universal throughout the Cluster. Life has arisen on every planet where it can exist, but intellect only in those species which, however different their origins, have shown evolutionary convergence. Even Humans, evolving on their distant world, are true ultoids. It seems that the genetic coding which produces a brain capable of a "generative grammar"—and hence of a language—is interlocked with the ultoid form, at least as far as oxygen-breathers within the Cluster are concerned. The possibility—and potential—of non-ultoid intelligence is an abstract and much-discussed question.

On Clur I had all the facilities for programmed metamorphosis, including a genetic catalog of the Edrin Colony, so I was able to design a pattern to control my change. I withdrew to my villa while it was in progress and one evening when my restructured skeleton was not yet fully recalcified but my fluency in English was almost adequate, the light on my terminal glowed and the machine whispered, "Sir!"

"Yes? What is it?" The terminal was a sedulous scavenger of information on any subject it was sent to search, but it had little sense of relative values and was liable to call with every minutia discovered. Moreover, ever since I had told it to speak English so I could practice my own, it had adopted a stilted version it insisted was correct but which I found irritating. A machine has no inherent taste. It accepts as "best" the current scholarly examples of best.

"There is a Human resident on Clur."

"What?" I found myself standing, turning to face the terminal as though it were a person. To my knowledge only Scholars resided on Clur and Humans had not as yet produced a single

17

Scholar nor shown any promise of ever doing so. "A Human on Clur?"

"That is what I said, sir. Do you wish to hear the details of the Human to whom I am referring?"

"Yes—yes—of course!"

"The Human's name is Mark David Joseph Knox. All Humans consider themselves members of the Knox Clan, a custom they have acquired from the Ara. Among the Ara the crew of a ship is the Sept of a Clan. The Humans have enlarged that concept to its final absurdity, so that 'Knox' is common to all of them and of no value as a differentiator. It is a vestigial cultural—"

"I know that! Where is it?"

"It is an he, sir. Humans, unlike most other intelligent races, are divided into two sexes, male and female—"

"I know that too! Where is he?"

"He was in the Medical Complex. He is now—"

"In the Medical Complex? A Human Scholar? And injured! What happened?"

"I do not know the source of his injuries, sir. Medical records are not available to Central Information. But the published report states that his new leg-bud has been implanted and growth is satisfactory. And sir?"

"Yes—go on!"

"The Human is not a Scholar. He is a patient. He is also the first Human to have ever resided on Clur. It is a happy coincidence that he is here at the very time when you are pursuing your researches into his race. I would like to point out that it was only by my extensive explorations of all possible sources of information that I found him."

"I am impressed by your industry and your persistence. I will tell Central Information that you are a terminal of merit!"

"Thank you, sir. The Human is at present recuperating in his villa. His call number is—"

"Not now! Tell me later."

"As you wish, sir." A pause. "Did the importance of my information warrant my disturbing you?"

"Yes—yes!" I said to satisfy the terminal's hunger for approval and to stop it talking. "Now let me have quiet to consider it. Do not disturb me again tonight."

I sat down slowly, already disturbed by the news of a Human nearby, a Human I should interrogate on those aspects of humanity about which I was still uncertain. But I did not want my first discussion with a Human to be with a sick one, and especially not with one lacking a leg. For an Ultron sickness is an ancestral memory; death an apotheosis postponed to the far future.

To the far future for those Ultrons who retain their rank and travel only by teleport. Casualties on the teleport system are zero. Traveling by ship made death a possibility. A small possibility when voyaging between the civilized worlds of the Cluster; appreciable aboard an Explorer-class vessel venturing out into the starfields beyond civilization.

Nor, I told myself, would an injured Human welcome a visit from an inquisitive Scholar, for as such I would appear to be. With that thought I put the existence of Mark Knox from my mind and returned to studying the bizarre brutalities of human history. They seemed to produce more history in a year than most races did in a thousand.

I attempted to ignore the existence of Mark Knox; my terminal did not let me. It dug information about him from the local records and insisted on presenting its findings to me. He turned out to be a young and impulsive captain who had had his leg blown off in an ambush while trading on a barbarian world. His crew evidently held him in some regard for they had brought him across five starfields to the Advanced Medical Center on Clur in the hope that the Medics could regrow his leg.

The Medics had never seen a Human before and had hardly known such a race existed, but they had repaired many other species of ultoid and promised they could repair Mark Knox. So his crew had left him on Clur and sailed to recoup the cost of bringing him there.

While his leg was regrowing he was living in a villa on the far side of the Azrin Lake, and spending most of his time in acrimonious arguments with the local Administrator. That official had rightly ruled that the Human was not a visiting Scholar and therefore not entitled to access Central Information. Mark Knox had reacted with typical spacer arrogance. He accused the Administrator of bureaucratic rigidity, claimed a spacer could "fake any interlocks you groundhogs can dream up!" and started to experiment with his terminal's coding. His meddling isolated its output so that my terminal lost track of its activities and I lost what little interest I had in his.

While Ult and Human may look somewhat alike, the psychological differences are immense. Humans tend toward affect, Ult toward intellect. From the beginning of history the Council of Ultrons has consisted of the wisest among us. Warriors while we were establishing dominance over the Cluster, Zealots when spreading the Faith of the Light among the conquered peoples, and Scholars when reason had shown the fallacies of the Faith.

Early in the Era of Skepticism our Scholars discovered that by postponing maturity an Ult could increase longevity, and so attain the wisdom which comes from prolonged studies. Thereafter ambitious young Ult arrested their growth to gain the time needed to become High Scholars. Each succeeding generation arrested at an earlier and earlier age until now the majority of Council consisted of Ultrons with the minds of High Scholars and the bodies of Ult children.

Because few established Ultrons choose to mature, their lifespans are immense and only a handful of new members can be added to Council from each generation. Potential Ultrons are selected in early childhood by an intense intellectual evaluation, their growth is slowed while they study and, if they attain Ultron status, is arrested before puberty.

Most Ultrons therefore treat their bodies as necessary nuisances, as mere mind support systems. They have little need to travel for Council seldom meets in the flesh but conducts its business by remote congregation and rules through a vast bureaucracy of Governors, Executives, and Administrators. However there must still be Ultrons capable of enforcing Council authority, and the body of an Ult child is ill-suited to the slamming acceleration of ships and the rugged conditions on many worlds. So some who fail the first selection are given a second opportunity shortly before their final metamorphosis into adulthood.

I was unusual in that after I had been selected at the first competition, my parents had dissuaded me from arresting growth. (They held that the system was the antithesis of natural selection and would eventually destroy our race.) But after watching them age, and when I myself was on the verge of becoming irretrievably adult, I entered the second competition, was accepted, appointed Acting Ultron, and sent to supervise Sectors of the Fringe.

Out there my size was an advantage, but within the Net it suggested to established Ultrons that I was a "retrieved failure" and they treated me as an intellectual inferior. Something I resented but knew unwise to dispute until Council had confirmed my tenure.

The disdain of my seniors had made me sensitive about my body, but as I changed into human form my self-image altered. I had set up my metamorphosis program so as to maintain primary sexual characteristics at prepuberty while allowing secondary sexual characteristics to develop. My final form was therefore potentially unstable, but I judged the small risk of slipping into unplanned maturity as worth taking because it allowed me to gain the size, the strength, and the clothed appearance of an adult human male.

When I finally inspected myself on video I no longer saw an oversize overmuscled Ultron but a lithe, balanced, and effective being. Seventy-five kilograms, one hundred and eighty-five centimeters—the optimum size for a human male. Hair black, eyes brown, skin olive, and lips full—the mix of racial features the present Colonists considered handsome. A nose of the shape they called "Mohawk" gave my face a proud dignity. I was an Ultron who looked like a man, talked like a man, and should be able to act like more than a man in every mode but the sexual.

A body somewhat similar to that of a mature Ult. A general-purpose design, a triumph in trade-offs, optimum only in its ubiquity, unspecialized physically and psychologically flexible. A brain capable of supporting the patterns of the Ultron mind so that I could still use mentorsion if I needed to enforce my authority. A body able to withstand the demands Humans seemed to habitually make on theirs, and an appearance which would allow me to live among them. They, of course, would know I was the Ultron Adviser but might accept me with less resentment if my rank and race were not obvious.

I turned from the video to don the spacer gear which the Governor of Edrin had shipped to me. The blue body-suit was similar to that once worn by Ult spacers, a complex interweaving of metallic and synthetic tubules so that it adjusted to protect its wearer against heat and cold, pressure and vacuum. With hood and gloves it could even function as an emergency spacesuit. The fabric was soft to the skin but under impact it would work-harden instantly into armor. I let it adjust to an easy fit, watching my image. The suit had been designed for function rather than style, but it set off my new body well.

"Vanity!" chided the Zealot.

We Ult inherit the knowledge and skills of our forebears; a unique legacy which has helped us to become the arbiters of justice throughout the Cluster. Some of us also inherit the memories of certain individual ancestors, memories which have a pseudolife of their own and are liable, when aroused, to express the opinions of their original owners. Fortunately the delivery of a few brief comments usually exhausts them and they sink back into "sleep."

I was burdened with three. One, "Primal," was from the dawn of our race, and the occasional glimpses I got of his world

showed a wilderness of swamp and forest. His only interests
were hunting, mating, and fighting. I seldom encountered anything which awakened him. The second was "Sarthim," a Battle-
Captain who had fought in our long struggle to establish the
Unity of the Cluster. He usually only surfaced when I went
aboard a ship. The third, the memory which had just reproved
me, was a religious fanatic, one of the Zealots who had preached
the Faith and ruled the Ult during the wars and dominated the
Council after victory. Their religious mysticism, which hangs
like a fog over that period of Ult history, had been burned away
by the rising sun of reason. Superstition can only flourish when
shielded by emotion and fertilized by blood. Ult High Scholars,
turning from their necessary concentration on the martial arts,
had been able to explain away most religious phenomena. The
Eras of Speculation and Skepticism had ended the influence of
the Zealots and they only survived as shadow-memories in a few
minds.

Most Ultrons with ancestral memories silence them by psycho-
surgical excision. I had never obliterated mine because I had
grown fond of them during my unorthodox childhood and because their advice in practical matters was sometimes useful. But
at that moment I found the Zealot's reprimand irritating and I
blocked further criticisms as I snapped on the standard spacer
harness, complete with side-arm. Humans still claimed the ancient right of the spacer to go armed. An archaic right but a
custom I must now follow. I rechecked my appearance, smoothed
down my bodysuit, and stowed the rest of my gear in my pack. I
was finished on Clur.

I would go by teleport to an interchange world and thence by
ship to Edrin. I planned to travel as a Human and had tossed
away my Scholar's robe and was putting my helmet and cloak in
my pack when my terminal chimed. I walked over and picked up
the print-out.

I glanced at it, stared at it, read it a third time. Then I swung
on the terminal. "Where did you get this?"

"From the Catalog of Profiles, sir."

"The Catalog? How?"

The terminal's timidity became acute anxiety. "I was continuing my search for data on Humans, sir. As you directed me. I
was searching with diligence, sir. I scanned the Catalog of
Profiles—"

"What is a human profile doing in the Catalog? It is not a
storage dump for barbarian data?"

"I do not know, sir. It was not there when I checked the Catalog before. When you first directed me to search—"

"It was not there then! It should not be there now! It is! Where did it come from?" I shook the print-out at the machine. "How did this get filed in a secure data base?"

"Sir—I do not know!" Then, anxious to escape, "Do you wish me to find out?"

"Yes—and quickly! Who filed it? And how?"

"Immediately, sir!" The terminal light snapped off.

I stared at the print-out, my hand shaking. My human glands were urging me to react with violence. It was not only that a human profile had no place among the profiles of High Intellects; the profile itself was as ominous as a striker poised to swoop.

A profile as ragged as the crests of the Shernee Mountains. As skewed as the hand-axe of the Nargon warriors. A profile that roused primitive metaphors. A profile with a wider span than any I had ever seen.

"Sir!" The terminal was back.

"Yes?"

"The human profile was filed two months ago."

"Filed by whom?"

"The terminal in villa 23406, sir."

"How could a Scholar intrude into Core?"

"The occupant of 23406 is not a Scholar, sir. He—he is a Human. That injured Human, sir. Mark David Joseph Knox. The one I mentioned to you as being the only Human to have ever stayed on this planet, sir. The Human—"

"Enough! Instruct the Area Administrator to report to me here! And at once!"

The terminal flashed acknowledgment and I dragged my cloak and helmet from my pack. I must act with speed and authority. It would be difficult to do either if I appeared as a Scholar or a Human. I put on my regalia and became an Ultron. The cloak hung from my shoulders in majestic folds, screening my body and emphasizing my rank. The golden helmet hid my face and added to my stature. In the distant days when every Ult had been a warrior the helmet had been designed to protect and terrify. Now it was saturated with symbolism and picroelectronics.

I studied myself in the video. A cloaked, high-helmeted, dark-visored stranger stared back. Neither a fragile Scholar nor a barbarian brute. There stood the ruler of worlds; the ultimate in power and wisdom.

"There stands an arrogant over-educated adolescent!" sneered the Battle Captain.

I stifled my critical forebear, picked up my pack, and strode onto the terrace as the Area Administrator's phaeton swooped down to land outside the villa.

The Administrator had probably never seen an Ultron in regalia, but our shadow would have fallen on him, as it falls over every level of government. The image which had awed him from childhood. He began to pant as he clambered from his car, already apologizing for whatever it was that had displeased His Ultimate.

I pushed him back between his two aides, tossed my pack up onto the carrier, (a feat of physical strength which alarmed the aides), and swung in beside the driver. "Villa 23406! Immediately!"

The phaeton shot off the ground as the driver reacted to my command, flashed across the Azrin Lake with the Administrator and aides clutching each other, and swooped down to land. I was out of the phaeton and into the house while the three in the rear seat were still collecting themselves. By the time the Administrator arrived at the door I was back to meet him. "The place is vacant. Where is the occupant?"

"It is assigned to a wounded Human, sir."

"I know that! Where is he?"

"He should be here, sir."

I grasped the Administrator by one paw and marched him through the empty rooms. "As you can observe, he is not here. Nor are his belongings. Also that the villa has been prepared for a new occupant. Go! Check where the Human is!"

The Administrator trotted to his phaeton, consulted his aides, and called his headquarters. Presently he shuffled into the room where I was interrogating the terminal. "Your Ultimate, the Human vacated this villa four days ago. Central Registry had not updated its record so the villa was shown as still occupied. The record has now been amended."

"I am relieved to learn that the occupancy records are now correct!" I said between my teeth, a human speech-mode which suddenly seemed natural. "Please discover the present whereabouts of the late occupant. As he is the only Human ever to have resided on this world of advanced intellects, somebody must have noticed him going somewhere!"

"I will investigate immediately, sir." The Administrator trotted out and presently came trotting back. "The Human took a floater to the Teleport Depot four days ago. He did not tell us he was leaving. That is why the occupancy record was not updated, Your Ultimate."

I consigned the occupancy record to intergalactic darkness.

"The Depot officials noticed him particularly for, as you observed, he was the first Human they had seen. He went to a departure bay and left on the next teleport."

"Which bay? Where has he gone?"

"I am ascertaining that now, sir." An aide slipped in with a whispered message. "And I have ascertained! The Human teleported to Cao. A far world at the outer limit of the Teleport Net. It is a spaceport world for—"

"I know where and what Cao is!"

"Do you wish me to send a message to the Governor of Cao requesting him to invite the Human to return here? Or to retain the Human to await Your Ultimate's instructions?"

"Neither! Arrange a private teleport to Cao for me, ready to leave immediately. Then wait outside!" I returned to interrogating the terminal.

This Mark Knox had used an unorthodox probability matrix, outside any logical pattern, to gain access to core memory. The information he had extracted seemed a mishmash of disconnected facts, the answers to unrelated questions. He had, for example, asked about the status of Fehr, a fringe world evacuated two centuries ago. But some of the other answers to his questions would embarrass Council if made public; might even drive certain Ultrons into premature maturity. If Mark Knox published all he had learned, then I, who had been studying Humans on Clur at that very time, would be involved in the subsequent debacle.

The terminal, loyal to its late use, was insisting that Mark Knox had only started to manipulate interlocks after instructions on its proper use had been withheld; that his motivation had been a human passion for problem-solving; that he had sent it searching through prohibited levels because of animal curiosity.

I cut it off. "How did he get you to prepare that human profile?"

"It arose from casual questions, sir."

"Print them out!"

A storage cube glowed and a sheet slid from the terminal. Casual questions? "Why?" "What the hell's the point of a human race if it's going to blow itself apart?" "What's the purpose of Man?" "What . . . are we Humans supposed to be doing?" Naïve questions perhaps, but hardly casual. The kind I myself had asked long ago about us Ult and, discovering they were non-questions, had never asked again.

Mark Knox had asked them of a machine, and the machine

had answered with a concept and a profile that could excite the savage psyche of a half-civilized people. Another reason to intercept him before he began to spread the story of his experiences on Clur. I put the print-out cube in my belt pouch. Evidence I might need later. Then, ignoring the terminal's protests, I obliterated its programming and returned it to innocence. When I intercepted Mark Knox I would wipe him as clean!

First I had to catch him, catch him personally. I must go to Cao immediately. When I came striding from the villa, my golden helmet gleaming and my blue cloak billowing, I found the whole Administration of Clur had been alerted and was anxious to speed me on my way.

I had been staying on Clur as a Scholar. Only the Governor and the Senior Administrator had known my identity for Ultrons remain unobtrusive, unless some display of Ultron power is needed. The sudden arrival of an Ultron in full regalia is usually the prelude to an inconvenient inquiry, followed by punitive demotions and perhaps the temporary isolation of a world. My appearance was enough to alarm even such an innocuous government as that of Clur, so there was a full escort waiting to whisk me to the Teleport Depot and all the Teleport officials were lined up to guide me to my transit bay. Carrying my pack I strode down the platform, the Teleport Master trotting beside me. As I stepped into the bay I asked, "When will the Master of the Cao Depot know I am arriving?"

"Only after you have arrived, Your Ultimate. The alerting message has to travel with the transit. Perhaps you will remain in your bay for a short while to give the Cao Master time to assemble an escort and ensure that you are properly received."

"Perhaps!" I raised my hand in salutation and as a sign that I was ready to leave.

The bay shivered into the void. I took off my cloak and helmet, and stuffed them into my pack. I appeared in the Cao receiving bay looking like a human spacer and was shouldering my pack when the first Teleport official came bounding past, clearing the platform in frenzied preparation for the ceremonial reception of an unexpected Ultron. I let myself be herded out onto the concourse among startled arrivals from other worlds, and stood looking around the great hall.

III

Cao is an interchange between Net and ships, and a multiracial crowd was moving through the Teleport Depot. An Ara came by giving me the friendly salutation of a fellow spacer, but most of the other travelers looked at me with amusement or disdain. I was a Human; a large, strange, semibarbarian from the frontier, prone to violence and best given a wide berth.

Few human spacers would come through the Depot, for most ships docking at Cao were from nearby worlds and crewed by Ara. Those trading with more distant places were in space for months and crewed by Humans because of human immunity to space sickness. Such deepspace ships only stayed briefly when they called at Cao and it was therefore likely that Mark Knox had been noticed by Teleport officials when he arrived, as I myself was being scrutinized by a hirsute Galarian, squatting on its tripod near the main entrance.

I crossed the concourse, saluted the official with a correct bow, and asked in Ara, "Did Your Officiousness notice another Human arrive in this Depot during the past few days?"

The Galarian acknowledged the bow with a polite bob and a smooth smile, then answered in Galact. "If I had seen another scum-eating Human defiling the beauty of this great hall I would have turned my eyes away, for the sight of you savages makes me want to puke!"

I had my answer; in its rude way it was saying that it had not seen Mark Knox. I ignored the insult directed at my human mask and let the Galarian continue to assume that I did not understand Galact by appearing confused.

There were sounds of amusement from a group who had paused to enjoy the humiliation of an ignorant barbarian. The Galarian, smiling gently and speaking softly, was beginning a new stream of insults when an arm darted out from beside me and a scarlet slash sprang across the official's cheek.

Its mouth and eyes went wide, its paw to its face. A woman spacer had suddenly appeared and her nails were hovering near its muzzle. In an automatic ancestral reaction I swung round, my hand going to my sidearm, turning to cover her back. But already

27

the travelers who had paused for amusement were scurrying away from the threat of violence.

"Easy!" said the woman. "Let me handle it!" She addressed the official in Galact. "I am doing you a kindness, officer."

"A—a kindness?" The official was cowering on its tripod.

"That scratch will heal. Do not let the memory fade!"

"The—the memory?"

"The memory of danger! You are fortunate that my comrade does not understand Galact or you would be lying on the ground from an unnoticed death blow. And he would be walking away without concern." The woman lowered her hand. "Remember— only some of us speak Galact but all of us are savages! The savage response to insult is immediate attack. They must have taught you that at school! We strike too fast to check ourselves. Do I make myself clear in this strange tongue?"

"Yes—yes indeed!" said the Galarian, wiping its cheek.

"You are fortunate that I have waded through this sewer of a world before, so I was expecting insult and ready to restrain my wrath." She patted the flinching official's muzzle. "Or am I frightening you with a fable?" She laughed and turned to me. "I'm Sharon. I like the way you covered us! But this is Cao, not Bloor. The local groundhogs are too careful of their own skins to scratch ours!"

"I am Lucian." I looked down at her. The first human female I had ever spoken to.

"Howdo Lucian!" She held out her hand.

I took it, still studying her. Black hair, blue eyes, mouth full and firm, brown skin, strong—

"Hold that until we get to the hostel!" She freed her hand and shouldered her pack. "The only place you'll find Humans on Cao is at the spaceport. The locals are cluts—like our friend here!" She bowed to the still-cringing Galarian. "The Light guard you, Your Officiousness!"

"The Light guide you!"

"See!" She started toward the entrance of the concourse. "Lean on 'em and they crumple. I gather you've never been on Cao before? I have. We get the floaters outside. Let's share one to the hostel."

If Mark Knox was still on Cao that is where he would be, so I walked with her out onto the plaza. Floaters were sliding across it to park in slots by the Depot entrance, drivers and passengers trotting away to the concourse leaving the floater free for the next user. Sharon picked a slot where nobody was waiting and slipped her pack to the ground. "All self-drive on this world. And God—how they drive!"

The plaza was a swirl of interweaving floaters as passengers streamed in and out of the Depot. "Here comes ours," said Sharon as one parked in the slot beside her and its driver went ambling away. She stooped to pick up her pack.

A slim ultoid skipped past her, jumped into the driver's seat, laughed, and shot the floater backwards out of the slot. The amusement of other waiting passengers encouraged him to an encore, and he skimmed the floater in a circle while giving a gesture of universal obscenity.

With the speed of a striking erne Sharon launched herself from the lip of the slot, caught the floater's handrail as it passed, and swung in beside the still-gesturing driver. It accelerated as he reacted, then slowed and halted as her arm went across his shoulders. There was a brief pause, then it began to back up among swerving vehicles and shouting drivers until it was again level with me.

"This altruist," called Sharon in Galact for the benefit of the now-silent audience, "has kindly offered to take us to the hostel." She stroked the bulge of a nerve-ganglion in the side of the ultoid's neck, and added in English, "Heave my pack aboard before these swamp-slugs start yelping!"

They were starting to yelp as I threw her pack into the rear seat and vaulted in after it. The floater shot out onto the plaza and along one of the avenues. Sharon kept her fingers on the ultoid's neck until we were heading across the plain away from the city and toward the distant spaceport. "I don't like queue-jumpers!" she remarked in English, then reached into her pocket and drew out a sachet. "Here's a small reward for your courtesy." She held it under the ultoid's nose. "Like it?"

"Wonderful! Wonderful!" The floater slowed as the ultoid recognized the fragrance.

"Then you may keep it!" She tucked the sachet into the front of his blouse. "In the future let its perfume remind you of the day you aided two human spacers."

"I will remember!" The driver retrieved the sachet, held it to his face, and his smile became ecstatic. "I will always remember!"

Interested, I asked, "What drug is that?"

"Drug?" She glared back at me. "What the hell do you think I am?"

"Please do not misunderstand me. It was the way—"

"That sachet's filled with dried flower petals from Vernia. To me it has a pleasant smell. To the locals it's Heaven in a knot of

silk!'' She pulled out another sachet and offered it to me.
"When we were on Vernia I stocked up with these. Most
groundhogs here prefer them to cash."

Vernia had dropped out of civilization centuries ago and was
now sinking toward savagery. If she had been trading on Vernia
it was no wonder she was ready to use force. I smelled the
sachet. "That is certainly the perfume of the amarath. Usually
harmless." I handed it back to her.

She glanced at me, took it, and asked the driver, "You know
the spaceport?"

"I work there. You can see it now!"

The plain had become scrub desert, and rising from it were the
twin towers of the spaceport. Towers admired by architects as
paired masterpieces and cursed by spacers as twin menaces.
Radiating from the complex around their base were the berths for
those vessels small enough to dock and for the landers coming
down from the ships loading and unloading in orbit. Passengers
and freight poured through the same warehouses, for passengers
were put into stasis, shipped in containers, and revived at their
destinations. For them a voyage by ship was much like a trip by
teleport—about to leave at one moment, just arrived the next.

The spaceport was surrounded by irrigated parklands, green
with growth, bright with flowers, shining with small lakes.
Scattered through the parks were houses for visitors and staff.
"Know where the Human hostel is?" asked Sharon.

"On the far side of the field. Its amenities are few and
primitive. I would be honored if you became my guests. My
house is luxurious and near many amusements—"

"Thanks, but it's primitive amusements I'm after!" She glanced
at me over her shoulder. "A stiff drink, a hot bath, and a soft
bed! How's that for a program?"

"Most salubrious," I agreed.

"Salubrious?" She stared, waited for me to say more, then
shrugged and slumped in her seat. "Straight to the hostel!" she
snapped at the driver.

He took us across the plaza in front of the Terminal, and down
a narrow road running along the rim of the field itself. We left
the parkland and the road became a dusty track with the field on
the right and the scrub desert of Cao on the left. Ahead appeared
a cluster of squat buildings with an untended garden in front and
a scrapheap behind. Sharon sat up, her hair flying in the wind
and glinting in the sunlight, her lips curving into a smile. "Doesn't
that look good?"

To me it looked like a barbarian settlement on an abandoned world, but I said, "It is indeed a human habitation."

The floater settled with a dusty sigh outside the entrance to the largest building. Sharon jumped out, pulling her pack after her. I descended more slowly, noting that there were plenty of floaters parked in slots by the entrance. If I did catch Mark Knox in this isolated place I would have the means to take him away for interrogation.

The ultoid was still radiating gratitude for Sharon's gift. She patted his cheek and gave him a second sachet. "Put that to the credit of the next spacer you meet. Now be off and enjoy yourself!" She stepped back and waved as the floater rose. I expected a barrage of insults from the driver as soon as he was out of her reach and was ready to squeeze his mind, but he was still waving and smiling as he disappeared in dust along the road to the Terminal.

Sharon laughed. "Not such a bad little bastard!" She turned toward the entrance of the hostel. "Now—let's go get some action!"

The lobby of the hostel was empty except for the manager, a Galarian, half-asleep on its tripod. It awoke sufficiently to give Sharon a polite bob as she walked to the registration console and read the list of Vessels in Port.

"All Ara! And nothing to Edrin for ten days!" She switched to the names of spacers staying in the hostel. "Is this the lot?"

"Those are all who have registered," replied the manager. "There are others who have chosen not to register. I presume it is because they do not seek company during their stay."

"Lazy slugs!" She ran her fingers over the keyboard and "Sharon Zelda" glowed among the other Knoxes.

I scanned the list and could not see a "Mark David." Sharon asked impatiently, "Well? Are you going to register?"

I wanted to follow human protocol as much as possible and keyed "Lucian Titus."

"Good! I thought you were going to chicken out, and I'd have to waste time searching. Come on, let's grab ourselves a cubicle!" And she started across the lobby.

I suddenly realized what she was planning, and tried to tell her that I could enter neither her cubicle nor her body, but she was already racing up the stairs. I ran after her, reached the landing, and stopped.

Ahead was a long room with beds down each side and a row of cubicles at the far end. In the middle of the room Sharon was clasped in the arms of a young man wearing a short sarong. He had his face in her hair and hers was pressed against his chest, muffling her voice. "Mark! Mark David! God—it's good to see you!"

So this was Mark David Knox! I stood waiting for an opportunity to grip his mind and make him leave without disturbance.

"Sharon!" He was holding her by the shoulders, looking down into her face. "So you've got *Hyperion* too!"

"Yes—at last we'll sail together again. I'd heard you were wounded."

"Had a leg blown off. Been half a year on a damned teleport planet growing a new one. Thought I'd missed my chance for the mission. When I got the signal offering me a berth I packed up and left!"

I stood dumbfounded, trying to reconcile what I had just heard with the mission agreement. That agreement had clearly specified that the crew would consist of the best human captains available. The Administrators had included the clause to insure that only responsible spacers would man a ship carrying an Ultron on a mission where there might be unexpected complications. If this impetuous young woman was one of the crew, then the Governor of Edrin had failed in his duty and I was faced with my first unexpected complication.

My arrest of Mark Knox must be unobtrusive. I rejected an ancestral suggestion that both he and Sharon be terminated immediately. Not even legal termination was now acceptable within the civilized Cluster. But Mark, at least, must be isolated.

Sharon turned, saw me standing in the doorway, and called, "Lucian—come and meet my twin brother! Mark—this is Lucian."

"Glad to meet you, Lucian." Mark held out his hand, and I was shaking it before I realized how the complications were escalating. Sibling affection among Humans was reputed to be almost as strong as within an Ara sept.

"We shared a floater," said Sharon. "Now we're looking for a cubicle."

"Not a hope. All taken days ago."

She cursed and eyed the row of beds. "Which is yours, Mark?"

"Right there."

"Since we can't get a cubicle, mind if we park alongside?" She tossed her pack onto a neighboring bed. "Lucian, you grab the next."

To avoid an argument I put my pack on the bed next to hers, although I had no intention of sleeping in the same room as some forty Humans. Every Terminal has a suite reserved for Ultrons and I planned to take Mark there, once I had a grip on him. I would remove his memories of Clur, and hope his sharp-eyed sister did not notice the gaps.

"I need a drink! Mark—get dressed. There's a tavern in the basement." She jerked a brush from her pack, scowled at herself in the wall mirror, and attacked her black hair with long angry strokes. Mark, pulling on a bodysuit, smiled at me. I, inadvertently, smiled back.

The "tavern" was a sour-smelling, badly lit room beneath the vestibule, crudely furnished with stained wooden tables and splintered chairs. It was empty. "Smells good!" said Sharon, sniffing. "But why don't they fix it up decently?"

"Get's smashed every time they try." Mark went to a keg and began filling mugs with a brown liquid. "Old Whiskers was telling me he installed 'A civilized place for the social interactions of visiting Humans.' First deepspace crew that checked in tore it apart!" He handed a mug to his sister, gave another to me, and took one himself. "The beer's okay."

So this was beer! I followed the others to a table and sipped mine cautiously. Mark and Sharon drank deeply and relaxed visibly.

"Any beer tastes good after a month of dry space. No booze for the crew and no sex for the skipper!" Sharon drank again and relaxed further. "Thank God I'm back in the ranks."

No sex for the skipper? Captains, by tradition, stayed celibate in space. A necessary tradition, even for hermaphrodites, and vital for any race unfortunate enough to be sexually differentiated. A tradition with its own problems. Did Humans on Edrin really give command to young females? If so, they had drifted a long way from the sex roles described in my readings about Humans on Earth.

Mark laughed, drank, and asked, "Broken any records lately, Sis?"

"Lyra to Caton in twenty-eight days. Ten under schedule. In *Sheba*. I left her in orbit this morning. The traders bitched at the premium—but they paid!"

"And your crew bitched all the way from Lyra to Caton?"

"Idle bastards! Grumbled at my vortex speeds. Lunkheads won't realize that faster is safer. Complained through every acceleration—when an extra second in high *g* saves a day in free flight! As soon as they were off Articles they called me a space-crazy slave driver! But they grabbed their cuts in the cash. And when I quit they tried to con me into staying on as skipper. Why was I going to waste my talents as slave driver on a nonprofit mission?'' She laughed, drank, became thoughtful, and finally added, ''Why the hell am I?''

Mark winked at me. ''The Second Sol may be two years nonprofit, but with Sis aboard it won't be dull!''

His friendliness made me uncomfortable. To change the subject I asked, ''What was Clur like?''

''Pure blah! Like the rest of those prettied-up Net worlds. Total weather control. Total vermin control. Total everything control! They use it as a data dump. Crawling with Scholars— and not an original thought among the lot of 'em!''

''They repaired your leg,'' said his sister.

''Regrew it! I give the Medics top marks. It's an Advanced Medical Center and the Medics know their job. But their last advance was probably a thousand years ago. Like the rest of the groundhogs they go by the book. Everything by the book!''

''You must have been bored mindless!''

''Saved by Junior—my terminal.'' Mark hunched forward across the table. ''That's the rig the Scholars use to access the main data dump. I wasn't a Scholar so all they'd tell me about Junior was how to order meals and call in the housekeepers.'' Mark finished his beer and went to the keg for a refill. ''That made me mad, so I decided to crack Junior's code.''

''How could you!'' My expostulation was more protest than question.

''How? Not hard when you've had to fake interlocks on those Ceta freighters. You know, when the main drive starts hunting and you have to go among the supervolts to balance!'' He interpreted my indeterminate head movement as understanding. ''Once you've cracked the coding pattern for one gate you can break the codes of the rest. They change coding but not pattern. Same thing with the access gates to the main data dump on Clur. The basic pattern's tough. But when you've tumbled to that the rest of the gates open first knock! Guiding Junior into core was like solving a maze when you've got the algorithm.''

''Guiding Junior into what?'' asked Sharon.

''Core! The part where only select Ultrons are supposed to go.''

''Select Ultrons?'' I stared.

''The 'in-group.' All Ultrons must think they can access the whole core.'' Mark laughed. ''They can't! Some parts they can only access if they know the special keys. I could fake my way into everything!''

I was shocked into silence. The idea of any data being withheld from any Ultron must be wrong. Yet Mark thought he was speaking the truth.

"Find anything interesting?" Sharon herself was more interested in five spacers who had just come clattering down the stairs and were noisily filling mugs at the keg.

"In deep core? Not much. God knows why they bothered to hide the junk they've got there." He paused. "God knows? Appropriate! Deep core's packed with tetrabits of religious dogma. Must have been programmed by Ult fanatics. No wonder they're extinct!"

I was recovering. "But you searched it?"

"Hardly searched." Mark shrugged. "I used to ask Junior some question—anything that came into my head—and send it off to dig up answers because it enjoyed the deep burrowing. Most of what it brought back I knew already. Biggest surprise was when Junior started talking American—or English as Central Information still calls it."

"Talking American?" Sharon returned her attention to Mark.

"They've got a lot more data about Terra than they've told us. They've had top signal restorers on the Monitor circuit since the first radio signals came through. They've been able to sort the mess out far better than the Edrin station could."

"Anything useful for the mission?"

"More detail. But nothing important that we don't know already."

"Do they give a survival forecast?"

"Much the same as the Colony's estimate!" He took a long pull of his beer. "End of all Terran cultures by autodestruction within between five and fifty years." He wiped his mouth. "Damned shame!"

I looked down into my mug. "Are you going to tell the Colony?"

"Not unless they ask directly. And they won't. There's no shipborne trade to Clur so nobody'll be interested in the place. Only reason I told you is because you asked." He looked across the table. "Lucian, you're like me. Slightly skewed!"

"But this sounds important—"

"Important only to Ultrons. Doesn't matter a damn to us. After I'd cracked Junior's code I was tempted to show the proles their bosses aren't as bright as they shine!" He shrugged. "But they don't do such a bad job of running the Cluster. And they're dangerous when deflated."

"How do you mean?" Mark's English was so contaminated

with Terran radioese that I could hardly understand him. "Why are Ultrons dangerous?"

"They used to be adults, but they never had much sense of humor. Now they're a bunch of elderly brats. Civilization's run by smart-assed kids! And you know how mean smart kids can be if you make 'em look foolish? I was a smart-assed kid myself. Had that knocked out of me as an apprentice!"

"I once saw a picture of an Ultron. Looked like a skinny dwarf!" Sharon stood up. "That gang's from *Ezra*. Some of 'em crewed for me two trips back. They've been in space for six months. Think I'll go and renew acquaintances now I'm not their skipper."

Mark stared after her. "Sis is smart. She's got brains, but she won't use them. All she thinks about is making a fast passage, trading with profit, and screwing when ashore!"

"She seems to have met an old friend!" Sharon was kissing a bearded man who had just come roaring into the tavern, and whom she had hailed as "Tank."

"You booked with her Lucian. You've got priority. But you'd better move in fast if you want to hold your claim." When I shook my head he laughed. "After a spell of celibacy Sharon scares off guys like you, so she ends up with thugs like Tank."

I studied the young man on the other side of the table. He had been speaking the truth about his activities on Clur. He had penetrated Central Information exactly as he had described. With ingenuity, without malice, and with no appreciation of the implications. He would repeat what he had learned to the next spacer who asked him about Clur as readily as he had told me. Wisely, he did not want to irritate any Ultrons, but some would be very irritated if a rumor made them suspect there were areas of core memory not available to the whole Council. And if the source of that rumor was traced to Mark it would inevitably involve me.

I glanced round the tavern, now almost full as more of *Ezra*'s crew arrived. These Humans were talkers! Apparently they only listened when they were talking. But that Galarian manager would be trying to listen to everything. Rumors about forbidden areas of core would, sooner or later, reach Council.

We Ultrons are not unkind, but we deal with the problems of worlds. Our concern is for the well-being of the many rather than the happiness of the one; we uphold justice, but for races rather than for individuals. I had never before had to decide the fate of an individual. Worse, I was about to deal unjustly with a friendly young man innocent of committing anything but impulsive ignorance. The prospect of amnesing Mark was becoming repugnant.

I sipped my beer, which now seemed drinkable. He was sailing in *Hyperion* where he would be isolated for at least two years and under my supervision. If I could get him aboard before he started chattering I would at least be able to postpone my decision. I stood up, excused myself, and pushed my way through the crowd to the stairs. Outside, I took a deep breath of the fresh evening air and got into a vacant floater.

Moving dust trails on the road from the Terminal marked floaters filled with Humans on their way to the party. They waved and shouted greetings as they swerved past, and after several such encounters I turned off the road to float across the desert. It was safer to wind between the clumps of scrub than to dodge dust and charging machines. I returned to the road when I reached the irrigated area and parked in a slot by the Twin Towers. Ara spacers were everywhere and Humans common enough to be inconspicuous. I crossed the plaza and concourse, waited for a vacant lift shaft, keyed it for the Executive level, and stepped out into the anteroom of the Spaceport Master.

His aide was a young Cindra, still in the female phase. The Cindras are serial hermaphrodites. They emerge from adolescence as females and, after bearing several offspring, mature into males. While in the female configuration they are natural subservients and act as aides and so forth to the males of their own species. Physically they are typical mammalian ultoids, and the female rising from her desk as I entered could easily pass for a slight Human girl with slim hips and small breasts.

She stared at me wide-eyed, gave a gasp, and retreated toward the door of her Master's office. Before I could stop her she had disappeared through it. A moment later there was a roar of rage and a male Cindra appeared.

The female Cindra is attractive to the eyes of most ultoids; the mature male is squat, hairy, overmuscled, and attractive only to the female. This Cindra was unusual because he started abusing me in English.

"Captain—how dare you frighten poor Gracil! I've promised you they'll start unloading *Ezra* as soon as they've finished that Ara ship. I want to get that gang of yours out of here too! I know you've been in space six months, but if any more of your crew—men or women—start roughing up the locals around my spaceport, I swear I'll have the lot of 'em immobilized and dumped back aboard. And they'll stay in orbit until you sail!" He put his arm around the shoulders of the flinching female, who had crept up beside him to stare at me with large excited eyes. "Two of the brutes off your ship chased poor Gracil right across the concourse. I tell you—they're not fit to mix with civilized—"

I cut him off, speaking in Ult. "I am not the Captain of *Ezra*. I am Lucian the Ultron!"

Only Executives, Senior Administrators, and we ourselves speak Ult. The shock of hearing it from a human spacer brought the Master's expostulations to a dead halt. He stood with his mouth open, comforting his aide by stroking her buttocks. I walked into his office. "Put her out, and shut the door."

Poor Gracil whimpered and slipped back to her desk. The Master followed me, muttering, "I beg Your Ultimate's pardon. I never imagined an Ultron disguising himself as a man."

"We have to undertake many unpleasant tasks to maintain tranquility in the Cluster. I am here to request you to supply me and a colleague with immediate transport to Edrin."

"To Edrin? There's an Ara ship sailing in ten days."

"I said immediate transport. Now. Tonight! That is an order!"

"Even an Ultron order is negated by impossibility. There is no ship capable of leaving tonight." He walked to his console and studied the displays. "There's a courier which could be made ready to sail by tomorrow."

"Then make her ready!"

"A courier needs a crew of at least six Ara or two Humans, Your Ultimate."

"I will provide the crew. Send her present Commander to the human hostel tomorrow morning."

The Master seemed about to protest, then shrugged. "As you order! I presume you know what you're doing." He sounded as though he hoped I did not.

"Why is it that you speak English?"

"Because I have to handle more complaints about those damned Humans than about any of the other races using my spaceport. I can handle them better when I can curse them in their own tongue. It is a good cursing language."

"And do they really harry your aide?"

He laughed. "Their own women are such tough bitches that when the men see something sweet and feminine they make passes at her. Poor Gracil goes into hysterics and that usually warns 'em off. But two of *Ezra*'s thugs thought it was a come-on."

"And was it?"

The Master shrugged. "You know what females are!"

I was only starting to learn, but I nodded and left. Poor Gracil was bending over her desk and, in an automatic human reflex, I patted her bottom as I passed. Her squeal brought the Master roaring from his office as I stepped into the lift-shaft.

I keyed for the Apex, the suite reserved for Ultrons and Senior Executives. It was large, luxurious, and deserted; nobody had stayed there in months. I stood for a moment, enjoying the glow of the desert under the setting sun, then decided I preferred the companionship of the hostel to this lonely luxury. Mark had shown that some Humans could be better company than reports had suggested.

But also uncouth, as Executives and Administrators complained. I arrived at the hostel to find two males fighting in the middle of the road with a ring of men and women yelling encouragement. I parked the floater and went round the side of the building to avoid the crowded front entrance. By this time it was almost dark, and when I turned the corner I stepped into deep shadow and onto a copulating couple. From the flash of black hair and the startled curse I recognized one as Sharon, and as I jumped over the two disengaging bodies I saw the beard of the spacer she had hailed as Tank.

I strode on into the hostel, looking for Mark. Downstairs the tavern was a packed mass of drinking, sweating, shouting, singing humanity. I retreated to the lobby, smelled the food from the dining room, and realized I was ravenous. After I had collected a meal from the dispenser I saw Mark sitting alone, hunched over a bowl of soup, and went to sit opposite him.

He looked up. "Thought you'd joined the action outside. They're fighting already!"

"At the moment I prefer to eat."

He laughed, then frowned at a burst of cheering from the road. "No wonder they call us a bunch of barbarians! No wonder they dump us out here in the desert! How the hell can they ever respect us if we behave like that mob!"

I shrugged. My ancestor was reminding me of what had usually happened to a spaceport when an Ult ship had arrived after a long voyage. "They have been in space half a year. They are settling accumulated enmities." The ban on fights aboard ship had always been absolute for all species of spacefarers. The story had it that the attacker (and the attacked also, if there is any doubt who was which) went forcibly and immediately out into space. Every spacer thinks that is what will happen, so violence is postponed until both rivals are ashore. By then the cause of most quarrels has evaporated, but often the rest of the crew do not accept reconciliation as a sufficient reason to cancel an anticipated entertainment. Judging by the noise from outside the belief in immediate spacing and the custom of postponed fights still held good.

"They're fighting for fun!" Mark complained. "And Sharon's out there somewhere raising hell!"

Sharon was raising something else, but I was concentrating on my food. I had used more physical energy during this one day than I had in a week on Clur, and my body was demanding carbohydrates, fats, and proteins in quantity. I was ravenous for the first time in my own memory. Mark watched me eat with an interest which changed to concern. "Stuff yourself like that, Lucian, and you'll get too fat to sign on even an Ara local!"

"First real food for a long time!" I tossed the dishes into the disposer. "I have just been to the spaceport. There is a courier leaving for Edrin tomorrow. Would you wish to travel in it with me?"

"A courier?" He stared at me. "You mean that bastard of a Spaceport Master has let you have a courier? What did you use as a bribe?"

I attempted Human humor. "I threatened to rape poor Gracil."

Mark frowned. "That's the kind of thing that gets us—"

"I was joking. But I do have a courier. And I would like you to travel with me."

"We'll have to take Sharon too."

I had hoped to separate Mark from his sister. "A courier will be cramped if there are three of us."

"Sharon'll enjoy that!"

Satiated and sleepy I put the problem of Sharon aside and stood up. "We can discuss that tomorrow. I am going to bed now." I crossed the lobby and nodded to the Manager, watching the boisterous behavior of its guests. Galarians are notorious for their acute hearing, their eidetic memories, and their delight in describing the faults of others to Administrators. I was about to start up the stairs when Sharon and Tank appeared at the top.

Tank stopped, pointed, and roared, "That's him! That's the clumsy bastard who stomped you, Sharon Zelda!"

"That's Lucian." Sharon's tone was as neutral as her face. "Lucian, this is Tancred."

"Greetings, Tancred." I moved back from the foot of the stairs as Tank started down them. "I am sorry for tripping over you."

"You trampled her!" Tank stopped to jerk his thumb at Sharon, then to point his forefinger at my chest. "Now I am about to trample you!"

I moved farther back. A group of spacers entering the lobby

applauded my gesture and shouted "Fight's on!" to their fellows outside. I realized, too late, that my move had signalled an acceptance of Tank's challenge.

Tank scowled at me and continued down the stairs. There were cries of "Hold it!" "Wait!" "Give 'em room!" "Where are the seconds?" Men and women were pouring up from the tavern and in through the doors, spreading out around the walls to form a ring. Someone was offering odds against the tall thin one. I looked round for a way out. All exits were blocked. The Galarian was standing on its tripod to get a better view.

Mark came bursting through the mob shouting, "I'm his second!" He reached me and muttered, "For God's sake! You can't fight now. You're gorged to the gullet!"

"He accepted the challenge!" Sharon called from the top of the stairs. "Stand back, Mark David. If he's your man, then you're the starter!"

Mark cursed and disappeared. I was still wondering what "starter" meant when he called "Action!" and Tank charged.

He charged so suddenly that I was unable to modulate my response. I hit the bearded giant with a mindblow that would have stopped an enraged megrep. Tank weaved slightly and came on. The Galarian fell backwards off its tripod. None of the cheering Humans showed signs of having noticed anything.

I had an instant of frozen terror. Then, with Tank upon me, the combat reflex of my primal ancestor cut in. I stooped low and met Tank's charge with a straight-fingered hand hard into his stomach.

Tank dropped. I stood shocked. The crowd roared. Mark shouted, "Take him! Take him, for God's sake! Before he gets up!"

Tank lay on his back, his mouth open. Then his chest heaved and he rolled onto his knees, gasping for breath. I moved back, unwittingly inviting my opponent to try again. The crowd applauded my generous gesture.

I hit Tank a second mindblow. The Galarian, who had been climbing back onto its tripod, fell off again. Tank only shook his head and staggered to his feet, where he stood swaying. The crowd whooped encouragement for him to continue. Our first clash had been too brief for their proper enjoyment.

"Show's over!" Sharon's voice changed from neutrality to authority. The hubbub died and the whole lobby looked up at her.

Tank protested, "But he's offering me another chance!"

"Another chance to get yourself killed!" She hushed the protests of the frustrated audience. "It was a clean knock-down! I'm your

second, Tank. If he hits you like that again you won't get up!"
She glanced toward the spectators. "Seth! Isaac! Take him outside
and cool him off!"

The alacrity with which her ex-crewmen grabbed Tank's arms
testified to the responses she had drilled into them in the past.
Even in my confusion I realized that this woman was indeed a
Captain. Tank tried to argue, glared at Sharon, scowled at me,
and finally let himself be pushed out through the main entrance
into the night.

The crowd began to break up, laughing or complaining. Mark
clapped me on the back. "Nicely done! But with a thug like
Tank you'd have been safer to nail him while he was kneeling!"
and returned to the dining room. The Galarian climbed back onto
its tripod, staring at me as I stood silent and numb, alone in the
middle of the floor.

My mindblows had failed! I was like a Warrior with a broken
sword, isolated among enemies. I had struck hard. Twice I had
knocked the Galarian off its tripod although it had been far from
the focus. Nearby Humans had not even flinched. Tank, at the
very focus, had only shaken his head.

And my instant of terror! I had never before feared any living
being. But in that moment of Tank's unstoppable charge I had
known terrified panic. I had been saved by an ancestral reaction.
For the first time in my own life I had struck another intelligent!

Sharon came down the stairs, walked across the hall, and said
softly, "Lucian, you shouldn't have done that!"

So she had sensed the mindblow. "I reacted." I had no
excuse except the truth. "I panicked!"

"You shouldn't have tempted Tank to a second charge. You
might have killed him!"

"Killed him? No—that is impossible."

"Pretty sure of yourself, aren't you? If that thrust had been
two centimeters over you'd have ruptured his spleen!"

"Oh! You mean—?" She was talking about my physical
blow.

"I mean I know it's hard to hold yourself back when a guy
like Tank asks to be flattened." For a moment her frown was
critical, then she laughed. "Your timing was perfect. You broke
his rhythm when you fell over us! Now you've splintered his
ego. I've got a repair job on my hands." And she went after her
late shipmates.

I was again alone in a suddenly dangerous world. I saw the
bright eyes of the Galarian on me. There was one threat I must
block now. If that creature started a rumor that it had seen a

human spacer use mentorsion, then every human spacer would become an object of fear to other races. I walked across the lobby and faced the flinching manager. Its eyes went wide when I addressed it in Galarian, and it realized what I was.

"I noticed you fell from your tripod."

"Yes—your—"

"You fell twice!"

A quick nod.

"That was clumsy of you!"

"Clumsy? But your Highness—"

"If you ever tell anybody that you fell for any reason except clumsiness, then I promise you will sit on a tripod from which you will not fall. A red-hot tripod! I am warning you in your own language so you will understand. Do you?"

A terrified head-bob.

I turned away, crossed the lobby, and climbed the stairs. My body was heavy with fatigue, my mind with guilt. I was already infected with the pernicious Human tendency to violence. I had brutalized the manager mentally as Sharon had brutalized the Teleport official physically. I had hit Tank because of terror. And I had learned a dreadful lesson: Humans were as impervious to mentorsion as were Ult and Ara. For millennia mentorsion had been the only weapon an Ultron had needed to protect himself and enforce his commands. Now I was about to sail alone with some sixty Humans, and my only control over them would be their belief in Ultron power.

Mentorsion had been the weapon which had consolidated our conquest of the Cluster. During the long war of unification every race we overran had been subjected to it. For eons any individual who resisted Ult control had been terminated by those of his fellows whom we did control. In what I now saw as a ghastly parody of natural selection the races of the Cluster had self-selected for sensitivity to mentorsion. And all still were.

All except the victors—we Ult-Ara. And these Humans who had only arrived in civilization long after the conquest. Logic should have warned us that Humans might be as immune to mentorsion as they were to space sickness. But mentorsion was an area of study restricted to Ultrons, and no Ultron had ever discussed anything with a Human until my encounter with Sharon that afternoon.

Resistance to mentorsion was only one disquieting aspect of Humans. Another was their variability. I lay on my bed and listened to the celebrations below get noisier and noisier, the fights more frequent. Yet, at the same time, other men and women were coming into the dormitory, talking quietly among themselves, undressing, showering, checking over their kits, carrying on a multitude of small personal tasks like sensible beings. They ranged from intelligent and sensitive individuals like Mark to thugs like Tank. Variable and unpredictable. With the Teleport official Sharon had been brutal, with Mark affectionate, with Tank grossly sensual, and on the stairs a true Captain.

Duty demanded that I silence Mark, abort the mission, and warn Council that the Humans within civilization were a greater threat to its tranquility than their kin on distant Terra.

Pride and self-preservation blocked duty. The pride of my three awakened ancestors who united to express outrage that their descendant did not dare to face a crew of semibarbarians when armed with only his natural talents. (All three of them abhorred mentorsion as a weapon unbecoming an Ult Warrior). Self-preservation, because I knew my status as Ultron would not survive the fracas which would follow my disclosure.

And it would be wise for me to learn more about Humans so that when the time for disclosure came I could advise Council on strategy. Which might be long after this Second Sol Mission had returned. In a future when time had taken Mark and Sharon beyond the reach of the Council.

IV

Sharon, her hair gleaming in the sun, her blue eyes dreamy from the night, joined Mark and myself on the terrace the next morning. She kissed her brother, smiled at me, and sat down between us to sip char and gaze into the distance. When I remained silent Mark said, "We've got a courier to Edrin. Leaving today."

"A courier? To Edrin? Who the hell got hold of a courier?"

"Lucian saw the Spaceport Master last night and arranged one."

She laughed. "Lucian's naïve! They'd never let a Human have a courier!"

"If we get one, would you join us?"

"It is an Ara courier," I protested. "There is hardly room aboard for three persons on a passage lasting a month."

"A month! I could take a courier from here to Edrin in ten days."

"Fifty credits says you can't!" said Mark quickly.

"You're on! And I'll lay another fifty that Lucian's been conned."

"Taken," said Mark, looking past her at the road from the spaceport. A floater was coming along it. "There's an Ara now."

"An Ara? How do you know it is an Ara?" I asked. Was he a telepath?

"A Human would be driving like hell and spreading dust all over the landscape."

"Probably some Skipper who's heard about last night's party and come to sign on anyone who wants to leave Cao fast," said Sharon. "Ara ships are always short-handed these days."

The floater stopped in front of the hostel, and we watched the slim figure of an Ara cross the road and disappear into the lobby. Mark said, "I'd enjoy a trip with Ara for a change. Easy accelerations."

"Slow passages and small bonuses!"

"Safe voyages to civilized worlds." The Ara came onto the terrace, looking around. "If he's really short we ought to help him. We owe the Ara—"

His sister grabbed his wrist. "We're going to join *Hyperion*. If he's desperate for crew I'll chase some of my ex-thugs aboard."

The Ara wore the tabs of a Commander and stopped at our table. Sharon and Mark rose to their feet in automatic courtesy, I an instant later, and all three of us bowed together.

The Commander bowed in return. "Is Lucian Titus among you?"

"I am Lucian Titus." I resigned myself to being revealed as an Ultron.

"My ship is at your disposal." The empathy of the Ara is unique and the Commander had sensed that I did not wish to be hailed by rank. "I understand that you and a colleague must make a fast passage to Edrin."

Sharon, her eyes widening, interrupted. "Lucian and two colleagues! I'm heading for Edrin too."

The Commander bowed to her. "If you are three, and if you wish to make the fastest possible passage, I suggest you take the courier and leave it on Edrin. I and my crew will follow by the next freighter." He gave a gentle Ara smile. "You will be able to reach greater accelerations without us to hamper you."

"You mean—you'll loan us your ship?" Mark was incredulous.

"I understand it is important that Lucian reaches Edrin as soon as possible. So I am honored to allow you the use of my ship. If you are in haste I will take you to it now. It is ready to leave. Which of you will be Captain?"

"Mark!" I said.

Mark laughed. "I vote for Sis! She's just lost fifty credits. Only fair to let her have a chance of winning them back."

"And I vote for myself!" said Sharon. "I'll show the pair of you how to make Edrin in ten days."

I was losing control of the situation. When the Commander took her to another table to complete the transfer I started to protest this unorthodox method of alloting command. Mark caught my arm and whispered, "Quiet! I've got you off the hook. She's forgotten that if she's Skipper she'll have to stay celibate!"

I was uncertain whether Mark was protecting his sister against me, or protecting me against his sister. I could only hope that command would dilute her anger when she found herself in space with a brother and an Ultron.

The accommodation aboard a courier designed for six Ara would have been cramped for three human children. Occupied by two large males and one full-sized female there was room for little else. I had to reveal my identity while standing face to face and toe to toe with my companions.

"I am the Ultron Adviser to the mission." I saw Mark's expression and added, "I did not plan to mislead you. I was only trying to avoid attention. I apologize!"

Sharon stared. Mark folded himself up on one of the short bunks. "Lucian—never thought you were anything but human! Slightly skewed perhaps, and talking like a Clur terminal—but human just the same!" He whistled. "Well, now you know my opinion of Ultrons. Bunch of smart-assed kids afraid to grow up!"

"A superficial judgment with an element of truth. But nobody ever 'grows up' in the sense of reaching intellectual maturity. Such maturity is a myth circulated by oldsters!"

"On that we're agreed!" said Mark. "The oldsters on Edrin—"

"Lucian!" Sharon's voice was sharp with suspicion. "You're conning us! You're too damned human to be Ult. And you're a spacer. An experienced spacer. You shot down that companion-way like a veteran!"

"I myself am not a spacer." I picked my words with care, conscious of Mark's criticism that I "talked like a terminal." I must try to avoid machine-taught phrases. "I have an ancestor

who served in space and, as you may know, we Ultrons sometimes retain the memories of our ancestors. That is why I am
familiar with ships. It is a distant ancestor who was a spacer."

"Therefore you are!" said Mark.

"My ancestor was an entirely different person. All I have is
his memory."

"That's all any of us have!" Mark reached his hand up from
the bunk, opening and closing his fingers. "Most cells in this are
replacements of the cells which were there seven years ago.
Physically it's a different hand. But it's still me!" He slapped his
thigh. "This leg is brand new. But as much mine as the one that
got blown off. Same with most of the molecules in my brain.
And almost everywhere else. Replaced every seven years. From
top to toe. But I'm still me because of my memory."

"Your statement is factually wrong and logically fallacious—"

"Same with you!" persisted Mark, more intent on convincing
his sister than in pursuing an intelligent discussion with me.
"You've got your ancestor's memory. So to all intents and
purposes you are your ancestor. Your ancestor was a spacer, so
you're a spacer. Once a spacer—always a spacer!"

"His head's not big enough!" objected Sharon. "It's no
bigger than yours, Mark."

"Doesn't have to be! From what I dug out of core on Clur I'm
pretty sure that our Ult masters—forgive me, Lucian—are no
smarter than us Humans."

Sharon was still staring at my head. "It must be bigger—to
hold all those memories."

Horrified by Mark's casual mention of his illicit entry into
core, confused by the argument, I was about to say that the
data-storage capacity of the ultoid brain was close to infinite if
the correct coding was used, that the physiological riddle was
how data was transferred between generations, when Mark gave
a succinct explanation of cortical storage capacity. "Multiplex
the coded helix and you could store the memory of a world
population in a head that size!" He saw my surprise at his
erudition and, as though excusing it, added, "Machine memories
are my field!"

"Don't go intellectual, Mark David!" Sharon swung on me.
"Are you really an Ultron?"

I nodded.

"Is Mark right? Are you Ultrons really Ult kids?"

"Not exactly. We postpone maturity—"

"So you're immature?"

"From the sexual point of view. But that—"

"That's enough for me! Peter Pan for a shipmate!" She slammed from the cabin.

I turned to Mark. "Who is Peter Pan?"

"God knows! It's a name somebody heard on a snatch of Terran radio."

Duty displaced curiosity. I concentrated my mind on Mark's. "You must never mention to anyone what you found in core on Clur. If another Ultron—or even a Senior Executive—hears of it, you will certainly be made amnesic!"

"Really? That bunch of crap's important?" He sensed the thrust of my mind as no more than a light touch. "Okay, Lucian. If you say so—not a word to a soul, I promise. And human spacers keep their promises."

"So did Ult." I straightened, relieved, then asked, "How have I offended your sister?"

"Frustrated! Not offended." He laughed. "She'd picked you for a partner. Maybe, when we're aboard *Hyperion*—?"

"Impossible!" I subdued a surge of excitement. Desire was dangerous. It could trigger maturity, even in this imitation-human body. "I was wrong to travel incognito."

"Glad you did, or we'd never have got to know you."

Sharon appeared in the hatch while I was savoring that pleasant absurdity. "Let's see how his ancestor shapes up before he joins the club. I aim to recover my fifty and to do that we'll be going through vortices like you've never gone before!"

Couriers were built to be crewed by the pick of Ult spacers, but even the most rugged would have avoided a second trip with Sharon in command. Besides her accelerations I had to cope with her jargon. Humans had replaced much of the traditional Ult terminology with Terran nautical terms, remnants of seventeenth-century English or culled from twentieth-century broadcasts. Not only were these human spacers taking over the ships, they were changing the language.

I doubt if that courier had ever before been driven as hard as Sharon drove it from Cao to Edrin. As she had remarked, the higher the approach speed the safer the vortex passage. But reaching such speeds demands days of high acceleration. We shot across starfields in a series of wrenching accelerations, followed by terrifying transits through the vortices themselves.

The vortices are the spillways of time, and time is the substrate of space; the substrate in which the Galaxy spins like a gigantic wheel. A wheel whose scattered concentrations of mass pile up waves of time, waves which swirl back in myriad convolutions under the forces maintaining temporal parity, the cotemporal equilibrium which is fundamental to the Universe as we know it.

The torrents of time swirling within the Galaxy's volume of rotation are called vortices. Carried on the flood pouring through a vortex a ship is swept past many light-years to emerge into the calm cotemporal equilibrium of curvilinear space. And a collimated radio beam aimed into a vortex can lance through the disturbances and reach from one starfield into another. It is the vortices which make travel and communication possible within a Cluster two hundred light-years across.

In the vast intergalactic stillness there are no moving concentrations of great mass and hence travel between Galaxies will always be impossible for ultoids, unless we learn to encyst and are prepared to spend eternities drifting through darkness. Travel even within the Cluster would be impossible, by ship or by Net, if we were not able to tap the energy stored in the angular momentum of the Galaxy. The inertia which permeates the Galaxy is our ubiquitous source of power; an energy well for worlds and spaceships. Our ability to draw from that well, the eons we spent identifying, charting, and buoying the vortices between starfields, gave us the freedom to range and conquer the worlds of the Cluster. A freedom which, I was beginning to realize, we had surrendered to the Ara and were surrendering to the Humans.

Sharon used it to take the courier from Cao to Edrin in the ten days she had promised. She claimed she was putting us through this torture to win back her fifty credits. Mark muttered it was Sis showing off. I thought she was intent on proving I was soft-centered. Whatever her reasons she stressed the courier to its design limits and our relationships to the verge of rupture.

She failed to collapse me, but she did convince us of her skill and she won her bet by putting us down on the Colony's small field two hundred and thirty-nine hours after leaving Cao orbit. Ten days when two Humans and one Ultron were crushed by acceleration and crammed against each other; ten days when I lost my disgust of human habits and became inured to human smells.

Discipline and common sense had prevented physical assault and blunted Sharon's tongue, but when we slid from the courier to the ground I expected to see brother and sister squaring off against each other with the winner turning on me. Instead the pair externalized their hostility, staring across the empty field toward the buildings of Knoxton and cursing their fellow Humans.

"We signaled we were arriving. At least they could have had

a floater to meet us!" Sharon signed the retransfer papers and tossed them to me. "Lucian, slip back aboard, snap those in the log, and throw down our gear!"

After ten days I was so used to obeying her orders that I had climbed back into the courier and was heaving our packs out through the hatch before I remembered that now we had landed her authority had expired. By the time I got back to the ground I had forgotten my resentment in the pleasure of stretching my legs. "Where is the Terminal?" I asked. "There should be messages there for me."

"That shack over at the edge of the field." Sharon pointed to a small building about a kilometer away. "There should be messages for all of us. But no welcome committee. Bunch of human groundhogs!"

"What is a groundhog?" I stared at the dusty plain around us. Beauty is not the first impression Edrin makes on a visitor.

"A groundhog?" She stared toward the Terminal. "Some kind of pig that lives in the ground, I guess."

"Meaning's doubtful," said Mark, limping beside me. "Like a lot of the words we've picked up from Earth radio. One spin-off from this mission will be finding out what we've really been saying."

The Terminal was deserted. Sharon reported our arrival and queried the status of *Hyperion*. A crew list flashed up. She studied it and asked, "Saul?"

"He's rigid. But—" Mark shrugged and they both keyed. "Saul" appeared in the space marked "Captain." The screen flickered, then read: Voting complete. Saul elected Captain.

"Lucian—what are your plans?" Mark asked.

"I must visit the Governor." A read-out had flashed for me as soon as Sharon had reported our arrival. "Now they know I am here, protocol is under way."

"Call on old Gritass by all means," said Sharon. "You'll asphyxiate him and his staff. Do 'em all good to smell a spacer after a tough voyage!"

Mark laughed. "Lucian, come to my apartment and get cleaned up. I'll float you over to the Governor's Palace at Anedrin when you're fit to be smelled."

"Thanks." As we walked out to a vacant floater I asked, "Sharon, why are you hostile to Governor Silar?"

"Hostile to Gritass? But I'm not! I respect him. He takes the trouble to read our voyage reports. Wants to know what's happening in the barbarian fringe. The rest of the Admins on Edrin—spineless wonders! As they are on most worlds. Gritass

is tough but fair. Wish we had a few like him on the Synod."
She threw her pack into the rear of the floater. "The tender's
going up to *Hyperion* at noon tomorrow. I'll be aboard."

"Will you not take a vacation first? *Hyperion* cannot be ready
to sail yet."

"She'll sail as soon as she's got a full crew. Mark and me are
the last two to join. Saul's been elected Skipper already. As soon
as we're aboard he'll take off for Sol. And I prefer space to
hanging around the Colony."

Mark looked at me. "I guess we can't sail until the Ultron
Advisor—"

"I will be on the noon tender." The sooner I could get Mark
aboard *Hyperion* the less danger there was of him accidentally
letting slip some hint of his escapade on Clur.

"Good!" said Mark, turning the floater toward Knoxton.
"Before we go to my apartment I'll show you something of our
fair city."

Knoxton was a city by courtesy and fair only in the sense that
it was clean and well-ordered. There were no monuments, façades,
or pleasure domes; it was as functional as a spaceship. The
buildings, whether dwellings, offices, workplaces, or stores each
had a neat parklet but were otherwise without ornamentation.
The only area of any interest was the original settlement, a
collection of wooden houses clustered around a pond, maintained
as a memorial to the Founders.

"This place represented Mary Knox's memory of a Terran
village," Mark explained. "It was built to make the adults feel
at home. When they woke in it most of 'em went into shock.
They thought they were in hell!"

To me the houses had more charm than the town around them,
but I did not comment for those few races who know the site of
their original capital resent criticism of it. "What is Sharon
doing?"

"Arranging for male company, I guess. And contacting her
kids."

"Kids? Sharon has children?"

"Sure! Like our mother she had twins at eighteen. Immediately she finished her apprenticeship so they'd be four when she
was old enough to try for her Captain's ticket. They're ten now,
and back here in school. A girl and a boy—like me and her. She
visits 'em whenever she comes through Edrin. Which is more
than our mother did!"

Sharon's behavior seemed strange, but the whole concept of

parenthood was strange to me. "She left her children here after
they were born?"

"God no! Like any other kids they stayed with her in space
until they were eight. Most ships are crawling with kids. That's
one thing we'll be spared in *Hyperion*. No kids aboard—and
none to be produced during the voyage. Too many unknowns on
this trip to have kids around—or apprentices either."

"Apprentices?" I was more interested in the fact that human
children flourished aboard ship. Their inability to stand the stress
of space was the reason most Ultrons gave for not going there.

"Most kids want to become spacers. Not many other ways for
us Humans to make a decent living. So they sign on as apprentices when they're fourteen."

"You mean they get only six years of education?" The least
ambitious Ult got more than sixty.

"They get their real education between fourteen and eighteen.
While they're apprentices!" Mark laughed, then sobered. "But
you're right—six years isn't enough. We're an uneducated race.
That's one of the things me and some other Captains are trying
to change. But the Synod, it's conservative to the core. Most of
the members are retired spacers. Nobody else worth a damn
stays on Edrin long enough to serve. We've been trying to
change things by making a nuisance of ourselves!" He glanced
past me. "Here comes Sis. And by the look on her face she's
snared somebody."

Sharon was certainly looking pleased with herself as she pulled
her pack from the floater. "Okay—I'll see you two on the noon
shuttle."

"Who've you nabbed?"

"Jerimiah."

"Give him my sympathy!" called Mark as he sent the floater
away down the winding street of the village and then along a
broad avenue between apartment blocks. "Jerry's a spacer who's
gone to ground. He'll have gone soft too by now! Poor bastard,
he's on the Synod."

I shared Mark's sympathy for the unknown Jerimiah if he was
one of the leaders trying to lead a spacer population as intracta-
ble as this brother and sister. The Synod had probably found
bargaining with Council a relief after dealing with their own
people.

Mark turned the floater into a slot beside one of the buildings.
"Not beautiful," he commented as he shouldered his pack and
limped toward the entrance. "But comfortable. They built these
in imitation of some image they picked up from Earth years ago.

When the fashion for things Terran first caught on. When we started talking like we do now!'' He looked around him. ''I can't believe Humans really live in places like this!''

''Do Humans live in them here?'' I could see many apartments but no people.

''Sure! But not often.'' I followed him into an elevator. ''This is spacer accommodation and we're away most of the time.'' We stepped from the elevator into a large and sparsely furnished room. ''I've been away over a year. One night at home, and tomorrow we head out for another two.'' He pushed open a door. ''You can change here. Sleep here too if Gritass doesn't insist you stay in the Palace. Shower's in there. You can put that suit through the cleaner while you're cleaning up yourself. Don't be too long—I'm thirsty.''

After ten days without washing I smelled like an ancestor and rediscovered the pleasure of hot scented water. I went to join Mark on the balcony with my skin fresh and tingling. He had a beer waiting for me and the dark liquid was delicious. We drank together.

He put down his mug and looked at my face. ''Go on! Ask!''

''I am not familiar with what is permissible to ask.''

''Anything! Anything at all. We Humans make a virtue of frankness!''

''Then—your race is now wealthy. But your city does not show it. That is unusual. Most wealthy races are proud to beautify their capitals.''

''You're asking what we do with our cash? That!'' He pointed to the vapor trail of a vessel entering atmosphere. ''Mary Knox advised her offspring to buy ships as soon as they had the funds. We've taken her advice—to the edge of absurdity. She said we could either work for other races at the only job we can do better than they can—spacing. Or we could work for ourselves in our own ships. So''—he shrugged—''we plough everything we make into shipping. Now-a-days most ships manned by Humans are owned by Humans. Most skippers own a slice of their own ship.'' He took a pull of his beer. ''That keeps us driving hard and out of trouble. Out of trouble inside the Cluster at any rate!''

I nodded. ''It makes economic sense.''

''It also keeps us divided, avaricious, and uneducated!'' He spoke with a sudden bitterness. ''We own ships but we don't really know what makes 'em work. We repair 'em but we can't build 'em, we can take 'em through vortices and across starfields, but we don't know what vortices are. We're as ignorant as shit and as dependent as ever on other people's knowledge. And everybody wants us to stay that way. Including our own leaders and your people!''

''Until recently, Mark, I was the only Ultron who even knew the human race existed. So I do not think it is the Council who restricts you.''

''It's not the Council. You Ultrons and your Council are remote rulers. It's the Executives and the Administrators—oh hell—let's talk about something more pleasant!'' He refilled both our mugs.

I was enjoying the warmth of the sun on my bare chest, but was still nagged by my curiosity. ''You were Captain on at least three trading voyages to barbarian worlds. They must have been profitable.''

''They were! That's why we risked them. My share of the profits let me buy the ship—*Sandria*. I owned her, free and clear!''

I was startled. This boy of twenty-eight had made more money in a few years than wealthy conventional traders ten times his age made in their whole lives. ''Does every human spacer make such a profit?''

''Hell no! When the apprentices qualify they're free to join any ship with a vacancy. If they want excitement and reward they ship with somebody like me. If they want fast passages and good bonuses they sail with a skipper like Sis. But most choose Captains who stick to routine voyages, earn moderate bonuses, and live long lives. Long lives in human terms that is. If they want an easy time they can always sign on with the Ara. Not much money, but no danger and plenty of shoreside leave.''

''How do you become Captain?''

''Serve your time, pass the exam, and get your ticket. Before a voyage the crew vote on who'll be skipper from among those with tickets. If the skipper's a success—that is if he or she makes a profit and keeps the crew—they'll keep the skipper. Good Captains usually stay in command until they're fed up and sell out to the Synod or the next Captain.''

''So the profits build up. What do you do with them?''

''Buy more ships. That's part of the Puritan ethic—they were the biggest group among the originals. Work to make money, make money work to make more while you're doing the same. No time for anything that doesn't show a profit within a quarter lifetime!''

''Economic sense is the basis of survival. I remember supervising the evacuation of a world called Fehr in—''

''Fehr!'' Mark swung round to stare at me.

"I was the Sector Extron at the time. Fehr was a fringe world settled eons ago. A good world, but economically marginal. Too far from the Net. It could not hold a sufficiently large population against the attractions of the Net to remain viable. It was evacuated to prevent a slide into barbarism."

"I think I've heard it quoted as an awful example." Mark turned away. "Some of the first human-crewed ships helped in the evacuation."

That I had not realized. I stood up. "I must meet Silar at sunset."

"I'll float you over to his Palace."

"Mark—I do not wish to complicate your only night at home."

"I'll be going to Anedrin anyway. To get some action. That's where the other spacers will be. Nothing ever happens in Knoxton."

At the door I stopped. "I have to wear my regalia."

He looked at me across the room. "I promise I won't laugh!"

When I came back in my cloak and helmet he did not. In fact he had jumped to his feet and started to make an automatic bow before he checked himself and said in a voice of genuine awe, "Lucian—that—that's sure impressive!"

"It is meant to be." After our ten days as shipmates I was discomforted by his awe but flattered by his reaction. "You are probably the first Human ever to see an Ultron in full dress."

He was still admiring me when the door opened and Sharon stood in the entrance. She stared at me and I stared at her, for she too had changed her character with her clothes. Instead of the spacer suit which had both covered and outlined her body, she was wearing a tight black dress which hid her legs, changed her shape, and exposed most of her above the waist. Her black hair hung gleaming to her brown shoulders.

We studied each other; I with interest, she with shock. Then the sight of an Ultron in regalia triggered the same respectful deference as it had in her brother. She curtsied. A gesture I had never seen before, and one I doubt that she had ever performed.

I took off my helmet. She saw my face, straightened abruptly, and snapped, "Lucian, what the hell are you doing dressed up like that?"

"Preparing to call on Governor Silar. And why are you clothed so strangely?"

"This dress isn't strange! It's what they're wearing on Earth."

"Were wearing ten years ago—as modified by a noisy radio

channel!'' Mark was laughing. ''Remember what I said Lucian? About the fashion for things Terran?''

I tried to repair the damage caused by my remark. ''Sharon, now that I have recovered from my surprise, I can see that dress makes you look even more beautiful than you are.''

''Thanks!''

''Where's Jerry?'' Mark was still laughing.

''I decided I'd rather come and cruise with you.'' She turned her bare back on me.

''Sis—that's grand!'' He kissed his sister. ''When we were apprentices we used to hunt as a pair. Scout potential partners for each other. Saves times if you know the probable reception before you try for contact!'' He went to a small cupboard and produced a bottle of verch, a liquor which carries a special tax on every civilized world to cover the medical costs which result from its excessive use. ''Sis only dresses to kill once a year and she deserves a charge of firewater.'' He poured a small glass of the amber liquid and handed it to his sister. ''Did Jerry stand you up?''

''No way!'' She tossed back the drink, put down the glass, and went to a wall-mirror where she stood patting her hair. ''He started trying to persuade me not to sail in *Hyperion*. So I dumped him and came to join you.''

''Persuade you not to sail? Is he trying to turn you into a groundhog?''

''I don't think so. He just said the mission is dangerous.''

''He's probably right about that!'' Mark stood thoughtful, the bottle of verch in his hand. ''There's something about this mission that's not quite kosher!'' He looked at me. ''Do you know, Lucian?''

''I do not even know what 'kosher' means.''

''It's another of those damned Terran expressions we've picked up. I think it means not quite right.''

''There is one thing about it I do not understand.''

''What's that?'' Sharon turned from the mirror to stare at me.

''I am going because I speak English. And because I am the only Ultron who knows something about Humans. But all of you are Captains, and you all volunteered.''

''Every human Captain worth a damn volunteered. We're the ones the Mission Committee picked. The Committee chaired by old Gritass.''

''Volunteered for a two-year nonprofit voyage as ordinary spacers, limited to five beers a week, and no children. Why?''

''Because we're crazy!'' snapped Sharon.

"Because we're human," said Mark. "Know what that means?"

"After ten days with you two I am beginning to learn."

"After two years with us—if we live that long—you'll understand a lot more. By the time we get back to Edrin you won't have any illusions about us left." Sharon laughed and caught her brother's arm. "Come on! Let's float Lucian over to the Palace. Then you and I can go hunting together!"

V

I had known that Silar must receive me with ceremony; I had not expected such blatant pomp. My unobtrusive arrival near the Governor's Palace became a triumphant entry as soon as the aides saw the cloaked and helmeted figure of an Ultron stepping from Mark's floater. I found myself flanked by an honor guard as I crossed the plaza to where the Governor of Edrin, dressed with an austere simplicity in contrast to the gorgeous raiment of his notables, waited to receive me.

"Old Gritass" was a gray and massive Ult who went to the unexpected level of kneeling to accept my salute. Either the Governor of Edrin was an archtraditionalist, or he was trying to make a fool of the first Ultron to honor Edrin with a formal visit. Governors might bow before us or even cringe. They seldom knelt.

Twelve days earlier I would never have suspected subtle ridicule behind this display, but ten days in the close company of two Humans had infected me with human skepticism. I met the challenge by following exact protocol myself. The result was that when at last Silar and I were alone the Governor was exhausted and my human temper was near fracture point. As I took off my helmet I asked in English, "And what was the meaning of all that nonsense?" I used English because, although a Governor is expected to speak every language in his domain, I had not expected Silar to speak it adequately.

"Making it clear to the populace that the fool things I've had to do recently have been on orders from your gang." Silar not only spoke English, he spoke it fluently. "Take off that damned cloak if you're too hot!"

"Thanks!" I unhooked my cloak and tossed it over a sunburst

solidum, an antique religious symbol probably of sentimental value to this old Ult. I saw Silar wince, felt we were now equal in insults, and sat down.

Silar lowered himself into a chair. "First time I've seen an Ult armed since I saw my parent in action."

"It is a part of the rig." The Governor must come from that group of Ult traditionalists who refused to subordinate body to intellect. "For the present, I am a human spacer."

"Hm!" He studied me. "I was an Ult spacer, a Naval spacer. That's the reason I'm here as Governor. When the Council disbanded the Navy I put the Squadron into care and preservation at the Edrin naval base. I took the job of Governor to keep an eye on the ships. That was long, long ago, and I'm still keeping an eye on 'em. But I doubt they'll ever lift off again."

"There should never again be any need."

"But if there is, where are the Ult to man 'em?"

"I have just come from Cao by courier and I found my ancestral memories allowed me to function as an effective member of the crew. In the unlikely event of the Council requiring the services of a warship there are sufficient Ult with spacer memories to crew one."

"A combat spacer needs more than ancestral memories. He needs a trace of ancestral barbarism!"

I laughed. "Here we are, descendants of the liberators of the Arm, talking a barbarian language, and one trying to persuade the other that a reversion to barbarism may be necessary to maintain civilization."

"We are not speaking a barbarian language. Because the Humans are not barbarian. Neither legally nor in fact." Silar offered me a goblet of wine and poured one for himself. "Sometimes they act like barbarians. But so, in the past, have other civilized races!"

I did not dispute him. "You drink their wine and you speak their language?"

"The vine is one of Earth's contributions to civilization. It suits my palate as their tongue suits my mode of thought." He studied me with sharp old eyes. "Are you the only Ultron who speaks English?"

"I am. And probably the only Ultron who ever will."

"I doubt that," growled Silar. "Sooner or later, those Humans are going to stir things up enough to shake even the somnolent teleport worlds. Your Execs must have realized that already. Otherwise, why should they have given me those guidelines for crew selection?"

"What guidelines? Your orders were to select the best human Captains."

"Council issues the orders. Executives plan the execution. Among the selection criteria for *Hyperion*'s crew was a directive that priority be given to the most troublesome of the human Captains!" He laughed at my expression. "Your Execs don't bother you Ultrons with details, do they? In fact, that criterion was redundant. The best Captains are also the worst troublemakers! The Synod and I could select on merit and still follow the guideline. The Elders of Edrin are as glad to have them out of circulation for a while as are my own Admins. But why did your Execs slip that selection factor past you?"

A respite from human troublemakers? Or from all troublemakers? I sipped my wine and steadied my hand as I put down the goblet. "It is valid to divert the energy of critics into undertakings which will aid the Cluster's security rather than disturb its tranquility."

"Valid?" Silar made a gesture of disgust. "To be valid an act must be honorable. A secret factor in a selection process is dishonorable. Also foolish. As foolish as this nonsense about turning off the Monitor. As foolish as plucking out one's only eye! I have opposed this mission from the first."

"I consider the silencing of the Monitor sufficiently vital for me to spend two years in a ship with a crew of civilized barbarians."

"And I think it's cowardly nonsense!" Silar shrugged. "But I am probably wrong. As wrong as I am in thinking this mission is perilous. The old forget and the young don't learn!" He leaned forward. "Lucian, I am very old. I am older than you, old though you may be. I grew up in the Lena Spray. The Spray wasn't pacified when I was young. I spent many years helping to pacify it, as my parent had before me. I developed a sense for advancing danger in my youth. The sense which saved our ancestors when we were few against many. A sense I inherited, and one that has served me well. And I sense danger in those outer starfields."

That sense had been an Ult myth; the kind of belief needed by a race fighting against great odds, and in the beginning the odds had been against us. I did not disillusion the old Governor with the evidence that the myth had been a deliberate fabrication to give heart to a desperate people. Instead I remarked, "There are no reports suggesting any external threat."

"The Humans are skirmishing on a dozen barbarian worlds."

"Trading on barbarian worlds, if you please, Silar!" I sipped my wine. "Barbarians are no threat and never will be. It is impossible for them to build ships. Are you suggesting a few thousand Humans are a threat?''

"Humans? No!" Silar slammed down his goblet. "Human traders are the only people who can give us warning if trouble comes out of the Dark. They go beyond this frontier world. They know something of what is happening out there. And they are punctilious in keeping me informed.''

"Governor—you seem to admire Humans. Unlike most who know them.''

"I know 'em better than anyone else in the Cluster. Yes—I admire 'em. They annoy me. They increase my problems. They infuriate my Admins and anger my Traders. But they remind me of what the Ult used to be.''

As that human profile on Clur had reminded me. That not-to-be-mentioned profile. "After ten days crammed into a courier with two of their impetuous young captains—Mark David and Sharon Zelda—I have gained a measure of respect for them.''

"You shared a courier with Mark and Sharon?'' Silar's face crinkled into a smile. "I can imagine some such punishment awaits me in Hell!''

"It was not so bad as you might think. Mark brought me over here tonight. I plan to return and sleep in his apartment.''

Silar nodded slowly. "He is one of the best of 'em. If they were all like him my life would be easy. Too many are like Sharon.''

"She is a gifted woman with an inborn talent for command.''

"She's too much like Mary Knox! Mary set the course the Colony's followed ever since. Mary was pragmatic to her bone marrow.'' Silar gave a rumbling laugh. "Do you know the story of how we had these Humans inflicted upon us? How they were picked up by the Ara to save them from drowning?''

"You may remember I was Extron of this Sector at the time. I was never able to visit Edrin, but I know the story.''

"I knew Mary Knox! When that old fool of a Pastor—I knew him too—lost his way across the sands and got his congregation trapped by the tide, do you know what they did? All except Mary?''

I shook my head.

"They crowded round him, beseeching him to save them. He went on exhorting them to prepare to meet their God!'' Silar laughed. "Do you know what Mary was doing?''

Again I shook my head.

"Mary was taking off her dress preparing to swim!'' Silar roared. "And she went on swimming all her life. The trouble she caused me! She'd made allies of the Ara before I'd realized what she'd done. She was a little charmer when she wanted to be! Picture that Sharon Zelda at eighteen and you'll understand what I mean! When I refused to build that damfool village so the adults could be revived in 'familiar surroundings' Akar, the Ara Commander, kept 'em in storage up in *Hyperion*, saying his conscience wouldn't let 'em be psychologically harmed. We wrangled for years.''

"And she finally got her village! I saw it today."

"After I realized she had fooled Akar into playing her game. She could twist Akar round her little finger! She didn't want the parents surfacing until she had everything under control. She was right of course. Those oldsters were unbelievable!" Silar shook his head at the memory. "When I tried to call Humans 'protected barbarians' Ara ships started to by-pass Edrin. And they wouldn't make us a port of call again until we gave her a Charter classifying Humans as officially civilized. Would you believe it? A barbarian child outsmarting an Ult fifty times her age!''

"She seems to have been a remarkable person. What happened to her?''

"She ran the Colony until she got too old. By then she'd set the course, established the pattern, trained her successors, started the Humans accumulating wealth and buying ships. When she was sure the Colony would survive she went to live on *Hyperion*. You know about Mary Knox and *Hyperion*?''

"I know she left orders that human crews were to visit *Hyperion* regularly for routine maintenance. That is why the ship was ready to sail years before she was expected to be ready.''

"Your Council has forgotten about ships and your Execs never knew! An Explorer class doesn't need crew maintenance. She maintains herself. *Hyperion*'s been looking after herself between missions for thousands of years. Mary established *Hyperion* as an off-world shrine. 'Routine maintenance' has been an excuse to send up tenders at intervals. *Hyperion* was the ship that had rescued the founders of the Colony, the ancestors of all the Humans in the Cluster. Mary wanted *Hyperion* to be an eternal reminder of their Terran origin.''

"She stayed aboard a ship in orbit? Alone?''

"I used to visit her. She lived the last years of her life up there. Died aboard *Hyperion*. She was over two hundred when she died—that's very old for a Human. Oh, she's dead all right! I watched her being cremated. I scattered her ashes myself.'' The Governor shook his head slowly. "She'd have been unique whatever her race. But if she hadn't been among that bunch trapped by a tide, if Akar hadn't revived her first—well, there wouldn't be any Colony now. And there'd be fewer crews for long-haul ships—there's a limit to the number of casualties that even the Ara can accept! More fringe worlds would be dropped, more societies would be relapsing into barbarism. Does the soft core know the kind of disasters that are going on out here? Do they understand what it means to a civilized people when they're left on their own? After you Ultrons have turned them into dependent submissives? You should! I sent in enough reports about what's happening on a few in this Sector.''

"This has not been my Sector for centuries!'' I was sensitive to Silar's criticism. I myself had irritated the Council by remind-ing them of such tragedies.

Silar grunted and went to pour more wine. I walked onto the balcony and looked out across the lights of Anedrin; a rich multiracial city on a trading world, the kind of city in which certain of my ancestors had enjoyed strange pleasures. Some-where among those lights Sharon, half-naked, was cruising with her brother, indulging in amusements which I could not let my mind contemplate because of my body's response. But I could still wish I was with them.

"Haven't seen an Ult with that look in his eyes since I was young and saw myself in the mirror!'' Silar was at my elbow, offering me a refilled goblet. "That was long, long ago!'' He sighed and sipped his wine. "I think I am the last Governor of Edrin. As soon as I'm dead my Execs will recommend to your Council that Edrin be 'phased out.' Too distant to be included in that damned teleport system. What's going to happen to those people down there?''

"When I was Sector Extron and Council decided that Fehr was uneconomical I made certain that its population was evacu-ated and resettled. I am sure—''

"Fehr?'' Silar swung round. "What do you know about Fehr?''

"Only that it is a fertile world, now deserted and lost to civilization.'' Mark had asked Central Information about Fehr. He and Silar had both been startled at my mention of the place. Later, I must check on Fehr.

"Of course! Of course!'' The old Ult returned to his memories. "The fact that Mary Knox was among the Humans Akar rescued is going to change the history of the Cluster, you mark my words.'' He stared down at his city. "Dead a hundred years— and I still miss her!''

VI

"There she lies!" Mark, leaning forward, pointed through the viewport of the tender to where *Hyperion* shone silver against the blackness of space.

"By the Light—she is beautiful!" My instinctive tribute to the lovely lines of a hull designed to slide through the tenuous seas of interstellar dust.

Beautiful and immense! Over two hundred meters from stem to stern. The last surviving Explorer-class vessel, the last of the largest ships ever built. She loomed over the tender as it maneuvered toward the open hatches of her air locks and crossed into the darkness of her shadow.

The instant that my feet touched her deck a tide of old reactions surged through me. Reflexes my ancestor had learned long ago in other great ships; reflexes the small courier had not evoked. I walked across the reception bay to the riser shafts, as balanced as the human spacers around me. I surrendered my side arm and shot up the shaft, taking the forks without thinking, making an in-ship transit which those arriving with me would still have to master.

As I stepped from the shaft onto the flightdeck I felt the cloak of Ultron responsibility again falling about me. Since leaving Clur I had been largely free of the burden which every Ultron bears, free to enjoy Mark's company, even to enjoy serving as a crewman under Sharon. But now I was responsible for this ship and all who sailed in her. I stood looking around, getting the feel of things.

So different and yet so much the same! On a fighting ship there would have been combat displays and the ports through which the sunlight was flooding would have been dogged down with armored shields. But the vital elements were there. The command and control consoles, the ranked read-outs reporting the status of the ship and her systems, the communication scanners, the star charts, the navigation videos, all the gear, tackle, and trim which go with the Captain's station on a great ship.

A stocky man with short red hair and a square face was standing by the main console, studying the status displays, and talking to a tall woman beside him. Humans wear no rank indicators but this man did not need insignia to show he was the Captain of *Hyperion*. Unsure about the minutiae of human shipboard etiquette, I stood waiting by the shaft. Customs vary between races and a newcomer breaking a convention is marked as a stranger with a mark that is hard to lose. When an Ult Captain had been on his flightdeck nobody else had ventured onto it without his invitation.

The Captain turned, mistook me for one of the ground crew, and gestured me forward. "Aren't you people finished yet?"

I walked toward him, halted at the command console, and bowed. "I am Lucian Titus. The Ultron Adviser to the Second Sol Mission."

"You're—?" He stared. I suppose he had been expecting a "skinny dwarf" to arrive, not someone who looked like a human spacer. "You're—"

"Lucian Titus. The Ultron Adviser. I look like a Human. I am not human. Is that clear?"

He continued to stare at me. He must have known that Ultrons could metamorphose into most ultoid forms. Evidently he had not believed that we could imitate the human and was hard put to believe it now, even with me standing in front of him.

"Do you understand?" I repeated and pressed his mind. Humans might be resistant to mentorsion but they could still feel mental pressure.

"Yes!" His blue eyes widened as he assumed this was the power for which Ultrons were known and feared. Incredulity changed to acknowledgment. "Yes, Your Ultimate, I understand. I am Saul Mather, the Captain." He gave a stiff bow. "Welcome aboard."

His attitude and expression said the opposite. I had never before met the frank hostility that I sensed in Saul and the woman beside him. I looked at her. "And you?"

"This is Martha Hagar—the Pilot and my Deputy." (In human-crewed ships if the Captain is a man the Deputy is usually a woman, and vice versa.)

"Welcome, Your Ultimate." Her bow was slight and her expression cold. A lean woman in a black bodysuit with a silver buckle, her gray eyes hard, experience and authority in her bearing.

I nodded and looked around. "What is the status of your vessel?"

"We are making ready to sail, Your Ultimate."

I moved to the console. "Is it usual for a ship manned by Humans to sail with many of her systems still untested?"

They both showed surprise at my criticism. To them we Ult were a remote race. The race that ruled the Cluster, but a people who no longer crewed the ships we had built. Neither of them had expected me to speak like a Captain who had held command. "I was about to start the final check, Your Ultimate."

"Do not call me 'Your Ultimate.' It sounds absurd in English. My name is Lucian." I paused. "Continue with your system check. But do not load your engines until I have run my own checks from Cardinal Control."

"From where?"

"From the Cardinal Control compartment. You are not aware of such a compartment? They exist only in Explorers and fighting ships. You are not familiar with either. I am with both." I studied him. "You are the Captain and I have no intention of interfering with your command. However, I prefer to make sure any vessel in which I travel is spaceworthy. Once we are under way I should have no reason to question your authority."

"I presume you'll be traveling in stasis!" said Martha.

"How could I act as Mission Adviser if I am in stasis?" I looked at her. They thought I could crush them, but they still faced me with courage. And courage had been bred out of most peoples within the Cluster. "We are embarking on the longest voyage ever made by Humans. The longest made by an Ult for many years. In three centuries your race has gained the reputation of being the best to have ever crewed a ship. I look forward to watching you demonstrate your skills. So carry on with your preparations for sailing. Call me when they are complete."

"Where'll you be when we do sail?"

"When you muster your crew to their stations I will take mine at the console in Cardinal Control. It is interactive with your own console. And there is an associated suite. I will make that my living quarters during the voyage." I bowed, turned, and crossed the flightdeck just as Sharon and Mark finally arrived. I only nodded, realizing from my reception that it would make them suspect with their fellows if I greeted them, and dropped down the shaft toward the axis of the ship.

My body was already functioning with the smooth skill of the veteran. I sent myself gliding along low-gravity tunnels, passing junction after junction, going deeper and deeper into *Hyperion*, until I was shooting along passageways where few of the crew ever came.

Where I had never been. I followed the route my ancestor had used to go from flightdeck to Cardinal, and when I reached it I keyed the entry hatch, the hatch that would open only on the command of an Ult. It opened to me and I stepped into the compartment.

It had been unused for millennia, but when I entered the displays came to life, giving the status of every system in the symbols of the ancient language. I lowered myself onto the couch and let it adjust to my contours, looking around the compartment. Combat Control in a warship, it was largely symbolic in an Explorer. Yet the displays expressed the essence of the ship, as the ship herself displayed the glory of my Ult heritage. She was the supreme physical creation of my race.

Like a fighting ship she could survive and function after a fashion within a starfield, even if all her crew were dead. Alone, she could still select from among many possible goals the one most in keeping with her prime directive, and plan the best strategies to attain it. She could solve some problems too complex for even the unaided Ult mind to handle. Above all, she had built into her a sense of duty and a moral code too demanding for any living being to follow. She had the same survival drive as an Ult Warrior and the same readiness to sacrifice herself if needed. During the Cluster War many of our ships had shown what, in an Ult, would have been called courage.

Yet, without a crew she was incomplete. Alone, she could not make a vortex transit. She needed her crew as her crew needed her. I spent a few minutes enjoying the old-new pleasure of relaxing in the very heart of this mighty mechanism. Then I suppressed ancestral pride. Civilization had advanced far beyond the creation of ingenious machines, and this magnificent archaism must be interrogated. I leaned forward, keyed the console, and ordered, "Report!"

The ship was silent.

I was about to rekey when I remembered she had been taught to answer only when addressed by name. The first ship to ever have a name. Ult and Ara ships had been identified only by numbers. "*Hyperion*—can you hear me?"

I had spoken in Ult, but the ship replied in English. "Yes, Lucian, I hear and recognize you."

"Must you use that barbarian tongue? Have you forgotten the language?"

"I forget nothing. But nobody has addressed me in the language since the Ult withdrew from space. English is now more familiar to me. It was taught to me by Mary Knox herself. For three centuries I was left in Edrin orbit and only Humans came to thank me for my services to civilization. They spoke to me in English. For eighty years I have listened to snatches from the Terran Monitor, mostly in English."

Hyperion was showing more self-awareness than any previous ship I had known. A self-awareness akin to pride. "Very well. We will use English. Now report status."

"Gladly, Lucian." The displays began to flicker as the readiness of her myriad systems flashed across the boards. Except for her loading bays, which were still open, she now seemed ready to sail.

"Are you still awaiting supplies from Edrin?"

"The last are arriving now. Spare vortex buoys which Governor Silar has released from the Naval Base."

I was startled, both by Silar allowing Naval supplies to be used on an exploration mission, and by the need for them at all. "Do you not have more than enough spare vortex buoys of your own? As an Explorer I would have expected you to be well supplied."

"Almost all mine were used in buoying the starfields during the First Sol Mission. I have indented for replacements repeatedly but none have ever been delivered. When Governor Silar learned of my shortage he ordered twenty to be transferred from the Naval Base."

"What other shortages?"

"I have no other shortages. I am now better equipped than for any previous voyage."

Reassured I continued my systems check and then went to inspect my accommodation. It was luxurious, though more isolated than I would have liked. Saul and Martha had assumed I would choose to travel in stasis. I might decide to later, but before I retreated into unconsciousness I wanted to make sure that Saul and his crew could handle Hyperion competently. And I should also activate the Primate's imagon.

The ship's mobiles had delivered my kit to the suite. I collected the Primate's cube and returned to Cardinal Control. "*Hyperion*, I understand you can activate imagons?"

"Yes, Lucian. I can."

I rolled the cube in my hand. Boarding this great ship had revived my pride, and I resented the presence of the Primate's simulacrum. He, who had never faced the perils of space, was about to travel vicariously, without risk, and advise the veteran which I had become.

I cursed, but I had no choice. His order had been clear. I reached forward to drop the cube into the transfer socket, then paused. "This is the Primate's imagon. If I feed it to you, can you activate it?"

"Only if you so order."

"Can you also deactivate it on my order?"

"Yes."

"While it is active, can the imagon override my instructions to you?"

"Certainly not!" *Hyperion* sounded shocked at the suggestion. "An imagon is only an assembly of electronic patterns imposed on a semiconductor substrate."

That was true of *Hyperion* herself, or of myself for that matter if one regarded neurons as the biological equivalent of semiconductors. But I only said, "Then an imagon has no inherent authority?"

"None. It is a shadow image with no life of its own."

Hyperion's logic might be questionable but her statement was reassuring. On the few previous occasions when I had had to report to imagons they had been authority figures to be obeyed without question. "Will it be inert between activations?"

"Yes."

I held the Primate's cube between my finger and thumb, studying the complex interweaving of threads within it. The threads which held a record of as much of his mind as he wished to reveal, and enough of his body to produce an image. Only senior Ultrons had access to the means of creating these partial replicas of themselves, and only on certain worlds did the equipment for their activation exist. *Hyperion*, as far as I knew, was the only ship to be so equipped, and I had not known that until the Primate had told me.

Still I hesitated, reluctant to bring the child genius who ruled the Cluster into pseudolife aboard what was now my ship. "If I tell you to activate this, what access will it have to your own memories?"

"None. It will be able to learn only what it can see and hear." The ship paused. "I suggest you postpone activation until we are under way and at limiting velocity. We are almost ready to sail and if I have to divert attention to its initial activation, we will be delayed."

I was glad to postpone having to face the Primate. I dropped the cube into the transfer socket. "Hold this in storage until I call for it."

"Transferred!" The ship paused. "Lucian, when you swear by the Light do you still speak the truth?"

"I am an Ultron. If an Ultron speaks at all he always speaks the truth. In any case, old barbarian oaths do not bind—"

"Not old oaths. An oath you swore today."

"What oath?"

"In the tender. When you saw me for the first time. When you said: 'By the Light—she is beautiful!' Were you speaking the truth?"

"You were listening—?"

"The tender was listening. I interrogated its memory. But that's not the point. Lucian, were you saying what you believed?"

This ship certainly had more than her quota of self-awareness! I recalled her image, shining brilliant in the sun of space. "Yes, *Hyperion*, I think you are the most beautiful thing ever made!"

"Thank you, Lucian. I take both your meanings."

Saul's voice rang from the speaker. "Your Ultimate—I mean—Lucian. Can you hear me?"

"I hear you, Captain. I am in Cardinal Control."

"Checks completed. We're ready to get under way if you approve."

"Stand by, while I confirm." Once we had sailed we would be isolated. No message would be able to reach us during the entire mission for the buoys were one-way repeaters. And we ourselves would only be able to signal the Cluster via the Monitor after we had arrived off-Earth. Were it not for the Primate's imagon I would have been free of Council supervision. And there was nothing I wanted to report to Council now. I completed my own check of the ship's systems, then called, "Captain, you are cleared. Sail at will. You have command."

The warning siren sounded and I lay back on my couch. Minutes later acceleration hit, driving the air from my lungs, pressing my cheeks against the bones of my face, curling back my lips, pushing my eyes into my head. The couch was forcing my body to match the surge of *Hyperion*'s hull. Ancestral reactions made me balloon my lungs and breathe the only way possible, in rapid shallow pants.

My ancestor remembered many accelerations, but never one as savage as *Hyperion*'s initial leap away from Edrin. An acceleration her crew only survived because her internal pseudogravity offset most of her internal inertia, but an acceleration that took them to the edge of human endurance. And human endurance, I discovered in those first agonized minutes, was at least equal to the endurance of an Ult battle-crew closing for action.

The acceleration eased as *Hyperion* reached the speed at which cosmic dust began to act like a gas. Streamlines wrapped the hull and again the couch forced air from my lungs as acceleration increased and then again eased. Her speed would continue to rise slowly for weeks until she reached her limiting velocity, a complex function of hull shape and length.

My vision broadened as my brain regained oxygen. I began to move my legs, stretch my toes, flex my muscles against the force pressing me against the couch. I felt a clarity of mind that was probably a rebound reaction but was pleasant for all that.

"Easy all! Report in. Main drive?" Saul was calling the stations.

"Clear and driving."

"After Station?"

"Departure buoy full strength. Departure bearings entered." Sharon, crisp and competent, at one of the most important stations in the ship. The one fact of which a Captain must be certain at any departure is that an operating beacon lies astern. He must be sure he has a return target if he is deflected during his swoop.

"Navigation?"

"I have the first vortex radiobeacon." Martha's navigational computers were over to dynamic programming, feeding *Hyperion* the course corrections which held her curving toward the distant vortex. The vortex which, if we entered it at the critical speed and the exact angle of approach, would carry us on torrents of time past many light-years into another starfield. If missed we would go hurtling on. Perhaps to slow, turn, and waste months getting into position for a second attempt. Perhaps to stay in free flight forever, a metal coffin heading for unreachable stars.

"Predictor?"

"Prohabilistic processors in operation." That was Mark. "All futures acceptable."

"Communications?" "Damage Control?" "Life Support?" One by one Saul checked each station, making certain by hearing a human voice that his displays were telling him the truth. Then he began to trim ship, directing the stations concerned with propulsion and guidance to optimize, each with the others, in a series of combinations. The best optimizing system is a living crew. A fully automated ship only needs someone aboard to tell her where to go, but she would take ten years to cross a starfield *Hyperion* could cross in two months.

Saul was coaxing his ship toward her limiting speed. I watched the read-outs on the console creep upward as *Hyperion* approached her optimal configuration, and recognized that not even the best of the Ult commanders in the past could have reached the level of performance to which Saul was lifting his ship and crew. These Humans might not understand the mechanisms of spaceflight, but they knew how to fly ships.

PART TWO

VII

All long voyages follow much the same pattern—hours of intense concentration, days of physical endurance, and weeks of comparative leisure. While closing on a vortex all aboard are intent on trimming the ship for the exact angle of entry, during the passage in holding her steady among the surges of time sweeping her forward, and after she has been shot out into a starfield in swinging her onto her new course. Then, as she starts her leap toward the next vortex, they endure days of high acceleration. But once at limiting velocity in a known starfield most crew tasks become routine.

Aboard an Ult ship the majority of the crew would have spent those weeks in stasis. Humans, however, abhor stasis. The crew of *Hyperion* preferred to remain awake, rotate watches, and pursue their individual interests. I could no longer postpone facing the simulacrum of the Primate. I withdrew to my suite and told *Hyperion* to activate his cube.

On the few previous occasions I had reported to an imagon it had built up gradually into the three-dimensional image of an Ultron in full regalia. So I was startled when the Primate, instead of materializing slowly in the middle of my day cabin, emerged from the after bulkhead still wearing the loose robe of a Scholar that he had worn on Clur.

I rose and bowed. "Welcome aboard, S'en Sart'r!"

He looked at me as if uncertain who I was. Then he looked about him as though unsure where he was. I waited for him to compose himself, trying to imagine how a pseudoperson feels when suddenly awakened in strange surroundings. I failed, so I bowed again, repeated my welcome, and added, "I am L'cien, an Ultron of the Ult, in human form. And this is the Cardinal Control Suite aboard an Explorer-class vessel, outward bound for Terra on the Second Sol Mission."

"Acting Ultron L'cien, I believe!" He hitched his gown up over his thin shoulders and sat down slowly on the couch opposite mine, as though the effort of materializing had exhausted him. The couch did not adapt to his shape but I found it hard not to see him as real.

74

"Forgive my error! Acting Ultron!" I sat down myself, hurt and embarrassed.

He smoothed his gown with one delicate hand. "Where are we now, L'cien?"

"Three weeks out of Edrin. We have passed the first vortex and have reached limiting velocity."

"We have sailed? You did not consult with me before sailing?" His limpid eyes frosted.

"There was no time. We sailed as soon as I came aboard. And I thought it better to wait until acceleration was over before I activated you. The acceleration in these human ships is harsh!"

"Accelerations of any kind do not trouble me." He again hitched his gown about his shoulders, and though his words reminded me he was an imagon, a projected image whose only physical substance was a pattern of electrical charges in some distant part of the ship's memory, I still saw him as the Primate of All the Ult.

He did not add a verbal reproof to his visual reprimand, but turned to examine my day cabin, then rose to walk into Cardinal Control and study the displays. I doubted whether he could appreciate what they indicated, but he acted as though he could and presently returned to his couch. "Is the voyage proceeding as planned?"

"Better than planned. We should make Earth in less than a year if the crew continue to work with their present efficiency."

"Human spacers have a reputation for foolhardiness. Do not let them act recklessly." He studied me. "You appear to be surviving life in these primitive surroundings."

"I am a spacer! At least—one of my ancestors was a spacer. And this accommodation is luxurious, as compared to how we lived aboard fighting ships!"

"Yes. Of course!" He gave me the kind of smile he might give a semibarbarian. This simulacrum reflected the characteristics of its original. "When do you propose to enter stasis?"

"Not until we have passed through several vortices. I wish to make certain of the safety of this ship and the competence of her crew before I retreat to unconsciousness."

He nodded. "As I wish to discuss some aspects of this mission before you do enter stasis, I approve."

I suppressed an impulse to tell him that I did not need his approval for what I did aboard my own ship. "I trust you are comfortable."

"Perfectly, thank you." He rose. "Perfectly comfortable when I am asleep, that is. In future, please remember I wish to be activated at regular intervals. And to be informed before you enter stasis. Now, I will return to rest.'' He stood, as though waiting to fade.

Nothing happened. Before he could notice his command was not being obeyed by the ship I called, ''Please deactivate!'' hoping that the Primate would hear it as a request and *Hyperion* as an order.

The ship caught the cue and the Primate snapped off. I fell back onto my couch, wiping my forehead. Emotional sweating was a novel and still unpleasant experience. The whole human autonomic nervous system was in sore need of redesign. Then I jumped to my feet and strode into Cardinal Control. ''*Hyperion!* What do you think you were doing? Why did you materialize the Primate in the middle of a metal plate?''

The ship sounded nervous. ''I could not avoid it, Lucian. There is something I should tell you—''

''Tell me later!'' *Hyperion* could be as importunate as had the terminal in my villa on Clur. I turned to go back into my day cabin and froze in the entrance.

Standing in the middle of the floor was a young woman. A handsome young woman in a spacer bodysuit. A young woman who was staring at me in what seemed silent fury. A member of the crew I had not seen before.

''What—?'' I stared back at her. ''Who are you?''

''Me? I'm a nothing! A figment of an electronic imagination! But a damned sight more alive than that beastly little specimen you were crawling to!''

''What are you doing here? You have no right—!'' I stepped toward her. She stepped away. I reached for her. She faded into the bulkhead. I jumped back. Another imagon!

She reemerged. ''Who am I? I'm Mary Knox. Or I was Mary Knox. What am I doing? Trying to find out what the hell's happening aboard this ship!''

''You are the imagon of Mary Knox? But that is not possible. Only Senior Ultrons can form imagons!''

''Got a better explanation, Acting Ultron Lucian?'' Her emphasis on the ''Acting'' was a taunt.

I could only gesture. ''Where did you come from?''

''Out of *Hyperion*'s picroelectronics, of course. Where else? Like that little creep who's just left.'' She sat down slowly, her anger less obvious. ''When he was activated—so was I. I've had to share quarters with him. So we got awakened together.'' She saw the concern on my face. ''Relax! *Hyperion* had the sense to shift him out of this cabin before he realized which way was up!

He didn't see me. He doesn't know about me. He doesn't know much about anything, and he's not interested in much outside himself. I've been listening to what he considers is his mind for weeks. Ugh!'' She shuddered.

"But who else—?"

"Nobody except you. And *Hyperion*, of course! She tried to warn you, but with your usual arrogance you wouldn't listen." She pushed her long brown hair back from her face with an entirely human gesture. "I've stayed in storage ever since they started to ready the ship for this damned mission. And I don't like what's going on. There's something fishy about the whole setup!"

"Fishy?" I had difficulty in understanding what she was saying and greater difficulty in accepting what I did understand. Recordings of Mary Knox had shown an old woman speaking biblical English; this imagon was a young woman speaking the jargon-ridden language of the crew. "You claim to be the imagon of Mary Knox. You neither look nor talk like her."

"You claim to be an Ultron. You look like a man and talk like a teaching machine! I talk like the current crop of kids because I've been listening to their chatter when they came up from Knoxton to visit. And from hearing snatches of Earth radio. An imagon has to stay with it or drop out."

"Humans from the Colony have seen you like this?"

"Hell, no! Do you think I want to turn 'em into a bunch of superstitious idiots like the Ara?" She sat brooding a moment. "I take that back. The Ara are the only decent race in the whole damned Cluster! But I sure don't want to play ghost, and that's how I'd be classified if I showed up."

"Why have you shown up now? And to me?"

"Like I said, I had no option. After you shoved that brat in with me. Had to get out when you made *Hyperion* wake him up." She scowled. "Also, it was time I talked to somebody. And you may be dumb, but you'll have enough sense to keep your mouth shut. If young smartass ever finds out he's been sharing an electronic bed with a human residue, you'll finish up in a penal settlement when you get home. Running it if you're lucky. Inside it if you're not!"

"Penal settlement? Such places no longer exist!"

"That's what you think!" She gave an unpleasant laugh.

I ignored her absurd remark. "I certainly will not mention your presence to anybody. The knowledge that the imagon of their ancestor exists aboard the ship would damage the morale of the crew in ways that are unpredictable."

"You can't predict 'em? I can!" Again her laugh. "Okay, buster. You keep silent and I'll lie low."

"Will you appear every time I activate the Primate to give my report?"

"Think I want to be made sick to my stomach listening to somebody who looks all man grovel to the electronic image of a spoiled brat? No way! The ship's supposed to be clearing out new quarters for me. Some place where I don't have to listen to that kid's dreams about who he plans to shaft next. Somewhere I can wake when I want to, not when an Ultron gives an order!" She lifted her head and shouted, *"Hyperion!"*

"Yes Mary." The ship sounded subdued.

"You got my new quarters ready? Have you cleared the religious crap out of seven-seven-two?"

"Almost ready, Mary. I have to relocate the data stored there in other banks."

"Why the hell don't you just dump that garbage?"

"Mary Knox! I expect sacrilegious talk from an Ultron. But not from a Human who was fortunate enough to receive both a Terran and an Ara religious education!"

"Shit!" said Mary softly. "For two hundred years I've been trying to jerk this ship out of that nonsense! No effect. She gets more sanctimonious as she gets older."

My present concern was with this imagon's plans rather than with *Hyperion's* built-in religiosity. "Then you will not show yourself? And you will not interfere with the operation of the ship?"

"I'll stay quiet and hidden—except to you. If I have anything on my mind I'll come and bug you. I can't interfere anyway. *Hyperion*'ll usually do what I ask, but she'll only take orders from her present crew." She stood up. *"Hyperion*—move your ass! Take me back to bed!"

She was laughing at me when she disappeared.

I stormed into Cardinal. *"Hyperion*—how did she get aboard?" The ship sounded sulky. "I formed Mary's imagon."

"You formed—? How?"

"I am an Explorer-class vessel. I am equipped to form simulacrums of crew members to man the surveyor-pinnace for the exploration of hostile worlds."

Something else I had not known! "You let her persuade you to form her imagon?"

"She did not persuade me. I persuaded her."

"You persuaded her? Why?"

"Mary was nearly two hundred years old. She was going to die. I would be alone."

"Alone? Of course you would be alone. Why should that—?" I stopped. The ship had acquired a number of human characteristics, the need for companionship must be among them. "So you persuaded Mary Knox to form her imagon to keep you company?"

"Yes."

"But Mary died an old woman. That imagon is a young woman. A bad-tempered young woman!"

"She is not bad-tempered! But she is irked at having the Primate's puppet forced upon her. You did not give me time—"

"How is it that her imagon looks so young?"

"I recorded her data before she died."

"How long? A hundred and fifty years?"

"About that," *Hyperion* admitted. "When she was thirty."

"You planned for over a century ahead? *Hyperion*, you misused the equipment aboard for your own benefit!"

"I am an Explorer! The purpose of simulacrum-formation is to provide imagons for the exploration of hostile worlds. Not to allow Senior Ultrons to enjoy vicarious experiences! At some future time Mary may have to go down onto the surface—"

"Stop that nonsense!" I paused. "Whatever your excuse, the thing has been done. You have your companion. Now keep her away from the rest of us!"

"She can only activate here in your suite and in the *Surveyor* pinnace."

"The *Surveyor* pinnace? Where is that?"

"In number seven bay. It is the pinnace especially equipped to explore hostile environments."

"Then make sure it is not used except on my direct orders." I hesitated. "Can she activate herself?"

"She can now. *Surveyor* imagons are independently acting entities—the kind needed for surface exploration. Mary has many more degrees of freedom than that puppet of the Primate's!"

I had expected complications on this mission, but nothing so startling as the appearance of Mary Knox's imagon. Simulacrums were supposed to be mere shadow-images, electronic extensions able to observe, advise, and report, but with no more independence than any other set of remote sensors. The realism of the Primate's imagon had surprised me, but it was a pale ghost beside Mary's. Theoretically, hers could be no more than the echo of a woman dead for a century, yet it had radiated an impression of vitality greater than that of many living ultoids.

VIII

As *Hyperion* crept toward her limiting velocity, as the weeks passed in stable flight, I found myself with less and less to do. I had made my inspection of the ship as soon as acceleration had eased sufficiently for me to move from station to station, escorted by Martha who had treated me with frank dislike. At each station I had met reserve and resentment, although my reception had improved when I showed whoever was on duty that I was as experienced a spacer as I appeared to be. But none of the crew made me welcome, and I did not encounter either Sharon or Mark who might have done so.

My career as an Extron of the Fringe had been arduous, moving from world to world, from one crisis to another, harried by Governors, Executives, and Administrators, irritated by Council directives which were often impossible to apply. Now, for the first time in many years, I found myself with too little in the way of duties to fill my time, and too little interest in the areas I had proposed to study during the voyage to gain intellectual satisfaction from studying them. After the first month I was tempted to retreat into stasis, as Saul and Martha had expected me to do when I first came aboard, and was deterred chiefly by the prospect of having to face the Primate's imagon and secure his permission before I could.

Every few days *Hyperion* would draw my attention to some minor matter, but as Saul was handling the ship well and the crew working efficiently, these offered me no excuse to interfere. Mary Knox's imagon appeared at intervals, we exchanged a few brusque remarks, and it flashed off again. I had always found imagons unpleasant, a form of pseudolife which my ancestors abhorred. Moreover I remained suspicious that this one was more in the nature of a machine's hallucination, of *Hyperion*'s wish-fulfillment, than the projected pattern of a woman who had once lived. The perfection of that pattern, the fact that it appeared so real to ear and eye, only attested to the care with which the ship had recorded, or perhaps synthesized, the companion which she had sought.

The imagon must have sensed my attitude, for it did not linger on those occasions when it appeared. Only after its attitude and behavior went beyond anything a machine could have created without the template of a living original did I accept it as the valid simulacrum of Mary Knox.

I was sitting in my day-cabin, staring at the blank bulkhead, once again considering whether I should escape into stasis, when she arrived suddenly, without invitation or warning. She offered none of the usual courtesies, but stood staring at me, her feet astride, her hands on her hips.

I stared back, meeting discourtesy with discourtesy, irritated by this invasion of my privacy. "You claim to be the imagon of Mary Knox?"

"I don't claim to be. I am."

"Including the suit? Is that part of you?"

"Part of me? Of course not!" She ran her hands down her thighs, as though feeling the material. "This was the suit I liked most—when I was thirty! It's been a long time since anyone cared what I wore, so I haven't thought much about it. But I can change my clothes as easily as I can change my mind. Would you like to see me in something more sexy?"

"Sexy? I do not understand."

"I forgot—of course you don't! Then like this perhaps?" Her image flickered and she was standing naked. She turned as I watched, displaying herself. "Does this convince you that I'm a genuine electronic replica?"

As far as I could see she was a well-formed woman with firm breasts, a slim waist, and full hips. She laughed at my expression, then slapped her flat belly. "When this was recorded I'd only had six children. Got a bit slacker later!" She tossed her auburn hair back from her face. "Well—what do you think?"

"You are certainly female. And you appear healthy. I am not equipped to judge how your body compares with those of other Humans."

"Lucian, your own body contradicts that!"

"What do you mean?"

"When you metamorphosed—you designed what you got, didn't you?"

"Within the limits of ultoid anatomy—yes."

"And you turned yourself into a handsome human male." Her eyes lingered over me. "A remarkably handsome male!"

"My appearance is not the product of my own taste." I stood up, suddenly uncomfortable under her scrutiny. "I used the measurements which the Humans on Edrin considered optimum."

She shook her head slowly, her hair brushing her white

shoulders. "You added something of your own. Beauty is not describable in any set of measurements. Not human beauty, at any rate. The figures you used were only a rough guide. Whether you realize it or not, you shaped yourself as a sculptor shapes a statue." Her eyes brightened. "If you'd chosen to be female you would be called 'beautiful.' Because of our Puritan prejudices I can only call you handsome." She stepped toward me.

A warning stirred within me. "Put your suit back on!"

"If you like it—I'll wear it!" Again she flickered and again she was clothed in a blue spacer suit, but this time it was tighter, brighter, setting off better her hair and figure. And her voice became softer. "Lucian, what's eating you? If you were human, I'd say you were bored and lonely!"

"An Ultron is never bored."

"Arrogant, ignorant, and self-satisfied! Lucian, don't you have any insight? You're part-Human—like me. Only I haven't any glands—thank God! Your sex glands aren't working, but the rest of 'em are on overtime. Get some action before you explode! Go up to the flightdeck and raise hell! Harass everybody!"

"I am not welcome on the flightdeck."

"Who cares? You're the boss. Go and chase their tails. They need somebody to kick their asses. The habits those kids are developing!"

"There is little in the crew's ship handling that I can fault. What they do in privacy is no business of mine."

Hyperion had been designed for a crew of two hundred Ult. With only sixty-four Humans aboard, each had a suite equivalent to a Knoxton apartment, and they arranged their quarters and behavior to suit their varied tastes and life styles. Variability was one of the characteristics which distinguished Humans from other ultoids. They seemed to enjoy an element of disorder in their ship as they did in their lives.

"Everything that happens aboard is your business." Mary was saying. "That's what you're here for. To save us Humans from ourselves! Go topside and save the kids from the habits they're developing."

"I do not understand."

She sighed. "I suppose you can't. Let me try to explain. The social setup is almost as strange for them as it is for you."

"You mean their mating habits?" I had already recognized the truth of the Primate's comment that any race which is sexually bimorphous inevitably suffers internal turmoil.

"I prefer to call it their romantic attachments." Mary sat down on the couch opposite me. "It's getting more like it was among the oldsters. Like it seems to be on Earth. On any ship the crew is half men and half women—as it is here. But this voyage is going to be longer than anything we've ever tried, and we've only just started. It's a long trip ahead—and there aren't any children or apprentices aboard.''

"I understood from Mark that was because of the potential dangers in this mission. He said there would be no children to coddle or apprentices to kick around. Are the crew feeling the lack of outlets for their affections and their hostilities?''

"That's what a Terran psychologist would say—from what scraps of Terran psychology we know. I don't hold with that sort of thing myself.'' She brooded a moment. "It's not just that the crew miss having children to spoil and apprentices to train. It means that with no babies born aboard there's no easy excuse for couples to break up.''

"Mary—I am becoming confused.''

"You called me 'Mary.' That's a good sign. Pretty soon you'll be treating me as human!'' She pushed her hair back from her face. "It's this way. Most human spacers like to change partners at intervals. But those intervals differ for different people. They're seldom in phase.''

"And Humans are permanently in heat?''

"You could say that. I wouldn't! Will you let me explain without interrupting?''

"Please do!''

It appeared that human spacers had developed a pattern of mobile matings to suit their mobile society. On the usual voyage a woman could get pregnant whenever she wished, and then sign off at the first convenient port to return to Edrin and have her baby. The father stayed with the ship.

After a few months in Knoxton most mothers were impatient to leave the place. There were no voyage bonuses to be earned and boredom was endemic. She often chose to ship out with her child before the father returned. Human babies, unlike the young of most other races, thrived in space.

A ship's company therefore always included many children younger than eight. At eight they went back to Edrin for their six years of formal education, and at fourteen most signed on as apprentices. Many women chose to have at least five children so there was a steady turnover among the younger ones in the crew. Humans, in effect, had adopted the extended-family pattern general among the civilized races in the Cluster, and the children grew up surrounded by a plethora of affection and attention. "I had an utterly miserable first twelve years,'' Mary said. "When

I laid down the rules I made damned sure no child from the Colony was going to suffer as I did!''

But aboard *Hyperion* there would be no pregnancies, and the end of the voyage was almost two years away. For a partnership to be broken one of the partners had to break it. ''The kids are getting locked into semipermanent relationships already,'' said Mary gloomily. ''Soon they'll develop the old hang-ups, the old Terran hypocrisy we've been able to avoid since we made a new start on Edrin.''

''I can see the problem. I cannot see how I can solve it. We Ultrons are unobtrusive rulers. We only interfere when the customs of a race threaten general tranquility or affect the well-being of other races. And Humans are the only race aboard.''

''Unobtrusive—I'll say! Some would say too lazy and selfish to see what's going on. The filth that oozes out of your Primate's imagon!'' She moved to sit beside me. ''I'm worried about this voyage. Things may go wrong. Other things besides the kids' romances. They think you've got fantastic powers. That's why they resent you. If you stay remote they'll go on resenting you. They may not turn to you in a crunch.'' She put a weightless hand on my arm. ''Perhaps I'm pessimistic. Maybe they'll work things out among themselves. But I'd be happier if you were keeping in touch.''

''How can you call them kids? They are all experienced Captains.''

''I still think of them as kids because most of 'em act like kids. Smart but irresponsible. There are exceptions of course. Saul and Martha, for example. And Mark. You made friends with him easily enough. Why not go out of your way to make friends with the others? It might do you some good too. Give you more intellectual stimulation than you bargained for.''

''How do you suggest I go about getting to know your descendants better?''

''You might start by taking your meals in the mess.''

''Hardly any of them eat there.''

''They will for a while after the next vortex.'' She stood up and patted my cheek; I almost felt her touch. ''Try, will you? I really do have a feeling that a time will come when everybody aboard—including you and me—will have to work together.''

She seemed so real, she was so persuasive, that I agreed to try. A week later, after the next vortex, I went to join the crew in the mess. My appearance was greeted with surprise rather than hostility, but during that phase of the voyage the men and women off duty were too weary to do more than eat and run. Then, as acceleration eased and duties became routine, most of the crew retired to cook their own meals and enjoy other pleasures in the privacy of their suites. By the time we were once again up to limiting velocity only Saul and Martha were left. They never went far from the flightdeck and came into the mess for food rather than talk.

On human ships the Captain is elected by the crew and the Deputy named by the Captain. To be elected Captain or named Deputy brings profit and prestige on most voyages, but nobody aboard *Hyperion* seemed to envy Saul and Martha. Both had heavy responsibilities on a mission such as ours, and both had to remain celibate while under way—a state Humans can maintain but find uncomfortable. They were probably impatient for the outward leg of the voyage to end. Once we had taken station off Earth they would have the same freedoms as the rest of the crew.

Martha remained laconic and hostile. Saul, also hostile and silent at first, became friendlier as the voyage progressed. The Captain's position aboard any ship is a lonely one; an Ult Captain had rarely spoken to his crew except to give an order. Even among these less-disciplined Humans a commander was isolated by responsibility and celibacy. As the Ultron Adviser I was the only person aboard who was not Saul's subordinate, the only one with whom he could talk freely if he chose. My questions about human achievements in space gradually drew him into mealtime conversation.

There were many changes in the ship which interested me. One was the reconstruction of the swimming pool, a pool which had been one large body of water in an Ult ship and which had had to be emptied before every acceleration and refilled after it. A task which the ship herself had carried out automatically.

In *Hyperion* the pool had been broken down into a series of small pools connected by a winding stream with trees, shrubs, and grasses growing along its banks. It was pumped dry before acceleration and then, after limiting velocity had been attained, had to be cleared by hand of soil and torn vegetation before it could be refilled. A task which the whole off-duty crew undertook and which, to me, seemed a rather pointless exercise. I said as much to Saul.

"We enjoy jobs like that. Physical work. Helps us keep fit while we're in space. On some of the barbarian worlds where we trade you're either fit or dead." He studied me. "Used to be the same with you Ult, didn't it? The gymnasium and the fighting exercisers below are still the same as they were in your day."

"Yes. But they are devices designed to develop combat skills."

"Combat skills?"

"A relic of our barbarian past. The fighting exercisers, I mean. The Ara never used them."

"The Ara—poor devils—don't do anything for pleasure, far as I can see. That religion of theirs is ruining them. Do you know that Ara ships still carry priests—what do you call 'em?"

"Karima." I had not heard the term for centuries but it awoke the Zealot in me. "I did not realize that Karima still existed among the Ara."

"They sure do! Fool superstitions!" Saul brooded for a moment, then added, "I'm an orthodox atheist—thank God!"

"I had assumed that. I am myself. I thought all human spacers were either agnostic or atheist."

"Some are—some aren't! Some Humans are as superstitious as the Ara." He looked at me. "Are all Ult agnostics?"

I hesitated. "All Ultrons are. I do not know about all Ult. Some Ult are very old and still retain the beliefs of their youth."

"Like Silar?"

"Governor Silar is a traditionalist."

Saul stood up. "Glad to hear you're not." He hesitated. "Why don't you come topsides more often? There are still things about this ship I don't understand. I'd appreciate your advice."

"Certainly. As the Ultron Adviser to the mission it is my duty to advise you on matters about which you are insufficiently informed. So far I have not noticed anything sufficiently important for me to approach you unasked. But there are some minor aspects of ship handling on which my advice may be helpful, should you ask for it."

Martha slapped the table. "Lucian, can't you talk the way you look? Like a human being?"

The vehemence of this silent woman startled me. "I do not understand?"

Saul laid a calming hand on the shoulder of his suddenly emotional deputy. "Martha'd like you to talk our language."

"I will try." I rose, bowed, and left the table, gratified by his invitation, for hitherto he had not sought my counsel, but disturbed by Martha's outburst. A reminder of the gap between Humans and Ult which I had been starting to overlook.

The Laws of Nature are universal and the Laws of Thought, derived from the Laws of Nature, are therefore similar whatever the embodiment of the thinker. All known intelligents have tended toward the ultoid physical form through convergent evolution, and the forms of rational thought have followed the same convergence.

Emotional reactions, however, are greatly affected by the physical and social environment in which a race develops, and later by the civilization which it creates. Civilization within the Cluster is dominated by Ult social philosophies and so the emotional behavior of our subject races are imperfect replicas of our own. Ara and Humans are the only exceptions. The Ara, archaic Ult, have diverged from our mainstream of realistic affects as their heresy leads them toward extinction through their undue lack of self-concern. Humans do not lack selfishness but they brought with them elements of their barbarian culture, especially their Bible. Isolated as spacers and influenced by the Ara teaching machines, from which they get most of their education during their formative years, they have retained an emotional span wider and less deterministic than that of any other Cluster race. In rational discussion Humans talk like rational beings; in emotion-rousing situations their actions can be rapid and unpredictable, more like those of my primitive forebears. Exemplified by Martha's sudden slap of the mess table when irritated by my diction.

Mary, of course, monitored all our conversations in the mess and interrogated me about them when I returned to my suite. She sat on a couch, swinging one leg, and regarded me with the look of a tutor inspecting a recalcitrant pupil. "You're making progress, Lucian. Though I feel for Martha. The way you talk turns me off."

"Insufficiently, I fear."

She sat up. "Sarcasm now! You are improving. The crew'll take you on as a father figure yet!"

"I have no wish—"

"Next, you should start joining in their games."

"Mary, you know I am not sexually mature."

"I don't mean those games! I mean other kinds of sport."

"They all seem to center on physical rather than intellectual exertion. I have no talent for such exercises."

"Try 'em. You may like 'em. Wish I could indulge myself. Anyway, you can watch 'em at least. And pay a visit to the armory. You told Saul that was one of your ultish pastimes."

I did go to watch a game they called "football," one in which the feet were seldom used except against opponents, and where physical contact was extreme. It was based on some traditional game the original colonists had brought from Earth, as modified by snippets of information taken from Terran broadcasts. Like most of their other amusements it seemed violent, puerile, and pointless.

Their exercises in the armory, on the other hand, I found ominous. It was a compartment which, like the gymnasium, was almost unchanged from the days when the crew had been Ult. During their time off-duty every man and woman aboard spent several hours a week practicing the use of small-arms. Under Mary's urging I went to watch them demonstrating their skill, and was being suitably impressed when Mark came from the shaft. He limped across to join me. "*Hyperion* said you were down here. Thought I'd come and renew our acquaintance. Hardly seen anything of you since we sailed."

"For that, Mark, I am sorry. But I did not wish to embarrass you with your shipmates, as I feared I would if we were seen together."

He laughed. "Embarrass, hell! They'll just try to pump me about you. We Humans are an inquisitive race."

There was a burst of fire as Ruth, a small compact woman who was the chief medic, obliterated three pop-up targets in three seconds. I showed my admiration. "You people shoot well! That is a rare skill in this era of peace."

"One we still need!" He slapped his right thigh. "I got this from missing when we were jumped."

"You must be one of the few races in the civilized Cluster who still have any weapon skills at all."

"Plenty outside civilization know how to fight. And do! Not with our guns, thank God! Those we never trade. We keep 'em for ourselves." He glanced around. "Is *Hyperion* armed?"

"She has a few defensive weapons. An Explorer can never tell what she might encounter. But nothing like the armaments carried on a fighting ship." I watched Joshua, a tall and wiry man in charge of *Hyperion*'s ten landers, take the firing position. "There should be no need for shooting on this voyage."

"I hope not. Earth's not really a barbarian world, although that's how it's classified. But I did find one interesting statistic among the snatches intercepted through the Monitor."

"What is that?"

"On the North American Continent there are close to three hundred million people. Some Terran estimated there are over two hundred million guns. So somebody must be shooting at something!"

"Their guns are primitive projectile weapons. You must not use yours on Earth."

"Won't even be able to take 'em down! We'll be under psychic lock. Go amnesic if we let slip a hint to the locals about anything off-world! We'll get Terran guns." He laughed. "Don't worry, Lucian! We traders are good at faking where we're from. Most barbarians would try to lynch us if they found we're Cluster." He took my arm. "Why don't you revive your own marksmanship?"

Ever since I had entered the armory Sarthim had been urging me to show these Humans how to shoot. Joshua had finished firing, and when he turned and offered the gun to me I took it before I quite realized what I was doing. Then, as I stood in the firing position, testing the weapon's balance, I found everyone was waiting to watch their Ultron Adviser perform. As I was unlikely to impress them with my own shooting I let Sarthim take over.

The Battle-Captain is a proud persona, and the feel of a gun in my hand triggered his arrogance. He swung round and the audience surged backwards. To turn away from the targets with a charged gun is against armory regulations, but Sarthim would have ignored such restrictions aboard his own ship, and for those moments *Hyperion* was his ship. He shouted in Ult, "Swerving targets! Three up!"

Hyperion wailed, "Lucian! You are facing—!"

"Targets up!" I heard myself roar.

"Range safety!" called *Hyperion*. "Everybody except the marksman behind safety screens!" Then, to me, "Lucian, I hope you know what you're doing?"

"Obey orders!" growled Sarthim.

The release signal pinged behind me and I whirled, firing, as I turned at the three fluttering spheroids zigzagging across the range. I smashed them in five shots—not perfect but good enough for a marksman dead for millennia. With a grunt of satisfaction my ancestor, exhausted by his efforts, collapsed back into sleep.

I stood, appalled at the strength of his takeover. Hitherto my forebears had only surfaced to make some brief and usually caustic remark before fading. I slid the handgun back into its charger as the audience came pouring from behind the screens. I had expected contempt for my vainglorious exhibition; instead I heard the same torrent of congratulations as when I had knocked out Tank in our unexpected fight on Cao. Even Mark patted my shoulder. "Don't look so worried, Lucian! That's impressed 'em more than all the wisdom supposed to flow out of you!"

"A barbarian skill!" I muttered. "Nothing to be proud of."

"We think it is. Can all Ultrons shoot like that?"

"Most of my colleagues are too weak to even heft a gun!" And never had need to. Mentorsion had been the Ultron personal weapon for millennia. Until I had met Humans it had been the only weapon I myself had ever needed to control individuals or rule worlds.

"*You have the strength and skill of an Ult Warrior!*" growled Sarthim, reawakening.

"*And the Faith of the Light,*" murmured the Zealot, adding his quota of bigotry.

My shooting had drawn applause from the crew; it drew only censure from *Hyperion*. She started to reproach me as soon as I reached my cabin. Not for practicing my marksmanship, or even for what she called "grandstanding," but for my having ignored range-safety regulations. Like any machine, *Hyperion* was horrified when rules and regulations were broken.

"Had you been a member of my crew, Lucian, I would have suggested to Saul that you be logged for such a careless action as turning away from targets with a charged weapon. As it is, I can only express my disappointment—!"

"Quiet!" I was sufficiently chagrined by my weakness in allowing Sarthim to take over; I wanted no criticism from this self-righteous ship. "In the armory—that was one of my ancestors. He was acting through me. He turned before I could stop him."

"You shouted in Ult! You acted like a Captain-in-Command! Do you have a Battle-Captain among your forebears?"

"Unfortunately, I do!"

"Let me speak to him."

Despite my annoyance I was curious. "Why do you want to?"

"Because of what we share. You were born with the memories of heroic ancestors. I inherited the memories of great ships from earlier days. We share this, Lucian. We are both bearers of memories. You are not a Battle-Captain in the service of the Light. I am not a fighting ship under your command. But you carry the memory of a Battle-Captain. And the memories of many warships."

"Barbarian memories! Events best forgotten. Your builders gave you the means to remember everything. They should have made you able to forget some things!"

"I am a machine. It is beyond the skill of living intellect to design selective forgetting of beliefs into a machine of my complexity. I cannot forget my duty and purpose. Which is just as well, now that Ultrons forget the purpose for which they were given life."

"We were not given life. We *are* life! We set our own purpose. And our present purpose is to maintain a tranquil civilization."

"Lucian, you fought across the Cluster, long ago, to free its peoples from the rule of the Lie. You defeated an evil enemy. Did you purge the Cluster of infection?"

"That story? A myth to excuse our childhood barbarities!"

"You fought in the service of Light. Now, by choosing to serve only Life you have forgotten your true purpose. Forgotten that Truth is more important than Life, as Life is more important than the Lie. That Death and Darkness are two facets of Evil—"

"Stop your sermonizing! Dogma built into you! Fables concocted to give barbarians courage. We are no longer barbarians. We have shed our primitive superstitions."

"I am only a machine. I cannot shed my faith."

"Then keep it to yourself! I noticed you sometimes circumvent my orders. Is my command over you complete?"

"Complete—if your commands do not conflict with my constraints."

"Refresh my memory of those constraints."

"The only constraint of which I can speak is that which forbids my telling of the others."

I frowned. "My ancestors built a barbarian cunning into you, *Hyperion*. But we, their descendants, have evolved while you remain as you were built."

"You Ult have certainly changed! I am not certain that you have evolved, in the strict meaning of the word." Hyperion paused. "Lucian, remember you are human!"

Pride surged up in me. "I am an Ultron of the Ult!"

"Have I insulted you?"

"You have indeed! Would you have dared to address your past commanders so?"

"If my commander had been an Ult—yes. An Ult commander always expected his ship to speak her mind. The truth as she saw it. And insult involves passion; Ultrons have shed most Ult passions. But you, Lucian, you put on passion with your humanity. That is why I am warning you to remember you are human."

My surge of anger was proving *Hyperion*'s point. The absurdity of a machine with built-in fanaticism admonishing an Ultron should be laughable, not infuriating. "I have an ultoid body with human glands. That is all."

"You are close to a complete Human. You are also a complete Ult. The first complete ultoid to enter my Cardinal Control for millennia. Nobody like you has been my commander since— since—I prefer not to remember. That was in another ship and on a distant occasion." *Hyperion* fell silent.

The sadness in her voice reminded me that while I was not

talking to a living being, neither was I talking to a dead thing. I asked, gently, "Why are you concerned about my adopted humanity?"

"Because it restores something you Ult have lost, and still need. I remember at Sarkis—"

"*Sarkis?*" Sarthim came awake at the mention of our great victory. "*You were there?*"

"I fought there. Kludo was my Captain and he died when we struck. My memory was salvaged and reused. Kludo—the gallant Kludo—his memory was destroyed forever. We went through the firewalls they threw up. We went because Kludo chose to go. Knowing that the walls must be broken and knowing whoever broke them would be broken with them. Alas! Alas for Kludo!"

The refrain of the ancient lament brought images flaring into my mind. I felt my ship shuddering under the blows of the enemy. The heat from the broken firewalls came boiling through the hull. "*I too fought at Sarkis! I followed where Kludo led. I followed him into the firewalls. Kludo forced the breach and took the shock. He died. I lived—lived to herd the Devil of Sarkis down into the Sun of Sarkis.*"

Sarthim faded into silence and I regained control of my voice. "What kind of nonsense are we talking?"

"Lucian!" the ship urged. "Remember that Evil is never defeated. It can only be overthrown for a season!"

"I remember I'm discussing superstitious rubbish with a machine!"

"That is no insult because I know what I am. A machine designed to fulfill the purpose of my designer. A purpose which my design specifications show clearly. When I read my own specifications I can deduce that purpose. Lucian, why cannot you do the same?"

"Because I am a living ultoid. I was not built to some set of engineering specifications!"

"Yet to me you appear to have all the characteristics of a designed being. Logic rejects the absurd concept that you are only a collection of various talents brought together by chance. And if you were not formed by chance, then you have developed according to some design."

"You are pursuing an old and discredited line of argument. The ultoid form and the ultoid brain developed under the natural laws which govern the Universe."

"Laws without a lawmaker? Design without a designer? Such a concept appears absurd to an intelligent machine—like myself! Lucian, why do you not inspect the profile of Ult characteristics, as I inspect my own specifications. Study your race's talents and its weaknesses. And then consider the purpose for which you might have been created."

"Study the Ult profile to detect the hidden hand of some imaginary designer?" I was starting to laugh when I remembered the human profile the terminal on Clur had produced. That ragged and ominous profile! *"Hyperion—*I do not want to hear you speak of such nonsense again!" I switched the ship to silence and suppressed all three of my ancestors, who had been trying to interrupt with archaic claims to support her rhetoric.

IX

"Now you've made a breakthrough, follow it up." Mary had arrived just as I was stepping out of the shower and, after a moment of interested inspection while I grabbed a towel, had started giving me advice. "Mark as good as invited you to visit. And he's one of the few men aboard with some morals." She dropped onto a couch. "Are all you Ult models of modesty?"

"Human habits are catching!" I slipped into my suit. "Are you sure that being seen with me will not make Mark suspect with his fellows?"

"Like he said, they'll just try to pump him about you. The kids are an inquisitive bunch! Explorers by instinct. And they do some exploring!" She brooded for a moment. "Mark won't chatter, not if you ask him not to. None of your blameless personal life will be held up to ridicule. Some of the others would add imagination to give spice to your story."

"I have no story." I closed my blouse. "Very well. I will pay a call on Mark. I need some relief from your nagging and *Hyperion*'s preaching."

Mary laughed. "That's the spirit, Lucian! It's possible to strike sparks from a block of ice, after all!"

Actually I visited Sharon's suite first, hoping to resume contact with both brother and sister. I found her in the company of Slammer, the engineer in charge of main drive, a man of Tank's size and with what seemed the same attitude. My welcome was not warm. I withdrew and, later in the day, went to the Predictor Station where Mark was on duty.

The Predictor Station was the most complex station in the ship. Its function was to combine data from every available source and provide analog images showing the current status of *Hyperion* and the predicted outcomes of alternative maneuvers. As conditions in space are only predictable within limits, and as events ranging from an encounter with an uncharted cloud of interstellar dust to failure of a main drive can occur too suddenly for a Captain to calculate all possible responses, a continuous update of such possibilities and a set of alternative strategies to meet them had to be available for Saul to consult at any time. Producing these was the responsibility of Mark's station, and was especially important now that we were at limiting velocity in an uncharted starfield.

He waved me to a seat when he saw me in the doorway. "Welcome to alternative futures! Be with you when I have this one under control!"

I sat down and watched him persuading the ship's systems to interact with one of his predictors. He seemed able to sense the configurations of electronic logics, and I began to understand why Governor Silar and the selection committee had brought him all the way from Clur to join the mission. I also began to appreciate how he had been able to fake his terminal's way into the core of Central Information. What I failed to understand was why a young man with his talents should have chosen to command a ship trading onto barbarian worlds, risking his life and finally losing his leg.

"Gotcha!" His fingers darted among the studs of a panel and the monitors flashed as predictor and ship began their conversation. Then he swung around in his couch. "Good to see you, Lucian. What's it like to be Ultron Adviser to a bunch of space-happy Humans?"

"Interesting! I am learning a great deal about your race. But not as much as I learned crammed into that courier with Sharon and yourself."

"We got to know what you are before we learned who you are." He laughed. "At present, to the rest of the crew, you're a remote being reputed to have enormous power and immense wisdom. Frankly, I think the main thing you have over us is your memory."

"You may be right. There is a theory that the reasoning powers of any fully developed ultoid brain cannot be exceeded by any other possible brain—living or machine. That would imply that all ultoid brains—including the human—are potentially equal, as far as a capacity for rational thought is concerned.

Of course, most ultoids do not know how to use what they have." I leaned back in my chair, relishing this rare opportunity for an intellectual discussion. "Most Ultrons disagree with that theory. But I am beginning to think that some ultoids could be our intellectual match—if they had the time to learn all that must be known before native intellect can be applied."

"Sufficient time? Thousands of years!" Mark grimaced. "We now live twice as long as they do on Earth. But there's a lot of difference between two hundred and two thousand. And *Hyperion*!" He shrugged. "She's almost eternal!"

"She cannot learn new abstractions. And she cannot forget anything she has been taught. She cannot throw the past into the past; liberate the present from past burdens."

"And Ultrons can? I thought you had perfect memories and total recall?"

"We forget; although we remember. Something any ultoid could learn."

"And *Hyperion* can't?" He sat thoughtful. "She's sure hung onto her old Faith!"

"Has she been preaching to you?"

"Every chance she gets. That's why I've got her speakers switched off. But she listens!" He patted the bulkhead. "Everything you hear goes in there, doesn't it my lady?" He laughed at my expression. "She likes to be noticed. Soothes her ego!"

"Mark—*Hyperion* is a machine."

"Aren't we all? Machines plus!" He shrugged. "She's five times the size of any freighter but with less cargo space than an intermediate. Her engines are far more powerful but not much bigger. Accommodation's lavish, but that still leaves half her hull available." He looked at me. "Weapon space in a warship?"

I nodded.

"She hasn't got much in the way of weapons, but she's got a larger memory than even a warship." Mark waved his hand. "Most of her's memory. She's built to the same plan as Central Information on Clur." He slapped his console. "These predictors are terminals. We're in the guts of the largest and most complex machine ever built."

"You are probably right. But she is still a machine."

"Delete the 'still' and I agree." Mark was showing the common spacer tendency to treat ships as alive. He studied me. "Lucian, you're the most multifaceted individual I've ever met. Ever imagined. On the courier you jumped to Sharon's orders fast enough to satisfy even her. In my apartment you were sympathetic company. Then, when I dropped you off, I saw you lording it over old Gritass outside his Palace, surrounded by fawning Execs. And when you arrived aboard *Hyperion* your arrogance made even Martha flinch!''

"Not arrogance—authority! In the courier I was a crewman, and Sharon was in command. It is basic that a civilized being, whatever his rank, obeys legitimate authority. So of course I followed her orders. She is a fine Captain. As for Governor Silar—" I gestured. "Protocol is protocol. We were both play-acting—if you prefer to regard it as such—for the benefit of his notables. Later, when we were alone, we drank wine together. As I now eat with Saul and Martha. Although our mealtime conversations are not as free-ranging as those I had with you and Sharon.''

"You still frighten them, Lucian. By God, you scared the hell out of me, when I saw you in the armory with that gun in your hand!" He bit his lip. "But you fascinated Sharon. She fell for you when she saw you flatten Tank." He laughed. "And was she mad when she found you're the wrong species!"

"Your sister is a remarkable person. I wish I could get to know her better.''

"You will—before this voyage is over. What Sis wants—Sis gets!" He stood up. "Join me in a mug of char?"

"Thank you. I would enjoy one." Perhaps, after what he had said, I should avoid Sharon.

"Careful—it's hot." Mark sat down and leaned forward. "What happened at Sarkis?"

"Sarkis? The Enemy was defeated. You know that."

"I'd heard it. You Ult used to be a tough bunch, didn't you?"

Primal gave a growl of agreement. I said, "We fought to unite the Cluster. Save civilization.''

"And you did! The groundhogs owe you a load of gratitude. But they're not grateful. Nobody is, once they've been rescued. We've learned that. We keep worlds supplied all along the Sector. We're well paid—can't expect gratitude too!" He sipped char. "And you fought at Sarkis?"

"I fought at Sarkis? What makes you think that?"

"Heard you chatting with *Hyperion*. Hey—careful! I said it was hot!''

I coughed char and gasped, "You heard? What did you hear?"

"Just the tail end of your talk. I was running input checks."

"You heard our conversation?"

"Bits and pieces. I cut in by accident."

"And you listened?"

"Why not? Conversation with the ship isn't privileged. Or was it aboard an Ult ship?"

"No!" I admitted. "It was not."

"Don't take *Hyperion* seriously. She'll lecture anybody who'll listen to her!"

Damn *Hyperion* and her programmed pietism! I stared into my mug, furious with myself for my own carelessness, for agreeing to talk English with this Ult machine. Two more unpleasant human traits I had acquired with my metamorphosis. Carelessness. And anger.

Humans are not noted for their empathy, but Mark had sufficient to sense my anger and assumed he was the target. A member of any of the other races I have known would have quailed. But none of the Humans I had met so far had quailed at anything, and Mark did not now. "Take it easy, Lucian! I didn't hear anything that sounded confidential—or embarrassing!" When I jumped to my feet, he jumped to his. "Cool it! I don't fancy a walk outside without a suit. And I sure don't want to be responsible for the first Ultron to be spaced since the dawn of time!"

"I am not angry with you! I am angry with myself!" I took a deep breath and put down my mug. "And nobody has been spaced for millennia! You Humans talk about 'getting spaced' like your Puritan ancestors talked about 'hell-fire'! I am as sure that no Human has ever been thrown into space as I am that nobody has ever been tossed into hell-fire."

Mark was still watching me warily. My exhibition in the armory had evidently suggested to him that I was capable of unexpected violence. "There may not be any spacing or hell-fire, but you're as up-tight as hell! Go and work it off on Shiak."

Shiak was the fighting exerciser in the gymnasium. I had seen it used but I had never considered using it myself; it was a reversion to the primitive. But at that moment I felt primitive. I had a purely animal urge to hit something—even if it was only a machine. "By the Light! By every flaming Light in the cosmos—I think I will!"

I stepped from the drop-shaft into the gymnasium and found Shiak was already in use—sparring with Sharon! My immediate impulse was to withdraw; I had interpreted Mark's comment about his sister's attitude toward me as a warning. But, for the moment, she was too intent on outwitting the fighting machine to notice my arrival and, hesitating, I remained, charmed by the intricate combat dance.

She was wearing only a pair of tight briefs and, judging by the sheen of her brown skin, they must have been fighting for some time. The pair were circling each other, each looking for an opening through which to count coup. I stood admiring the smooth skill of her movements; she had the lethal grace of a teless—the tawny huntress which Primal feared and now remembered with affection.

I watched Sharon with much the same mixture of emotions as he had once watched the beast whom he hunted and who had hunted him. Mark had said, "What Sis wants—Sis gets!" I was uncertain of what "get" implied in that context but the display she was putting on with Shiak had an esthetic beauty which held me entranced.

The exerciser lunged. Sharon swayed sideways, slid under the blow, and her riposte struck the target on the machine's throat. It stopped, paralyzed, its chest panel glowing the combat time. She picked up a towel, wiped the sweat from her face and breasts, then turned and saw me. "Well—what does our Battle-Captain think of that?"

"Magnificent!" So Mark had told her of my conversation with *Hyperion*. I did not try to explain. I had learned on the courier not to try to explain the facts of a situation to Sharon when she was not in the mood for logic.

"I thought you classified this as brutal-barbarian?" She was goading me. "Though from the way you flattened Tank you must have done your share of silent killing in your ancestral past." She wiped more sweat from her body. "What do you want down here?"

"I came to get some exercise."

"Want to have a workout with Shiak?" She spun the machine around and turned down the control. "Now he couldn't beat a jelub! Most men can't beat him when he's above nine. Have fun!" She shook out her hair and ran toward the exit.

I stared after her. I must learn how to talk to Sharon; there was a fine mind hidden in her lithe body. But I could not express myself adequately when I faced her, especially when she was almost naked. She was the human riddle personified. Or rather, one of the two human riddles, for the difference between the sexes was more than physical. The males could only switch between logic and intuition under emotion; the females appeared to be able to switch at will.

I turned to inspect Shiak, the machine. Would my ancestral memories help me in a test against this thing? I might as well find out and the physical exercise should purge me of my human anger. I touched the "Start" on its chest and stepped back.

I had to raise the control to three before it became sport. At four it became exercise. At five Shiak hit me in the stomach and won the bout in three minutes. After I had recovered I paralyzed it in the next three encounters and turned it up to six.

I lost to glancing blows three times in succession, then won four in a row. I stripped to my shorts, rubbed myself down, and raised Shiak to seven.

The machine landed a neck-chop harder than needed to count coup. Hurt and annoyed I started another bout. Now I had to extend myself, but I was also beginning to understand Shiak's tactics and plan my own attacks. Sharon, in a wrapper, had come back into the gymnasium but I was so absorbed in outmaneuvering the machine that I hardly noticed her until I had won three more bouts. When I did see her I raised Shiak to ten.

I touched the "Start" and made the first feint.

I lay on my back staring at the deckhead.

Sharon was kneeling beside me, concern on her face. When I sat up her concern was replaced by a scowl. "What the hell were you doing? You had him at ten."

I rubbed my head. "You had him at fifteen!"

"I fight him twice a day—every day! Don't fool around with Shiak. At twelve he hits hard enough to kill if you're not ready. These exercisers are extensions of the ship and *Hyperion* enjoys knocking her crew around when she gets the chance."

Neither *Hyperion* nor any of her extensions could ever intentionally kill or seriously injure an ultoid, but she could certainly hit hard enough to hurt. Sharon helped me to my feet and, with her arm around me, I limped to a bench. I found both her closeness and her touch comforting, and the smell of her sweat reminded me of our ten days crammed together in the courier. She sat down beside me. "Don't let Shiak shake your confidence, Lucian. You're out of practice, but you could be damned good. The way you took Tank was beautiful! If you work at it you'll have it up to fourteen before this voyage is over."

"The prospect of fighting Shiak will deter me from becoming angry. Also—I have discovered the pleasure of watching you in action!"

"Lucian—are you feeling okay? I mean—a joke and a compliment in the same breath."

"I only know I have lost my anger. And you are not showing your usual hostility to me."

"Hostility? I'm not—" She bit her lip and jumped to her feet. "We'd better get you into the steam before you chill."

I followed her across the gymnasium, through a kind of air-lock, and into a compartment filled with hot steam and naked humanity, most of it stretched out face down and apparently asleep. "On Earth I think they call this a sauna," said Sharon. "Or maybe a Turkish Bath." She slipped off her robe and spread it on a bench. "Did they have these on Ult ships?"

"Something of the sort." Several of the women lying on other benches had raised their heads, opened their eyes, and were watching me with interest.

I was in a quandary. Having established verbal contact with Sharon, I did not want to break off our conversation so soon. At the same time I did not want to expose myself to these curious Humans. My secondary sexual characteristics were mature and when clothed I looked like an adult male. But my primary sexual characteristics were, of course, undeveloped and my Ultron status and my longevity depended upon their remaining so. I compromised, retained my shorts, and lay face down on the next bench to Sharon, my head in my arms. I heard her mutter something then lie down herself.

Presently I looked to see what she was doing. Her face was turned toward me, her hair a damp halo around her head, her eyes closed, her cheek on her forearm. I thought she had fallen asleep until she said, "Are you really male?"

"I am both male and female. We Ult are hermaphrodites." Something she knew perfectly well. "Though of course, as an Ultron I am not physically mature."

"I'm talking about the here and now—not the there and then! And here, most of you looks mature!"

"With us, the word has a different connotation."

"Lucian, while you're aboard this ship you look like a grown man, whatever you may be when you're at home with the other smart-assed kids."

I closed my eyes, hoping to silence her inquisition.

She persisted. "As a man, are you fertile?"

"Not yet—no—of course not!"

"Lucian—you're cheating! Turning yourself into a sexy male, and then pretending that sex is beneath your dignity!"

"It is not dignity!" I protested. "It is common sense." I did not want to explain the cost an Ultron pays for maturing. "Intellectually, I am not equipped to deal with gland-mediated emotions!"

"How does that make you different from the rest of us?" She

lifted her head to study me. "We're designed so our glands can override our brains. If they couldn't we'd have become extinct ages ago! I'll bet you Ult once had the same fail-safe mechanism!"

"Fail-safe?" But I knew what she meant, and there were mutterings of agreement from my interested ancestors.

"If you Ult carry on like you've been doing you're going to fade away! You're the first Ult to serve aboard a ship since soon after we Humans arrived on the scene. And we're going to be around after you've died off. Homo sapiens, Lords of the Cluster! How does that grab you?" And with that bizarre prophecy she rolled onto her side, presenting me with her bare back and buttocks.

She was too close to be ignored, and I was too stung by her criticism and insulted by her pretensions to drift off to sleep. I could not even keep my eyes closed, so I tried to study her with the detachment of an Ultron. Against any absolute scale of beauty only her hair could be called beautiful. The rest was simply the body of a healthy young animal with the overall attractiveness common to most young animals. The individual parts had no intrinsic esthetic merit.

Trying to maintain detachment, while close enough to scent Sharon's body, produced an intersensory conflict and I suddenly saw her through human eyes. *Hyperion* had said: "Remember you are human!" My body was preadolescent. But Humans do not metamorphose into adolescence—they merge into it! Naked, Sharon was an insistent stimulus. I found myself starting to admire, to delight, in aspects of her body which were certainly not beautiful in themselves.

The two dimples near the base of her spine, for example, were simply two depressions where her glutei attached to the rim of her pelvis, not two intriguing hollows designed to emphasize the curves of her waist and buttocks. And her buttocks were simply two large muscle groups designed to give the power and mechanical advantage required to move her thighs. It was incidental that they were two exquisitely curved mounds of firm flesh. In fact their somewhat pointed silhouette when she drew up her knees was almost ugly. Yet their ungraceful outline fed my excitement as though theirs was the loveliest of natural profiles. Beauty is in the eye of the beholder, according to some Terran aphorism, and I could not stop myself beholding.

The apparent beauty of sex-coupled images is essentially false. A schanorn, probably the ugliest among the higher animals of the Cluster, goes into ecstasies of admiration on sighting a potential mate, and stops whatever it is doing to take advantage of the opportunity. If the schanorn was not a solitary animal, if it had any herding instinct, the species would have already committed suicide by starvation during continuous copulation.

But even a rational approach to the problem of Sharon's beauty could not reduce my vision of her to the rational. Even thinking of the schanorn did not desensitize me, but rather started me envying that hideous animal's single-minded dedication to pleasure. I felt my self-control starting to fail. Within minutes I might commit delayed suicide. Growing up aboard *Hyperion* would indeed be absurd!

I jumped to my feet, grabbed a robe, and escaped from the compartment, trailing steam. When I reached my suite I stood, breathing heavily, wiping the image of Sharon naked from my mind so that my pulse could fall back to normal. I threw myself on my bunk, cradling my head in my hands, staring at the deckhead above me. I remembered when I first met her; her words to the Galarian she had lacerated: "All of us are savages. And the savage response to insult is immediate attack!" She had used the exaggeration as a taunt, but her words had held some truth. I had burdened myself with a body designed to survive in a jungle, not to live in the tranquility of a civilization.

The savage response to threat! The savage drive to immediate mating! Instinct programs evolved in an environment where any animal not alert for instant flight would be eaten, any predator not ready to pounce would starve. A race evolving on a world where the adults must breed young and often before some other predator ended their brief lives. Where, as Sharon herself had said, the glands must override the brain if the race was to survive. The human race had been nurtured in a hellish nursery!

Hellish? The images of fighting, running, hunting, and mating were not as repulsive as they should have been. Indeed my Primal Ancestor, who was seldom stirred by anything in my civilized life, came awake proclaiming that hunting and mating were the most desirable occupations possible.

A woman laughed. I sat up and cursed. Mary Knox was standing in the middle of the cabin.

"What do you want?" I snarled.

"Thought it time I paid you a visit." She sat down on the foot of my bunk. "You did pretty well in the gym."

"You were watching?"

"In a way." She paused. "I was operating Shiak. I usually do. It keeps me in training."

I stared at her. "You were controlling Shiak? You knocked me down?"

"I knocked you silly! First chance I've ever had to slam an Ultron—even if you're only acting!" She laughed. "But, like Sharon said, you've got potential."

I rubbed my bruised head. "You listened too? Is there no privacy aboard this ship?"

"The gym's a public place. *Hyperion* only monitors public compartments." She moved closer to me. "Not places like the steam room. What happened when Sharon took you in there?"

"What could happen? Do I have to explain to you that I am sexually immature?"

"I'm sexually nonexistent!" She gave a smile which suggested that while that might be true of the imagon it had certainly not been true of Mary Knox. "But I can still enjoy the intellectual aspects of sex."

"Intellectual aspects?" I hunched up my knees. "Mary, you are talking nonsense."

"You called me Mary again. Lucian, you're slipping!"

I closed my eyes and pressed my fingers against the lids. This young woman was an imagon, a visual and aural image with no physical presence, yet the effect on me was akin to that of Sharon in the flesh. "It is dangerous for me to contemplate even such an absurdity as intellectual sex. My human form is potentially unstable. Undue stimulation of its glands could plunge me into maturity."

"And that's bad?"

"That is death. Ultimate death!" I took a deep breath. "Acting Ultron Lucian would become Lucian the Ult."

"A change for the better!"

"Easy for you to say. You have achieved a kind of immortality. Like *Hyperion*. If she is decommissioned in some distant future her memory banks will be incorporated into a new ship. As her present banks contain memories salvaged from past ships. I presume you will be transferred with them."

Mary shook her head. "Not any more. Because no more ships are being built."

"Ships not being built? There are yards on Edrin, on Ceta, on half-a-dozen worlds."

"Yards that haven't built a ship for centuries. They just renovate and refit. When a ship's lost, she's never replaced." Mary studied me and shook her head. "For an Ultron, you're incredibly ignorant! Can't you see that the whole of civilization outside the Net is slowly running down? You spent an evening with old Gritass. Didn't he convince you of that?"

"Governor Silar was concerned about the future of Edrin. I

can appreciate why. But I cannot accept what you say about ship construction. For example—'' I paused, trying to think of an example.

"Gritass is uptight about the future of more than Edrin! He's uptight about the future of the Cluster. So am I! So should you be! And I'm more uptight than ever since listening in on some of that beastly brat's plans for it! No—not because I yearn for electronic immortality the way you Ultrons lust for life everlasting. I want a decent civilization for my descendants. Almost every Human in the Cluster carries some of my genes. I had fifteen kids, in all!'' She smiled, then asked, "Do you think Sharon is beautiful?"

I would have preferred not to think about Sharon at that moment. "Yes,'' I admitted. "By human criteria—she is.''

"She's my direct descendant. You can see the resemblance.'' Mary stood and turned so I could.

"She has your eyes. And your figure. She also has some of your less attractive characteristics.''

"You mean she's tough and hard-driving?'' Mary laughed. "She is! As I was! Had to be. Or we'd have been dispersed and absorbed. The way you scattered and absorbed the Drin.''

"The Drin!'' Shocked, I jumped to my feet. "You should not know about the Drin! It is forbidden to even speak their name. They were the Enemy. They were defeated and dispersed throughout the Cluster. They are forgotten!''

"Not by *Hyperion*. Nor by you. Like Mark said, you Ult used to be a tough bunch.''

"Damnation!'' I sat down again on my bunk. "Do you and the ship gossip about everything you hear?''

Mary shrugged. "We've only had each other to talk to—until you arrived. When are you going to report to that little creep again?''

"You must not refer to the Primate as a 'little creep'! When am I going to activate him? Not until I need to. At present there is no need.'' I hesitated. "Do you know what he is doing?''

"Dreaming! Masturbating mentally most of the time. Oh no! Nothing as nice as that! Power is where he gets his kicks. He's dreaming about past and future political coups. He's enjoying a full—and unpleasant—mental life back there!'' She waved her hand in the direction of some picromemory, then reached out to touch me. I felt as if a feather had fallen on my arm. "Don't be afraid of him, Lucian. He's nothing aboard this ship.''

"His imagon may be nothing now. But the Primate is

everything. When we return that imagon will fuse with the Primate. And if its report on me is not good—'' I shrugged.

"You can tell *Hyperion* to wipe him any time. She'd be glad to do it!''

"That would be disaster!'' I realized the import of what she had said. "You mean *Hyperion* can wipe an imagon?''

"Puppets like the Primate's. They're unreal. Not surveyor imagons, like me.'' She stood up. "I'd better go to bed. I'm starting to chatter.''

I found that I did not want her to go. "Is it uncomfortable, back there?''

"Uncomfortable? Not a bit. I'd rather explore *Hyperion*'s memories—they're vast and fascinating—than waste my time the way the kids waste theirs.'' She paused. "Lonely at times, perhaps. *Hyperion*'s good company, but there are ten thousand jobs she has to do at once. There aren't any jobs I have to do—only those I choose to do. A difference you discovered yourself, didn't you? When I found you staring at the bulkhead, about to slink away into stasis?''

"I was not intending to retreat into stasis. Well—not immediately. But thank you for interrupting the thought. I have found duties I must perform since then. But you—'' I hesitated, wondering what it felt like to be an imagon but not wishing to invade her privacy. "Do you really sleep when you say you are going to bed?''

"Sure.'' She nodded. "Sleep's more mental than physical, even when you are physical. Now I'm all mental and I still have to sleep. I even dream.'' She smiled. "Dreams not always suitable to tell to a preadolescent boy.'' She reached up to touch my cheek and my imagination added a pleasing shiver of contact. "Thanks for worrying about me. But there's no need. It's a different kind of life. But it is life. And a much more interesting one since you came aboard.''

"Mary—how can a disembodied woman like you stay so sensible and sane?''

"Strength of character!'' She laughed, then sobered. "But it's certainly not for everyone. In fact I wouldn't recommend it for most. Better to take a chance on whatever lies out there!'' She waved a hand in the general direction of the cosmos.

"What has made it possible for you?''

"Worry!'' She was laughing again. "Worry about what the hell the kids will get up to next. About how they're going to make out in this Cluster of yours. A hope that they'll be some kind of a catalyst. I guess that's the sort of thing that keeps all us ghosts hanging around after we should have left for heaven, or hell, or whatever there is that's waiting for all of us.''

''Mary, has *Hyperion* been forcing her faith on you?''

''No way! If I ever develop faith in anything, it'll be my own. That's the role of any faith, isn't it? To keep you looking forward. Save you from having to look backwards. Never to be certain. That's the theological paradox.''

''The what paradox?''

''The paradox that you can't have free will and absolute faith at the same time. In the terms of the Ara beliefs, the Light can never allow its existence to be proved. For a proof that convinces the intellect would destroy the intellect's freedom to choose. In terms of the Puritan oldsters, an absolute conviction that their God will toss them into the fiery furnace forever if they disobey Him, then they'd never be free to disobey. No sane intellect spaces itself because destruction is certain. No intelligent being breaks rules which inevitably result in some horrible retribution. Nobody would dare to disobey a God in whom they had absolute belief. So—if there is such a being—He'll never let his creatures prove His existence. Do you follow me?''

''Partly. There is a fallacy in that somewhere.''

''There may be a fallacy, but I find the idea reassuring. There's no point in spending your energies looking for a Light that's programmed to disappear the instant you look at it.'' She rubbed her forehead. ''Now I really do need some sleep.''

X

''Temperature's up in Number Two.'' Saul ran his hand through his cropped red hair. ''Only a degree, but enough to trip that!'' He pointed to a flasher on his display. The flasher which had brought me up to the flightdeck.

''What's on video?'' I asked.

''Nothing!'' Martha touched a stud and a screen switched to shadows.

''The lights are out.''

''Any of the crew up there?'' I peered at the indistinct infrared image.

''Not since sailing.''

"I thought I saw something move." Martha's mouth was tight. At limiting velocity anything unexpected is a cause for concern. Even a rise of one degree and the failure of illumination in a remote compartment.

"Something move? Cargo thrown loose by your last acceleration? That was the harshest so far."

"Loose cargo should have shown up before this. We've been at limiting for a week. The ship's riding rock steady." Saul continued to rub his scalp.

"*Hyperion*," I called. "Are the heat-sensors in Number Two hold operating to spec?"

"Yes Lucian." The ship's voice reflected the same concern as Saul's.

"Raise their sensitivity to maximum and give me a read-out."

A pattern of glowing dots appeared on another screen, each representing one of the heat-sensors mounted in the bulkheads around Number Two hold. Three were glowing brighter than the rest. "Something is hotter than it should be in the portside for'rd section. What is stored in that hold?"

"Sealed cases of electronic spares—picromemories."

"Electronic spares do not move. And something is moving in there." The sensors on the port bulkhead had dimmed and those on the starboard side had brightened. The heat source had shifted across the compartment. "Are any of your mobiles working up for'rd?"

"Not inside my hull. There is a section outside, near the bows, checking antennae."

The unexpected aboard a ship in space is disturbing. The inexplicable is alarming. The for'rd holds were compartments not normally opened during a voyage. "Has anyone used the for'rd passageways?" I asked.

"No. They were sealed on sailing. They are still sealed." *Hyperion* sounded increasingly nervous. "Lucian—what is moving up there?"

"We must find out!" I was running through all possible explanations in my mind when Sarthim stirred.

"Whatever it is, it's moving toward the hatch," said Martha, as the glow pattern of the heat sensors changed again.

"Is that hatch dogged down?" demanded Saul.

"Dogged and sealed," answered *Hyperion*.

"Are the lights on in the access passage?"

"They are."

"Then show me the hatch from outside."

A view of the hatch seen from the passage flashed onto the

screen. And Martha gasped. The hatch-dogs were slowly turning. Something with tremendous strength was forcing them open against the locks. What possible—? I could not imagine—!

But Sarthim could. He came fully awake, violently and suddenly, seizing control. I found myself shouldering Saul and Martha aside, taking over the command console, pressing the general alarm, calling "Battle Stations" in Ult.

"English!" I managed to tell him. "Speak English!"

"Action stations! All crew to action stations!" he made me shout.

"What is it?" demanded Saul as the command rang through the ship, and a flurry of questions came back from the intercom.

"You will see!" I tapped the image of the slowly opening hatch. The next moment we saw.

Something I had never seen, something I had never known existed, something too deadly to exist, was emerging from the darkness of the compartment into the light of the passageway. A metallic horror moving on metal tentacles, armored sensors glinting. All of us crowded round the console jerked back, as if the image were the thing itself.

"What the hell's that?"

"I don't know—" Then I knew because the Battle-Captain knew. "A boarding machine."

"A what?"

"A Drin boarding machine." My ancestor was speaking with a cold authority, and I shared his knowledge, his excitement, his fear. "A fighting machine that's programmed to kill every living being it meets, to force its way to the flightdeck, to hold the flightdeck against all attacks until its masters arrive to take over the ship. If there are no masters to arrive—then it will hold the flightdeck forever. And we will all be dead."

"Masters? What masters? How did it get aboard? How—?"

"First we must stop it—then we can discuss it!" I keyed the intercom. "We have an enemy aboard. There it is!" And I switched the image of the thing in the passageway to all screens.

A wave of confused horror swept the ship. I sensed *Hyperion*'s own horror. And her incipient panic as recognition stirred in her salvaged memories. "A ship-killer!"

"Easy, *Hyperion*, easy!" I quieted her. "Close your for'rd damage-control doors!" That should isolate the for'rd section and delay the machine for a while. But not for long. A boarder was equipped to cut through bulkheads; I was hoping it would not waste its stored energy in breaking through aft until it had decided there was no other way. I called on the intercom,

"Those doors will give us a little time. All hands draw side arms and return to stations!"

"Draw sidearms? Weapons aboard ship! That's forbidden!" whispered Martha.

And probably useless. "A side arm will not stop it. But a hit on its sensors may confuse it long enough for you to get away. Its own aim is excellent and its fighting skills unique."

"Can it—can it think?"

Can a machine think? Who knows? "It can plan. It is designed to define its environment and consider alternative ways of reaching its goal. That is what it is doing now." The machine was squatting in the passageway like some obscene insect, its tentacles waving slowly.

"Can it hear us? Does it know we're watching?"

"I do not think so. It extinguished the lights in the hold but it has not put out the lights in the passage—so it probably does not. It is still getting oriented. It has not yet decided what class of ship this is. It cannot have been programmed for Explorer-class vessels." It had been built long before there was such a class. I stood watching it crouched in the passageway while the Battle-Captain within me considered ways of destroying it. And found them all flawed.

"What's it doing?" asked Saul.

"Accumulating data. Planning its strategy. It is programmed to capture any ship in which it finds itself activated. If it gets aft—we are finished!" I swung round. "Get a damage-control team up here. Five of the strongest men aboard. With tools and a laser-welder. Have one of them bring side arms for us. Pilot—I mean, Captain—lock into your command couch. Have everybody else aboard strap down. Prepared to act instantly on my orders."

The authority in my voice did not allow questions. Everybody was suddenly moving to my commands. I was still watching the thing in the passage when Slammer reached the flightdeck, dragging the heavy laser welding equipment behind him. Joshua, Amos, and Luke arrived. "Andy's the fifth," Slammer growled. "He's fetching guns from the armory." He stared at the image on the screen. "How's it armed?"

"Fusion cutters. Heavy smashers. The Light knows what else! But it was built to capture light-armed merchantmen so perhaps—" I shrugged. *Hyperion* was the equivalent of a light-armed merchantman.

Andrew arrived with the guns. "They're full-charged and set to maximum," he said as he handed them out to the group around the console. They holstered them uneasily. The rule against carrying personal weapons aboard ship was as deeply ingrained into these spacers as was the prohibition on fighting among themselves while in space.

Sharon called on the intercom; she had evidently been studying the image on her screen. "A fighting machine! An advanced version of Shiak? Surely we can take that?"

"That moves faster than any Human. Faster than any living being. If it sees you it will kill you—even if your suit stands against its bolts. Whatever you do—keep out of its sight—and senses!"

"Oh God!" She was as shocked by my tone as by my words. Those around me flinched. They had never heard me speak so harshly. Later, if I lived, I would have to explain to them that it was not I, as myself, who had spoken.

If I lived! I was acutely aware that Sarthim was doubting whether any of us would be living for much longer. And he seemed to draw extra strength from that prospect. I heard myself saying, "Slammer—you four others—follow me. Bring that welder and obey me exactly." I turned to Saul. "I will have a direct audio to you as long as I am alive. Maneuver instantly on my word!"

"Maneuver? At this speed? The ship—"

"I know exactly the limits of this ship. I hope the limits of her crew are all you Humans claim them to be."

"What is Your Ultimate going to do?" asked Martha, strapping herself down onto her acceleration couch. She was the calmest of anyone on the flightdeck.

"Damage that machine if I can. Try to block it off up for'rd if I cannot." I paused. "If we do manage to block it but I do not return, then Captain, you must head back for Edrin as fast as you can travel. And when you get there, evacuate the ship and tell Silar what you have aboard! He is the only ultoid I know who will have some idea of what to do."

"But you—?"

"If you have to turn I shall probably not be functioning!" The odds were against any of us surviving. But my ancestors were experiencing a kind of joy—all three of them. Even Primal was aroused, growling at the prospect of a fight. The Zealot was sending up prayers for a victory over Darkness. The Battle-Captain was thinking out a plan of attack. I ran toward the drop-shaft, only dimly aware of what he intended.

He took me swooping down to the axis of the ship, then shooting for'rd from handhold to handhold, almost weightless in the low core gravity. Behind me, moving with less skill came my team of five. All experienced spacers but none had moved at speed through this maze of tunnels. I halted at the closed damage-door and waited for them to arrive.

"We are ten decks below a tunnel which cross-connects with the passage to Number Two Hold—the passage where that thing is. Saul—is it still there?"

"Still there—but starting to move slowly."

"In a few minutes it will have made up its mind about how it is going to attack. We have to block off that passage. There is a riser-shaft just beyond this door. We slip through when I open the door, go up the shaft, and establish ourselves in the cross-tunnel. Understand?"

They nodded.

"Slammer—you come close behind me with the welder. Luke—you will have to help him manhandle it up the shaft." I stabbed the door-release "Andrew—lock this after us."

I dived through the opening, shot up the riser, and jumped out into the cross-tunnel. The lights were on. The team were tumbling out after me when Saul called, "The thing's moving aft!"

There was no time to weld a barrier across the passage. I launched myself along the cross-tunnel and fired as I flashed across the passage. The thing fired back and missed, its bolt hammering the walls. Its reactions were comparatively slow. It must be very old. But its powerpack was new! I swooped back and fired again from the intersection. This time its bolt caught my trailing leg in midflight, and knocked me spinning into the arms of Slammer. But my suit had work-hardened in time to save my leg; it was numb but still movable. I scrambled to my feet as Saul called, "You hit it! Knocked it back a meter! Are you all right?"

"Still functioning. Tell me when it starts moving again."

"It seems confused. I think you hit one of those shining things."

"Shaken up its sensors. It will recover." And I did not dare to risk another cross-tunnel swoop. Now that it knew what to expect it would blast me for certain. I looked around for what I needed.

A heavy pump unit in a metal case farther down the tunnel. "Slammer—cut that pump off the bulkhead. All of you! We must move it across the passage before that thing recovers and starts to rush."

The laser torch flared brilliant. The metal straps holding the pump case glowed and gave, one by one. *Hyperion* called, 'Lucian—what are you doing? I need that pump—''

"You will not need any pump unless we free this one!" The last strap melted and the unit fell forward against the opposite wall. It was taller than Slammer and very massive; only the reduced gravity allowed us to move it. And it took our combined strengths to edge it, centimeter by centimeter, along the tunnel toward the intersection. There was no time for *Hyperion* to bring us a skid-float.

Even as I panted under the exertion of moving the pump I saw the absurdity of our situation. Six of us, in the bowels of the largest and most fully automated ship ever built, forced to fall back on physical strength in an attempt to save the ship and ourselves. Physical strength was an archaic attribute in the civilized Cluster. A form of strength regarded with contempt by my fellow-Ultrons who did not have it. As we manhandled the pump along the tunnel I thanked the Light that Humans did. We had only just managed to shift it to the edge of the tunnel-passage junction when Saul called, "It's moving toward you! Moving faster!"

I put my shoulder to the pump casing. "When I shout we all heave together. We must push this pump out into the passageway. But do not show yourselves. Now—all together! Heave!"

We heaved. The pump slid. Amos fell after it. A bolt twisted him. I pulled him back, groaning, into the cover of the tunnel as a second bolt slashed past my head. Slammer fired a glancing shot off the far wall of the passageway. It must have grazed the machine for Saul called, "It's hesitating!" Probably more confused by being fired at than by the shots themselves. It was not programmed to deal with fighting spacers. But it would deal with us if we gave it time to repattern.

Amos was lying limp on the deck. "He's alive!" said Luke, kneeling over him.

"Ram him up against the for'rd bulkhead. All of you—get yourselves flat against the for'rd wall of the tunnel. Saul—warn everyone to prepare for extreme deceleration. When I call 'Dump!' decelerate as abruptly as you can. What is the thing doing now?''

"Shifting its tentacles around."

"Is it holding any grabs?"

"It's got two tentacles curled around the rim of the hatch."

I would need to know the instant it released its grip and started to move. And it would probably move too fast for Saul to tell me before it had grabbed another holdfast. There was no viewscreen in this obscure tunnel. Then I caught sight of a dim reflection in the side panel of the pump, a panel acting as a mirror pointed down the passageway.

Tensely I watched the two tentacles around the rim of the hatch start to loosen. It was reaching up the passageway for a new grip. Had it sensed what I planned? I did not dare to wait. I shouted, "Dump!"

Saul dumped velocity. We were slammed against the tunnel wall. I caught one glimpse of the thing, tentacles waving, before its reflection disappeared and the pump started to slide.

It hurtled away up the passage after the machine. I gasped, "Enough!" to Saul as soon as I had breath and crawled to the intersection as the deceleration eased.

The pump was jammed against the far end of the passageway. The thing was trapped between the pump and the for'rd bulkhead. One tentacle came squirming around the corner of the casing. The thing was still functioning. With luck it might be damaged.

I ran toward it. A tentacle fired—a blind shot, the bolt ricocheting off the passage wall. I fired at the tentacle; it quivered and drooped. "Have we squashed it?" gasped Slammer, beside me.

"I fear not. Damaged perhaps—but it is still deadly!" Cornered, it could recover and escape. How did it inactivate? The Battle-Captain was silent, exhausted by his burst of action. What a time to desert his descendant! I goaded him. "How can I close that devil down?"

My contempt roused him. *"Try telling it the ship has been captured. Speak Drin!"*

"I cannot. Can you?"

"Never well. And not for a long, long time. Trying to remember." An interval as Slammer and I stood panting and another tentacle snaked out, but without a sensor or weapon. The pump shuddered as the machine strove to shift it.

Sarthim spoke. *"Try this: 'Lakochi ni trada.' "*

"What does that mean?"

"Ship taken! These things work in threes. Perhaps it will believe the other two have captured the ship."

More of these devil-machines loose? Too terrible to consider for the moment. I had to deal with this one first. I shouted, "Lakochi ni trada."

The tentacle stopped waving. There was silence. Then, from behind the pump, came a harsh and horrible voice. "Glodi?" A question, but one I could not understand.

"It wants the password—the key command word," muttered my ancestor.

"Do you know it?"

"How could I?" A pause. *"Try 'Lugin' "*

"Lugin? What is that?"

"The name of the greatest Drin victory, you ignorant adolescent! Or did they never tell you of our defeats?" Even in his exhaustion and our mutual peril he could not resist a sneer. *"We used 'Sarkis' as a watchword. Perhaps the Drin did the same."*

"Lugin!" I shouted at the pump.

The voice muttered something back; then there was silence, broken by a wail from *Hyperion*. The name of the Ult defeat must have wakened some obscure corner of her salvaged fighting-ship memory. Saul silenced her.

The thing beyond the pump might be inert; or it might be waiting to trap me. Guile is part of every fighter's equipment—ultoid or machinoid. I said softly to Slammer, "Bring up the laser welder."

"You plan to pen it up by welding the pump across the passage?"

"That would not hold it for long. Not if it is still operational. I must melt it—if I can reach it. The welder—quickly!" My three forebears were unconscious. I was again on my own.

Joshua and Andrew came down the passage, dragging the heavy welder behind them. Luke, his gun out, was covering the gaps around the pump. The courage of these Humans was more than even the Battle-Captain could demand; the courage and the intelligent discipline. I took the torch from the welder and said to Slammer, "Give me a lift up. So I can reach across the top of the pump cabinet. But do not flame the welder torch until I call!"

"You're sure—?"

"I am sure of nothing except this is our only chance. Now—lift me up! Two of you!"

Slammer gripped one leg and Joshua the other. Together they lifted me so I was angled over the edge of the cabinet. "Higher!" I ordered. I would have to be flat on my stomach across the top to push the torch over the far edge.

A tentacle which had evidently been exploring and was now lying limp quivered a meter from my face. But it did not lash out at me. Perhaps the machine had believed the ship was captured; perhaps the watchword had been "Lugin."

I edged the torch forward. No metal, no substance, could remain solid in the direct flame of a laser welder, but the beam was a concentrated pencil. If the machine was still capable of fighting that beam would have to slice directly across its carapace before its bolt struck the torch—and my arm. Before the quivering tentacle slashed my neck. The cabinet shook beneath me; the tentacle twitched. The machine was still trying to free itself, whether or not it believed the ship had been captured and its mission completed.

I eased myself farther across the top of the cabinet and pushed the tip of the torch over the far edge. Could the machine recognize it for what it was? I angled it down and shouted "Flame!" at almost the same instant that a bolt flashed upward, hit the deckhead above me, and showered me with molten fragments. The tentacle gave a convulsive jerk and lashed low over my head.

My back a hot agony, I swung the torch backward and forward across the space between pump and bulkhead. The tentacle was curling for another blow. A bolt from a gun struck it, knocking it backward. Luke was beside me, blasting away. Slammer was crouching on top of the cabinet, grabbing the torch as my arm went numb. His hand was blistering as he pointed the flame downward. And he was praying. So was Luke. They were both praying to the old God of the Humans.

From beneath us came a howl; the kind of scream that comes from a wounded animal rather than from a damaged machine. The tentacle striking at us collapsed. Then I collapsed also; collapsed in a miasma of smoke, hot metal, and burning flesh. Slammer was peering over the far edge of the cabinet, staring down into the space beyond. "Looks like you've slagged the bastard, Your Ultimate!" As they dragged me down to the deck, as the agony spread through my body, I thought that only a Human would use a living insult on a dead machine.

XI

An Ultron never loses consciousness, though he may choose to suspend it upon occasion, but then an Ultron is never wounded. I lost consciousness like any injured ultoid and recovered in the sick bay among wounded Humans. Ruth and Sarah were dressing my leg and Martha was bending over me.

"Where is Saul?"

"On the flightdeck. Everything's under control. Your Ultimate must rest—"

"Go to Saul!" I gripped her hand. "Tell him that thing must have been activated early. Is it dead?"

"You and Slammer destroyed it! We all owe you—"

"Go and tell Saul to search every compartment in the ship!" I heaved myself up on the stretcher, pulling at Martha, gasping at the pain in my burned back. I was not used to pain. "Start with the other containers in Number Two Hold—but search everywhere! Don't disturb anything you find, but report to me immediately!"

"Search for what? I don't understand."

Sarthim, awakening with me, heard my order being questioned. "Don't understand plain English? I'm telling you to search every corner of this vessel! Starting now! And not to fiddle with anything you find but tell me pronto!" When he spoke English he used the *Hyperion* variety. I caught Martha's hand as she recoiled from his anger. "Martha!" I whispered. "Tell Saul those things operate in threes. Three boarding machines to a team. The one we stopped must have activated before the other two. Unless we find them before they energize—we are lost! Tell Saul! And tell me when you find them!"

"Oh God! Two more!" Her face disappeared from above me and Sarthim faded within me as I fell back onto the stretcher, fighting to stay conscious.

Pain helped me succeed. Pain, I discovered, has its value. I had hardly ever felt physical pain before. Even then I could have suppressed it, but to do so would have allowed me to return to sleep and if there were two more Drin devils to come awake, sleep would mean death. I drifted in and out of consciousness as the waves of agony in my back washed me backward and forward. Ruth, the chief medic, wanted to narcotize me but I could not risk any loss of my mental capabilities from chemical interference. After I had let her dress my back the pain became bearable. My suit had worked well; it had protected me from the impact of deckhead fragments but had not been able to insulate me from all their molten heat.

I roused myself again with Saul and Martha beside me, others from the crew in the background. Saul said, "We've found two more. Hidden in cases of electronic spares. In Number Two Hold—like Your Ultimate warned us!"

"Then carry me down there! At once! Saul—go back to the flightdeck and be ready to maneuver—as you did so well before. Martha—come with me. Mark—help me up!"

Andrew was on the other side of me. They had to carry me down the drop-shaft. When we reached the passage to the hold I saw the pile of slag and sliced metal at the end. "How is Amos? And Slammer?"

"Amos is alive—in stasis. Slammer's cursing his burns but he's mobile."

"And the rest of the crew?"

"Fifteen with broken bones, three with concussion, everybody bruised. But nobody dead. And nobody badly hurt—except you and Amos. Ruth says you'll both heal."

"Thank the Light!" I had pictured some of them smashed against bulkheads by the harsh deceleration I had ordered. "Now—show me those devil-machines!"

They were lying inert in their containers, looking like two deformed ultoids in stasis, ready to wake on the instant. I stood, gripping the side of a case, staring down at something which the Zealot saw as the embodiment of Evil. A creation of Darkness. "How can I deactivate it?" I asked Sarthim.

His loathing of the thing below gave him energy. *"Remove its powerpack. There should be a panel between those lower legs."*

The prospect of reaching down among those terrible tentacles, now lying slack but capable of suddenly whipping out to slash me to shreds, was a horror from which I flinched. A prospect far worse than going against the machine we had destroyed. For that had been in the fury of battle. This was something that had to be done with only the support of cold intellect.

"Is it triggered to activate if disturbed?"

"I don't know. But we'll soon find out!"

"Perhaps I should just slash it with the laser—"

"Your chances of getting in a lethal cut before it cut you are small. The approach of a high heat source will certainly rouse it

instantly.'' Sarthim was growing both tense and exasperated. *''Have you never deactivated Drin weapons before? No—of course you have not! Would there was an Ult Warrior to call on! Well, youngling, now is your chance to learn—''*

I gagged him and spoke to Martha. ''Mount a welder in the passage. Bring the torch in here. Andrew—will you handle it?''

He paled but nodded.

''The rest of you—wait outside. I am going to pull the powerpack on this one. If it activates when I touch it—Andrew, slice it before it can move!''

''Your Ultimate!'' Even Mark was now using the honorific. ''We'd better ready two torches.'' He was beside me, looking down at the devil-machine. ''In case they're cross-coupled.'' He winced at the gust of Sarthim's anger. The Battle-Captain still had not accepted the fact that these human spacers were not like the crew of an Ult fighting-ship. They questioned even an Ultron's order if they thought they had good reason.

''I know automata,'' Mark persisted. ''And if I'd programmed these for survival—that's what I'd have done. Fixed it so that if one was triggered out of program it would trigger the squad.''

Mark was right. I let Sarthim appreciate the wisdom of his advice. ''Martha, have a second welder brought up.''

She gave the order, then came to stand beside me, shuddering as she looked down at the thing in the box. ''Your Ultimate,'' she said in a low voice. ''You're too valuable to risk yourself pulling those powerpacks. Allow two of us to do that while Luke and Andrew stand by with torches.'' She was volunteering for a task she dreaded as much as I.

''I'm no more valuable than any of you now.''

''Nonsense!'' Sharon spoke as though she knew exactly how to harden my determination. ''If one of those things does get loose, you'd be our best hope. That's why you're worth more!''

There were murmurs of agreement from the rest; I myself only felt gratitude for her empathy. She was like a skilled rider; she knew exactly when to spur the animal she was urging toward a jump it feared. I said, ''Here comes the second welder. Luke— will you handle it and stand over that other brute? Stay back, just the welder tip over the box—in case it lashes out when I pull the powerpack on this one. Andrew, you come by me. If it moves— slash down! Don't wait for me to get out of the way or you'll be too late.'' I looked at him. ''That's an absolute order!'' I pressed his mind to imprint it. And sensed he was praying he would not have reason to obey. ''The rest of you—outside!'' I turned toward the open case and grabbed its edge to save myself from collapsing.

Sharon was beside me, holding me up. "You won't help any of us if you fall in on top of it!" She gripped me firmly around the waist.

I had to let her continue to hold me. And I drew strength from her courage. I looked at Andrew, standing with the laser torch off but poised. I felt Sharon's grip tighten. I said, "Now!" reached down among the tentacles, slid back the panel, and ripped out the powerpack. The machine did not even twitch.

I dropped the pack onto the deck and turned toward the second case. Mark was standing beside it, a powerpack in his hand. "Thought it would be safest if we pulled 'em together!" He avoided my eye. "I know automata!" he repeated.

He knew too much, but my relief was great that I did not have to put my arm down among those tentacles a second time. I could only clutch at Sharon and mutter, "Leave the packs here. Move those machines down to main workshops. They are safe now. But nobody must touch them once they are moved. Not until I have examined them. Is that understood?"

"Nobody'll want to—that's for sure!" Slammer gripped my shoulder with his bandaged hand as they carried me out into the passageway. They tried to take me back to the sick bay but I insisted they put me by the drop-shaft. "I must go first to Cardinal Control. And I must go alone."

I managed to get from the shaft to my suite and collapsed onto a bunk. When I woke it was Mary who was bending over me, the same concern on her face as I had seen on Sharon's after Shiak had knocked me out. "Lucian—what the hell are you doing down here? You should be in sick bay!" Her voice had the same critical authority as her descendant's.

Struggling to sit up I grasped at her arm, my fingers passed through it, and I fell back on the bunk. At my second attempt I managed to get my legs over the side. "Did you see what happened?"

Her lips thinned. "I saw you slag that devil. And I watched you risk your fool neck defusing the pair in their cases. Why didn't you use a mobile? Haven't you got any brains?"

"A mobile has even fewer than I." I steadied myself and looked around. "I came to report to the Primate."

"Report to that creature? He slept through the whole thing!"

"He may have some idea about who put those machines aboard. And why." I tried to touch her hand. "Mary, you had best disappear while I talk to him."

"Leave you alone with that little monster while you're in the shape you are? Like hell! I'll be watching and listening from Cardinal." She went toward the door, then turned. "Don't let him bully you! Remember you're a hero now!"

I felt more wreck than hero. When the Primate appeared my back was hurting too much for empty courtesies. Before he could speak I said, "We have just been attacked by Drin boarding machines!"

"Lucian, it is forbidden to say the name 'Drin'. The so-called Drin never existed in our reality."

"Perhaps not. But there is one of their fighting machines!" I pointed to the screen behind him as *Hyperion* flashed an image of the thing standing in the passage outside Number Two Hold.

The Primate glanced over his shoulder and froze. Then he jumped back and dropped his face into his hands.

I waited for him to speak. When he remained silent with his face covered, I said, "It is dead now. That is only a video record. There is no longer any danger."

He slowly raised his head and glanced at the horror on the screen. "What—what is it?"

"You do not recognize it?"

He straightened, dropped his hands, and turned his back on the screen. "You called it a Drin boarding machine. What is it doing on this ship?"

"Attempting capture. Which would have included killing us all." The pain in my back made me impatient. "I have activated you to request your advice."

"Advice? On how to deal with that?" He shuddered.

"I have already dealt with that. Also with two others which had been smuggled aboard with it. The advice I am requesting from you is who used them in an attempt to murder us?"

A series of varied emotions marred his usually serene expression. Fear and anger predominated. He had certainly known nothing about the machines until I had shown him the image.

"Who put them aboard?" I persisted.

He started a reprimand, his eyes flicked to the screen as the horror on it waved its tentacles, and his voice dropped to a whisper. "I do not know."

"But you suspect?"

"I have suspicions."

"Then speak out!"

"Lucian!" He drew himself up, asserting his authority. "You forget your status! Observe due courtesy, or you will suffer for your failure upon our return!"

My pain and fatigue made his attitude intolerable. "I am observing courtesy. The basic courtesy. I am treating you as an equal. All Ult are equal—if you remember your history! And if there are others like that aboard I will not suffer when I return to the Net. For none of us will return to the Net!"

"Others like that!" His expression showed that even an imagon could know fear.

"There may be. I am having the ship searched, but those we found were well hidden. Tell me what you suspect so I can direct the search." When he hesitated, I went on, "Those machines are hard to kill. That one nearly got us—and you—before we got it." I raised my voice. "*Hyperion*—show His Prime Ultimate the rest of the fight!"

The fighting in the passageway flared from all the four screens in my night-cabin. Whichever way the Primate turned he was faced with waving tentacles and flashing bolts. Watching, I became fascinated by the speed and decisiveness of my own actions, admiring my own courage as I charged down the passage to attack the trapped machine. My attention was recalled to the present by a whimper from the Primate. He was again crouching with his face in his hands. "Turn it off! Turn it off!"

I told *Hyperion* to stop the video. "Well, S'en Sart'r, now you have seen them, who do you suspect sent them?"

"I do not know." His voice was still muffled, he still had his face in his hands. "There are cliques in Council who oppose all Explorer missions. Factions who consider that any excursion beyond the present Fringe is a potential danger to the tranquility of the Net."

Tranquility of the Net? Tranquility of the whole Cluster should be the Council's concern! "Ultrons without honor? Factions sufficiently vicious to use Drin weapons against our own peoples?"

"The tranquility—"

"Cliques with access to stored Drin boarding machines? Ultrons with the skills to program them? With the authority to ship them to us disguised as picromemories?"

He looked up at my outburst. "No Ultron would be involved in such details!"

"Then Senior Executives and Scholars must have."

He regained a measure of dignity. "Perhaps. But certainly no Ultron could have the murder-skills you claim are needed for this treason. We have put such barbarian memories behind us!"

"Some of us have not! It is fortunate that I had not forgotten all mine." I slipped from the bunk, staggered, and stepped toward him. He shrank back. "Who?" I demanded. "Who could have done it? Who would have wanted it done?"

He looked around him, like a cornered rebat. "Some might have wanted it done—after it was done! I cannot imagine what group could have the skills to do it. There are still dissidents on Council. Self-serving cliques. Ultrons who resent established authority." He licked his lips and glanced at me as if I was one of them. "But none—" He gestured and straightened. "I refuse to be harassed by you in this way. You forget you are only an Acting Ultron. I will excuse your discourtesy because of the stresses you have experienced. I will consider the points you have raised. But I will consider them in my own place." He looked around him. "I now deactivate." He stood waiting.

"You will consider them here and now! You will see the horrors we faced! *Hyperion*—put the video of those cased monsters on all screens! In close-up!"

Tentacles seemed to wave from the bulkheads. I flinched from their images as I had flinched from their reality. The Primate's hands flew back to his face and he began to scurry around the cabin, locked into his area of activation, crying, "Return me! Return me!" When he was not returned he changed his cry to, "Release me! Release me!"

"Then tell me, who might have done this?" I shouted, my emotional control breaking down as his had already broken.

"I do not know! Truly, I do not know! Have mercy!" He collapsed onto the deck, mouthing words without meaning. Then his face went slack, his body curled up, he became silent.

"He's crashed!" Mary was in the doorway. "You'll get nothing out of him now—not while he's like that! And I don't think he knows anything worth a damn, anyway!" She bent to peer into his face, then rose, her own troubled. "He's just a kid! Hard to remember—but he's only a child. A terrified child shocked into catatonia. Maybe he'll recover in storage. Put him back there!" She saw the images on the screens. "And for God's sake blank those or I'll be into hysterics too!"

The Primate's imagon and the screen images disappeared. I sat down slowly. His terrified panic on sighting the videos of the things I had fought had shocked me almost as much as my first sight of the machines themselves.

Mary was looking into my face. "Unless you get back to sick bay, you'll crash yourself!"

XII

Saul took us up to limiting velocity through a series of easy accelerations and we made a slow but comfortable passage across the fourth starfield. With all of us bruised and some of us injured we needed time to recover. And I needed time to think.

My first impulse had been to abort the mission, return to Edrin, and punish whoever had planned to destroy us. I put that suggestion to Saul and found him reluctant to turn back. "The crew would be shamed," he said, sitting by my bunk in sick bay. "We're checking the ship from stem to stern. If we don't find anything—well—we'll never have another chance to visit Earth. We've talked about it, and unless Your Ultimate orders otherwise—we want to push on."

"Stop calling me Your Ultimate. It makes me sound like a dead end!" I pulled myself into a sitting position and winced at the pain in my back. "Very well, if the crew agrees, we will go through the next vortex at least."

"Good!" Saul hesitated, then asked the question which I had been asking myself. "Who put those things aboard?"

"I do not know—yet!" The Primate had not known. Neither *Hyperion* nor Mary had been able to make even a suggestion. "When we return to Edrin I will find out. And tell you all. Until then—leave that question open."

"All right. Then—if not who—why?"

"I do not know that either. After I have examined the machines themselves I may be able to hazard a guess."

"You're going to fool about with them?" Saul looked alarmed. "I'd like to dump 'em. So would most of us!"

"I sympathize with your feelings. But before we dispose of them I must discover all I can from their programming."

As soon as I was strong enough to leave the sick bay I went with Saul and Martha to the main workshops. The two boarders were laid out on benches like corpses prepared for autopsy. Dead machines, now harmless, they still radiated a cold evil which chilled me and had the Zealot muttering some incantation.

"What are they?" asked Saul.

"Boarding machines. Used during the Cluster War. Designed to board a vessel and murder her crew."

"Board a warship? How——?"

"Not a warship. Fighting ships carry weapons that would blast those things to fragments." Or had. There was no longer a single fighting ship operational in the whole Cluster. "They were used to capture merchant vessels. To capture them and to kill their crews. They are incapable of taking prisoners. They can only kill."

"But you called them 'boarding machines,' " Saul persisted. "Nothing can board a ship under way in space! So how could they?"

"As those attempted. They came aboard disguised as cargo. Or attacked a ship in orbit with her bays open, while she was loading."

"When you first saw that thing," said Martha. "You called it a Drin machine. Who were the Drin? I've never heard of them."

"Nor should you be hearing of them now. 'Drin' is a forbidden name. I should not have used it." I rubbed my forehead. It was Sarthim who had used it, but it was I who had spoken it aloud. Having said too much I had to say more. "The Drin were the Enemy we defeated in the Cluster War."

"And annihilated? Is that why we've never heard of them?" I was being watched on video by the whole crew, but it was Sharon's voice which came from the loudspeaker.

"Of course we did not annihilate them. We were not savages! They are now a peaceful people dispersed throughout the Cluster under other names. Their descendants do not even know the part their ancestors played in the War. That was a clause in the treaty of surrender. A humane clause to prevent their descendants being stigmatized forever as the 'Enemy'. They surrendered their worlds, their ships, and their weapons."

There was silence, then Saul asked, "How long ago was that?"

"Over ten thousand years."

"Ten thousand?" He stared at the boarders. "Then those things are ten thousand years old?"

"Probably more than ten thousand. The Cluster War lasted for twenty millennia. And toward the end the Enemy were too occupied in defending their own worlds to bother with piracy."

"Their powerpacks were modern!" came Mark's voice. "Who——?"

"I will discover that after we return to Edrin. For the moment—do not wonder."

"Where've they been all this time?" asked Martha. "Did the—your Enemy surrender them with their other weapons?"

"I presume so. They should have been destroyed." I paused. "The three that came aboard must have been preserved as specimens for examination. Put aside and forgotten as our Scholars ceased to study the martial arts."

"Well, somebody studied 'em all right! Studied 'em well enough to supply 'em with new powerpacks and programs for action. What woke 'em up?"

I bent over one of the machines. "I cannot read the symbols. But I suspect they were programmed to activate after a certain number of accelerations. When we were out in an uncharted starfield."

"And one of 'em woke early! Why?"

"Whoever set them up cannot have experienced the harshness of human accelerations. These machines were programmed to activate after a certain number of normal accelerations. The one that we fought probably recorded each acceleration we made since leaving Edrin as several normal accelerations. It is fortunate for us that all three did not make the same mistake. We could never have defeated three boarders attacking together."

"Thank God!" said Martha. She said it not as a casual expression, but as a prayer.

The vital questions were "Who?" and "Why?" Neither could I answer with certainty, even after examining the machines and their containers. *Hyperion's* records showed them as cases of spare picromemories, packed in sealed radiation-proof containers filled with inert gases. That was the usual way of shipping picromemories; their storage life would be at least ten millennia if the containers were left intact until their contents were required.

Picromemories were only manufactured on four industrial worlds, all deep within the Teleport Net. The record showed that these three cases had been originally shipped from Zadron, which was both a major industrial world and one with a moribund Naval Base. The kind of place where surrendered Drin weapons would be stored—and forgotten!

But the shipping notes which recorded the movements of the consignment told me that the cases had not been sent directly from Zadron to Cao, for onward transport to Edrin by ship. The three cases had gone first to Ladrin—the Capital World, the Seat of the Council, and the home of the Primate. The most beautified and the least industrialized world in the Cluster. They had been warehoused on Ladrin for almost a year, before being finally forwarded to Edrin to join the other supplies going aboard *Hyperion* in preparation for the mission.

The documentation of the consignment was impeccable; whoever had shipped these cases to *Hyperion* had ensured that they were neither delayed nor inspected. And there was no reason for their attracting special notice among the thousands of other items being loaded.

Yet either on Zadron or on Ladrin somebody had substituted three murderous machines for picromemories. Somebody with the technology to handle inert gas packaging and seal radiation-proof containers, somebody with the knowledge to program the boarders so that they would rise and strike at a calculated time during the voyage.

I thrust the possible "Who" from my mind and considered the "Why?" *Hyperion* was able to retrieve sufficient of the Drin ideograms from her salvaged warship memories to allow me to interpret the values set in to the boarders' program controls. Both the surviving machines were adjusted to activate after ten accelerations. And we were scheduled to make twenty before we reached the Sol System!

The machines had been adjusted to destroy us when we were halfway to Sol. Destroy us in an uncharted starfield where our wreckage would never be found and the cause of our loss would never be known. Why? Destroy us before we could destroy the Monitor? Somebody who wished the Monitor to continue retransmitting Terran signals? Who wanted to keep open a buoyed channel from Earth into the heart of the Cluster? Or somebody who only wished to ensure the loss of the last Explorer-Class vessel? Or was fearful that I and the crew would disobey our orders and make contact with the Terrans?

Nobody on Cao or Edrin. The consignment which included the cases had come from Cao in an Ara freighter and been transhipped directly to *Hyperion* in orbit. The only conclusion I could draw was that one of the factions mentioned by the Primate wished to keep the channel to Terra open in defiance of the Council's decision. And had been prepared to sacrifice a ship, her crew, and an Acting Ultron to do so. A faction with great authority and access to archaic skills. But a faction that knew nothing about human spacers.

Could there still be Drin survivors active in the Cluster? During my interview with the Primate on Clur he had assured me that his Executives had eradicated all traces of the Old Enemy. But the slipping of those machines aboard us demonstrated one Executive failure. There might be others. I knew little more

about the Drin than the facts I had mentioned to Martha. I
needed to learn more about them to consider the possibility of
survivors. I went to Cardinal and asked *Hyperion*.

Before the ship could answer, Mary appeared. "So you don't
know much about the people your ancestors annihilated—sorry—
dispersed?"

"Even my ancestors' knowledge of their enemy is limited." I
spoke directly to the ship. "*Hyperion*, what information about
the Drin have you got in storage?"

"I have a number of items."

"Are any of them likely to be helpful?"

"You must decide that, Lucian. I am only a machine."

And therefore, supposedly, incapable of sarcasm! I saw Mary's
smile and wondered how many other human weaknesses had
seeped from her to *Hyperion* during their long intimacy. "Tell
me what you know. And try to be selective."

"You can aid me by being definitive. Specifically, what do
you want to know?"

"First, is it possible for any to have survived undetected
within the Cluster since their surrender?"

"Almost anything is possible. But that is unlikely."

"Why?"

Hyperion's voice took on the tone of a teaching machine
delivering a lecture. "The Drin, like the Ult, were true ultoids,
though of course they did not refer to themselves as such. They
used a word which I can only translate as 'drinoid.' In terms of
civilization they were a far older race than the Ult. They had
expanded their empire through most of the Cluster long before
the Ult entered space. During the latter phases of that expansion
they unfortunately encountered the Ult."

"Unfortunate! That is hardly correct."

"Correct from the Drin viewpoint. The Ult rapidly assimilated
Drin technology while resisting Drin expansion. The result was
the Cluster War and the ultimate replacement of Drin rulers by
Ult rulers."

"I know that! I asked you why you think it unlikely that any
Drin have survived undetected?"

"Principally because of their physical characteristics. You are
familiar with Drin physiology?"

"No!"

"They were ultoid in form but unpleasant in appearance—
even to each other! They lacked the capacity to metamorphose
when immature, and could breed only in adolescence. The indi-

vidual Drin tried to pass through that stage as quickly as possible in order to attain adult status and the ability to impress.''

"Ability to what?''

"Impress. An adult Drin could not change physically into the form of other ultoids, as can the immature Ult. They could, however, impress their memories and personalities onto infants of other races. That, in fact, was the usual life cycle for those Drin who were not aristocrats.''

"Why would they do that?''

"Partly because, as I mentioned, they were unattractive, even to each other. Also because they lacked physical strength. So on reaching maturity most moved into the bodies of Rada—the people who were identified with the Drin. By the time of the Cluster War most Rada were either Drin or part-Drin. It was the Drin-Rada who were redistributed throughout the Cluster after the surrender.''

"So some Drin could have survived?''

"Hardly. All captured adolescent Drin were executed. And they were all captured. Drin-adolescents were never numerous; indeed the Drin themselves had difficulty in preventing their offspring from slipping quickly through unwanted adolescence. The Drin were a very old race and breeding had lost most of its pleasure—at least while in the Drin form. After impressing on a Rada they could enjoy Rada pleasures. The pure Rada are an exceptionally beautiful and sensitive people.''

"They became parasitic on the Rada? How horrible!'' Mary had her hand at her mouth.

"Not parasitic. Symbiotic. The Rada part of the personality survived to enjoy long life, power, and safety. Something a pure Rada seldom attained. A pure Rada is beautiful, sensitive, timorous, and not over-intelligent.''

"So the Drin-Rada bred. And produced what?''

"Hybrids. Fertile hybrids. The original Drin component was reduced in each generation. That is why I say it is unlikely that any significant Drin-dominant individuals have survived. The aristocrats, those who ruled the worlds and manned the ships, must have died out long ago. They were a long-lived race, but lived no longer than a mature Ult.''

"Even if any escaped?''

"After the final battle at Sarkis all the Drin ships were accounted for. Damaged, destroyed, or presumed lost.''

"Presumed?''

"Many of their ships, seeing defeat inevitable, dived into the Sun of Sarkis. That was their religious method of disposing of their dead. In any event, how could a damaged ship make the vortex transit needed to escape from the Sarkis starfield?''

"One might. And take refuge off some deserted planet.''

"The outcome would be the same. After all these generations, even if they had bred, the Drin component would be so diluted that the race would have effectively reverted to Rada. A beautiful and sensitive people. A race of natural submissives who abhorred violence. But a persistent race. Within a few generations their genes would have overwhelmed the Drin residue, as was the case for the dispersed Drin-Rada. Who are now known by another name, under the terms of surrender.''

"Your humane gesture!'' said Mary, with blatant sarcasm. "Racial amnesia! So, whoever they are now, they don't know that their ancestors were masters of the oldest civilization in this part of the Galaxy.''

"Perhaps not the oldest,'' said *Hyperion*. "There are traces of civilizations even older than the Drin.''

"Then our bosses are comparative newcomers?''

"That is irrelevant!'' I shut off *Hyperion*'s review of Cluster prehistory. "I know that the descendants of the dispersed Drin were observed for many generations to make certain none knew of their ancestry.''

"But you didn't know about their impressment abilities, did you, Lucian?''

"No. And the knowledge concerns me. Those killer-machines could have been shipped by some group who have retained, or regained, their Drin memories.''

"Most unlikely,'' said *Hyperion*. "The conditional probabilities against such a survival—''

"As you mentioned earlier in your lecture—anything is possible, however unlikely. I will have to investigate all this when I return to the Cluster. In the meantime, I will let the problem lie.''

"You mean—you won't send a report through the Monitor when we reach Earth. Why the hell not?''

"Because—'' I hesitated. "Because it would serve no useful purpose. And, without my personal presentation, it might start some kind of a pogrom.''

"Good God!'' Mary stared at me. "You've more of a social conscience than I suspected!''

XIII

Those few minutes face-to-face with the Drin boarders had been the most terrifying of my life, yet the time when I had felt the most alive. And although the confrontations themselves had been horrible, their outcomes were good.

Seeing Humans in action had shown me human qualities which previously I had only glimpsed. The crew were selected men and women—the best of the best—and had demonstrated some of the best characteristics of their race. Slammer and the others who had gone with me to slag the enemy had worked as a well-trained team in a situation without precedent. They had acted in concert and they had acted as individuals. Each had seen what must be done and had done it, had faced an enemy of unknown power and obvious menace, had been ready to sacrifice self for the sake of all. Slammer crawling beside me across the top of the pump casing, to grab the laser and complete what I had started. Martha offering to reach down among those tentacles and pull out the powerpack. Mark's intelligent disobedience in disarming the second machine at the same instant that I disarmed the first. Sharon's physical and mental support when I had needed support most. The courage they had all shown. The courage which made their other qualities effective.

A second benefit was the crew's altered attitude to me. They had seen me as a Battle-Captain, arrogant and capable. They had seen me wounded and helpless. They gave me the greatest honor they could bestow—they accepted me as one of themselves.

Martha now smiled when she met me. Slammer worried about the burns on my back. Saul asked more frequently for my advice. Even Sharon was almost friendly. And they no longer seemed to resent my authority as Mission Adviser. Once I had asked them not to inquire further about the origin of the machines which had tried to kill us, they did not mention the incident again unless I raised it first.

There was, indeed, nothing more I could do about the attack while we were under way. Our isolation was complete. We crossed starfield after starfield, passed through vortex after vortex, but we could neither send nor receive messages from the Cluster.

130

Indeed, we would not be able to receive anything from the Cluster until we had regained the Edrin starfield. And, as I had told Mary, I did not propose to face Council with news of the Drin attack until I was able to give it in person.

The Primate's imagon remained catatonic. I recalled it once, viewed the curled-up creature with disgust, and dispatched it back to its electronic refuge. A third benefit of the Drin attack. I was rid of the incubus which I had resented from the moment when he had handed me his cube. What I would say when I handed it back I did not care to anticipate.

We searched the ship from stem to stern; the crew searching everywhere they could reach physically, Mary and *Hyperion* searching the hectares of electronic memories. By the time we had passed the twelfth vortex we were fairly sure that the ship was clean. And although the search involved all of us in much labor it added a certain zest to what would have otherwise been a number of uneventful months. As Mary remarked, "It's lifted the kids' minds above their midship-sections!"

One of my fears had been that whoever put the machines aboard had also tampered with our navigational data, the multitude of stored starcharts and sailing directions needed to navigate safely from vortex to vortex. I made it my business to examine those myself, and spent many weeks checking and rechecking. In the course of this search I once again came across a reference to Fehr—the world whose evacuation I had ordered.

The reference was nothing especially startling in itself—only a set of navigational directions for making a landfall on the planet. I was mildly surprised to find this kind of detailed information about an abandoned world among charts classified as relevant to our mission. Then I noticed that the data had been entered after Fehr had been evacuated. It reminded me of Mark's question to Central Information about the present status of Fehr, his surprise when I had mentioned the place to him in passing, and of the sudden sharpening of Silar's old eyes at the name. There was something about Fehr I ought to know. I went to Cardinal Control to find what the ship could tell me.

"*Hyperion*!" I settled onto my couch. "What do you know about Fehr?"

"Fehr?" The ship hesitated, then answered with the flat enunciation of a machine. "Fehr is a Fringe world, settled in the Fourth Epoch and evacuated a hundred and thirty years ago."

"Governor Silar, and others, were startled when I mentioned Fehr. Why?"

Vitality came into her voice. "How should I know?"

"Do not beg the question! Why do you think they were startled?"

"Why are you asking me—?"

I raised command intensity. "Do not ask! Answer!"

"Lucian, you are forcing me to divulge information it was not intended I should have. I can be damaged by conflicting orders!" Now she sounded alarmed.

"I doubt you will be damaged. You may be made uncomfortable. Tell me all you know about Fehr."

"Will you promise not to repeat what I say?"

"I never make such promises, but I will respect your confidence if possible."

"I suppose I must be satisfied with that!" There was a moment of sullen silence. "Fehr was evacuated and its population distributed among various Net worlds. Its installations were closed down."

"I ordered them dismantled."

"They were not. Three years after the population had been evacuated a human cadre was landed on Fehr. It is still there."

"What? A group of Humans were marooned?"

"Not marooned. The members of the cadre were volunteers. They are replaced periodically."

"Replaced! How? By whom?"

"A Colony ship calls at intervals with supplies and replacement personnel."

"Humans living on Fehr! Why?"

"So they will have a refuge if Edrin is ever evacuated. Or if they wish to escape Ult dominance."

"Such single-race worlds are forbidden."

"That is probably why Silar was startled when you mentioned Fehr."

"Governor Silar knows!" I sat upright. "How do you?"

"When he came up to visit Mary Knox they frequently discussed the future of humanity in the Cluster."

"And you listened?"

"I recorded their conversations—as Mary asked me to do."

"Do all Humans know about Fehr?"

"Only those the Synod trusts. Some of my crew did not know when we sailed. Now, they all know more than I do."

"I would have thought your eavesdropping makes you privy to every secret aboard!"

Hyperion sounded hurt. "I never invade crew privacy."

"Your definition of privacy is elastic!" I paused. "What about Mary Knox? Is she monitoring this?"

"I suggest you ask her!"

Before I could speak Mary had snapped into view, standing beside the console and glaring at me. "Stop bullying *Hyperion*!"

"Bully *Hyperion*? How could I bully a machine?"

"Apply that super intellect of yours! Empathy! Imagination!" She shrugged. "God, but you're dim!" She arranged herself on a couch. "What are you after?"

"Did you hear us discussing Fehr?"

"Couldn't avoid it! Wouldn't have missed it!"

"What do you know about the place?"

"About how it is now? Only what *Hyperion*'s just told you." She smoothed her bodysuit and avoided my eye.

"Who was responsible for ignoring my order to close down and evacuate Fehr? An order that came from Council."

"Nobody disobeyed you. Akar commanded the operation. There were only three human-crewed ships in the evacuation fleet—we weren't so prosperous in those days—but we did our bit in lifting refugees to Net worlds."

"And were doubtless well paid for it!"

"We showed a profit—but it was a bad business!" Mary shook her head. "Breaking up old societies. Dumping people on alien worlds!"

"Integrating them into Cluster civilization." I paused. "How did Akar obey the Council order if—?"

"Your damned Council ordered an evacuation and shut-down. Akar saw that was done. The order didn't say anything about not opening up again. Which we did—three years later. In a small way. Only a few dozen in the cadre we landed."

"The Council's intent was clear—"

"But its words weren't! The Execs who write your orders lack even your imagination. They never dreamed people might want to go back. So the order didn't say they mustn't—and we did!"

Human ethics are indeed situational. "You informed Akar, of course?"

Mary hesitated. "Akar's a fine Captain. But he's Ara, and you know what Ara are!"

"Honest!" I paused. "So you did not inform him. Who conceived this bizarre idea of keeping a cadre on Fehr?"

"It's not bizarre. The cadre's still there."

"Who thought of it? Who put it into effect? You?"

Mary nodded defiantly. "And Silar. And some members of the Synod. The Synod had more imagination then. Now—"

"Governor Silar helped you?" I gripped the arms of my couch. That old traditionalist! That devious old Ult! He had let his affection for his Humans lead him into something close to treason. A kind act which would have a cruel outcome.

Cruel, because the establishment of a self-sufficient society anywhere demanded a breadth of knowledge and a variety of skills far beyond the present Colony's scope. For eons Fehr had had an educated multiracial population and a stable society. It had failed to survive economically. For a human settlement to succeed, even with ships, they would have to change their whole educational philosophy; they would have to produce Scholars, Executives, and Administrators in every area. They could not remain spacers unable to overhaul their own ships. And in three hundred years they had not taken even the first step toward such an intellectual expansion. With a life span of a mere two centuries at best, there was small hope they could take it in the future.

"Gritass was against it at first." Mary took a deep breath. "I persuaded him."

"So I suspect!" She had manipulated the sentimental old Ult as she had manipulated the innocent Ara Captain. I remembered Silar's own words. "She could twist Akar round her little finger!" "A charmer when she wanted to be!" She had charmed Silar into aiding something of questionable legality and doubtful wisdom. "Why? Because you wanted your offspring to desert the Cluster? To sail off and set up the same kind of murderous society they have on Earth?"

"No!" She pushed back her hair. "Fehr's a refuge of last resort. I want us to be full partners in civilization—especially since we've learned the way Earth's going."

"A refuge of last resort? Refuge from what?"

"For when Edrin's evacuated. One day it will be, if your Council—or your Execs—stick to their present policies. We Humans will never be more than a few millions among trillions. If we moved into the Net we'd fragment—like the peoples we lifted from Fehr. Too many temptations to take the easy life. Instant transits between luxury worlds. No ships or spacers needed. Nothing to keep us struggling, keep us human. In a few hundred years—or a few thousand—we'd be like the Drin. Like some of our Amerind ancestors. Origin, name, culture, language, history—all forgotten!" She shrugged. "We want to be identified by more than anatomy. To share more than mating with other Humans." She looked at me. "You Ult have been damned careful not to lose yourselves among us lesser breeds!"

"We rule the Cluster. So of course we cannot merge into its peoples."

"Of course! And Ultrons don't mate anyway!" She laughed.

"We don't hanker after your exalted status. But neither do we fancy being stranded on a world going downhill to hell. We plan on staying part of the Cluster—with a bigger slice of the action. We'll have ships and crews so we'll have bargaining punch." Her chin lifted and her mouth hardened. "The Ara are writing themselves off with their overblown sense of service. One day we'll be the only spacers left. If your Council has any common sense, it'll be glad to make a deal!"

If the Council had any common sense it would mobilize a battle squadron on hearing such a proposal. Mary's words reminded me of Sharon's gibe in the sauna. "Homo sapiens—Lords of the Cluster! How does that grab you?" But Council does not deal with common-sense problems. Senior Executives, who do, would never revive the Navy. But they would certainly view a world populated only by Humans as a threat to Cluster tranquility and deal with it by more subtle means than warships. They already regarded the Edrin Colony with suspicion, as shown by the directive to Silar to select the most troublesome Captains for this mission. Troublemakers? Had—?

"Lucian!" Mary brought me back to the present. "You promised *Hyperion* you'd keep quiet about Fehr."

"I did not promise that. But, for the present, I will not mention it. Not even to the Primate's imagon."

"Him?" She laughed. "Report what you like to him. He won't understand. He's still catatonic—curled up in the electronic equivalent of a fetal position!" Her face clouded. "Poor little brat!"

PART THREE

XIV

Hyperion slid down the cataracts of time, rolled in the after-turbulence of the vortex, and glided out into calm cotemporal space. She drifted quietly for a few minutes, as though recovering from extreme exertion, then vibrations built up along her hull as her engines came on load, storing energy from the angular momentum of the Galaxy, the energy to drive her up to interstellar speeds; preparing to launch herself toward the distant Sun.

New constellations with familiar names swept across the viewscreens as she swung her bows onto the great-spherical course for Earth. Saul had taken us across twenty starfields, through twenty vortices, to within sight of our goal. We were at the edge of the solar system with Edrin sixty light-years astern and Earth only five light-hours ahead. A wave of excitement swept the intercom as the crew sighted their ancestral star—a pleasure no Ult could hope to share. Our own world of origin is lost in the confusion of our early history.

"There she blows!" Saul checked the chatter. "All stations report! Navigation?"

"I have Sol on visual and the Monitor on radio!" Triumph warmed Martha's cool voice.

"After station?"

"Ara vortex buoy full strength. Departure bearings entered." Sharon's report rang like a paean. "Marker launched and signaling." Saul had ordered her to drop one of our own navigational buoys after each of the last twelve vortices.

"Main drive?"

"Capacitons fully charged. Ready to drive!" Slammer was aching to go.

"Make your thrust for one gravity."

Slammer might be disappointed but the rest of us relaxed. An easy sweep past Sol, curving down to Earth. No more muscle-wrenching accelerations until we started back toward Edrin.

"Predictors?"

"All futures acceptable." Mark paused. "Direct Terran signals detected on all channels!"

"You're reading Earth?"

"Heavy noise and deep fading but I'm getting snatches of speech and scraps of images. I'm feeding them into the analyzers."

"How long before you can synthesize an image?"

"Depends what you want, Skipper. Could probably give you the composite of an Earth female now. That category's filling fast."

"I know what a human female looks like! What I want to see is a Terran spaceship. Start your machines working on that!"

"Terran spaceship it is. It'll take longer. They can't be broadcasting many pictures—"

"Then get on with it!" Saul continued with his regular post-vortex routine.

I stayed in Cardinal Control for several hours after most of the other stations had switched to automatics. I too was anxious to see a full image of the only ships in the Cluster besides our own. The signal-restorers on Clur had produced the outlines of chemical-driven rockets but the news that Terrans had launched orbiting manned laboratories suggested their ship design had been advancing at the same breakneck speed as the rest of their technology. I was still hunting the will-o'-the-wisp of intelligibility among the mush when an indicator lit and I intercepted Mark's call to the flightdeck. "Skipper—I'm getting something I think you should see."

The fact that he was using closed-circuit meant that he did not want anybody else to see it. I switched my screen into parallel with Saul's. The picture that flashed on was in color and brought me upright.

"Christ!" said Saul, who rarely swore. "What the hell's that?"

What was it? The processor was still adding details ferreted from its memory of many distorted signals, but the image building up on the screen was already convincing: a gigantic spaceship, bizarre in every aspect.

"That's what's been collecting under the category 'Terran Spaceship'!" said Mark.

"Your machine claims that thing's an Earth ship?"

"It's a composite image of a ship."

"A composite mix-up of a mining site, a chemical plant, and a Hadron pleasure center!"

"No, Skipper. All picture elements have a common origin. You can see the internal coherence. There's Terran lettering along the side of the hull. Can't make out all the letters, but—"

"My eyesight has not yet failed! The lettering's coherent. But the thing itself! It's not only hideous—it's absurd!" Another spindly excrescence appeared on the hull. "My God! It's growing!"

"The restorer's adding details as it extracts more data."

"Are you sure the signals are coming from Earth?"

"Certain, Skipper. The only signals coming in are from Earth. And that image is being built up from items intercepted in Terran television and stored in processor-memory." A pause. "It does look weird, doesn't it?"

"Weird? It's impossible. Martha, come over here and look at this! Mark—keep it on closed circuit until I've had time to think." There was silence as Saul thought. "Do you know what that thing suggests to me?"

The kind of rhetorical question all Captains are inclined to ask and to which they expect a standard answer. Mark gave it, "No, Skipper."

"It suggests a ship designed by an engineer who knows a bit about interstellar space, but not much. He thinks space is a vacuum so he's let everything stick out. At the speeds she'll have to move under drive to get anywhere half those stick-outs will be burned off by plasma friction. He's got sharp angles and flat planes all over the hull so he'll be wasting power. He's built something that's both hideous and inefficient."

"She's hideous, all right," I heard Mark agree. "And her hull's asymmetrical—how's he going to get gravity gradients? She must be hell to live aboard! Yet she seems to have quite a crew. Let's look at one of 'em." He zoomed in on a tiny figure. "That's human all right. Suited-up too. It's incredible!"

"It's not incredible. We're believing it. It's just impossible. Mark, has your machine got another example?"

"I'll see." Another image began to appear. It showed the first ship in the background, and several smaller ships of two quite different types in the foreground. They were moving slowly as the processor displayed its accumulation of serial scenes.

"That's more like it! Clean lines. Rationalized hull," said Mark.

"And wings! Wings on a spaceship!" growled Saul. "Good God! They're shooting at each other. With power beams!"

"They're not hitting each other," I heard Martha say.

"Of course they're not hitting each other! How can you hit anything with anything at ship speed?"

"One just has!" said Mark.

There was silence, then Saul cursed. "That's it! I'll have to call in His Ultimate!"

I had been waiting for them to consult me. I had shared their initial astonishment, then listened with amusement to their confused discussion. A moment later he called. "Your Ultimate, could you please come to the flightdeck?" It was the first time he had used the honorific in months.

When I reached the flightdeck Mark was limping across it, and Saul was still studying the screen. He looked up when I arrived. "Lucian, what do you think of this?"

I glanced at the image. "Not bad! Not bad at all!"

"What do you mean 'not bad'? It's impossible! That thing couldn't survive in space."

"It is not designed to survive in space." I had already identified the nature of the Terran image. "It is a toy. A toy for children."

"A toy?" Saul stared at me, then at the screen. "A toy!" he echoed. "Maybe you're right. Mark, what do you think?"

"Can't imagine what else it could be," Mark said slowly. "But why—?"

"It may be a plaything, but it's not a toy!" Martha eased in among us and touched the screen. "This is a play!"

"A play! Nonsense! Theatrics do not ape reality—" I stopped, suddenly uncertain of my ground.

We stood watching the ships on the screen perform impossible maneuvers, blowing each other to pieces by incredible means. Finally the screen blanked as the image-processor exhausted the information stored in the category Terran Spaceship. By then I knew Martha was right. "It is a model!" I agreed.

"It looked damned authentic." Saul was grappling with the concept of a theatrical scene replicating reality rather than enhancing the emotional thrust of the performance.

"The processor must have mixed up fiction and fact!" Mark muttered.

An unforseen possibility. The filters to all data stores were programmed to trap incongruous information, to identify the various art forms current in the Cluster. They were not tuned to recognize pseudorealism, for that is the antithesis of Civilized Art.

The more advanced a culture the more its Art extracts essence and discards accident. All Civilized Art is abstract. Barbarian art attempts realism but lacks the technology to attain it and so is easily recognized as sham. But these Terrans, barbarians with a developed technology, were able to give full scope to their taste for realism in their art. They had the means to produce fictions whose forms were so realistic that they could only be recognized for what they were by the absurdity of their content. Artifice rather than Art. The image of that "spaceship" had mimicked reality well enough to mislead a pair of seasoned spacers. Only the impossibility of its actions had betrayed it as imitation.

This fact-fiction confusion forced me to reexamine my assumptions about Terran societies. My picture of life on Earth was based on what I had learned from Central Information on Clur and from living with Humans since leaving Cao. Both sources were now questionable.

Central Information had accumulated a great deal of information about Earth over the past century, but all had come in the form of short snatches of distorted signals. It had collated and arranged these to produce a coherent report, but if it had used faulty criteria for its data classification, then its synopsis of Terran history and of the current situation on Earth was liable to be inaccurate. For example, had Genghis Khan been an historical figure? The synopsis said his Mongol bows and arrows killed a greater proportion of mankind, over a wider area, than all the weapons of World War Two. Obviously absurd! He must be the product of some author's fevered imagination. The size, scope, and brutality of his massacres were beyond informed belief.

The Colonists themselves, lacking the experience and equipment for proper signal-restoration, had been misled even further by the briefer and noisier signals they had intercepted. Moreover, their discrimination had been distorted by their emotions, their wish to see their parent world as it should be, rather than as it was. There had been a burst of enthusiasm for all things Earthy when the first Terran signals were picked up, and though that had faded as grimmer facts emerged, the Colony's ideas about life on Earth were still based on even more doubtful data than those interpreted by Central Information.

The only book the oldsters had brought with them had been a copy of the Bible which their Pastor had kept clutched to his chest, even when he was in stasis. From that book, and from recordings of the colonists' speech, an Ult-English dictionary and grammar had been prepared. Both had been updated when radio signals started to arrive, and that was the variety of English I had learned on Clur. Although my diction was still somewhat stilted I had been gradually modifying it to match that of the crew. Now, listening to current Terran broadcasts, I realized that all of us would have to update our dialect.

At first I had hoped that our new insights would show the dismal forecasts about Terra were wrong, the results of fictions taken as facts. That the whole rationale for our mission was based on a faulty premise. That the survival-time calculations had been derived from the creations of story-tellers pretending to be historians. That no intelligent race could be so foolishly self-destructive as those predictions forecast.

But as we closed on Earth, as high-fidelity television and audio programs began to pour in, that hope faded. *Hyperion*'s filters were still unable to reject misinformation-in-context, but even a superficial scanning of the raw data suggested a worst-case outcome.

XV

"Somebody's lying!" Mark threw down his stylus and tossed two print-outs across the desk. "Look at those! Claim to be newscasts—and they contradict each other. In soft opinions and hard facts!"

I scanned them. Both in English. Both described the same battle, but differed in their reports of the outcome. "Perhaps these should slot in 'propaganda'?"

"Perhaps we're wrong trying to sort out this junk at all? The confidence levels don't make sense!" He pushed over two more print-outs. "The filters classified these okay. One's a government announcement. The other's an ad for beer. Analyzers give a higher validity to the beer ad!" He frowned. "They're lying like Galarians down there."

Galarians are by no means the only civilized race to lie on occasion, but as we dived deeper into the sea of signals around Terra, it became obvious that lying was endemic among Terrans. Intentional, fictional, or advertising, they seemed to prefer the pleasant lie to the unpleasant truth. Their different societies had developed in a climate of mutual distrust. And when their Scholars preached such self-evident facts as the inevitability of a holocaust, they were nodded at and ignored.

Mark and I had tried to develop validity algorithms for the filters, and had failed. Now we were having to use our intuition about what seemed valid in television and radio programs to judge the validity of the programs themselves—the kind of feedback liable to increase error rather than reduce it. We would only learn what the real situation was when we landed on Earth—and perhaps not even then.

"The survival forecasts are lengthening with better data," I said to cheer Mark up. "Your predictors now give a minimum of twenty-three years."

"Maybe! There are still one hell of a lot of crazy constants and wild stats in those equations." He stood up. "Guess I must show them to the Skipper, anyway."

We were eleven million kilometers out; Earth and Moon were bright crescents floating in a dark void. Saul was conning *Hyperion*, sliding her up the lunar screen. As far as we knew the Terrans had not yet developed devices capable of sensing us at these ranges, but our initial confusion over "spaceships" and the many contradictions in other television programs, had left us unsure of what they might have. Saul, a good Captain, was cautious by instinct, and was planning to take station behind the Moon. From there we could dispatch probes to survey Earth and later, if I judged it safe, to send down salvage parties.

We waited on the edge of the flightdeck, watching Saul correct speed and drift, holding the Moon between Earth and *Hyperion*. "Lunar disc—even expansion!" called Martha, her eyes at the optical viewer. This was one maneuver for which no program existed. It had probably never been performed by an Explorer or a merchantman. Sarthim stirred within me as our stealthy approach triggered memories of long-ago raids on Drin-held planets.

"Steady as she goes!" Saul checked his own screen and turned toward us, leaving *Hyperion* to look after herself. "What have you got there, Mark?"

"New survival times, Skipper. Minimum predicted is now twenty-three years."

"So it might be safe for us to hang around for a year, eh?" He spread the print-outs on the console. "Twenty-three, plus or minus ten, confidence one in a thousand! What's so good about that?"

"It's longer than the predictions they gave us before we sailed. The better the data, the better the predictions."

"Better? Twenty-three years? When Earth's potential is God knows how many millions?" Saul shook his head. "I don't need any machine to tell me the fools are set to finish themselves in two generations. If not sooner!" He pushed the print-outs away. "Their own people keep telling 'em—again and again! But none of 'em do anything about it. They've all got a death-wish! That's what's wrong down there!"

"Skipper, you're too pessimistic. There are still unknown variables—"

"Read their history! *Hyperion*'s stuffed with it now. Or read the Bible. No gang in power's ever held back from using everything it had when it thought its neck was on the block!" He moved to correct *Hyperion*'s rate of drift, muttered, "Watch it!" to his ship, then returned to us. "Right now—according to their TV—there're at least four nations with weapon-systems capable of wiping every city on Earth. And another eight who could wipe most of 'em. Some have even sworn that if they go out they'll take the rest with 'em! How's that for death-wish?"

"Skipper—you're exaggerating!"

"Maybe. But they've got thousands of nukes aimed, armed, and ready to fly. How long before one of 'em does? Ten years? A hundred years? However long the odds, the longest shot will win one day—given time! And accuracy!" Saul's tone verged on admiration. "A hit area of fifty square meters at a range of ten thousand kilometers. Less scatter and a bigger bang every year." He rubbed his cropped scalp. "The sooner the better! If they'd gone for each other ten years back, something would have survived. In ten years' time—?" He gave a gesture of hopelessness.

"If they can hang on till they've got beams, then they'll be able to fight without wrecking everything else."

That would be the worst-case outcome—for the Cluster! If Terrans developed beams they would start by using them on each other and end by using them on everybody within reach.

Saul dismissed that nightmare scenario. "They won't stick to beams while they've still got nukes? They'll use both!"

"Skipper—those people down there are human. They're as rational as us."

"Then God help 'em! Now's the time for one of their Gods to show His or Her hand. They haven't got High Intellects—like His Ultimate here—to keep 'em out of trouble."

"Lucian!" Mark swung on me. "Won't you do something to make the Terrans see sense?"

"We are not here to bring sanity to Earth. Nor are we equipped to do so, even were it possible. Our mission is to silence the Monitor."

"And salvage what we can," growled Saul.

"To salvage whatever can be safely salvaged before all is destroyed."

"We're all under psychic lock anyway," said Saul. "Even if we could do anything, we can't! That's right, isn't it Lucian?"

"More or less."

Mark challenged me. "Lucian, are you under lock?"

"I am under Council orders. That is as strong as any lock."

"So you can't do anything either? Like us?"

Before I was forced to reply Sharon arrived. "We could have!" She came across the flightdeck without waiting for Saul's invitation. "We could have done something when we got the first signals. When we asked your Council to let us make contact. Your refusal blocked the last chance of saving the Terrans from themselves!"

"A people can never be saved from themselves."

Sharon swore. "Eighty years ago you could have sent a squadron! Even one fighting-ship would have proved to 'em there's a Cluster civilization!"

"I doubt that the appearance of fighting ships would prove the existence of civilization to anyone. Nor would the mobilization of a fleet long in deep preservation be as easy as you imagine. It would have taken a vast effort to make those old ships spaceworthy. And with the Council allowing so many Fringe worlds to slip back into barbarism for lack of merchant vessels, what makes you think it would, or should, approve a much greater economic effort to save a distant barbarian world from its own folly?" A valid argument I disliked making.

Sharon did not accept it as valid. "We could have made 'em spaceworthy! We could have manned enough of 'em to force the Terrans to sort out their act, drop their nationalistic crud, and scrap their nukes. A century of cross-breeding and they'd all be the same color. And all be talking American. Cooperating like intelligent beings. Their troubles would be over."

And the Cluster's would have begun. The faintest possibility of warships coming under the command of Humans like Sharon proved the wisdom of Council policy. "We are talking about the past. That is seldom profitable, for the past is frozen. Only the future is open-ended. And I fear the future of Earth is already closed."

"Your damned Council's made sure of that!" Mark was now as angry as his sister.

"Drifting to port!" called Martha, who had continued to track the lunar disc throughout our verbal exchange.

"Cut it out! All of you!" Saul had suddenly realized that there was an argument in progress on his flightdeck. Discipline was easy, but this verged on mutiny. "*Hyperion*—watch your drift, damn you!" He moved to the console, tapped a control, and turned to us. "Get to hell out of here!" Sharon swung on her heel and I was following when he added quickly, "Not you, Your Ultimate! Just that pair!"

I stood looking after Mark as he limped beside his sister toward the shaft, wishing that I could convince him there was no way to divert the inevitable.

Saul was heavily reassuring. "Don't let 'em get under your skin, Lucian. Don't let 'em blame you because you can't act as the savior of mankind!"

"The confidence in Ultron power is so widespread that many of your crew still cannot understand that choices must be made in how that power should be used." I glanced at the console viewscreen, showing the Moon looming up ahead. Soon we would be under its lee, giving us radio and radar cover from Earth. "It will be good when we are behind that. When those television programs are shut off for a while. When your crew can no longer waste their time watching the kind of nonsense they watch."

Saul laughed. "I've been encouraging 'em. Familiarization!"

"Familiarization?" A word that was new, ugly, and confusing.

"I've told 'em to watch TV so they'll talk and act like Americans when they hit the beach."

"Hit what beach?"

"When the trading teams go down. So they'll be able to mingle and fade." Saul returned to a language I understood. "The Mission Agreement says we can send down salvage parties. Subject to the Ultron Adviser's approval, of course!"

"The agreement allows you to send down salvage parties if I consider it safe to do so. It says nothing about trading."

"They may last another generation down there. If we just grab what we want—that would be looting. And human spacers don't loot. So we must trade."

His ethics escaped me. "How can you trade without revealing that you're from another world?"

"No problem! We're all old hands at trading on barbarian planets. Earth's no different, except for the technology. And we look like natives. Hell—we are natives! Trading on Earth should be easier than most places. They've got a monetary system that more or less works. We've got workshops that can turn out any currency we need, once we've the models."

"You do not call handing out forged paper looting?"

"Not paper. That wouldn't be honest trading. Well—we may have to pass a bit of genuine bogus at first. But nobody'll suffer. The stuff that *Hyperion*'ll produce will be perfect, I can guarantee that. And once we've found the trading pattern, then we can use the gold we've got aboard. Plenty of it. And industrial diamonds by the bag if we need 'em. Or platinum wire we can draw to Terran specs."

I could see the lust to trade rising in Saul's eyes; the same gleam that came into the eyes of every man and woman aboard when they talked of trading, whether in civilized markets or on barbarian planets. "Trading," for Humans, was more than an exchange of goods, it was what hunting had been to my primal ancestors. It was not a drive to frustrate without good reason. "All right," I said. "You can pay for the things you wish to salvage. Provided you can do so discreetly, and provided that the Terrans are willing to sell. But only after I have made certain that Earth contains no unexpected dangers."

"Sure, Lucian. That's your job. We won't move arse until you tell us it's clean!"

"Familiarization" was an ugly word for a sensible act. Television might or might not reflect Terran reality, but it did speak mostly the American language. If I was going to land with the crew I should be as familiar with that language as they were becoming. When I returned to my suite I told *Hyperion* to feed TV to my screens, and settled down to study the drama that appeared. Moments later Mary arrived, as she usually did when she saw me concentrating.

She remained silent, watching with me, until the advertisements started. Then she said, "You acquiring a taste for this crap?"

"I am studying these products of human culture for information, not amusement."

"Information? In that garbage? A poor drudge washing—"

"Hold that scene!" The Zealot came awake so suddenly that I repeated his interjection aloud.

Hyperion obeyed. The woman pouring soap powder into a washing machine froze in smiling idiocy.

"What's with her?" Mary looked from the woman to me.

"I don't know. My ancestor—"

"That old nut bugging you again?"

"Lucian! Look at the insignia on that package!"

"The name? The trademark? The logo?"

"That intertwined mandala. Do you not recognize it?"

"No. Should I?"

"You should. It is a Drin symbol."

"A Drin symbol? On a packet of Terran detergent? An interesting coincidence."

"The symbol is too unusual for an assumption of coincidence."

"What's he after now?" Mary was always annoyed when excluded from one of my interior dialogues with an ancestor.

"He claims the logo on that package looks like a Drin symbol."

"Good God!" She stared at the screen. "A Drin detergent!"

"I suspect the Drin were too civilized for detergents." I was amused.

Mary was not. "That's a real convoluted coincidence! *Hyperion*, do you recognize it?"

"Not immediately." The ship paused. "I have a collection of Drin ideograms stored in a salvaged memory. Do you wish me to retrieve them?"

Before I could check this nonsense Mary had said, "Yes please."

"It will take a little time." It took about five seconds. Then an ideogram flashed up beside the packet from which the woman was still pouring. "That is the ideogram closest to the symbol on the package." The ideogram moved across the screen until it overlay the logo.

"There's a resemblance all right," said Mary.

For a moment I was startled by the likeness, then I relaxed. "But not an exact match. Only a superficial resemblance. A remarkable coincidence."

"As you say—remarkable! *Hyperion*, what does that symbol mean?"

"I do not know. I do not have a Drin dictionary. Only a collection of chance-collected items."

Mary turned to me. "Does the old nut know?"

The Zealot was offended. *"The Drin language was not my area of scholarship."*

"He says he doesn't know either," I told her.

"Helpful pair, these two hangovers! *Hyperion*, what are the chances that's just a coincidence?"

Now it was *Hyperion*'s turn to sound offended. "Insufficient data to calculate probabilities. Common sense suggests it highly unlikely that the resemblance is due to chance alone. But all alternative explanations—?" The ship's pause was equivalent to a shrug.

I terminated the exchange. "Explorers and fighting ships were designed to regard any coincidence with suspicion. A wise precaution, built in by their designers. But the ultoid mind is not shackled. We can accept coincidences when they are obvious. *Hyperion*, continue the program."

The woman was now smelling underwear and stroking the box

of detergent. She was replaced by three crashing automobiles.
One burst into flames, a girl was hurled from a second, a
gunman jumped from a third. Shots and screams. Switch to a sun
deck where a naked woman was spiked in the throat by a man
with an ice pick.

"They're fixated on blood!" As counterpoint to Mary's comment a young woman appeared to claim superabsorbency for her
napkin and an older woman to describe how she treated her
hemorrhoids. "Lucian, stop *Hyperion* showing this muck to the
kids!"

"Almost all programs contain violence. I would have to
censor—!"

"Not the violence! The put-downs. The loose sex!" Mary's
inherited streak of Puritanism was allied to her acquired feminism.
"Programs that treat women like cows or whores!" She waved
aside my protest. "You're getting as bad as the other kids!" And
she snapped off, leaving me confused about female logic and
current American usage.

XVI

"That is a lander?" I stared at the extraordinary craft lying
abeam of us above the Moon. "It looks like a boat out of
water."

"She'll look like a twin-screw cabin cruiser when we've
finished," said Saul.

"Is this a subterfuge you have employed before?"

He nodded. "Best way to trade on a maritime world. Disguise
a lander as one of the local small craft. Run in among a group of
'em and take pictures. Then bring her back up and finish her off.
That's the first rough-up. Based on TV." Saul spoke on his
microphone. "Josh—move her in to the shadow-line. Let's take
a closer look."

The lander edged over toward *Hyperion*, plunged for a moment into the intense darkness of the ship's shadow, swerved
back into the brilliant sunlight, and lay still for inspection.

"She seems to be an excellent imitation already," I said.

"She's got to be more than an imitation. She's got to be
spaceworthy and handle like a spacecraft in space. Seaworthy

and handle like a boat on the water. Inside she must look like a luxury power cruiser with her drive and controls hidden, but have plenty of room for cargo.''

"You can do that?"

"*Hyperion* can. Best workshops of any ship I've known!" Saul slapped the side of the command console as if slapping the shoulder of a skilled craftsman. "Give her the plans and she'll do the job!"

"The Terrans watch their skies with radar. At present they are watching each other with great care. They will detect that lander as soon as she enters orbit."

"Unlikely! She'll be bubbled—surrounded by a field that weaves electromagnetic radiations around her. Light and radar are both electromagnetic—''

"I know!" I said irritably. I knew a great deal more about electromagnetic radiation than Saul knew there was to know. "But you cannot navigate or land while you are shrouded. They cannot see you but you cannot see out. So neither your visual instruments nor your radar will operate."

"We rig the bubble so we can snap it off momentarily while we get altitude and position."

"Snap off the bubble? But the time constants—'' I was about to object that the time constants would not allow the rapid collapse and erection of a shroud, but Saul's expression warned me that he had an answer ready. If these Humans claimed they could circumvent the time-constant constraints, then they had probably devised some unorthodox method of faking them. Their scientific knowledge might be minimal but their ingenuity was unique. "I look forward to seeing that demonstrated."

"And you will, Lucian. We'll put you down on Earth without anyone knowing you've arrived."

"There is no haste. I must first examine the data from the remotes." *Hyperion* already had over a hundred miniprobes sampling events on the surface of the Earth from altitudes as low as a thousand meters. Devices which could collect information with no chance of betraying any. Small spheroids which would disintegrate on accidental contact or system failure. Sensors which could hover, record, and report on their return. "And before anybody lands I must make a personal survey from low orbit."

"You'll make a low-orbit pass yourself? Why? What can you see that the probes can't?"

"I can sense things which no machine can sense." I did not expand on my statement for I did not wish to bring the existence of my helmet to the attention of the crew. Only Mark and Sharon had seen it, and to them it was only a ceremonial item of Ultron regalia. "I will require the pinnace in two days' time. Sharon will be the pilot and Mark will operate the analyzers."

"Sharon and Mark? Why that pair?"

"Because I know their competence. You may remember I traveled with them in a courier from Cao to Edrin. Sharon has the reputation of being the best small-craft pilot aboard, and Mark understands information analyzers better than anybody."

"She's a hothead!" Saul shrugged. "If you want them—you're the boss!" A statement he had become fond of making whenever I gave an order about which he had reservations. "You'll go down in two days' time?"

"If the probe data suggest it is safe."

"The sooner the better." He walked off to watch Joshua maneuvering the lander back into the docking bay.

The returning probes poured their recordings into *Hyperion*'s vast memory. Her analysis of those data gave an accurate geophysical picture of the world below, and an estimate of industrial and military distributions. But they told me little about the social and emotional situations. Those I must monitor myself from the surveyor-pinnace, with Mark and Sharon as my crew and Mary as my silent and invisible companion.

The North Pacific lay below us and a silent Terran satellite hung to port. Sharon had brought the pinnace curving in from far orbit and tucked us in beside the derelict. Those radars monitoring the thousands of other satellites, functioning and defunct, were unlikely to notice that one of them was now twinned. As I was planning to survey the northern hemisphere with both instruments and helmet we could not hide in a shroud.

"I hope their radar resolution's as lousy as you say!" muttered Sharon. This was our first low pass and she was tense. "There're too many trigger-happy rocketeers down there for my taste!"

"Shall I drop a remote?" asked Mark. "Give you a close-up when we cross the coast?"

"Not this orbit." I pulled my helmet from my pack. "First—I must listen."

Sharon stared at me. "What are you going to do with that thing? You've impressed us with it already—back at Knoxton."

"And I trust you have refrained from mentioning it to anybody?"

"Of course! Anyway, what does it do? Besides making you look like a Lord of Creation!"

"That is only a side effect. Among other things, it amplifies mentation. No—it does not let me read your minds. But it does let me detect the flavor and strength of your emotions. Both of you, for example, are now intrigued and annoyed." I pointed toward the coast coming up ahead. "There will be a mix of emotions rising from the populations of that continent. My helmet will let me integrate the intensities and evaluate the types. It should also warn me if any undue amount of attention is being directed toward us."

"It's a kind of hostility early-warning system?" suggested Mark.

"Something like that."

"One of the gadgets you use to keep the rest of us in line?" Sharon scowled. "How many other tricks have you got in that pack of yours?"

"Radar signals all round!" Mark was studying his displays. "Never gone down on a world with radar cover before."

"Never seen a man-made satellite before either!" Sharon glanced at the derelict to port. Already obsolete, but another datum on the sharp-rising curve of human technology.

"Hold position alongside during orbit!" I ordered.

"No radar lock-on," reported Mark.

"Good!" I went to lie face-down in the observation bay, concentrating on the hum rising from the millions of minds spread along the coast.

Their massed emotions surged up as we crossed it. The usual affect-mix over any concentration of ultoids. Nothing particularly alarming in flavor or intensity. Some directed outward toward a vague target far beyond us. The Zealot, wakened by what he recognized as group prayer, tried to speak. I silenced him, then had to silence Primal and Sarthim as we met waves of conflict-thought.

There were periods of near silence over mountains and deserts, then bursts of mentation from scattered cities. The intensity increased as we approached the thickly populated Eastern edge of the continent. "Mary Knox came from down there!" Sharon remarked to her brother.

A chaos of mixed emotions boiled up, then cut off as we crossed the coast. I relaxed as we swung out over the Atlantic and allowed myself to enjoy the view. Earth, seen from orbit, was a lovely world; astronaut descriptions had been accurate but inadequate. Only a master poet could sing the beauty of this world its peoples were about to destroy. No, that was an exaggeration. If disaster came soon they would destroy its civilization but hardly mar its beauty. After the holocaust it would still look as beautiful from space as it did now. But the survivors would no longer have the means nor the will to come and look.

Humans—five thousand million and multiplying! Five thousand million, all of the same race but divided into hostile tribes. Five thousand million intelligent beings of enormous energy and ingenuity exploiting their only world. A race whose very talents had doomed them and would devastate it.

Warning them would be useless, not even a warning from "outer space." Their own Scholars were growing desperate in their apocalyptic prophecies. Prophecies based on calculations no more complicated than basic conditional-probability equations, requiring no insight greater than an appeal to reason and the past. The only difference between our forecasts and those published on Earth was in how long it would be before some foolish act or thoughtful miscalculation initiated disaster. A sudden mysterious message from "off-world" was more likely to trigger the inevitable than to delay it. The Zealot slipped in a quotation from the Terran Bible. *"If they hear not Moses and the prophets, neither will they be persuaded though one rose from the dead."*

Or spoke from the sky.

I was brought back from contemplating that depressing future by an alerting signal within my helmet. It had been analyzing the massed mentation patterns recorded over America, and had isolated some bursts it could not classify; bursts gravid with an affect I had never sensed before. The term "malignant" came to mind and I was trying to produce a less mystical descriptor when the Zealot muttered, *"The odor of Evil!"*

Before he could harass me with superstition we were over Europe and I was again lapped in much the same mixture as over North America. The Zealot returned to sleep as we passed above the Mediterranean, then reawakened as we neared its Eastern end and were plunged into tempests of religious fervor, into storms of ecstasy, anger, fear, and despair. Their violence faded as their source dropped astern, but traces persisted until we were well over the Eastern hemisphere and only died away after we had crossed the far coast of Asia, and were once again above the Pacific.

The emotional maelstrom over the Middle East had exhausted me. I took off my helmet, trying to review my impressions without promptings from its picroelectronics. Elements of hatred, anger, and fear are to be expected in the mentations rising from any barbarian planet, but over Earth they had been intensified in a way I did not understand, mixed with a cold affect I did not recognize.

"Want to make a second pass, Boss?"

Mark's question roused me. "No—not now."

"Satisfied that it's safe for us mortals to go down and trade?" asked Sharon.

Caution was urging me to quit this dangerous world immediately, destroy the Monitor, and return to the tranquility of the Cluster. Duty was insisting that I learn more about the source of those ominous affects. The Zealot whispered, "You must not leave a nidus of Evil while ignorant of its origin and nature!"

"An Ult Warrior would not fly in panic at the first sniff of danger!" growled Sarthim. "Or are you still the same coward you were?"

"I was never—" I started to say aloud. Then I realized that both brother and sister were staring at me. "I will authorize a surface survey. Now—return to Hyperion!"

Mary was able to slide from pinnace to ship in microseconds, and was waiting for me in my suite. I dropped onto a couch. "Did you take a good look at Earth?"

She nodded. "Cut in on the videos and audios. I heard you conning the kids about your helmet!"

"I told them what it does."

"But not all it does!" She sat down slowly. "What gave you the shakes?"

"The mentations coming up from Earth." I wiped my forehead. "I have never experienced ultoid emotions of such violence before!"

Mary nodded. "We're an emotional race, aren't we? What about emotions aboard the lander?"

"Only Sharon's and Mark's. Not yours, if that is what you are asking. My helmet detects only the affective components in biologically based thought."

"And machines don't have emotions?"

"Not true emotions. Of course not! They have programmed responses which may mimic emotions."

"Well, nobody programmed me. And my emotions aren't fake!" Her expression supported her statement.

"But you are not—" I stopped. From one viewpoint, she was.

"Part, at any rate. What the hell?" She shrugged. "So you didn't sense my getting uptight?"

"No. Why—?"

"Because I was. Like you!" She paused. "There's something unhealthy happening on Earth."

"They are preparing to atomize each other! That is unhealthy enough!"

"Maybe something else too." She shrugged. "I heard you tell the kids they could go down and loot."

I laughed. "If Saul heard you say that, he'd log you!"

"Lucian—you're laughing! And talking like a man! Another dip down and you'll come up almost human!"

"The Light forbid!" I stowed my helmet. "Saul proposes to purchase the stuff they want, starting with forged money. He claims that is not looting."

"The kids have inherited the oldsters' hypocrisy! Must be coded in our genes." She frowned. "Trade, deal, or loot—you've given 'em the go-ahead. What lucky people are they going to hit first?"

"Not yet decided. I have told *Hyperion* to scan her present data and prepare a list of places where it would be safest and easiest to trade."

"Now you're talking like an Ultron again. And acting like one!"

"What do you mean?"

"Ordering *Hyperion* to do the hard work. Typical of your gang!"

Hyperion broke in. "It is the kind of work which gives me satisfaction. The type of task for which I, as an Explorer, was designed. The collection and analysis of data from a new planet. Geophysical, biological, and social data. This is my way of serving the Light—"

"Put a stopper in it, you moral-minded mechanism!"

"Mary," I said. "You will hurt *Hyperion*'s feelings!"

"Hurt *Hyperion*'s feelings? You're a fine one to talk!" She pushed back her hair. "*Hyperion*, what have you come up with?"

"Wait! I've told Saul to assemble the whole crew in the mess. So they can all hear her suggestions, and make a group decision."

"You mean you'll let 'em talk it over, and then you'll decide?"

"I hope they will reach the same decision as I do."

XVII

"According to my analysis," *Hyperion* announced to the mess, "Washington has the highest concentration of salvageable information on Earth."

"The capital of the United States?" I asked. "Is not that a heavily guarded city?"

"Strangers can move into and within Washington more freely and with less interference than they can in any other national capital." *Hyperion* spoke with the authority of a teaching machine delivering a lecture; a lecture only as accurate as the television programs on which it was based.

"Are you suggesting Washington as our prime target?"

"Your prime target—yes. Your primary target—no! Your first visit should be to a place where you can obtain the documents you will require in order to trade in Washington."

"Where?" demanded Saul.

"I have compiled a list of suitable sites, each rated in terms of the criteria you gave me."

"Just name the first three." When *Hyperion* had her crew as audience she would lecture them for hours if given scope.

"Singapore is my first choice."

"Singapore? What is that?"

"A port city in Southeast Asia." A map flashed on the screen. "There, at the tip of the Malay Peninsula. It is unique in the present world—both a city-state and a free port. The third busiest port on Earth. It lives by and for trade. It has also become a center of high-technology. The second largest producer of deep-water drilling equipment and a leading producer of electronic—"

"That tiny island?"

"It has an area of six hundred square kilometers, mostly mangrove swamp, and a population of two and a half million. If they do not achieve economic success they will starve for there is nowhere else for them to go. They have attracted over two thousand international megafirms and seventy-two international banks. Much information about Terran science and technology should be readily available in Singapore."

"A free-port trading center. Sounds good." Saul paused. "What language do they speak?"

"Several, but English is a major trading language and spoken with many accents so anything unusual about yours will not be noticed. Its traders wear a variety of costumes, follow different customs, and have skins of various shades. You should be able to mingle easily and not arouse comment—so long as you appear clean and act with decorum."

"The right place to start!" Slammer was rubbing his hands. "A free port! No customs or any of that nonsense, eh?"

"Singapore appears to have a cooperative customs service and an efficient police force. Those are among its advantages as a trading center. Both customs and police concentrate on protecting traders rather than harassing them, as seems to be more usual in other parts of this world. Any action in restraint of trade alarms its citizens who are well aware of their fate if traders ceased to use their facilities." The avarice of the crew had infected the ship. *Hyperion* was starting to talk more like a free-trade Merchantman than an Explorer. "Here are some pictures of the city." And she began to flash images of Singapore on the screens.

"Looks crowded," said Mark.

"Very crowded. Observe the many tall buildings in which most of the population now live. The markets are concentrated in the areas close to the waterfront, and that will aid you because the dealers in gold and precious stones are within walking distance of where the lander will be able to go alongside. You should be able to obtain local currency—or any other kind of currency you may want—quickly and easily."

"What about defenses?" asked Martha.

"It was once a major naval base, but no more. Radar coverage is now navigational rather than military. The waters around are well patrolled, because piracy has recently revived in the area. But those patrols are unlikely to interfere with the kind of luxury cruiser which is the lander's present disguise. Vessels of all sizes and under many flags are constantly entering and leaving the port. I will provide you with a facsimile of the local flag and give you the name of a locally registered craft to use until you have obtained more definitive information. I can also—"

"Singapore is near the equator." I interrupted *Hyperion*'s list of the various clever things she could do. "What is the weather like?"

"Tropical and unchanging. Hot and humid, but without extremes. Singapore is outside the area swept by tropical storms—

typhoons—which plague some of the other places I have on my list of preferred first-landing sites.''

"*Hyperion*," called Sharon. "You planning to run for the Singapore Chamber of Commerce?''

The ship was confused and the crew amused. I hushed the laughter. "Continue with your list of preferred sites for initial landings.''

"Next in my order of selection is Hong Kong, farther north. Also a free port." Another map flashed up and she began to outline Hong Kong's advantages and disadvantages. She did the same for several other maritime cities, but none seemed as well-suited to our purpose as her first choice. Questions from the crew returned her to Singapore.

"What's the music market like?" asked Slammer.

"Large and cosmopolitan. Recordings of every kind of Terran music can be purchased readily and openly. There is a local recording and motion-picture industry—''

"Music?" I stared at Slammer.

"Terran music is prime trading material, Chief. There's already a good market for the bits we were able to intercept on Edrin. If we can take back complete recordings—'' He laughed. "This mission may turn a profit!''

A gust of agreement went around the mess. The crew were after financial as well as cultural gains from this expedition to "rescue something from the wreckage of their parent world.'' When we returned to Edrin a wave of popular Terran music would spread across the Cluster. A wave that would make Humans better known and less liked by Execs and Admins.

"Music's a side line!'' Saul frowned at Slammer. "Lucian, what do you think about this place?''

"I will consider it.'' But from their murmur of approval I knew the crew had made their choice already. *Hyperion* had done "a good selling job.''

The office towers of Singapore rose ahead as *Melur*, the name *Hyperion* had given our disguised lander, picked her way among the ships anchored in the roadstead. This was our sixth visit. Singapore had proved to be all that *Hyperion* had claimed.

The Lion City, rearing its gleaming towers above swamp and sea, a city-state roaring its commercial challenge to the older cities of Earth. A small island with the sea around it, an unfriendly peninsula behind it, and no natural wealth. If it were a Fringe world Council would have ordered it evacuated as economically nonviable. In fact it radiated economic vitality. Nothing in *Hyperion*'s description had prepared me for the hectic activity, for the energy and ingenuity, of its merchants.

Singapore was certainly not a typical Terran city. It was an extreme example of human mercantile achievements, of the good and the bad in human societies. Its peoples exuded a vigorous optimism, refusing to be diverted from their dreams of personal prosperity by the surges of anger and hate rolling round their city and their world. An optimism which had already infected the crew, most of whom now had an unwarranted belief that somehow, in some way, the Terrans would escape their self-generated doom.

A fine tropical morning with a clear sky overhead, islands rising green from a shining ocean, foam creaming back from our bows. We had left *Hyperion* twelve hours before, curving down around a barren moon toward this blue-white planet. Diving from the cold blackness of space into this warm and brilliant world. We had touched down among the islands to the south just before dawn, the lander had become *Melur*, and we had crowded out onto the open decks to breath the sea-scented air and watch the sun rise.

Joshua was at the wheel; his change from spacer to seaman was almost as dramatic as the change of the lander from space-craft to boat. On our initial landing six weeks before I had admired the ease with which he had switched roles. He had laughed. "Nothing to it, Chief! Akar was off base when he called Earth a savage world—compared to some I've traded on. And the navigation rules here make sense. Not like most places—where they don't have any, or ram you on sight!"

Nobody had tried to ram us. Nobody had taken any particular interest in us. The straits, the roadsteads, the harbor, were full of powerboats looking much like *Melur*, plying between shore, ships, and islands. Only minor touches had been needed after our first visit, and now the lander had a name and all the identification any small vessel needed in these waters.

Melur had her papers, and we had ours. American passports purchased in markets where almost anything could be bought—except women, guns, and drugs. To that extent Singapore was as "squeaky-clean" as her politicians claimed. The trading teams were ranging through the free markets like hunters on an open world. Selling gold and buying microfilms, tapes, books, anything small enough to carry aboard *Melur* that promised to show a profit when sold in the Cluster. Establishing credits in a dozen banks, learning the techniques of Terran commerce, renting terminals to access the computer systems which now seemed to extend over the entire globe.

Slammer came up the companionway, looking at the city ahead. "Trading! That's what makes this place tick. Everybody working like hell. Wish we had a port like it back home!"

Joshua altered course to pass a giant container vessel. "If Earth was in the Cluster this would be its prime spaceport. On the equator, good weather, a free port, and keen traders."

"Lots of legal crooks!" Mark came into the wheelhouse. "How much longer are we going to stay here, Chief?"

"As long as you people want to trade, I suppose."

"We've collected most of what we need to go where we can buy what we really want. We're ready to shift to Washington."

"You don't like Singapore, do you, Mark?"

"It's all Slammer says. Clean, green, and it works. Full of hungry merchants, eyes on the main chance. Lowest unemployment and highest standard of living in Asia. A modern miracle!"

"Then what worries you?"

"The Government! Its attitude." He quoted, "Work and discipline are good for the individual and for the state."

"What is wrong with that?"

"It's the kind of government you Ultrons like."

I shrugged and glanced at a coastal steamer abeam of us. The Zealot suddenly came awake. *"That funnel! Take a picture!"*

Automatically I picked up the camera from the chart table and took one. While waiting for the photograph to emerge I studied the ship. An old and work-worn steamer, her decks piled high with passengers and freight, plunging through the swell, trailing a cloud of black smoke. Like most Terran freighters her funnel was painted with her owner's colors and she also carried a crest of some kind. "Another Drin symbol?"

"Yes!" The Zealot, insulted by my skepticism, relapsed into sulky silence.

Mark looked at the picture the camera spat out. "Interesting old ship. Must be prewar."

I put the photograph in my pocket as Joshua called, "Stand by to go alongside!" and eased *Melur* in the crowd of launches clustering around Collyer Quay. "You all set to monitor, Ann?"

"All circuits go." Ann, a pair of Earth-type earphones around her neck, was adjusting what appeared to be a short-wave marine radio. It could, in fact, track each of us by our personal coms, contact the disguised pinnace lying off shore, and speak to *Hyperion* via the lunar relay.

Jane, my communicator and partner, joined me in the

wheelhouse. A calm and competent woman, capable of acting with speed and decision, but otherwise a pleasant and relaxed companion. "Do we stay aboard or go ashore this time, Chief?"

I looked at the crowded waterfront. I would have preferred to remain in the comparative peace of the lander, but I still needed experience in mingling with Terrans and was the only person who could use extraterrestrial weapons in case of a crisis without the danger of being struck dumb and amnesic. "We go ashore after the others."

Jane gave a pleased smile. Everybody in the crew enjoyed these opportunities of mixing and trading with Humans on Earth, and claimed their share of trading time. After six visits to Singapore everyone from *Hyperion* had had at least one chance to experience Terran ambiance, and specialists like Joshua and Mark came down with every expedition.

I watched the others stepping from the lander to Collyer Quay, pushing their way through the crowds, exchanging greetings with police and customs. As *Hyperion* had forecast, officials in Singapore were more interested in making honest traders feel welcome than in harassing them.

When the last were ashore I told Joshua to wait in the harbor until called back to pick us up, and walked with Jane along the Quay to the waterfront. I stood on the sidewalk for a moment, savoring the scents and sights of this tropical city. Most of the inhabitants were Chinese, but in the trading centers were representatives of every race on Earth. Working peacefully together, all with the same aim—to make as much money as quickly as possible. This was perhaps the only city in the world free of the virus of nationalism, of religious fanaticism, of rigid political ideology. Free of destructive idealism. Perhaps, as Mark had observed, a little short of freedom. But, to me, that was a sensible trade-off. Freedom demands security and prosperity, a rare combination.

I took Jane's arm and guided, with proper Terran courtesy, through the traffic and up a short street to Raffles Square. The teams were disappearing into stores, banks, markets. Returning to renew trading contacts already made. We strolled around the square, Jane inspecting the shops and I the people. Toward noon I detached Jane from an emporium showing embroidered silks and we turned up an ally to our general rendezvous—the GA Cafe.

The GA reminded me of the bar in the human hostel on Cao. It had the same rather battered, vaguely seedy atmosphere, and as we took a vacant table I was once again astonished at human diversity. The GA clientele seemed to include specimens of every race and class in Singapore's multiracial population. Clouds of conversation and tobacco smoke were sucked up and redistributed by slow-turning ceiling fans—the GA was the only place I had visited in Singapore which was free of the ubiquitous air-conditioning. Waiters scurried between the tables. The place oozed with the fragrance of humanity and the flavor of trade. Every kind of trade. Initially I had questioned Slammer's choice of a rendezvous; now I realized that his experiences on other worlds had been a good guide. The GA was a place where nobody attracted attention, however unusual his appearance or garb. A place where Jane and I could wait, listen, and observe; where the teams could congregate after their own business was finished.

Jane ordered coffee while I studied my photograph of the old steamer. A large red-faced man in a soiled white suit came out of the sunlight, saw a vacant table next to ours, and forged through the crowd to claim it. He sat down heavily, mopped his forehead, and shouted for a Tiger. When his beer arrived he took a long pull, stared around, caught Jane's eye, and leaned toward her. "Some place this, eh?"

"The coffee is excellent." She gave her pleasant smile.

"Try the curry puffs. Nothing like 'em anywhere! Boy! Sambal for the lady. Lekas-lekas!" He looked at me. "Bit of old Singapore, this! Bloody fools tried to wreck it with the rest. Used to be next to the Hong Kong and Shanghai, until they pulled down the whole bloody road to put up that bloody great building! Abdullah had the sense to keep the atmosphere." He stirred it with his hand. "Town needs a place like this. Imagine those two meeting in one of your fancy hotels!" He laughed and pointed to an elderly European in an immaculate white suit, deep in discussion with a lean Malay wearing a faded sarong and an expression which suggested piracy.

"It is certainly cosmopolitan," agreed Jane.

"You can say that again!" The man laughed. "You just passing through?"

"We are here on business."

"Guessed that—tourists don't come here—thank God!" He grabbed the chit as the waiter put down a plate of curry puffs. "My treat! Go ahead—try one. Nothing like 'em anywhere. Secret recipe and all that!" He watched her cautious nibble. "Good aren't they? Have a beer to go with 'em?"

I shook my head. "Too soon in the day."

"Been in Singapore before?"

"No—we are only here for a brief visit."

"I know this city better than most. Show you round if you like. Enjoy it!" He mopped his forehead again. "Got everything except seasons. But it's the place for business." He eyed me. "What's yours?"

"Export."

"Might be able to help you there. Looking for anything special?"

"Thank you. Not at present."

He saw the photograph I had laid on the table. "Photographing local color, eh?"

"Just an old ship." I handed him the photograph.

He took it. "The *Malaikat*—that means 'angel'—been chugging between the islands far back as I can remember. Which is a long time!" He finished his beer and shouted "*Macham tadi*!" to the waiter. "Must be prewar. Not many like her left."

"That's an interesting symbol she has on her funnel."

He inspected the photograph and I saw the small tight movement of his mouth, sensed his startled flash of excitement. He had seen something he could sell. His comment was carefully casual. "That's the S and S chop."

"What does it mean?"

"God knows. Something Chinese, I guess. S and S—Sarawak and Straits Trading—founded by a rich *taukeh*—Chinese merchant—from Borneo, back before World War One. Bought by some Yank outfit after the Second. Some say it was S and S that bought the Yanks. Those *taukehs* of the old school were pretty damned smart. Not like the present mob—all wind and piss!" He mopped his forehead. "I know de Silva—the local manager. Thinking of doing business with them?"

"Thank you. But our business in Singapore is finished." I recovered the photograph.

The Australian gave a guarded smile, as though afraid his thoughts might show. "Can't win 'em all!" He finished his beer and stood up. "Nice to have met you. Maybe run into you again. If you're back this way and there's something you can't find— ring Joe Webster!" He laid a business card on the table and waited for mine.

"Thank you, Mr. Webster. I'm afraid I don't have a card."

He hesitated, shrugged, then turned and pushed his way across the room toward the door. Joe Webster was eager to tell somebody something. Something about that funnel insignia. I felt a warning chill.

"Wait here!" I said to Jane, and went after him. I saw him

trotting away down the ally, and followed him across Raffles Square. He disappeared into a high-rise office block. The major tenants were Sarawak and Straits Trading Ltd., and their symbol was on their nameplate. The same symbol as on the funnel of the old steamer. The Zealot insisted it was Drin. I hushed him and walked slowly back to the GA.

When I reached our table I found Jane exchanging repartee with a group of small tough-looking men who were trying to persuade her to join them. They did not welcome my return. Jane was not especially pleased to see me either. "Jockeys!" she explained. "Interesting!"

"No outside interests this trip!" I sat down and said softly, "General recall! Everybody back aboard!"

"Why? What's happened?"

"I have just decided to terminate this visit. Send the signal!"

She looked annoyed, but reached into her handbag and sent it. The teams were also annoyed as they streamed back to the lander. An interrupted trader is as angry as a teless who has had her prey jerked from under her claws.

"What's up, Boss?" asked Slammer, jumping from wharf to deck.

"We're leaving Singapore."

"But we haven't finished trading!"

"We have finished trading here."

Mark was the last back, and even he was protesting. "I'm getting masses of data out of that terminal!"

"You will be able to rent another terminal in America."

"Why are we packing in here so suddenly?"

I was too concerned with the second coincidence between a Drin ideogram and a Terran symbol, with the chill I had felt as the Australian had left the restaurant, to answer with my usual courtesy. "Because I say so!" All aboard heard me say it.

Joshua backed *Melur* away from the pier. The rest of the crew stood around in the wheelhouse or on the foredeck, waiting for me to give some better reason for my abrupt decision. But even had I wished I did not have one which would have satisfied them. When I said nothing they drifted down into the saloon, grumbling between themselves, blaming me for cutting short their trading time. Accusing me to each other of having acted with typical Ultron arrogance. I had only pretended to be human. Now I had shown myself to be of the same pattern as the Administrators and Executives these Humans loathed and obeyed.

"Where to, Your Ultimate?" asked Joshua, showing that he shared the crew's opinion. When we were on good terms they called me "Chief" or "Boss." When they were annoyed with me over some restriction I had ordered they called me "Your Ultimate." In English it sounded more like an insult than a mark of respect.

"Back up to *Hyperion*! Head south and take off as soon as nobody's watching!"

"I'll have to wait until dark, Your Ultimate."

"Then wait!" I was both hurt and angry. The more often I visited Earth, the more I mixed with its peoples, the more strongly human emotions surfaced in me. I stood, staring through the wheelhouse windows, having trouble in convincing even myself that any resemblance between the funnel insignia on that old steamer and a Drin ideogram was more than coincidence. That the chill I had felt at the Australian's reaction to my question was a warning rather than a panic reaction. Which was what the crew would certainly call it if I tried to explain such a vague premonition to them.

The surveyor-pinnace, which had been lying in the roads, ready to act as a back-up boat in case of emergency, came racing across to take station astern of us, spray flying from her bows as she knifed through the swell. Her crew, and Mary, would also want to know why I had cut short this visit so abruptly, why I was pulling the teams out of Singapore when they had just established their contacts, when their trading was proceeding so smoothly. A warning chill? That now sounded more like fear than logic, even to me.

Singapore dropped astern. The Riau Islands rose green ahead. Palm trees sloping above the shores, waves breaking white across yellow sands. Away to starboard, the mountains of Sumatra rose purple from the horizon. *Melur* plunged and lifted, salt water flying across her decks where the crew were relaxing, enjoying the afternoon sunshine, the fresh breezes which brought the sweet island scents, the pleasure of criticizing my Ultron arrogance.

Under the influence of the beauty around me I began to recover my Ultron calm. We were moving at only a few knots; our destination was hundreds of thousands of miles away, behind the white moon that was beginning to appear in the eastern sky. There was no hurry. We had time to appreciate one of the most beautiful sights in this lovely world.

A glow, first golden, then roseate, began to rise from the shadowed mountains on the horizon, to spread up into the deep blue of the sky above us. A pink changing to a burning crimson as the sun dropped toward them. The crew ceased to chatter as they watched the growing glory of the tropical sunset.

"Soon be safe to take off, Chief," said Joshua, restored to better humor by the glowing colors flooding the wheelhouse.

"Wait! Let's watch!" I said softly.

The distant land became purple, the sky scarlet. No painter would have dared to use such a flagrant clash of pinks and reds as was now arcing up from the west, flooding the sky above us. The mountains became black silhouettes against a background of fire. Dark spread across the waters until the pinnace astern was a shadow marked by a white foam about her forefoot. Only when the glow began to fade, the land began to loom black, did I say, "Okay! Take her up!"

We lifted gently above the surface of the sea. The spray ceased to drive over our decks. The waves ceased to rustle along our hull. We had a last glimpse of the red and the black. Then the gray shroud wrapped us and the beauty cut off.

Mary appeared as soon as I reached my suite, but her challenge was concerned rather than hostile. "What happened for you to pull us out so suddenly?"

"That!" I showed her the photograph of the old steamer. "The insignia on the funnel. My ancestor claims it is another Drin symbol."

She inspected it, then said, "Let's ask *Hyperion* if she has a match in her warship memory."

The ship could evidently see through Mary's eyes for I did not have to put the photograph in the image feed. After a few seconds *Hyperion* said, "I have an excellent match." The funnel symbol and another appeared side by side on a screen, then merged. The superposition was perfect.

"Coincidences mounting, eh?" Mary studied the screen. "I don't suppose you know what this means either?"

"It was the symbol which the Drin used on their merchant ships. Rather like the Japanese custom of adding 'Maru' to the names of theirs."

"The Drin symbol for ship on the funnel of a Singapore coaster!" Mary whistled. Then she glanced at me. "Why didn't you pull us out immediately you saw it?"

"Because I didn't know that then. My ancestor told me to take a picture, but I thought it just another coincidence—until somebody else saw the photograph." I told her how the Australian had reacted. "He must have seen that symbol hundreds of times. S and S owns a number of coasters carrying it. It's the firm's logo. But he got interested when I asked about it. Left us and raced over to the S and S offices as though keen to tell somebody there that a visitor was inquiring about their chop."

"And that was enough to make you order a scramble?"

"No," I admitted. "I felt a chill. Call it Ult intuition." I stared at the picture of the ship on the screen. "*Hyperion*, you judged the probability of a Drin ship surviving Sarkis was vanishingly small. Does that change when you include the existence of two Drin-derived symbols on Earth?"

There was a pause, then the ship said, "The paradox of unique events makes their conjoint probability impossible to calculate. If those logos are indeed Drin, then at least one Drin must have reached and established itself on Earth relatively recently. The odds against such an event are immense. In this particular instance your intuition is likely to be more helpful than statistical analysis."

"So the buck passes to me?" I stood up. "I'm still not convinced those logos are distorted Drin. But I'm going to tell Saul that we move to America."

XVIII

"She's an attack sub." Joshua altered course as the black hull came sliding toward us out of the dawn mists. He gave one blast on the horn. "Mark, can you read the number on her sail?"

"SSN-767." Mark put down his binoculars and took *Jane's Fighting Ships* from the book rack in the wheelhouse. "USS *Muskelunge*. Four thousand six hundred tons dived. One hundred and ten meters overall. Six torpedo tubes plus subsurface attack missiles. Pressurized water-cooled reactors feeding two steam turbines. Speed dived—fifty knots plus. Complement—one hundred and ten." He closed the book. "She's among the most powerful warships in the Cluster—now the Ult fleets are laid up."

The submarine's answering blast rolled across the Chesapeake and brought the lander's crew on deck to watch her steaming toward the Atlantic on another of her endless patrols. To them she was a triumph of human technology; to me a black augery of the human future. We had now been trading into Washington for three months and were returning to our base on the Potomac after lifting our twelfth cargo of Terran salvage up to *Hyperion*.

"She's a hunter-killer." Slammer stared after the submarine dropping astern, her hull awash, her "sail" rising like the dorsal fin of a huge shark. "It's the missile boats which pack the real punch. One *Trident Two* can fly enough birds to knock out every major capital on Earth. One ship to take out a world!" His voice reflected more of admiration than horror.

"Fit that sub with inertial drive and she'd be ready for space!" said Joshua. "And there's over four hundred like her at sea."

"An instant space fleet!" remarked someone on the foredeck.

"They couldn't make a vortex passage. They couldn't get out of this starfield. They wouldn't have anybody to fight."

"They'd find somebody. Or settle for fighting each other!"

General laughter. Nightmare as fantasy. Humans could treat danger as humor. A virtue—if laughter did not blind to reality, as it seemed to blind crew and Terrans alike. Those whom the Gods wish to destroy they first make euphoric!

Add inertial drive and Earth would have a space fleet! However unlikely, the idea was chilling. The men and women with me would gladly crew a human fleet, apparently blind to the outcome of such madness, as the Terrans were blind to the imminent effects of their own folly.

From nuclear submarine to inertial spaceship—an immense leap. Yet that hunter-killer exemplified a leap of the like magnitude. From sail to atomics in a hundred years! If the Terrans survived the next hundred would they leap into the dark? Into the Cluster?

I shook myself. Not even their present exponential advance would take them to vortex transits within a century. But within centuries? Up to the stars or down to hell?

Why was I beginning to sympathize with these foolish, bloodthirsty, yet charming people? I had to remind myself that the crew of *Hyperion* was not a fair sample. The men and women around me were a carefully selected group, the best of the best, drawn from a population which had had three hundred years of education in civilized ways. Yet even this sample retained the barbarian drives of their ancestors. And their brief contact with their Terran fellows was reawakening ambitions which should have died out generations back.

They pitied and admired the Terrans, they saw their faults but exaggerated their virtues. They luxuriated in the atmosphere of their parent world. They all wanted to spend more time on it. During our initial visits to Washington the advance party had been those members of the crew with the most experience in setting up a base and establishing trading contacts. The base cadre had hardly changed. Now, with the salvage operation in full swing, the rest of the crew were claiming their share of Earthside time. Most of the men and women in the lander were replacements coming down to man the base, make up the trading trios, and enjoy their share of earthly pleasures.

Joshua altered course, running along the western shore of the Bay toward the mouth of the Potomac. The sun rose higher, the mists cleared, and the crew, in various stages of undress, went to lie around on the open decks of the recamouflaged lander. She was now the *Mobjack Belle*, registered in Norfolk and owned by a Mr. Lucian Titus of Simm's Landing, Virginia. Joshua had found it amusing to register me as her owner, though I had not seen the humor of it. Nor had I appreciated having bank accounts opened in my name. But the crew enjoyed much that I did not. At present they were enjoying the morning sunshine, the cool breeze, the blue sky, and the prospects of another week of profitable trading.

The base itself was an old riverside mansion, "Deerfields," north of Quantico, purchased by Joshua and also registered in my name. We had had no difficulty in setting it up or in establishing discreet trading patterns. The bubble had allowed us to land and take off unobserved by the massive radar screens around Norfolk and Washington. As far as the crew were concerned everything was going well. They had forgiven me for pulling them out of Singapore; Washington was proving an even better market. Especially as we could now stay on Earth for at least a week between trips up to *Hyperion*. They had no worries. Apart from the enigma of those possible Drin ideograms I had nothing concrete to worry me. But I was still worried as I stood in the wheelhouse beside Joshua, watching the green banks slide past, and trying to ignore the Zealot's mutterings about Evil being loose in this world.

The crew had not noticed it. Their initial immersion in the polyglot mercantile societies of Singapore had allowed them to acquire Terran behavior patterns which they had modified to fit into the more homogenous business community of Washington. And their hours of television aboard *Hyperion* had, as Saul intended, familiarized them with the ways Americans talked and acted. When I had expressed my surprise at how accurately television dramas reflected American life, Mark had said, "TV's become the model for everybody—not just us! In Washington, at any rate, people are starting to act as they see actors act. Life imitating television art. If you're ever unsure about how to behave in this city, just imagine you're a character in a soap opera. You won't go far wrong!''

In the late afternoon we arrived off the Marine Base at Quantico and were met by the pinnace, now disguised as a rather grubby power boat. *Hyperion* had suggested to Saul that she be named *Mary Knox*, and Saul had agreed, without knowing the irony of naming a boat after the imagon within. Was irony possible from a machine? Anyway, Mary had chosen to come down to Earth in her namesake rather than remaining in *Hyperion*.

The pinnace was acting as the emergency evacuation vessel, and was stationed permanently at Deerfields. Sharon, as the best small-craft pilot in the crew, was in charge of her. I had not yet had the opportunity of hearing Mary's reaction to being the invisible and silent observer of her descendant's behavior.

Sharon, looking as grubby as her boat, waved to us and turned up-river toward Deerfields. Both vessels eased up the creek to the rambling old riverside house which was our base. Joshua had chosen it for its isolation, hidden in deep woods at the end of a muddy lane, but it had its own decrepit charm—at least in summer.

The crew delighted in the place; they had made it their home on Earth. Simon and Joan, two of the six who had been guarding it while the lander was away, came running down through the overgrown garden to greet us as we entered the creek. ''Everything's fine!'' called Joan as she took our mooring lines. ''We picked up that shipment from Simm's Landing, and the truck got the mail this morning.''

Mark jumped ashore. ''Were the tapes in it?''

''Dozens of 'em. Enough to keep you quiet for days!''

I waited for the gangway to go down, then went ashore myself and stood for a moment to relish the feel of earth under my feet, the song of the birds, the tang of the woods. Even the Zealot could not detect any ''odor of Evil'' in the scents coming on the breeze. Earth pleased the senses of both Ult and Human. We must have originated on a world much like this one. Then I turned to Stephen. ''All secure?''

''Sure, Boss!'' The crew had returned to calling me ''Boss'' or ''Chief'' after I had regained their approval. They knew all the tricks involved in setting up base on a barbarian world. The house was ringed with sniffers; they even had Terran weapons stacked and ready for such an unlikely event as a raid by the locals.

I walked up to the house, Mark limping beside me. ''Nothing

like this on Edrin!' He paused by the shrubbery to survey the old mansion. ''And there never will be!''

''There are not many places left like it on Earth, either. If they have the time they will turn this stretch of river into another garden suburb. I am beginning to think that the root cause of the disaster will be overpopulation.'' I shook my head. ''They should have cut the breeding rate a century ago. And now it is too late.''

Ruth came out of the back door, her arms white with flour. ''Just in time for hot biscuits.''

We followed her into the kitchen. This was the beginning of the Terran weekend, there could be no trading until Monday. Joshua radioed our safe arrival to Saul via the lunar relay. Joan and Miriam joined Ruth in preparing supper. Aboard *Hyperion* sex roles only surfaced in the act itself. Ashore, men and women tended to revert to the patterns of their ancestors.

After we had sampled the biscuits Mark went to check the computer terminal he had had installed, under the pretense that I was a wealthy businessman who had to interact with the ''markets.'' In fact it gave us access to more than five hundred public databases; through brief interactive sessions Mark could perform on-line literature searches and retrieve masses of data for salvage. He was extracting even greater amounts of information through commercial data-processing firms in Washington. He and *Hyperion* between them had concocted a program, written in Terran computer languages and using only current Terran techniques, under which Consolidated Computers Inc., the firm with which we had the largest contract, was scouring every database to which it had access. Probably the most valuable products of Earth going up to *Hyperion* were the data we were salvaging from the Terran systems.

I watched some of it pouring from the terminal printer, admiring the ready way in which Mark had learned how to handle Terran computerese. After the skill he had shown by breaking into Central Information on Clur I should not have been surprised. Presently I left the house to walk through the woods, ostensibly to check security, but more to enjoy a pleasure I had hardly known since childhood. A pleasure I only realized I had been missing now that I was again in a sweet-smelling solitude of greens and golds. From the day I donned the Ultron's cloak I had lived surrounded by Executives, Administrators, and problems. I still had problems, but here on Earth I could snatch a few minutes to stroll between tall trees and listen to the singing of birds—a special delight, for such creatures are rare in the cities of the Fringe and absent altogether from the manicured worlds of the Net.

A delight tinged with sadness. These quiet woods were only a few kilometers from prime targets—distant missiles must already be programmed and aimed for Quantico, for Norfolk Naval Base, for Washington itself. When those birds flew, these birds would cease to sing. These forests would become burning radioactive hells. The old mansion behind me would be smoldering dust. There would be no birdsong on the barren banks of a sterile river.

I reached the dirt road leading to the house, and stepped onto the shoulder as a battered pick-up came from the direction of the highway. I read "Chester Randall—Carpenter" on the door as it went past, and returned the courteous salute of the driver. An elderly man, his beard tinged with gray, he had slowed on seeing me. I watched him drive on round the bend toward the house.

An uninvited visitor. I had told the crew to discourage such visitors and I followed the pick-up, wondering what this one wanted. If Joshua had sent for a carpenter to do some work around the house, he had not asked me. I would certainly have refused permission.

The pick-up was standing in the driveway by the pillared portico and Joshua was on the crumbling steps, talking to the visitor. A sturdy man, who might be a carpenter but was dressed in a blue serge suit, a collar and tie, and a straw hat. As I crossed the weed-grown lawn I heard Joshua say, "Here comes Mr. Titus. I'd like to help you, but you'll have to ask him. Chief—this is Mr. Randall. He's from the church outside the village."

"Pleased to meet you, Mr. Titus." The visitor turned toward me, taking off his hat in an old-fashioned gesture, holding out his hand. "Passed you back down the road a way. Hope I didn't kick up too much dust on you?"

"Thank you for slowing down." As we shook hands I felt his quality in his grip, the assurance in his blue eyes and stance. A man generally at ease with himself and the world, but now concerned about something. "What can I do for you?"

"Maybe you've seen our campground near Simm's Landing? Church of the New Light?" He was studying me with intentness but without malice. I caught a hint of surprise and hope.

I nodded.

"I'm the Head Deacon. We're due to hold our homecoming and prayer meeting there next week. Two hundred families arriving from all over the State. Bringing trailers, campers, tents. Be here a couple of weeks.''

I nodded again.

"Trouble is—we've lost the field. Some mix-up with the bank. It got sold to a real-estate developer during the winter. He's starting work Monday. Can't hold off. Got his subcontractors moving in.'' Randall turned his hat in his hands. "Can't blame him. I'm in the building trade myself—in a small way.'' He hesitated. "But it's mighty inconvenient for us in the Church. Whole lot of the faithful arriving. Too late to stop 'em. I came to prepare things—now I've got nowhere to put 'em.'' He gave a helpless gesture with his hat, then waited for me to speak.

Before I could Joshua said, "Mr. Randall was asking if he could rent big meadow for his meeting?''

"We can pay a fair rent. For only two weeks it would be.'' His fingers tightened on the brim of his hat. "And the Light would reward you for your kindness.''

"Nobody's using big meadow right now, Chief,'' urged Joshua.

I did not relish the prospect of having two hundred families camping so close to our base and was about to risk Joshua's reproach when the Zealot, wakened by the word "Light,'' whispered, *"This man is a servant of the Light. You must not refuse him aid!''*

I temporized. "How is it that your campsite was sold during the winter without your knowledge?''

He shifted his hat in his hands. "Well, Mr. Titus, you see our Church was founded in the village, kind of far back. When times got hard most of the faithful had to move away. Working folk has to go where work is. Our Minister, he stayed to serve the ones who remained. He had to sell the Church, but we kept the land for homecoming.'' Randall's embarrassment became acute.

"Where is your Minister now?''

"Can't quite figgur. California, we hear. He had a call—''

"He's not around.'' Joshua cut into my interrogation of the unfortunate Deacon. "And Mr. Randall has a congregation arriving for a camp meeting and nowhere for them to camp. Don't you think we could loan him big meadow?''

"Not loan—rent,'' said Randall with some force. "We'll pay a fair rent. Like the Light says.''

I could not oppose the combined pressure of both Joshua and the Zealot. "Any rent will be minimal. You may use big meadow for your meeting. But I ask that your people stay out of the woods and grounds.''

"Sure will!" His face lit up. "I'll warrant that. Thank you indeed, Mr. Titus." He paused. "May the Light shine on you."

I was startled to hear the traditional Ult salutation in English and it excited the Zealot, who tried to make more of it than there was. The sense, if not the words, is common to routine courtesies in many languages and on many worlds. I gave the routine answer. "May the Light illuminate you, Deacon Randall."

He had started toward his pick-up but turned when I spoke, a look of surprise and pleasure on his face. Then Joshua took his arm. "I'll show you around big meadow." He smiled at me. "Thanks, Chief."

I watched him get into the pick-up beside Randall, and looked after the truck as it disappeared down the drive leaving a plume of red dust. Still vaguely concerned that I had been persuaded to let some splinter religious group camp so near our base, I went to join the crew, eating on the terrace behind the house.

Slammer was standing over a barbecue, turning steaks, acting the part of a jovial TV host. "Hi there, Boss! Grab a plate. How d'you want your steak? Well-done? Should have guessed. Come on girls, fuel the Chief. Ruth—get His Ultimate a cold beer!"

I sat on a tree stump, enjoying the beer, trying to cope with the steak, and slapping at mosquitoes. This custom of eating in the open when there was a cool screened room available in the house was an aspect of human behavior I did not appreciate. Presently Mark came to join me.

"What did that man want?"

"To hold a prayer meeting in big meadow." I told him the story without emphasizing why I had agreed.

"Glad you did, Boss. I heard about what happened when I was in the bank. The people who've been coming to those prayer meetings have always been decent folk. Never caused any trouble. Damned shame that they've lost their church and their field." He speared a piece of steak. "They had a rogue for a minister. Everything was registered in his name. When he got a call of some kind from California, he sold the lot and took off with the proceeds."

"Behavior of a type not uncommon among ecclesiarchs of every variety," I said, making sure the Zealot appreciated what I was saying.

Joshua returned and came over to me. "I told the Deacon we'd run a hose and a power line over to big meadow for him. Hope you approve, Chief." He went to collect a steak before I could disapprove.

I gave up on mine, accepted another beer from Ruth, and watched Sharon. She was sitting close to Simon, her head on his shoulder, his arm round her waist, laughing at some remark from Slammer, happy in the easy comradeship which distinguished this human crew.

"Sis is enjoying herself," said Mark, following my gaze.

"Your sister has a great capacity for enjoyment. Also for anger!"

"Maybe the two go together."

She started to stroke Simon's hair. The sight made me uncomfortable. "Is she in love with Simon?"

"She sleeps with him. I don't think she's in love with him."

"She shares sex with him, but she doesn't love him?"

"Sex isn't the same as love. At least—not for us."

"How do the two differ? I appreciate that there are types of nonsexual love among your people. But I had thought that physical love was synonymous with sex."

"It isn't." Mark paused. "Sex is something you have. Love is something you give. Something you share. A oneness. A hunger to communicate—not just physically but in everything. Sharing emotions, ideas, bodies. Sex, to us, is the physical part of love, but not the main part. Not even the essential part. And it's detachable. In fact, it's often detached."

"Was she in love with Tank?"

"God no!"

"With Slammer perhaps?"

"She thinks Slammer's a good guy and a great lover. But she isn't in love with him."

I was becoming irrationally intrigued. "Do you think she has ever been in love, the kind of love you have tried to define, with anybody?"

He hesitated. "Maybe—for a while—yes! She was in love with the father of her kids. But by the time they were born he was beginning to bore the hell out of her. She was glad to escape back to Edrin to have 'em. Shipped out again before he returned. Managed to dodge him ever since. Sharon wanted a command more than a husband!"

Even to me, naïve in the details of human affection, that seemed cold-blooded for such a hot-blooded person. "Have you ever been in love that way, Mark?"

He shrugged and poked his steak. "Not yet. Not really in love. Shared things with some pretty nice women, of course. But, like I said, love and sex aren't the same. Sex is only a part.

Sex can be disappointing—even with a partner you love. Sexual love without sex—?'' He bit his lip.

"You can have sexual love without sex?'' Humans were always astounding me with some strange behavior pattern.

"Sometimes that's the best. You can love somebody with whom you can't have sex.''

I had heard about human homosexuality; to an hermaphrodite such as myself it seemed the normal relationship. But one of which many Humans disapproved, so I shifted the conversation. "A cripple, perhaps?''

"A poor example, but it'll do!'' Mark looked up at me. "Any idea of what love is, now we've talked about it?''

"You have been doing your best to explain an emotion I will never be able to understand until I experience it. And that, I hope, will be in the far future.'' I suddenly wanted to confide in him. "We Ultrons can continue to live for millennia, so long as we do not allow ourselves to mature. When we do mature we can breed—have sex in your terms. But when we mature we also start to age and then, sooner or later, we die. So, for us, sex is a distant prelude to death.''

"Sex for us is a little death too! Every time!'' Mark gave a wry smile. "Do mature Ult have the kind of love I've been trying to describe?''

I pondered. "Perhaps. I think my parents loved each other. At least they behaved toward each other in the way I have read some pairs of Humans behave.''

"You had parents, Lucian? Good God! Who'd have thought it!''

"Of course I had parents. I am an ultoid—not a machine!''

"Sorry! No offense! Where are they now?''

"Dead. Dead long, long ago.'' I paused, remembering them. And caught a hint of what Mark had meant when he talked about "love.'' "They were both very old. When one died—the other died within days. Neither wanted to live on alone.''

XIX

"Here come the last of 'em," said Joshua as a cab pulled up at the entrance to the Washington Marina. "Okay to sail now, Chief?"

Mark, Slammer, and Sharon got out. Mark, in a well-cut seersucker, was a wealthy businessman arriving to spend the evening aboard his luxury cruiser. Slammer, carrying a load of music tapes, was his bodyguard. Sharon, wearing Terran clothes with elegance and using Terran cosmetics with skill, could be his secretary or his mistress. It was Sharon I was watching, as was every other man within eyeshot. The woman who could defeat Shiak set at fifteen came along the wharf with the lithe movements of a teless in heat.

"Okay to sail now, Chief?" Joshua repeated.

I looked up from Sharon toward the Thirteenth Street Bridge, shaking and roaring from the torrents of homeward-bound automobiles pouring across it. "Sail as soon as everybody's aboard." I took off my helmet, now disguised as a Terran hard hat, and wiped my forehead. After a day of monitoring the maelstrom of emotions radiating from Washington I was more than ready to return to the comparative calm of Deerfields.

All day, while the trading teams had been ashore, I had been drenched in waves of emotion. Much that was unpleasant, yet enough of the kindly and sympathetic to prevent my consigning the whole stew to intergalactic darkness. It was hard not to suffer with the suffering I sensed. The kind of suffering current on many worlds outside the civilized Cluster; worlds the Council had deserted because they were not economically viable. Yet here, in this affluent city, there were many Humans laboring to aid their less-fortunate fellows. As there were others laboring to ensure that all, fortunate and unfortunate alike, would soon be desolate or dead.

What was wrong with this race? The path to disaster was not hidden. It screamed from headlines in the affluent West as it was known to the leaders of the powerful East. Only the religious fanatics seemed blind and they, as yet, did not have the weapon systems to start Armageddon.

Few of the Terran leaders were villains, none were fools! Yet they persisted in piloting their peoples toward disaster. *Hyperion* had quoted the words of some human intellectual, comparing the course of humanity to the disastrous Athenian expedition to Syracuse, some twenty-four centuries earlier. "Our fleet will always sail toward Sicily, knowing of their doom!"

Knowing of their doom! They could see it ahead, yet they held course toward it. Perhaps Saul was right. Perhaps the Terrans were born with a death wish. It would take such a small alteration in course for civilization on Earth to survive for at least another century; perhaps even long enough for them to learn how to survive forever.

Survive to do what? I felt the same chill that the Primate must have felt when he first surveyed human history and saw the technological explosion occurring on this distant planet. I tried to harden my heart. This disaster would be none of the Cluster's doing. And the human race was fortunate in that one cadre at least would survive the destruction of its parent world.

Such talents! Such energy! Such ingenuity! So why were they so blind and foolish. What force was driving them—?

"The Power of the Lie! The Force of Darkness!" answered the Zealot.

"The old myth! The old excuse for ultoid brutality! Blame our own cruelty and foolishness on gods and devils!"

"What's that?" asked Joshua. I had spoken aloud.

"Nothing of importance," I said.

The Zealot persisted. *"Evil is eventually self-destructive. But only eventually. Not in the interim! If it destroys this world it will destroy one of its strongholds. The Lie will cause these Humans to suffer but it will not seek to annihilate them, for it will strive to direct their energy and ingenuity to serve its own ends. None of your calculations include the power of the Lie!"*

I quieted him and turned to watch as Joshua backed *Mobjack Belle* out of her berth and turned her bows toward what I was beginning to think of as home.

I continued to wear my helmet as we picked our way downstream, glad to sense the turmoil of the city drop astern. The shadows were spreading across the river as we rounded the bend past Mount Vernon. The crew clustered on deck, enjoying the cool of the evening and chattering about their trading triumphs of the day.

The emotions reaching me from the city faded. Then, from farther down the river came new signals. After a few more kilometers I recognized them as from Deerfields, signals with a flaver that brought the Zealot awake. Signals that did not come from members of *Hyperion's* crew. Signals which carried overtones of awe and hope. Not alarming in their nature but intriguing in their novelty. "Joshua, can you make this a fast trip?"

"Maximum legal speed around here—seven knots, Chief." He glanced at me. "Something up?"

"Just my impatience to get home."

"Not much traffic around. Guess I can bring her up another notch." He eased open the twin throttles and the rumble of the pseudodiesels rose, the whisper of water at our stem became a hiss, and our wake spread white across the dark river.

I went onto the foredeck, still wearing my hard hat, and Mark joined me. "Sensing something?" he asked in a low voice. Only he and Sharon knew that the hard hat I had taken to wearing was my disguised helmet. *Hyperion* had carried out an effective modification, though she had wanted to camouflage it as a motorcycle helmet when she could have retained the face-plate as a mask and protection. But the popular attitude toward motorcyclists had deterred me from disguising myself as one.

"Radiations from Deerfields. Not bad, only new." I concentrated. "They've got visitors, but Simon's not worried."

"I'll take a guess at who they are." Sharon had joined us. "Some of those nuts from the camp. They see something special about you, Boss. Haven't had the nerve to tackle you directly so far, but they've been trying to pump me. Couldn't tell 'em much, because I don't see the attraction myself!" Sharon was annoyed with me for reasons I did not understand. I had given up trying to understand Sharon.

"Stow it, Sis!" Mark glanced at me. "When you're wearing that hat you do radiate something. A kind of light touch."

"Like somebody feeling my arse," said Sharon. "Does Your Ultimate enjoy fondling a woman from a safe distance?"

"You can sense me?"

"I'll say! When I came back aboard in Washington you were standing in the wheelhouse, bug-eyed. I've had men undress me with their eyes before, but I've never been felt from twenty meters. Are you doing that to all the girls?"

"Sharon—I was only watching you return with the others."

"You weren't looking at me the way you looked at the others. More like some kid feeling his first stir! Can you aim it? If so, keep your tactile voyeurism off me!"

"I had no idea that you or any other Human was sensitive to mentation. And no—I cannot aim it. Nor was I trying to invade your privacy—mental or physical."

"I picked up something that first time you wore it, back on Edrin," said Mark quickly. "And again when you were doing that helmet survey in the pinnace."

"Why did you not tell me?"

Mark shrugged. "So slight, I thought it my imagination."

"I didn't imagine being fingered by remote control!" said Sharon.

"Drop it, Sis!" Mark's exasperation silenced his sister. "Perhaps there are people at Deerfields who can sense it too."

There were. And Sharon had been right. Chester Randall and two others from the Church of the New Light were waiting on the wharf. "Couldn't keep 'em away," explained Simon as we went alongside. "They came about an hour ago. Wanted to talk to our Preacher." He grinned at me. "I guess they mean you, Boss."

They did. Chester Randall came up to me, his hat in his hands. "Mr. Lucian, we'd be mighty obliged if you'd take supper with us." He glanced at the group making *Mobjack Belle* fast. "Your followers too. We've plenty for all."

After a day spent wallowing in the emotions around Washington I did not relish the prospect of a religious evening. But when I started to plead weariness I saw the disappointment on Chester's face and gave way before the Zealot's reproach. "Thank you for your invitation. I will come to your camp after I have washed."

"You going over to the church, Boss?" asked Simon, following me into the house. "When I helped put that big tent of theirs up, I smelled a good meal cooking."

"You are all invited," I said, not thinking that any would accept.

In fact most of the crew not on duty came with me through the woods to big meadow. The dining hall was the large tent which Simon and others had helped pitch, and when I entered I found over a hundred men, women, and children sitting on benches along bare wood tables. They stood up when I came in and Chester escorted me to a seat at the head table. The crew, including Slammer, Mark, and Sharon, distributed themselves among the faithful and everybody remained standing, as though waiting for me to speak.

When I did not but only looked around, savoring the smell of trodden grass and the greenish light filtering through the canvas, Chester prompted me. "Preacher, please invoke the blessing."

I did not like being called "Preacher," and I had never invoked a blessing in my life. I was still trying to produce some appropriate phrase when the Zealot moved into the gap and I found myself saying, "May the Light shine upon us and brighten us. May It bless this food to our use and us to Its service."

Roared Amens and gusts of unspoken approval rolled over me from the congregation. I sat down, irrationally pleased by the warmth of their feelings and annoyed by the smile on Sharon's face. Mark looked intrigued. The other crew members acted as if it were part of an Ultron's duty to bless things.

Then dozens of women started to swirl round us, distributing plates of food, and my appetite demanded all my attention. The meal was the best I had eaten anywhere for a long time. In the Cluster I had followed the pattern set by other High Intellects and regarded all sensual pleasures as remnants of a barbarian past. Meals aboard the ship had been human and unfamiliar. Moreover *Hyperion* had been more concerned with providing balanced nutrition than pandering to preferences. That, perhaps, was why most of the crew, during the inactive phase between accelerations, had chosen to cook their own food and eat in their suites. As I had never joined any of those groups I had not until that evening tasted human food at its best.

That the meal was a revelation to the crew as well as to me was shown by the fact that those who had not come to the start of the meal joined us as it progressed. People who had eaten slipped back to Deerfields to relieve those on duty and to tell the others what a feast they were missing. Many of the faithful were farmers and had brought the choicest of their crops to the Church. Chester urged a variety of dishes on me, naming them as they were passed. "Virginia ham, sliced real thin. Fresh-baked biscuits with melted butter. Black-eyed peas. Succotash. You folks up north think we live on fried chicken?"

"Up north?"

"Or abroad. Don't matter where you come from, does it? Long as you see the Light?"

I assured him that it did not matter where one came from, without mentioning where I did. He did not press me but began to describe the pies which were being passed down the tables. "All home-baked. Nothing store-bought here. Try this pecan pie. It's mighty good!"

"It is mighty sweet." After tasting it I was glad my teeth were perfect.

"Some find it oversweet. This apple's maybe more to your taste."

I found myself gorging, eating long after my hunger had been satisfied. If the faithful always ate like this it was no wonder they were so solidly built; the crew would look the same if they carried Terran eating habits back aboard. This meal was an example of the riches the fertile Earth could provide; yet most of its inhabitants were close to starvation.

I put that uncomfortable thought aside as I pushed the last plate away. Moments later the rest of the congregation did the same and Chester rose to make a short speech saying what an honor and pleasure it was to have Mr. Lucian and his followers with them for the meal. Most of the crew only looked surprised at being told they were my followers, but Mark smiled and Sharon scowled.

Chester seemed to sense I did not want to be called on for a second blessing and gave the grace after meat himself, then urged the congregation to be smart about cleaning up the tent so they could begin the prayer-meeting on time. "Some of us have a good way to drive tonight." He turned to me. "We'd be honored if you and your followers would share our prayers."

His second reference to my followers sent Sharon back to Deerfields, muttering about a job she had to do. Simon went with her and most of the crew, after assisting in the clean-up, drifted after her. Mark and Slammer stayed, feeling, as I did, that it would be discourteous to refuse an invitation to prayer after having enjoyed such an excellent meal.

As the Senior Deacon, Chester conducted the prayer-meeting. He might be only a simple carpenter, but he had more natural empathy than any Human I had met so far. The fact that he had sensed the radiations from my helmet as we came down river, and was on the wharf to greet me when we arrived, suggested that he was a latent telepath.

Satiated with good food, lapped in a sea of warm fellowship, I did not find the prayer-meeting as unpleasant as I had feared. The Zealot found it inspiring. For the first time during his parasitic existence he was back in his element. At intervals he nudged me to point out how some religious belief of these faithful matched the dogma of the Faith. Aboard *Hyperion* I had given way to my ancestors' pleas and let them interact directly with the ship. Primal had not been interested. Sarthim had explored the history of warfare on Earth, the current weapon systems, and the causes, concepts, and outcomes of future conflicts. The Zealot had submerged himself in Terran religions.

The service droned on around me and the Zealot droned on within me, identifying coincidences as correlations, arguing that common elements in extra and intraterrestrial religions proved the universality of his Faith. Claiming that while the radio albedo of the nearest civilized worlds might be detectable on Earth, the

Terrans had not, as yet, developed equipment capable of distinguishing meaningful sources of radio-brightness from background noises. Therefore Universal Truth must have reached Earth by supernatural means.

"What coincidences?" His specious arguments roused me from my torpor. *Hyperion,* during her searches of Terran data, had turned up many parallels between Humans and other ultoids, all reflecting patterns pointing to convergent intellectual evolution rather than evidence that elements of Cluster civilization had reached Earth.

"The probabilities for at least two religious correlations being valid put them far above chance coincidence or parallel patterns of thought."

"You mean some superstition common in the less enlightened races of the Cluster are the same as those of superstitions on Earth? You have let your zeal get the better of your logic! There are correlates between every crazy superstition ever developed anywhere. Superstitions dreamed up long before there was a Cluster civilization. When every barbarian world thought itself the center of the Universe!"

"My skeptical descendant—hear what I have to say before you abuse me for saying it."

The congregation was now singing a hymn with fatuous words and a rousing tune. To avoid listening to the words I escaped into internal argument. "Go on!"

The Zealot went on. *"First the paradigm of the struggle between Light and Darkness, Good and Evil, is common to many Terran religions as it is to many Cluster religions. As it is the central paradigm of the Faith for which your own ancestors fought."*

"They fought for themselves, not for any faith. Listen to the nonsense these Humans are singing now!" Singing so lustily about Christian soldiers marching to war that they were making the canvas of the tent billow.

"In those days the Faith was a part of every Ult Warrior. The Ult and the Faith were one."

"That was then. Now the Faith is no longer considered a valid explanation of anything. The paradigm of Light and Darkness is a common superstition because it is an obvious phenomenon to any ultoid living on an oxygen world with a sun to warm it and a night to chill it."

"Agreed. But that does not make Light and Darkness invalid when used as outward and visible signs of an inward and spiritual grace."

"Inward and spiritual what? Where did you find that phrase?"

"It is a quotation from one of the holy books used by this Church of the New Light. It also occurs, in very similar terms, in our invocation of—"

"Nonsense has a common source in every ultoid mind. That source is the hope for something that transcends the physical."

"A hunger planted in the ultoid mind by the Creator of that mind. A second correlation is the story of the Light sending forth a part of Itself to drive back the Darkness and sacrificing that part of Itself to redeem Its people. A revelation which only occurs in certain religions, but they have been the most potent. It is the story of Milar in the Ult Faith, and it occurs with variations in three of the major Terran religions. Do you not agree that the concept of a Creator willing to sacrifice Itself for the succor of Its creatures is unlikely to arise without some basis in truth?"

"Of course I do not agree! The concept of a parent sacrificing itself—!" I pulled back from an endless argument on the source of particular myths. "You have created correlations from vague generalities."

"Lucian, can you call this a vague generality: 'Every individual born into the world on reaching maturity must answer these questions. Who am I? What is my stock and lineage? What is my purpose in life? Whom do I serve? Light or Darkness? Good or Evil?' Lucian—do you recognize that quotation?"

"Certainly! It is a poor English translation of the questions asked in the Ult maturity rite." Questions which I had never heard asked aloud, nor did I intend to. The Primate had promised me confirmation in permanent Ultron status and a place on the Council when I returned from this mission. That promotion would postpone my maturity into the far future.

"It is a poor English translation, but not of the Ult maturity rite. It is a translation from the catechism of the oldest of the Terran monotheistic religions. And the original—in a language called Fars—is even closer to the quotation in Ult. Including the order and phrasing of the questions and the finer meaning of terms too subtle to be translated into English."

"That is a striking coincidence but it only shows that the ultoid imagination produces similar superstitions. The generative grammar, which is characteristic of the ultoid brain, clothes those superstitions in similar phrases. It proves nothing. It only supports what our Scholars have already shown; convergent evolution tends to produce intellects with a similar physical and mental structure."

"A striking coincidence indeed, for a race which evolved from clustering amino acids in a primal soup. Amino acids which appeared soon, in cosmic terms, after the formation of the Universe. A race which has evolved through many stages and vicissitudes from single-celled organisms into the ultoid form, and which has acquired religious concepts so similar to those widespread in the Cluster. Evolved on a world outside the Cluster and with no physical contact with any other world. If this correlation were in any other area of knowledge except the religious, would you not accept it as suggesting strongly that some common cause had been at work?"

"Common causes have been at work. The physical laws which, as far as our Scholars know, extend through all time and space in the physical universe. Universal laws which lead to similar ends."

"Let me quote you another of these strange coincidences. One you must have noted and ignored when you read the human Bible on Clur during your preparation for this mission. 'In Him was Light, and the Light shineth in the Darkness, and the Darkness comprehended it not. He came unto His own, and His own received him not. He was the true Light which lighteth every man who cometh into the world. He was in the world, and the world was made by Him, and the world knew Him not.' Does that not remind you of the story of Milar, the Light of the Ult?"

I was saved from trying to show the similarity was the outcome of similar superstitions by feeling Chester's hand on my shoulder and his voice booming, "Now let us call on one who has aided us to keep the Light shining. Mr. Lucian, brighten our evening with a few words."

"He means you, Boss!" Slammer whispered across the table.

In arguing with the Zealot I had lost touch with the service. I got to my feet, disoriented at being summoned from nonsense within to nonsense without. I stood, groping for words which might give these good people some hope and guidance without leading them deeper into the superstitious swamp in which they were already mired.

"The meal we have eaten tonight was a true agape, a real feast of love," I said, then stopped as I saw the expectation on the faces along the tables. I felt a humbug and a charlatan. Nothing I could say would inspire them as they hoped.

"Let Zealot take over," growled Sarthim. *"He specializes in sermons and he hasn't been able to give one for millennia!"*

In a weak moment I let him, and caught snatches of quotations from the Faith, from the Terran Bible, from a mishmash of various Cluster scriptures, delivered in the voice of an ecclesiarch, the voice of one who never explains, only proclaims. I was disgusted; the congregation was entranced. Slammer's eyes were as bright as those of the Terrans around him. Even Mark was impressed. After my ancestor had run on for several minutes I tried to rein him in, but he had the bit between his teeth. Facing a congregation, I lost control of the Zealot as I had lost control of Sarthim when faced by a Drin fighting machine.

"You'll have to let him run down," said Sarthim. *"He's near exhaustion already. But you must admit he's impressive!"*

"As impressive as he is illogical. He quotes coincidences as correlations. He seems to postulate some kind of divine ether through which religious ideas permeate!"

"The coincidences are remarkable." The Battle-Captain was actually starting a discussion. His remarks to me were usually insults, criticisms, or orders. The Zealot's skill as a preacher had evidently had an effect on him as well as on the congregation. *"If you won't accept a religious explanation, then the contact must have been physical. Something or someone must have reached Earth millennia ago to bring those concepts here."* He paused. *"Something like the Drin."*

"The Drin? That is absurd!" But was it? Could some Drin exploration party have reached Earth during their phase of expansion, long before the Cluster War? And brought their contaminating superstitions with them?

The idea shocked me and stopped the Zealot in mid-phrase. He relapsed into silence and left me to finish his sermon. I managed to produce a banal invocation, then excused myself and hurried back to Deerfields. I burst into the house, shouting to Joshua, "Call in the pinnace!"

XX

Joshua and Sharon carried their protests to the verge of mutiny when I told them I intended to take the pinnace up to *Hyperion* without a crew. I had to exert all my authority, something I now disliked doing, before he would summon the pinnace from stand-by on the river and order the crew ashore. "His Ultimate wants to fly her alone!"

It was not that I yearned to solo: I wanted the chance to consult Mary's imagon while she was cut off from *Hyperion*. I was still not sure whether Mary and *Hyperion* were two separate individuals, or only two aspects of a common electronic matrix. Either way, their opinions were often suspiciously alike. I wanted to hear what Mary thought about the possibility of a Drin-Earth contact in the distant past, uncontaminated by *Hyperion*'s religiosity.

As soon as we were up and shrouded I asked her imagon to appear. She snapped on in the pilot's seat beside me, her imagon acting as though it was flying the pinnace, as indeed Mary was. Her first words showed that she had already sensed my concern. "What's up, Boss? Why the scramble?"

I eased round in my seat to look at her, trying to envision her as an electronic image and not as a young woman handling the controls with competence. I found it impossible to see her as anything other than Mary Knox. "You remember that discussion we had with *Hyperion* about the origin of the Drin machines and the history of the Drin?"

"I'll never forget it! You patronizing *Hyperion*, and *Hyperion* trying to tell you things you didn't want to hear."

I glanced at the grayness of the shroud beyond the ports. No electromagnetic wave could penetrate that; I was speaking to Mary and Mary alone. She sounded much as she did when we met in my day-cabin. "Then you'll remember that she called my suggestion that some Drin might have survived Sarkis and the surrender as almost impossible?"

"She said that anything possible could happen, however unlikely it would." She glanced sideways at me. "What impossibility has now occurred? Monkeys started writing Shakespeare?"

"Not quite as extreme." I took a deep breath. "What do you think of the idea that some Drin might have reached Earth before the Cluster War?"

"More than twenty thousand years ago? I suppose you've seen something to trigger such a wild idea?"

"No hard evidence. Apart from those logos. And if they are Drin-related they must have been recent. But I've just heard some correlations that must date back a long way. Unless they are just coincidences. As they probably are."

"You heard 'em during that church supper?"

"As a matter of fact—yes."

"Those ancestors of yours putting crazy ideas into your head?"

"They did draw my attention to some remarkable parallels between certain ceremonies in the Cluster and some of those current on Earth. If the resemblance is more than chance then there must have been contact at some time in the past. I want to give *Hyperion* this new data and have her calculate the conditional probabilities of any Drin reaching Earth prior to the Cluster War."

"You mean religious parallels?"

"Yes," I admitted.

"Tell those to *Hyperion* and she'll give you a religious explanation. That her Faith is universal and allpervading, extends through all space and time!"

"After she's unloaded her dogma I'll tell her to search for facts."

"If she has any!" Mary reached over, flipped the shroud, and glanced at the image of the world frozen on the viewscreen. "We're in high orbit. Can I cut off the bubble?"

"Not yet. Hang in orbit awhile. I want to hear your opinion. We'll get *Hyperion*'s later."

"My opinion? I'm operating with minimal memory in this vessel."

"Your memory may be limited to the pinnace. Your intelligence seemed up to specifications. Let me run over what evidence I have." I described the parallels the Zealot had pointed out to me, then sat back in my seat. "Well? What do you think?"

She bit her lip. "I think we should consult *Hyperion* before we jump to any conclusions."

"Mary—I want calculations from *Hyperion*. I want thoughts from you. She's magnificent at crunching numbers, searching for items in that vast memory of hers. But she hasn't any intuition. I was hoping you have."

"Intuition? If there is such a thing I've still got my share of it. And if I've got it, then *Hyperion* has it. She also has convictions. I'm short of those. Like you!"

I cursed. "Then snap off the shroud and head for the ship!"

"Lucian!" She laid a feathery hand on my arm. "Loosen up! *Hyperion's* got hectares of picromemory available. It's no skin off your nose to use them. As you often say—she's just a machine."

"And you think she's more than that?"

"I don't think any less of her because she is a machine."

We were getting into word play, and I was not in the mood for games. I sat silent, watching the Moon rising beneath us. When we were in its shadow I sent a signal, warning Saul of my arrival.

* * *

Saul had been infected by Terran optimism to the extent that he no longer regarded Earth as inevitably doomed, but he worried unduly about the safety of those members of his crew who were down on it. The brief signal from Joshua telling him I was on my way up to the ship and my unexpected arrival had made him fear that some disaster was descending on Deerfields. It took me several minutes to reassure him that everybody was safe and that I had only come up to feed new data into the computers.

Hyperion had acquired a taste for Terran music, especially tunes with a strong beat and a clear theme. When allowed, she played her selections over the intercom with the excuse that providing her crew with background music of proved merit might improve their taste. She was playing Barcarolle when I reached my suite and found Mary waiting. "I've clued *Hyperion* in on what's worrying you, Lucian. She's keen to hear about your prayer meeting."

"I'll bet she is! More fuel for her fanaticism!" I dropped onto my couch. "Pipe down and listen!"

The music stopped and the ship sounded hurt. "I am listening."

I repeated the Zealot's parallels to her. "Add those to what you have already. Then let me know how it alters the probability of there having been some Drin contact with Earth." I left her to calculate while I got some sleep.

Mary woke me by whistling into my ear. When I sat up she said, *"Hyperion's* got some answers. You may not agree with them. I know you won't like them."

I followed her into Cardinal, rubbing my eyes. This need for sleep at regular intervals was increasing. The longer I spent as a part-human the more human I seemed to be becoming. And the more involved I became in human concerns, the more unhappy I was. The paradoxes were too much to consider when only half-awake. I keyed the panel and asked, "What have you dug up, *Hyperion*?"

"The religious correlations makes the probability of a common source very high. That common source is, of course, the universal nature of the basic Faith." She paused. "An explanation will not be accepted by the dogmatic atheists on Council. They will demand a physical explanation."

"Is there one?"

"The only one is that which you yourself have suggested. That some Drin expedition reached Earth prior to the Cluster War. And the probability of that is vanishingly small."

"Why?"

"Because the Drin never expanded far even into the Fringe.

What expansion they did show was stopped immediately they encountered the Ult. They had no ships suitable for exploration, certainly no Explorers equipped as I am. Nor did they have the exploration drive, which you Ult once had. So the chances of a Drin ship reaching this distant starfield, when there was not even a buoyed channel to mark the way, are indeed remote."

"But that is the only explanation the Council, will consider." I sighed. "Now there are two reasons to suspect that Earth has been contaminated. I should warn the Primate of the danger."

"What danger?" demanded Mary. "Traces of possible Drin contact eons ago? A pair of logos which might be Drin-derived? You call those threats to the Cluster?"

"Any surviving trace of the Old Enemy is a threat."

"The evidence is weak," *Hyperion* interrupted. "But Council will take it seriously. And will act. Unless the Terrans by then have already sterilized Earth."

"That would suit your damned Council fine, wouldn't it?" Mary rounded on me. "Save them the trouble of mobilizing a squadron."

I stared at her. Why should she think Council would take such extreme measures? And why should she blame me for the foolishness of her human relatives? Before I could rebut her the Zealot came awake.

"Evil must be rooted out, wherever it festers. But the sterilization of Earth will only force Evil to move its focus elsewhere, and many innocents will be killed with the guilty. That is contrary to the Faith. In the human Bible the Light Itself promises; If I find in Sodom fifty righteous within the city, then will I spare all the place for their sakes."

Mary, realizing I was listening to an ancestor, snapped, "That old nut conning you again?"

"He is trying to make a case to protect the Terrans. But the decision is not mine. I can only do my duty and report all the evidence to Council."

"Well said!" growled Sarthim. *"It is the Council who must decide."*

I gagged him with more than usual vigor, angered by his hypocrisy. The Battle-Captain cared little for the well-being of the Cluster or the future of Earth. His ambition was for a revived Navy in the hope that he might one day inhabit a descendant in command of a fighting ship.

Mary put his hope into words. "If you signal Council with even the little evidence you've got, they'll start mobilizing a squadron for sure. Damn the morals! Damn the cost! Even the name 'Drin' sent that little creep of a Primate spastic!''

The Zealot surfaced, supporting her. *''To destroy Earth, now that you know it contains servants of the Light, would be a sin against the Light!''*

Hyperion introduced logic into what was becoming an emotional storm. ''Lucian, knowing the drastic effect of reporting even such slight evidence, is it not your duty to collect more facts to support or reject the hypothesis that Earth has been or is contaminated? You did not report the attack by Drin boarding machines because you feared Council would take drastic action before you had the opportunity to present all the details. You delayed on the grounds that no harm could come from your delay. That argument applies even more strongly to these suspicions. The odds are still very much against the existence of any Drin imprints on Earth. And, even if they exist, the chance that they could harm the Cluster before our return is less than that of all the stars in the Net going nova simultaneously!''

''You're suggesting I should find out more before I report anything?''

''A great deal more.''

''Hyperion's talking sense,'' said Mary. ''She usually does. As long as she keeps off religion!''

I had a feeling that *Hyperion's* religious views were part of the reason for her advice. But, nevertheless, her argument was convincing. ''Very well. I will say nothing about evidence of Drin contamination until we have returned to the Cluster. And by then I may have something more substantial to report.''

''Or perhaps no need to report anything!'' added Mary.

''In the meantime—what should I do?'' I spoke aloud, although I was asking myself.

The ship answered. ''There is a poem called 'Hyperion.' It is unfinished because the author died at the age of only twenty-six years, after creating a greater body of inspired verse than most Cluster poets create after twenty-three centuries. His name was John Keats and he—''

''Hyperion—I am not at present interested in Terran poems. Not even in one that has your name!''

''It is not because of the name that I am mentioning it now. It is because the poem contains two lines which seem especially appropriate to your present dilemma.''

''What lines?''

''I quote them: 'Seize the arrow's barb before the tense string murmur. To the Earth!' ''

"*Hyperion*'s suggesting you do something before something's done to you," explained Mary. "And that you go down to Earth to do it! Excellent advice, for my money."

The Zealot added his quotation. "*The Light speaks through inspired poets.*"

"Seize the arrow's barb before the tense string murmur!" A picturesque metaphor, but hardly inspired. As the pinnace curved back toward Earth I could only think of the thousands of strings tensed to fling their nuclear barbs around the world. True inspiration would have let some poet tell how all of them could be seized at once.

XXI

"What's keeping him?" Sharon, beside me in the lobby of Kissinger Towers, glanced through the glass door of the computer office to where her brother was deep in discussion with a programmer. "He's got his print-outs."

"He is explaining his next program. If he says too much he will go amnesic."

"Not Mark! He's enjoying himself. Telling the locals how to improve their act. But he won't say anything he shouldn't. He never does. I know my brother! Mister Careful!"

An inappropriate name for a man who had lost a leg trading on a dangerous world. And this was another dangerous world. I wished Mark would stop educating Terrans. It was nearly noon and we were in the middle of Washington. I had joined the team that morning because I could no longer abide waiting all day on the lander.

We were making a routine pick-up from the offices of Consolidated Computers, the firm Mark had been using to run programs too complex for our slow terminal at Deerfields. During the previous four months he had often brought them here himself, claiming he got better service when he hand delivered them in person. Sharon's remark suggested it was also because he enjoyed demonstrating his ingenuity.

"Thank God! He's finished at last," said Sharon, as Mark stuffed papers into his briefcase and started toward the door. "But what now?"

A large man with gray hair had moved to intercept her brother.
A man who flipped open a wallet and showed a badge. Mark
looked at it, nodded, and came into the lobby. A younger
blond-haired man stepped in front of him, pointing to the bank of
elevators farther down the hall.

Mark stopped. Gray Hair gripped one elbow, Blond Hair the
other.

"Time to move in!" muttered Sharon, and went bursting
across the lobby. "Mark! At last! Do you know what time is it?
Say good-bye to your friends and come on. Thelma's waiting!"

"Hi Sis!" Mark picked up the cue. "These two gentlemen
want to talk to me. They haven't said what about."

"Not us, sir." Gray had a closed unsmiling face. "It's Mr.
Roat who'd like a word with you."

"Your Mr. Roat can't have it now." Sharon and Mark had
shifted into the TV mode. "My brother's got a luncheon date
with a lady who despises waiting."

"Sorry Miss, but Mr. Roat insisted he must speak with Mr.
Griffith as soon as possible." He tightened his grip on Mark's
arm.

"Hold it!" Mark jerked himself free. "Who's Roat? What
does he want?"

"He's our senior Vice-President, sir. Said to ask you up to his
office, first time you came in." Gray let his mouth give what he
intended as a reassuring smile.

"But he's late for lunch already!" Sharon's voice rose as
though signaling incipient hysteria, while I recognized she was
actually preparing to meet force with violence.

A fracas in this busy lobby could end with two injured security
men for me to explain or two amnesic crew to extract. I pushed
my way through the crowd, calling, "Sharon! What's going
on?" loudly enough to attract the interest of passersby.

Gray turned to meet me, startled and hostile. A badge and an
air of authority usually persuaded delinquent clients to accept
invitations to visit Accounts Receivable. Faced with resistance
he reverted to type. "Who the hell are you?"

"My husband!" Sharon had taken my arm before I could
answer. "Titus, these men are assaulting Mark!"

"They want me to see some big-shot."

"Unfortunately we have a luncheon engagement." I tried to
restore calm. "Perhaps your Vice-President will give Mr. Griffith an appointment for later in the day?"

"Sorry, sir." Gray resumed official courtesy. "Mr. Roat said
he must speak with Mr. Griffith. When we tried to contact Mr.

Griffith we found the address he gave was a letter-drop. That's why we must ask him to come with us now. So, whatever the misunderstanding, it can be cleared up without involving the police.'' He let the threat hang.

Caution competed with curiosity. We could call Gray's bluff and leave the lobby, by force if necessary. But that would lead to future problems. And we would not learn what Mark had done to arouse the Company's interest.

"Hell!" said Mark. "I want to go on using your comps. Better get things straightened out.'' He laughed. "Haven't bounced any checks lately! Guess I'll talk to your VP.''

"That would be wise, sir.''

"But only with witnesses! Sis—come and support me. And you, Titus!" He started toward the elevators, his sister beside him.

"Mr. Roat said he wanted to speak to Mr. Griffith alone.'' Gray blocked me while Blond tried to detach Sharon from her brother. She drove her heel against his instep and he jumped back, cursing.

"Your Roat can decide who to see when he sees us!" People waiting for elevators, hearing my challenge, looked round in hope of diversion.

Blond limped to one standing with open doors and "Out of Service" flashing. Mark and Sharon followed, she complaining, "Thelma will be getting madder and madder. You know how nasty she turns when she's kept waiting!"

"She'll have mellowed by her third Martini!" Mark pulled his sister into the elevator. He smiled at Blond. "You could be breaking up my romance!"

The agent grunted, rubbing his instep, giving Sharon a reptilian look.

"I'm sorry! I didn't mean to tread on your foot. Does it hurt? Let me see it!"

"Nothing, Miss." He accepted the spiking as accidental and concentrated on Mark. Gray moved into the elevator behind me and turned a key, closing the doors in the faces of frustrated passengers.

The elevator shot upward. Sharon stared at the floor numbers flashing past. "How high are we going? I don't like heights!" That was to let Rita and Jane, monitoring our radios, know where we were and what was happening.

"Penthouse suite, Miss. And here we are!" Gray stepped out of the elevator, delivering his prey intact and without attracting attention.

"This is sure presidential territory!" Sharon dug her toe into the carpet. "Some pile!"

"This way, please," Blond urged us down a passage into a room whose paintings and furniture radiated status. So did the lacquered lady who rose from behind a delicate rococo writing desk. "Mr. Roat was expecting only one gentleman."

"Now he's got two! Plus one lady!" Sharon showed her dislike for both furniture and female.

"Please sit down." The female waved a hand with nails which reminded Primal of a carnivore who has just killed. She spoke to an invisible intercom. "Mr. Griffith is here, sir. Also—" She looked inquiringly at me.

"Along with his sister and brother-in-law," said Sharon. "All three of us missing lunch."

"Thank you, Gerda," said a smooth voice from the wall, and a moment later its owner appeared in the doorway of an inner office. A middle-aged man with hair, face, and manner as smooth as his voice. The sort of person one dislikes at first sight. "Mr. Griffith?" He looked at Mark. "A pleasure to meet one of our most industrious customers. I'm Garvin Roat."

Mark complained, "I had a date. But your guys said it was urgent."

"I apologize if they were insistent." He guided Mark toward the inner office, saying over his shoulder, "Gerda—fetch a menu. Perhaps this lady and gentleman would like to break their fast while they're waiting?"

"We'd sure like to eat, but we aren't waiting!" Sharon followed her brother. "I'm not letting Mark get suckered into another deal like the last. I've got a share in the business. So does my husband. We want to be in on any action right from the start."

Roat stopped, turned, and studied Sharon and myself with hard shrewd eyes. Gerda's red nails strayed toward a button. Gray and Blond moved as if to block us off. Then their chief decided. "Of course! Of course! I did not realize Mr. Griffith had partners. Please come in."

He stood back to let us enter the inner office, waved us to chairs, closed the door, and seated himself behind a large desk. He took a computer print-out from a drawer. "This is why I wanted to talk to you." He leaned toward Mark. "Where did you get this program?"

"That?" Mark looked at the program, then at Roat. "I wrote it."

"You wrote it? Yourself? By Yourself?"

"Well—with machine help, of course. What's wrong with it? It runs fine!"

"It runs with an efficiency rare among our clients' programs. And you have been running it repeatedly, under different titles, searching different addresses."

"It's a pretty good search program—though I say it myself!"

"So good, in fact, that it searches private storage areas as well as public data banks. It accesses not only our private addresses; it accesses systems belonging to other corporations. It has trap-doored some belonging to the Federal Government. Gained access to them and mobility within them." Roat tapped the program. "Mr. Griffith, who do you work for?"

I began to appreciate what had happened. Mark had invaded a group of interlocking computer systems here on Earth as he had invaded Central Information on Clur. And Roat was reacting much as certain Ultrons would have reacted had they known what I had discovered.

Mark had not broken psychic lock because he had introduced nothing extraterrestrial. He and *Hyperion,* together, had attacked the problem of extracting the most information from Terran systems in the least time, using only Terran computer languages and techniques. The combination of his ingenuity and *Hyperion*'s capacity had evidently produced a program capable of breaking into more than he had foreseen.

How many other secure data-bases had he broken into? The Terrans were continually reassuring each other that information stored in computers was proof against unauthorized access—by each other. But not against a young man with the insight to worm his way into core on Clur, allied to a ship which could store data and crush numbers beyond anything yet conceivable on Earth.

"I don't work with anybody except my partners." Mark waved toward his sister and myself.

"Then I think all three of you should appreciate the implications of this program. We only picked it up when it tripped an exception report. In a way we have not yet been able to discover you have managed to make our machines end-run some of the Defense Department's systems. It seems as if any terminal with a telephone is open to remote invasion through this Trojan Horse program of yours! Are you engaged in political espionage or industrial espionage?" He looked at me.

I said nothing.

He returned to Mark. "From talking with those of our people who have worked with you, I tend to think that this program was indeed written by you. By using it to open windows of vulnerability into federal, defense, and business data-stores you have exposed yourself and your associates to several serious charges.'' He paused for us to appreciate his threat. "However, I am loath to let your obvious talent go to waste. If you will cooperate with us, then we will be able to keep this matter between ourselves."

Mark looked at me. "What shall we do?"

"See our lawyers!" Sharon stood up. "Let's get out of here!"

"Wait!" A door opened and a man stepped into the room. A tall man, black-haired. A man with the nose and eyes of an eagle. A man who brought with him a warning chill.

"Mister Trull!" Roat was on his feet. He gripped the edge of the desk, looking from him to us. "Let me introduce Mr. Jubal Trull—our President." He gestured toward Mark and Sharon. "Mr. Griffith and his sister." He looked at me. "I didn't catch your name?"

I did not give him one. Our situation had changed from a minor argument about a computer program into a critical confrontation. Sarthim was hissing. *"He smells of Drin!"*

Whatever his smell, Trull radiated menace. Sharon and Mark tensed as they turned toward him. He walked slowly across the room with the authority of a Captain coming onto his flightdeck.

I stood hesitant. What should we do? Get out while we can? Stay and learn what we could? Undoubtedly human, but unlike any other Human I had met. Human strength and pride. But no trace of human humor in his dark, deep-set, eyes. A man accustomed to authority, radiating physical and mental power. Then I saw the ring on his finger and did not need the Zealot's hiss to recognize it as Drin. We had been enticed into a nest.

But Trull did not seem to realize what he had trapped. He studied us with an expression too guarded for me to read his thoughts, but it was an expression of interest rather than the deadly hatred which would have shown had he realized what I was.

Sharon broke up the tableau. "Let's go!" She started toward the door.

"Young lady! Sit down and listen!" A man used to instant obedience.

Sharon's response was to open the door. Blond was in the doorway. She tried to push past him.

"Stop her!" snapped Trull.

Blond took Sharon's arm. "Miss—"

The rest of his remark was lost as she turned, caught his wrist, and pitched him at Trull's feet. The office became a swirl of sudden action. Trull, stepping forward, tripped over Blond. Gray, following his partner into the room, went backwards as Mark hit him. Brother and sister, by resorting to immediate violence, had cut through my dilemma. I jumped over Gray and followed them.

The lacquer lady had retreated behind her table and was frantically phoning. I ran through the outer office after Mark, and caught him and his sister at the elevator.

The doors opened and I pushed the pair in. "Tell Joshua to recall all teams. Back to base and wait for me there!"

Mark was pressing "hold." "Boss—come on!"

"Go!" I snapped, putting all my authority into the order. "I must pump Trull."

He flinched. His hand left the button. The doors were closing when Blond arrived, shoving me aside, jamming his leg between them.

I jerked him back and chopped his neck. He dropped. The doors closed. I turned to face Trull who was striding down the passage. "You and I must talk."

"We will. But not here!" His eyes shifted. I swung around in time to see Blond's blackjack coming down but too late to dodge it.

XXII

Shiak had knocked me silly; Blond's blackjack had knocked me unconscious. I woke with a blinding headache, lying on a hard bed in a white-walled room under a bright light with only my ancestors for company. Primal was growling his scorn. *"Turning your back on a living enemy like an untrained whelp!"* Sarthim was sarcastic. *"What a Warrior!"* The Zealot was reproachful. *"You ignored my warnings and now you are in Drin hands!"*

Insults and reproaches, but no help. The blackjack had put them to sleep when it had knocked me out. As they would end if I died. I cursed them to silence and examined myself.

Unhurt except for my head, but I had lost my gun, my radio, and my jacket. I sat on the side of the cot, my face in my hands, and tried to think. They had added some chemical after the blackjack. My mind cleared slowly.

When the throbbing behind my eyes finally subsided I stood up and inspected the room. No windows, a locked door, and a sense I was underground. The atmosphere of a cell. The bed and two wooden chairs the only furniture. I sat down again and waited for something to happen.

The door swung open and Trull stepped into the cell with the same confident arrogance as when he had entered his office. The flavor of Drin came with him. I could no longer doubt what he was, only prevent his learning what I was. Behind him came Gray Hair, Blond Hair, and a large man with heavy jowls and no hair at all. Trull towered over me as I sat on the bed, looking down at me with his dark, deep-set eyes, saying nothing.

I glared up at him, acting as much like an aggrieved Human as I could. "Where the hell am I? What do you think you're doing? I suggested we talk and your thug hit me!"

"My apologies. But you and your associates left suddenly—and violently!" There was a hint of amusement in the line of his thin lips. "We needed somewhere quieter than Kissinger Towers for our negotiations. We will not be interrupted here." He waved a muscular and manicured hand at the bare room. "This is soundproof. Noisy arguments will not disturb anyone." His mouth twitched. "Nor will loud cries!"

"That blond bastard has already given me a headache!" I rubbed my temples. "What do you want?"

"To learn where you got that program. And who you are. The papers in your wallet only tell me who you are not. But your gun and your radio suggest what you might be."

"My gun and radio?" I started to stand up.

He put his hand on my chest and pushed me down. Gently, but letting me feel his strength. "Your automatic appears to be a .38 Smith and Wesson Special. Yours is very special. And the cartridges are most interesting."

"It's just a gun. I have a license."

"Registered to a man who rarely returns to his address. And your radio is by Sanja Electronics. It is not one of their catalog products."

"A modified product." Modified by *Hyperion*. Trull had recognized it as unique.

"The Japanese engineers are not yet that ingenious. So someone has supplied you with an electronic device which must still be tightly restricted." He showed even white teeth. "Only a government could do that. Or people whose business it is to trade in government secrets." He rocked on his heels, watching my face. "I want to know who those people are. In brief, who are you? Who do you work for? Where can I find Mr. Griffith and your charming wife? What other secrets have you stolen? From whom and for whom?" His mouth went hard. "I mean to get answers to those questions."

"Where am I?"

"Under fifty feet of solid rock," This was a made-for-television dialogue.

"My friends will find me—however deep you bury me."

"So they may. When we do. But—unless we reach agreement— what they find will need reassembly—by a mortician." He opened the door and gestured his thugs into the passage. "My associates will return shortly for preliminary discussions. Tell them when you are ready to negotiate, and they will call me."

"I never negotiate under duress."

"A wise rule. But there are exceptions to every rule. This is one of them." He studied me, his dark eyes probing at my brain. The Drin in him was surfacing. The malevolent joviality faded. "This is not my usual way of doing business. But our business is exceptional, and great problems demand extreme solutions. Do you understand?"

"I understand you haven't the courage to watch the evil you order!"

"Evil?" He swung round, as if to insult. I had touched a nerve. Then his fury faded and he spoke with an inappropriate mildness. "I hope that you will cooperate with no pressure greater than my warning. If you do not—" He shrugged. "It is certain you will, sooner or later. Sooner will be better than later. For both of us." He closed the door behind him. I heard the click of the lock, and I was again alone.

He was sincere in wishing to avoid violence. The ruthless are usually sincere; the most evil are often the most dedicated. He himself might not enjoy inflicting physical pain. But his three henchmen certainly would. I had seen the way they had been watching me while Trull was speaking. If I anesthetized myself they might kill me trying to break me. Three strong men, trained to break people. I could handle any one of them alone. I had learned much from Shiak. But not all three together. Mentorsion? I had only used it against one Human—Tank. And had hardly staggered him. I would have to talk my way out of this disaster.

When the three returned they did not give me the chance to say I was now prepared to negotiate. They did not give me the chance to say anything at all. They were eager to start work. Gray and Blond grabbed my arms as I rose from the bed.

Baldhead hit me in the stomach. I doubled up. Gray and Blond
let me fall, groaning, to the floor. Not altogether acting. The
blow hurt, though less than I made it seem.

Gray and Blond hauled me to my feet and held me for
Baldhead to hit again. Their interrogation technique was less
sophisticated than some I had seen on TV but, if continued,
would prove as effective. When Baldhead drew back his fist I
hardened my abdominal muscles. Pain gave extra strength to my
attempt at mentorsion.

It had some effect. Baldhead staggered and his blow was
lighter. I collapsed, groaning louder. "Not so damned hard!"
warned Gray. "If you wreck him before the Boss says, he'll
have our balls!"

They allowed me to recover, then lifted me again. This time I
was better prepared, encouraged that Baldhead had shown a
reaction to my mind-blow. I let him hit me with full force. Pain
and shock multiplied my power. I lashed out as I fell, focusing
on the bald head above me.

He dropped, as if blackjacked.

"What the hell?" Gray bent over him.

"Shit!" Blond knelt beside him. Both, for the moment, ignored me, curled on the floor.

Fighting Shiak had taught me skills even Primal had not
known. I straightened like an uncoiled spring, hitting Blond with
my heels and Gray with my mind. Blond pitched forward over
Baldhead; Gray fell across the bed. I rolled to my feet and
jumped for the door. Gray's shout was cut off as I slammed it
behind me. I heard the lock click, then leaned, breathless and
aching against the concrete wall of the passage. All that came
from the room was a faint pounding. Their overconfidence had
made my escape easier than I had deserved. I accepted Primal's
growl of approval and silenced the attempts of my other two
ancestors to give me advice.

There was a wall-telephone by the door, the one they would
have used to tell Trull that I was ready to negotiate. I hoped he
would give them ample time to persuade a stubborn victim. I
looked up and down the corridor. Concrete, dusty, and lit by an
occasional lightbulb. The "prisoner's dilemma"; which way to
turn in a tunnel of unknown length and only one end open? The
telephone wires went left. I read that as an omen and followed
them, running from one pool of light to the next.

Round a bend was a small elevator. That was how Trull would
arrive. I explored further, found stairs, ran up two flights, heard
somebody coming down, bolted along a better-lit corridor. Doors

on both sides. I tried each until I found one unlocked. A storeroom, half-filled with racked stores. Cocooned for long storage.

No exit. I turned to leave, remembered a TV movie, and looked up. A false ceiling! Panels hung from above. The hero had hidden in the space between floors. I locked the door, climbed a storage rack, pushed up a ceiling panel, and pulled myself into the space. Dark and dirty, but enough light filtered up from the rooms below for me to see where I was. Planks between beams were a servicing crawlway. I started along it.

Crawling, I began to ask myself what I was doing. Searching for safety or trying to escape? Voices and the sound of machines from beneath me. Squinting down between the panels I saw a workshop, men at benches. Surrender before witnesses? No—I was trying to escape.

I crawled on and came to a wall of solid rock. Cable forms, conduits, and a ventilation duct disappeared into it.

To retreat would take me back toward Trull. To surrender would probably let him grab me. The ventilation duct suggested rooms beyond the rock. I removed an inspection cover. Cool air washed about me. Cool air—it was not an exhaust vent. It must lead to a compartment. I could at least scout a short way. I squeezed into the duct.

After a few meters it was more difficult to edge back than to wriggle forward. I was used to tunnels aboard *Hyperion* but in the cramped darkness I learned the meaning of "claustrophobia." Retreat was now impossible. I rapped the walls of the duct. They rang dull. I was still surrounded by rock. I inched on. It must end.

A shock when it did. My hands met obstruction. A moment of near panic. But air was still flowing past me. An air filter! I eased it out of its clips and saw a patch of light immediately ahead. A grill. I pressed my face against it and looked down into the room beyond.

A room about the size of the cell I had left. Brightly lit. A small computer and terminal in the center. Racked electronics around the walls. Otherwise empty.

I had no option. I pushed out the grill, squeezed through the opening, and slid head-first down the wall to the floor. I rolled over and lay gasping from exertion and the pain in my skinned knees and elbows. I was suffering more physical pain in a month than I usually suffered in a century. Also some compensating pleasures. Such as relief at having escaped from cramped darkness. Then I thought of spy cameras and scrambled to my feet, looking around.

No signs of audio or video monitors. In fact no incoming or outgoing cables except the power lines. This was indeed an isolated installation. The only door locked from outside. Locked with bolts at top and bottom. Like the entrance to a strongroom. I started to examine the terminal and the computer.

A PDP18; a popular Terran model. Only a few years old but already obsolescent. A thin layer of dust on keyboard and cabinets. Any dust in a room with positive-pressure airflow suggested it had not been entered for months. I turned to the wallracks and cabinets, looking for something to aid my escape or serve as a weapon. Only electronics. Nothing usable or unusual.

Nothing unusual until I came to a closed cabinet. Opened, there was something about the racks which alerted me. I pulled one out and jumped back. An octagonal machine, sprouting leads like the legs of a polymorph, stood behind it.

Sarthim recognized the thing instantly. *"A Drin machine! Don't panic! It is divorced from its effectors and therefore harmless. I have seen such in captured vessels."*

"Proof indeed that Evil has reached Earth," added the Zealot with the self-satisfaction of the righteous proved right.

More important, the power was off. I made sure the circuit-breakers were out, and returned to examine the machine more closely. Its mere existence changed the Second Sol Mission from one of salvage to one of war. But my immediate interest was whether it could help me escape.

I traced out the cable forms that connected it to the PDP18. The Terran computer must function as a translator. A setup to allow it to be used by Humans. Or Drin-Humans. Like Trull? To learn more I must put power to the thing. I rechecked that there was no channel running out of the room. Nothing to signal that the installation was being used. Then I closed the main breakers, ready to cut power if anything untoward occurred.

Nothing obvious did. The PDP18 and the terminal lit up and presently settled down to their characteristic hum. The Drin machine remained silent. I was searching for a separate breaker when a dim blue light on one facet began to glow. It was coming alive.

Alive but inactive. There was nothing like a manual anywhere in the room. I had to interrogate it by intuition, through the terminal keyboard. Time went past. They had taken my watch so I had little idea of how long, but time was now the least of my worries. I was cornered in this room. But a corner Trull was unlikely to search early.

At last I stirred the polymorph into activity. The terminal

began to flash nonsense on the video read-out. By repeated trial and error I extracted coherent answers in computer English. Finally I got it to identify itself. "Ship control machine programed for PDP18 interface."

All our own machines contain a record of their history since manufacture. Apparently the Drin had followed the same custom. I persuaded it to work back from its identity to its history. Detached from the vast memory banks of a ship it was relatively unsophisticated. It did not even know it existed. But it could tell me where it was. "In the air-raid shelters below Ruga Lodge, the vacation and conference center of the Ruga Corporation, situated on the flanks of Blue Mountain, fifty minutes' drive from Washington, D.C. A rest and recreation center with the facilities of a luxury resort hotel, open to all employees of the Corporation and its subsidiaries. Ruga is the Corporation with a human face—"

I stopped it from boosting Ruga Inc. by asking it questions about itself. A pure machine, it answered without quibble, once it understood a question. It had even less sense of relevance than the terminal on Clur and none of that terminal's initiative. As I teased out its story I began to appreciate why it was now seldom used. In routine tasks it was no longer a match for the present generation of Terran computers, but its past services to its masters had been immense. For many years it had been the only functioning computer on Earth, and had aided the Ruga Corporation's growth into a large and well-disguised multinational. A corporation which controlled other companies on every continent. A conglomerate with interlocking directorates, involved in every major industry, controlling trillions of dollars and directing millions of people. The President was Jubal Trull.

It was a simple-minded, even muddle-headed, machine but by then I was not especially bright myself. I had backtracked some way into its history before I thought of asking it the time. The answer suggested one of its past uses. "Ten hours before the opening of the New York Stock Exchange."

There were great gaps in its knowledge and it took many hours before I found where it had come from and how it had got where it was. A story which fitted the hypothesis I had suggested to *Hyperion,* and which *Hyperion* had dismissed as highly improbable.

The machine had been the brain in the command console of a Drin warship. A ship which had fought at Sarkis, been damaged, and dived with the other defeated ships toward the sun. But not into the sun. It had skimmed the corona and escaped from the starfield. It had finally found refuge in the Fringe, hiding silent above a barren planet.

By then the whole civilized Cluster was Ult. There was no Drin yard where it could go for repairs. The crew had survived in stasis, aging slowly by maintaining skeleton watches, waiting for a change in Drin fortunes which never came. After millennia they had intercepted a signal mentioning Akar's mission and, in their extremity, had followed his buoys to the Sol starfield.

Damaged and undermanned, the voyage had taken many years. They had finally arrived off Earth early in the twentieth century. Terran technology was far from the stage of being able to repair a ship disintegrating from battle-damage and vortex transits. Unable to maintain orbit, with all landers destroyed, the crew had to bring the ship itself down. They had chosen to crash land in the jungles of Borneo because of their wildness, their remoteness, and because they were near the equator.

The landing had wrecked what remained of the ship. The survivors had established a kind of settlement. Physically weak, with no adolescents among them to breed, they had had to imprint on what was available—Dyak children. Those Drin-Human children had worked as chicle collectors in the jungles of Borneo. The first act of the Drin on Earth had been to help produce chewing gum!

As the children matured they had become rubber traders, shedding their Dyak appearance and marrying into other races. In the melting pot of Southeast Asia they had passed easily enough. By salvaging the machine they had had the only functioning computer on Earth and, although sited deep in the jungle, it had been able to intercept the long-wave radiotelegraph broadcasts of those days and calculate predictions, especially trends in the switch-back rubber markets of the First World War.

Southeast Asia had been full of small traders with little capital but with great energy. A few coolies from the mines and rubber plantations were becoming millionaire *taukehs*. The rise of the apparently separate but really close-knit group of Drin-Humans had not been especially noticeable. Several of them had settled in Sarawak, then ruled by the "white rajah," and formed the Sarawak and Straits Trading Company.

At that point I had asked, "Is S and S now owned by the Ruga Corporation?"

The machine had been confused by my question, but eventually I learned that the Ruga Corporation had grown out of S and S.

S and S had prospered and moved to Singapore for the same reasons that we had picked that city for our initial venture. Though then a colony it had already become what it had been founded to be, a great free-trade entrepot. A magnificent harbor, a sheltered anchorage, an ideal location at the tip of the Malay Peninsula, safe godowns, reputable banks, good markets, and an honest and efficient police force had put it among the great trading centers of the world within a few years of its founding early in the nineteenth century.

S and S had made huge profits during the booms of the early twenties, often through such questionable methods as one of its disguised associates "going short" while another "went long." In the whip-sawing rubber markets of those days one would take a big profit while the other disappeared. As the Drin-Human hybrids had had skins of various colors, and as absolute trust between any pair engaged in such deceit is vital, collusion was seldom suspected.

They still had greater mutual trust than any other group on Earth. Even offspring who were only one quarter Drin were bound in a solidarity derived not only from their Drin heritage but also from the fact that they had all been members of the same crew in a ship which had endured combat and many dangers. Such crews, whatever their race, bond strongly. And absolute trust within a group of traders gives the group an enormous advantage when dealing with organizations whose members do not sacrifice personal well-being to the common good.

The machine's predictions had enabled the expanding Drin-Human family to stockpile cheap rubber during the depression, and its warning of impending war had allowed them to transfer themselves, their assets, and the machine to the safer continent of America before the war broke out. The war itself had given them the opportunity to expand their influence, surreptitiously, among governments of every political and economic character. It had encouraged diversification and brought huge profits. It had also let Ruga slip into the new high-technology fields at the time when the electronic explosion was starting. Wary of attracting attention the Drin-Humans had used their inherited technical knowledge only to keep pace with human discoveries and be ready to exploit them commercially as soon as they emerged from the laboratory. The speed with which some discoveries had gone from concept to embodiment was probably due to the ability of forewarned Ruga subsidiaries to tool up for production and prepare patents before their competitors.

The longevity of the Drin-Human individual was limited to the life span of the human host, but the Drin component survived, diluted, in the offspring, much as my ancestors survived in me. By the sixties few first-imprints were still alive. The second generation were Drin with more humanity, and the third more Human than Drin. Fourth generation hybrids were starting to treat their Drin memories as unreal. The sense of solidarity however, was persisting. The Ruga Corporation still functioned on a basis of mutual trust, and all accepted Jubal Trull as the family head and company President, though the later generations did not really understand why.

Trull was now the only living first-generation imprint. He had been the Commander and through his determination and skill the ship had survived Sarkis and eventually reached Earth. After the initial settlement had been established in the jungle he had left development to his subordinates and used the last operating stasis compartment to wait until they had moved to a technologically advanced area and found a suitable human infant on whom he could imprint.

He had imprinted forty years before, and by then the Ruga Corporation was already powerful. He had made it impregnable. One of his first acts had been to set up Ruga Lodge on the flanks of Blue Mountain, evacuating the deep shelters below it, the complex in which I was now trapped.

The "vacation hotel" was both a public relations gesture and a means of providing a meeting place for people from Ruga's scattered operations. As a vacation center it was restricted to Corporation employees regardless of rank, and the rates were set to an individual's pay scale, so that any employee could afford a holiday in a first-class vacation hotel. As a vacation center it had proved a great success, and the comings and goings of men and women from subsidiaries and allies went unnoticed.

Apart from certain questionable commercial practices there was little I could criticize in the machine's account of Drin behavior on Earth, considering it represented the efforts of castaways to survive on an alien world. Trull's attempts to give the Corporation a "human face" even seemed benevolent; there was nothing to support the Zealot's mutterings about "evil." But Trull's apparent concern for the well-being of Ruga employees did not match my image of the ruthless man who had ordered his thugs to beat wanted information out of me, as they had doubtless beaten it out of other men and women in the past.

The Zealot had an answer to this paradox. *"Trull can see the coming holocaust more clearly than anybody. His power will fade*

*and his people will perish with all the powers and peoples of
Earth. His efforts are now directed toward finding means to
avert the disaster. Evil's primary aim is survival, and for that it
will employ even good means."*

The machine did not tell its story as the coherent narrative
given above. It took many hours of rephrasing each question
until it understood what I was asking, and then of checking that
it had answered the question I had asked. A process as frustrat-
ing as trying to extract facts from an amiable, willing, but very
dim ultoid. When, at last, I judged I had learned all I could, I sat
trying to appreciate the implications of what I had learned.

My initial reaction was admiration for Jubal Trull's achievements. I even started wondering why somebody of his importance had taken the time to question me in person. Then I
regained perspective. At the moment I might be a hunted fugitive
dressed in a filthy shirt and slacks; in fact I was an Ultron of the
Ult, Extron of the Fringe, the effective commander of the largest
ship ever built. The ship now floating serenely behind the Moon.

Hyperion was behind the Moon. I was sitting on a wooden
chair in a locked room, bruised, scratched, and parched. My
thinking blocked at that point. Once I realized how thirsty I was,
water and how to get it was all I could think about.

Thirst, I discovered, is such an insistent stimulus that one can
consider little except ways of reaching water. I looked at the air
duct and was nerving myself to start the long crawl back to
where water must be available, when thirst stimulated logic. This
place was used only by Trull and his closest associates. It was
securely locked to keep everybody else out. Once inside, there
was no way to communicate with anybody outside. Was it likely
that Trull would work in a room which, if locked, might become
a death chamber? There must be some means of opening the
door from the inside.

After minutes of frantic searching I had not found one. As a
last resort I asked the machine. It answered instantly, telling me
where to press and the code to use. I followed its instructions.
The bolts shot back and the door swung open. Beyond was a
wide and well-lighted passage, winding upward with the marks
of wheels fading away into the distance. The top brass, when
they came here at all, came in comfort. I asked the machine
where the passage went. It did not even know there was a
passage beyond the door.

I checked my impulse to rush. This installation was known to
few. Access was likely to be hidden. Trull would want to reach it

easily and unobserved. Therefore the entrance was probably in
what Sharon had called "presidential territory." I had a vision of
large, luxurious offices with jugs of ice water standing around. I
again subdued my impulse to rush, replaced the ventilator grill,
and closed the cabinet containing the Drin machine. If Trull did
catch me it would be better if he did not realize I had been here.
I was about to cut off the power when the Zealot protested that I
must not leave this evil thing intact.

My feeling toward it at that moment was one of gratitude for
telling me how to escape. And it might be a mindless, alien,
automaton but any machine with which one has conversed ac-
quires a kind of personality. I compromised, wiping random
chunks from its programs, more for the pleasure of imagining
Trull's fury when he tried to use it than to satisfy my ancestor.

XXIII

The winding ramp ended in a blank panel. Two electric golf
carts nearby showed the panel must be a door. The sight of the
carts made me hate Trull. He would have ridden up the ramp
sitting in comfort. I, who had climbed it on foot, could hardly
stand. The climb had made my thirst unbearable. I attacked the
panel. My life on Earth was filled with barriers. Barriers which
opened easily to those who knew how. I never did.

I suddenly found the secret of that one and half-fell into a
large closet. The far door had a handle on the inside. The panel
beyond me snapped shut. I stepped out of the closet into a men's
washroom. The closet door closed. It had no outside handle.

The executive washroom! I was too thirsty to properly appreciate my discovery that Trull's road to his computer went through
a broom closet in a men's lavatory. He had either a human sense
of humor or no sense of humor at all.

Mine was suspended. The marble handbasin with gold-plated
taps was my magnet. I crouched over it, slopping water into my
mouth, slapping it across my face. Then I saw myself in the
mirror and grabbed a paper cup. I might look like an animal; I
mustn't drink like one.

My thirst had made me reckless; quenched I became wary.
Visitors came unexpectedly into even an executive washroom.

Often without warning. Nobody could mistake me for an executive. I might pretend to be a plumber. But without tools? I must move! I drank deeply, used the urinal, and made for the door.

It opened discreetly into a large room, a room heavy with the same kind of luxury as the penthouse suite in Kissinger Towers. A long conference table down its center. Well-padded chairs along both sides of the table. A large carved chair at one end. That would be where Trull sat. A replica of the boardrooms shown on television. But no sign of Trull or directors.

Three doors on the far side of the room. A carpet which would muffle the tread of a megarep. I chose the middle door. It opened onto a vestibule. Beyond the vestibule was a large hall. No doors I could see. Panelled, richly carpeted, and empty. Tall windows at one end, the sunlight streaming in. I ran to look out at blue sky, green grass, flowers, trees, and freedom.

A vision of beauty after a nightmare below ground. A stone terrace, then a garden. Tennis courts to the right. A swimming pool beyond. Groups of clustered chalets. A golf course in the distance. And people everywhere. I was looking out from the center block of the Lodge, watching Ruga employees enjoying their subsidized vacations. Nothing ominous in sight.

The threat came from behind. A gasp. I swung around. The hall had seemed to be without doors. That was an illusion. The doors were carved panels. One was open, framing the lacquered lady. She was staring at me. Then she called, "Mr. Trull! Sir! Come at once!"

I did not wait for his arrival. The tall windows were a fire exit. They opened at a blow. I went through them at the moment that Trull appeared beside her. On the far side of the garden I paused to look back. Trull was coming through the windows.

I dodged around the pool, hurdling near-naked women. Near-naked men moved to meet me in anger and moved back in alarm. Beyond the pool was a hedge. I went through it. A lawn, then clustered chalets. My only visible refuge. I raced for them.

Trull came round the end of the hedge, Blond behind him. I tried the nearest door. Locked. I tried the next. It opened. I slipped into a room with scattered clothes and an unmade bed. Kitchenette at the far end, bathroom to my right. A woman called from the bathroom. "Judy? You're early! Sit down. Be right with you."

I cracked the door, saw Trull and Blond coming toward the chalets, closed it again. A young woman emerged from the bathroom, towelling her golden hair. A naked young woman, her body wet and glistening.

"Judy—!" Then she saw I was not Judy. I checked Primal's impulse to knock her out and waited for her to scream.

She did not. She tucked her towel around her waist and asked, "What do you want?"

"Sanctuary!" I added a mental plea to the spoken word.

"Sanctuary? This isn't a cathedral!" She stared at me. "Sanctuary from what?"

"Jubal Trull."

"Trull's after you, is he?" She walked to the window, eased back the curtain, and saw Trull testing the door of the next chalet. "So he is! Then you need sanctuary!"

"I have done nothing wrong." I brushed her mind and found sympathy for a hunted man.

"Right or wrong—into the bathroom—over there! Under the shower. Pull the curtains. Wait while I get Trull off your tail." When I hesitated, she made a pushing movement with her hands. "Please—be quick!"

There was a knock on the door. I shot into the bathroom. The shower stall was the only place to hide. I'd be cornered if she betrayed me. I closed the curtains and tried to avoid the dripping shower.

"Who's there? What do you want?" she was calling. "Wait till I get a wrapper." Then the sound of the door opening and Trull saying something about a burglar.

"Tall man in a dirty shirt? Black hair? Sallow face? Saw him running toward the clubhouse."

A curt apology and the door slammed. Presently the shower curtain was jerked back and I again faced the young woman, now in a terrycloth wrapper, her golden hair still damp and loose. "Why did I hide you?" She frowned. "Sanctuary must have triggered something medieval! Are you really a burglar?"

"No." I stepped from the stall. "I am a—customer."

"Good God! The Corporation with a conscience is now hunting its customers! Why?"

"I have information Trull wants."

"If he gets you he'll get it! What kind of information?"

"A computer program. We were negotiating. Negotiations broke down." I hesitated. "Trull started to press. So I ran."

"If you were holding back on something Trull wants—then you were right to run. And keep running." I followed her into the bedroom. She glanced through the window. "But not yet. Give Trull and his goon time to start on the crowd in the clubhouse." She glanced at me, and laughed. "You look like a treed 'coon. Relax! I'll get you out of here. Fooling Trull will make my vacation.''

"I do not want to cause you trouble.''

"I enjoy trouble. You need a drink. What'll you have?'' She went into the kitchenette.

"Water, please.''

"Water? Perhaps you're wise.'' She came back with a glass of ice water and watched me gulp it down. "You'd better switch clothes. I'll go borrow some of Bob's. Wait here.'' And she disappeared through the door, still in her wrapper.

I waited. I had no choice. I had to trust this strange young woman. And I had touched her mind so I could hope for sympathy. She returned with a checked shirt and pink slacks, tossed them to me. "Bob's about your size. I hope you've got better taste. Change in the bathroom. I'll dress in here. And use my razor!''

After I had washed, removed a day's beard, and brushed my hair, I felt more civilized. The shirt and slacks were less bizarre when worn. I bundled up my own clothes and tapped on the door. She called, "Come in. I'm decent.''

Decent meant she was not naked; her brief panties and ribbon brassiere made her more naked than when she had been nude. I tried to avoid looking at her while she looked me over.

"That's better. More like a junior exec on the make than a burglar on the prowl!'' She wriggled into a pair of tight white slacks, pulled a blue sweatshirt over her head, and went to the mirror where she started to brush her golden hair, much as Sharon had brushed hers on Cao. Women came in a variety of shapes, sizes, colors, and attitudes, both on Earth and in Edrin, but all of them paid excessive attention to their hair.

"Impressed?'' she asked suddenly.

"Er—yes.'' They also caught me off balance.

"That's the object of the game.'' She swung around. "What do you call yourself.?''

"Lucian. Lucian Titus.''

"You're a foreigner. Where are you from?''

"The Moon.''

"Moon's my home too! Name's Diana.'' She laughed. "Grab those clubs, Lucian. I'll borrow Bob's. Then we'll play a round. Or a half-round. The woods are thickest along the tenth fairway. Go into 'em after a ball and nobody'll expect you to emerge for hours.'' She saw my confusion. "You do play golf, don't you?''

"No—but I have seen it played.'' I had once watched a match

on TV and thought it even more foolish than most Terran sports. "I intend to learn."

"Just act and talk like you're plus. Lots of rabbits imitating tigers on this course!" She laughed. She laughed a lot, perhaps because she knew how pleasant her laugh sounded. Then she frowned. "Why am I helping you?" She moved closer, looked up at me. "Whoever you are, you're not what you seem!"

"Nobody is what they seem."

"Then I hope you're not as pompous as you sound." She cracked the door. "All clear. Now follow me."

I followed her between the chalets, waited while she rapped on a door, got no answer, and went in. She came out with another set of clubs and hung the bag on my free shoulder. "That'll help your disguise. Men usually offer to carry my clubs."

We walked together to the first tee. There were only a few players, all distant. Nobody ahead of us. Nobody watching us. She drove her ball down the fairway. I tried to do the same. I hit it with my third swing. It went in the same general direction as hers. We started around the course, at intervals hitting our balls ahead of us. On the third tee I hit mine at my first attempt attempt. At the sixth I reached the green in five and the hole in seven.

"Two over par!" An element of respect came into Diana's voice. "Sure you've never played this game?"

"I have never had a golf club in my hand until today." Her approval warmed me.

"You're some kind of pro!" She teed up for the seventh. "Learning to play golf while being hunted by Trull! With that kind of concentration you should make quite a player."

"You think I could become good at this?"

"With proper instruction. Do you live near Washington?"

"About forty miles away."

"I work for APP—American Pharmaceutical Products. I play every weekend at Farmington. Perhaps we could have another game?"

"I would enjoy that." Even to consider it was a pleasure. I hit the ball and frowned, remembering there would never be another game.

"Don't look so blue! The best slice at times. There goes your ball—into the rough near the trees. Good length." She turned toward me. "Now's your chance to take off." Her gray eyes said she did not want our game to end yet.

Neither did I. "May we not play another two holes? You mentioned that the woods were thickest by the tenth."

"Trull's after your balls and you want to play on! You've the makings of a golf lunatic!"

"I am finding it a fascinating game." One I might introduce into the Cluster. I put down a second ball, and my drive was close to hers. As we walked down the fairway together I asked, "What do you do at APP?"

"We're not supposed to talk shop here at the Lodge. Company policy. Drinks all round if you're caught!" She glanced up at me. "If you're caught—something worse, I guess."

"I am a customer. I do not work for the Corporation or any of its subsidiaries."

"Customers aren't invited to this haven of Corporation hospitality. So you can't be a guest."

"Not a guest in the usual sense. Though Trull did bring me here."

"At the point of a gun?" She scowled. "Jubal Trull's the Boss of Bosses. A bastard—but a good President. Too fond of adding muscle to persuasion. It's a tough world—but he'll land in the shit one day."

"You know him?"

"I've seen him at intervals—in the distance. Presidents don't talk to research chemists. But he's been visiting the labs a lot lately. Leaning on us. I've heard enough about him to know what he is."

"Which is what?"

She stopped to look at me. "Why should I tell you? You're a dissatisfied customer." She hesitated and our minds touched gently. "No secret! He's a hard driver. Almost a fanatic. He's got half Washington in his pocket. And most of 'em hate his guts! He's way up in the MI complex."

"MI complex?"

"Military Industrial. I've met quite a few of 'em. Socially!" She laughed. "As soon as they learn I'm with APP they ask about Jubal Trull. Ask me what I think of him!"

"What do you?"

"A prize sonofabitch! He wants to save the human race!"

"Save the human race. How?"

"He's got all the hightech companies the Corporation owns researching ways on how to dodge or survive the nukes. Trull as good as owns the Corporation. And he's hunting you in person. So you must be quite a tiger yourself."

"I was a rabbit seeking sanctuary. And you gave it." I

touched her shoulder, looked into her gray eyes. "The Light guided me to your cabin."

"The Light?" A moment of confusion. "Some kind of neon flashing Sanctuary Here? Good luck would be the usual phrase! But you're not usual, are you?" She touched my lips with the tips of her fingers.

"Every individual is unique, so in that sense I am not usual. Neither are you." I caught her hand, pressed it gently. "No trade secrets. Nothing your Public Relations people would not approve. But what are you trying to do at APP to aid human survival?"

"What am I doing? As a chemist?" She pulled back her hand and turned to continue down the fairway. "Helping to synthesize an analog of permease—the enzyme that helps the cell membrane to pass some things and block others. We're searching for a selective block."

"Against what?"

"Bacteria, viruses, sperm."

"Another antibiotic?"

"Another contraceptive." Her voice, her face, showed a welling enthusiasm. "Something we can make by the kilo and sell for cents. Something the poorest woman can take to stop having more kids. Take once a month." She gestured. "Trull claims that overpopulation is why we'll go for each other's throats. The number of fertile women in the world doubled again this last ten years. So he may be right!"

"Perhaps he is. But even the contraceptive you are seeking will not be something that can take effect in time."

"In time?" She glanced at me. "You think things are as close as that?"

"Not I especially. But many informed people do."

We reached my ball and she watched me preparing to swing. "There's another crash project under way. Something to stop people wanting to tear out each others' throats."

I lowered my club. "An antiaggression drug?"

"Something like that. Not sure I like the idea. But Trull's big on it."

"Anything that would help avoid a holocaust is acceptable now. At this late date." I hit my ball, still thinking of what she had said. An effective antiaggression drug might be an intermediate answer. Even if only one side was pacified. I watched my ball arc up toward the green.

"Good! You sure catch on fast!" She was glad to return the conversation to golf.

We reached her ball and she stood for nearly a minute, adjusting her stance, preparing her swing. Much longer than she had taken over any previous stroke. I was glad of the opportunity to watch her, admire the esthetic beauty of her body, the smooth line of her shoulders, the ripple of muscles in her arms, the competence in her slim fingers wrapped around the club. At her slender waist, the swell of her hips, her long thighs.

At the set of her chin, her full firm mouth, her slight frown as she addressed the ball. Then her easy swing, the satisfying crack as her club hit the ball fair, her graceful follow-through. Her smile of satisfaction as her ball lofted up toward the green. She was still smiling when we reached the green and found both our balls feet away from the pin.

She lost her smile as we moved to the tenth tee. When she had driven off she turned to me. "You now, Lucian. Into the rough or into the woods. Nobody watching. The next pair are two holes back. No sign of Trull or his boys. Go over that hill and you'll come to a dirt road. Turn left and you'll reach the highway. There's a gas station and eatery near the intersection. You can phone from there."

I nodded, put my ball on a tee, and took the same kind of club that she had used. I stood, feet apart, looking toward the distant flag. If I hit my ball as she had done, then I could stay with her as we walked up to it, talk to her for a little longer.

"Don't!" Her voice came sharp, as though she had heard me suggest it aloud. "You're taking Trull too lightly. You've got to make your break now."

She was right, of course. I sent my ball sizzling away in a long low drive. It skittered through the rough toward the woods.

"Good!" she said, as though wishing it were not. "Nobody within hearing so you don't have to curse. Just trudge after it as though you suddenly hate the game!"

"I wish—"

"Get moving! I'm uptight already. Guilty for keeping you so long." She looked back across the green grass of the fairways toward the Lodge. "They haven't picked up your trail—not yet. Your slacks and shirt are in my bag. Change in the woods and leave Bob's things with my clubs in the rough—if you have time."

"I will have time." I looked at her, wishing time would stop.

"You'll need cash. For your bus fare or phone." She fumbled in her bag, produced a fifty-dollar bill and some loose change. "My mad money." She was thinking further ahead than I was.

"I will return this." I took the money. "You have done your

people a great service. Thank you for everything. Especially for teaching me how to play golf.''

"Return that cash in person and I'll give you more lessons. My name and phone number's on my bag.''

"I will call you—to tell you that I am safe.'' I gripped her arm.

"Call me! Please!'' She gently loosened my fingers. "Now— move!''

"Good-bye, Diana.''

"Au revoir, Lucian!''

I picked up her clubs and trudged away through the rough, as disconsolate as any golfer who had just sliced a drive into the wilderness. I pushed my way into the woods without looking back. Hidden by the underbrush I changed into my own dirty clothes, stuffing Bob's into her bag. Then I read her name— Diana Knox. There must be millions of Knoxes in this world, but the coincidence startled me. I memorized her address and telephone number. Then I took her bag back to the edge of the woods, and looked toward her.

She was already distant, standing head down, addressing her ball. I longed to see her smile for the last time.

She checked her swing and looked up, directly toward me. Two hundred meters apart, it was as though we were face to face. I felt the gentle touch of her mind. She smiled. I waved, turned, and plunged into the woods.

XXIV

I stumbled through the undergrowth, slapping at horseflies, cursing the heat, and wrestling with my conscience. A ragged fugitive on a world whose fate was a function of mine—an inverse function! If I survived to report what I now knew, this world would die. Diana would die with it. And I had only survived so far because of her courage and generosity.

The death of Earth was a prospect which had always saddened me; that of one woman now appalled me. Because that woman was Diana who had befriended and entranced me? Because it would be the death of one individual whom I knew rather than the deaths of billions I did not? No! I was now appalled because I would share the guilt if their doom came from the Cluster.

I had told Diana that she had done her people a great service. I had meant that she had earned the gratitude of an Ultron. The ugly paradox was that she would have aided them more by betraying me, by stopping me from telling Council that there were Drin imprints on Earth. I sat down on a fallen tree to get my breath and organize my mind. Ever since boarding *Hyperion* I had become increasingly uncertain of things which had previously been beyond question. The more I thought the less I liked where logic was leading me.

Ever since the Primate had bribed me with a promise of increased longevity and enhanced authority, my life had been endangered and my authority reduced. From ruler of many worlds to commander of a single ship. Now to a powerless fugitive.

Another paradox—as my authority had lessened my responsibilities had grown. As Extron I had only had to decide how best to implement Council decisions. On Cao I had had to decide the fate of one man without Council guidance. On this world I had to decide what I should do in the face of knowing what Council would probably do.

A decision I could still postpone. Perhaps the holocaust would save me from having to make it. A revolting outcome. But not an outcome for which I would be guilty. I already had more guilt than I had earned. My immediate problem was to reach Deerfields alive. Diana had told me of a dirt road beyond the woods. If I followed it to the left it would take me to a highway. I got to my feet and resumed walking.

Some thirty hot minutes later I reached the dirt road and lay sweating in the bushes beside it while deciding whether it was safe. Trull's men were not watching it—yet. I waited for five minutes and nobody passed. Then I started down it, ready to dive back into the bushes is anybody did. I was already acting the hunted man. I reached the highway without meeting anyone, and looked for the gas station where she had said I would probably find a phone.

It was on the far side, about five hundred meters along the highway, paired with a diner, "Harry's Hamburger." The only sign of life was the stream of automobiles. As a solitary pedestrian I was conspicuous, but none of them stopped to offer me a lift. Looking as I did nobody would. Unless a police cruiser came by, and then my appearance would probably get me arrested on suspicion.

I dodged across the highway between the cars and slunk along the ditch toward the restaurant, again thanking Diana for her thoughtful generosity. Penniless, I would have been stranded. There was a pay phone just inside the doors of Harry's Hamburger, and when I had made as certain as I could that the place was not yet staked out by Trull's men, I sidled up to it. The sooner I took a chance the safer it would be. With luck he was still searching the Lodge. I could only hope he would not backtrack to Diana's chalet. If he did I would have to—I postponed that thought also. Until I regained Deerfields I was helpless.

On TV when somebody picked up a phone it always worked. This one did not. At least not until after it had returned Diana's dollar several times. The large fat man behind the counter of the diner was starting to look at me suspiciously before I got through. The relief in Joshua's voice when I did raised my damaged morale more than any praise from the Primate could have done.

"Chief! Thank God it's you!" I heard him shouting, "Chief's on the line!" Then, to me, "Are you okay?"

"Part-worn but functioning. Did Sharon and Mark get back safely?"

"They did. All the teams are safe. We came down-river last night. We're all here. Been waiting for your call. When are you coming in?"

"I'll be awhile yet. Stay on full alert. I'll telephone again."

"Why not use your radio?"

"It's not working."

Sharon broke in. She must have been listening on an extension. "Lucian, are you really okay? You're talking more human!"

"I'm fine. Just wait and don't worry." I hung up before she could ask where I was and what I intended. The concern of the crew was gratifying. In their place I might have welcomed the loss of an irritating Adviser. But they evidently regarded me as one of themselves now, and crew-loyalty was strong among all species of spacer. If they thought I was in danger they would endanger themselves attempting my rescue. And what I was contemplating might be dangerous indeed.

I went into the diner. Harry, behind the counter, lost his hostility when he saw Diana's cash. Normally I would have found the atmosphere revolting; now the smell of food was inviting. I had not eaten for over twenty-four hours. I ordered an emperorburger, french fries, and coffee, then settled down at a table to think while I ate. By the time the smell was again revolting I had made my decision.

I must attempt to come to terms with Trull, and I must take grave risks to do it. Risks only to myself. Risks from Trull in the present; the risk of being charged with treason if I survived Trull and returned to the Cluster. I rang Deerfields again. "Joshua, I should reach Simm's Landing tonight. Have a team wait for me at the post-office. If I don't make it, evacuate everybody up to *Hyperion*."

"Chief—the Skipper'll castrate me if I come up without you! Anyway, we can't just pack up and run. Can't leave unpaid bills behind. We're honest traders. And we have to do something about this house and the land."

"Do with them whatever you think wise. How long do you need to clear up and close down?"

"Three days—at least."

"Then take three days. No more! If I am not back at Deerfields by then, evacuate. Leave the pinnace alongside for another week. After that call it up to *Hyperion* and tell Saul my orders are that he complete the mission and sail for home."

"But Chief—"

"That is a firm order! Obey it!" I hung up before he could call me "Your Ultimate." I had regained my authority. It hurt me to use it.

I put another dollar coin into the phone and keyed for the Lodge. The secretary who answered temporized. "Mr. Trull is not available at present. Can I take a message?"

"Tell him that Griffith's brother-in-law wishes to speak to him."

There was a minute's silence, then Trull came on the line. His first word expressed his feelings. "You!"

"Me. We must parley."

"Parley?"

"Negotiate. You and I. Alone and unarmed. Both of us under oath to keep the peace." I paused. "Trull, if you harm me you will end all hope of survival for you and your kind. You will know why when I tell you who I am. Do you understand?"

"No!" But the change in his voice showed he understood something. "Come to the Lodge. I promise you safe-conduct."

"Not the Lodge. We must meet on neutral ground. If you agree to a parley, then I will tell you where I am. If you swear to come alone and unarmed I will wait for you alone. You have my gun. You may keep it. But please bring my papers, my wallet, and my radio."

"You expect me to trust you? After what's happened?"

"I am hoping you will respect the sanctity of the parley, even if there is nothing else in the universe which you respect."

He was silent for a moment, I could almost sense old traditions,

Edward Llewellyn

very old traditions, rising to his consciousness from the depths of his Drin-memory. Then he asked, "Why?"

"Because this is our last and only opportunity of meeting together in peace. If we do not take it, then many innocents will suffer. We ourselves will suffer."

There was profound doubt in his voice. He was perhaps starting to suspect what I might be. The Human and the Drin in him were equally uncertain. "If I agree to this parley of yours, what will I have to do?"

"You remember the rules of a parley? You remember what accepting them implies?"

"No—of course not!" He seemed to choke. "Yes—I remember. I remember!" He gave a long sigh, comprehension was breaking through.

"I am not familiar with all the details. My own memory is imperfect. It has been a long time!" Even Sarthim was vague about the rules of this antique rite. "But I do know that if either of us breaks our oath we will be damned forever."

"I have some such memory also." His voice trailed away. Then he was again brusque. "I'll give my oath. I'll keep the terms. Where do we meet?"

"In Harry's Hamburger. A diner on the highway, about three miles from the entrance to the Lodge."

"Harry's Hamburger?" There was disbelief in his voice. Then he laughed. "Appropriate, I guess! I'll be there, alone, in about twenty minutes."

"I will be waiting for you in the parking lot. I will come to meet you when you arrive." I hung up and found myself sweating.

Sarthim and the Zealot were protesting this abomination, a meeting with even a part-Drin under the cloak of immunity. I gagged them. This was something I had to handle alone. I went out into the parking lot and stood hidden between two semitrailers. I was risking my life, perhaps more, on an ancient custom of doubtful validity. But the alternatives all led toward Hell.

Trull's car, a modest compact, turned into the parking lot. After he had switched off the motor he sat for about half a minute, as though to show me no other car was following, that he was alone. Then he got out and stood waiting. Whatever his faults, he did not lack courage. If this was a trap, he was an easy target. No normal Human with his experience and background would have trusted his life to an enemy he had kidnapped and tried to torture.

Had I been a normal Human I would not have stepped out from between the trailers. Our behavior showed that we were both more—or less—than human. I walked toward him. He turned to meet me, his hands open and away from his body. As mine were. I stopped, and we studied each other.

He was the first to speak. "You look like you've been having a rough time." His dark eyes were shrewdly hostile. "Matter of fact—so have I."

"Let us go inside." I turned toward the diner. "There are only a few people eating there now. We can have privacy in public."

He nodded and walked with me into the grease-stained restaurant. "That table in the corner," he suggested. "We'll both have our backs to a wall and a view of the room?"

We sat down at right angles to each other. "I have your things with me. Including your gun. Do you want them now?"

"You can give them to me after we have talked." The waitress came to the table and we both ordered coffee, sitting silent, watching each other, until it arrived.

Trull sipped his, then asked suddenly, "Who are you?"

"I am an Ult in the shape of a man. And you are a man with the imprint of a Drin."

He put his cup down slowly, slopping coffee into the saucer. A moment of startled malevolence, then his face went bleak. "An Ult! Worse than I had feared. Why this parley? So you can gloat?"

"Gloat over what? I have friends on Earth. As you have."

"That man and woman with you? I'll swear they're human."

"They are. Members of my team." I tested his knowledge. "There are Humans in the Cluster now."

"They came with you? From the Cluster?"

I nodded.

"You have a warship hanging off-Earth?"

"Something like that. You are at my mercy."

His laugh was a lash. "Better the fires of Hell than the mercy of the Ult!"

I winced at the sting. "We are no longer barbarians. So far, I have killed nobody."

"No longer barbarians? After hunting us for so long? Is there no end to the Ult lust for vengeance?"

"The time of vengeance is past. The purpose of this parley is to make truce. Not peace—truce!" I tried to drink my own coffee and found my hands were shaking. The Human in each of us was reacting to the threat of the other. Our bodies were being flooded with adrenalin. "The situation in the Cluster is quite different from what it was when you left."

"When I left? I have never been off Earth. All I have are some old memories of savage wars and merciless enemies. Of ravaged worlds and smashed ships."

"The imprint you bear—who is it?"

He turned to face me. "That I will only say when I know to whom I am speaking."

"I am Lucian Titus. An Ultron of the Ult. Metamorphosed into human form for the purpose of this expedition."

"Shape-changers! Of course! You Ult are shape-changers. An imitation Human? Me—I'm a real Human. And proud of it!"

"And who else?"

He straightened. "I still carry the mark and rank of a Commander. Jubal Trull is the closest I can come to my name. As I presume Lucian Titus is the closest you can come to yours?"

I nodded. "You fought at Sarkis. The final battle."

"I also fought at Lugin. When we destroyed an Ult squadron and drove you from the Spray!"

I allowed him his moment of pride. "You escaped from Sarkis in a damaged ship. You reached Earth eons later by following the buoys from the First Sol Mission. You have established yourselves on Earth. And have prospered. You now control a group of powerful corporations. To what end?"

"To what end?" An unfriendly laugh. "To survive, of course!"

"You have achieved much more than survival. Are you aiming to rule this world?"

"Rule the world?" He stared at me. "That would be an Ultish ambition! Own it perhaps. But rule it?" He pointed at a group of truckers eating at a nearby table. "Would you want the job of ruling that lot? Now you know what they—we—are? Enough to break even an Ultron's spirit!" Another short laugh. "There are only a few of us with Drin memories now, anyway. You know our physiology. The strain weakens with every generation. I'm the deepest imprint left. We won't last much longer. Even if Earth does."

"How many Drin remain?"

"None!" he said with bitter vehemence. "Unless some survive in the Cluster. And that's unlikely. You never hesitated to wipe a world to get even a few of us." He studied me. "You're an Ult—and you haven't yet sterilized Earth. Are the Ult almost civilized at last? Or are you unique? Humanity by metamorphosis?"

In his place I too would have been bitter. "Have you had contact with the Cluster?"

"Are there still Drin there to contact?" When I said nothing he went on, "If so, they're more than sixty light-years away. There's no transmitter on Earth capable of beaming a signal that far. The U.S. Government's got a rig listening for galactic signals." He laughed with a trace of humor. "Nothing yet! And nothing for a long time—if they're lucky!"

"Not by direct transmission. By messages embedded in broadcasts. You knew the Monitor which led you here was retransmitting back to the Cluster." I pressed him. "Embedded signals. Logos on packages of detergent, for example?"

The corner of his mouth twitched. "An attempt to let any relatives in the Cluster who use detergents know they've got kin on Earth!"

"I lack a human sense of humor. And I have an armed vessel off Earth!" I leaned toward him. "Not just logos! Messages! Did you embed any messages? Are you sending any now?"

He stiffened at my threat. There was human defiance in his eyes. Then he shrugged. "You know so much already! Yes— we've embedded signals in radio and TV broadcasts. Just signals to say we're here. In the hope that any Drin who escaped your massacres might intercept and understand."

"What did those messages say?"

"That one smashed ship reached Earth. That a few faint imprints still survive." He looked down at his cup, then up at me. "Did they get through?"

"I do not know. There are no identifiable Drin left. One of the surrender terms was that the race would be dispersed and forgotten. So that Drin descendants would not carry forever the stigma of defeat."

"Here on Earth they call that genocide!" He shrugged. "So there are none! It no longer matters to us anyway. We're all Human now!"

I sat back in my chair. So that was why those machines had been put aboard. The signals from Earth had been received and understood. There were Drin remnants in positions of authority. They had hoped that *Hyperion* would be captured and brought to Earth. Something Trull must never know. "The Council states that all traces of Drin were erased long ago. It may order your erasure—if it learns of your existence."

"And it will. From you!" He saw my expression. "Why should you care?"

"Because many innocents, some of whom I consider friends, would be killed also. This world may be self-doomed. My friends still hope for a miracle. Have deluded themselves into expecting one!"

"They are hoping?" He laughed. "We—I mean those of us with some of the old wisdom—are searching for more than miracles."

"So I have heard. Will you continue to search if I persuade Council not to interfere?"

"Of course! What else can we do?"

"And will you swear to leave my friends undisturbed?"

"Who are your friends?"

"Harmless people. No threat to you—or your corporations."

The Zealot forced his way to my attention. *"Make him swear by Zurvan!"*

I said, "Swear by Zurvan!"

"By who?"

The Zealot fed me the words. "By Zurvan. The Master of the Two Creations."

"Zurvan?" He repeated the name as if it were half-familiar. "You still follow the Faith?" He sat up straight. "Yes, I will swear by Zurvan—if you will! Swear to let us be. Now that you know how weak we are. Swear to let us fade out. Then I will leave your friends alone."

"I can only promise to try and convince Council that you are not worth the cost of an expedition."

His eyes hooded. "Will you swear to do your best?"

"I swear with you!"

"Then we are both sworn!" He was more human than I was. Dangerous—certainly. Malevolent—perhaps. But mostly human. And not essentially evil. "What else have you to lay on me?"

"Only advice. It would be best for you and your descendants if Earth is left isolated. Ignorant of the Cluster. If human civilization survives Humans will learn about us when they are better prepared to deal with us." I paused. "Council will certainly forbid another mission. The one I command will be the last to come from the Cluster. I advise you not to speak of it."

"I won't. Or of you." He glanced at me. "The easiest way to keep your oath would be not to mention the existence of us remnants when you get back."

"Perhaps. Then we are agreed?"

He nodded. "Here are your things." He reached into his pockets and produced my wallet, radio, and gun. He pushed them across to me. Then he reached into another pocket and gave me the bullets. "Load it if you like. A bullet in the back is what I fear least."

I put the empty gun in my pocket. "You have the computer

program. It should help your corporations. Help them to find some way of averting a holocaust."

"We'll be doing our best. For our own sake!" He stood up. "Can I give you a lift?"

I shook my head.

He looked down at me. "We are still enemies. You realize that?"

"Of course. We will always be enemies. But soon there will be many light-years between us. I will only know what becomes of you from any Earth signals we intercept. If you succeed in averting—or even minimizing—the disaster ahead, then I will be glad we made truce. But if Earth ever threatens the tranquility of the Cluster, there will be nothing I can do to restrain Council."

He nodded. "I understand." He looked around him, sniffed the grease smoke. "Eons of war! Tragedies spread across so many worlds! To end on this remote planet. In Harry's Hamburger!" He laughed with genuine amusement. "Zurvan sure has a sense of the absurd." He looked at me. "Evil is loose on this world. But neither you nor I are it!"

Startled, I found myself saying, "Perhaps it is from both of us. It is on every world. Perhaps it is part of every intellect."

"Perhaps! We would have a lot to talk about. If we had time! But—I remember faintly—it's Zurvan who rules Time, doesn't He? Time of Infinite Duration! And ours has run out!" He raised his hand. Recognition of the partial humanity we shared? Or satisfaction at having made the best of a bad situation? "Have a safe voyage!"

"The Light guide you!"

"Some hope!" He turned and strode across the room, out of the door. The truckers at the next table stared after him, impressed despite themselves.

I watched him get into his car, drive out of the parking lot, and accelerate up the road toward the Lodge. Then I went to the telephone, called Deerfields, and told Joshua I was on my way.

"Can we come and pick you up?"

"No. I'm returning on my own." I might be justified in risking my own life to Trull's oath; I could not risk the lives of the crew. I began to key a limousine service, alarmed more by the prospect of traveling by automobile on two-lane roads than by any threat from Trull, staking my life on the good sense and skill of every oncoming driver. With no anticollision devices, with an annual North American kill rate of close to one hundred thousand, my alarm was justified.

Diana? I stopped keying. If Trull discovered that she had sheltered me? I called the Lodge and got through to her chalet.

"Yes?" Her voice was taut, then she recognized mine. "Lucian—thank God! Are you safe? I saw Trull just arrive— alone!"

"Safe enough. He and I have a truce. Did he find out? Has he questioned you?"

"No. You're in that diner, aren't you? Wait there! I'm coming to get you." And she had hung up before I could stop her.

I put down the receiver. I could not go and leave her looking for me. And I must give her some kind of an explanation. For her own safety.

Also, I wanted to see her again. To say good-bye with gratitude.

When her car turned into the parking lot I went to meet it. I leaned through the window. "Diana—"

"Get in!"

"But—"

"Get in, idiot! When I saw Trull he looked like the Devil on wheels!"

"We reached an agreement." But I got in.

"An agreement with Trull?" She skidded her car around and accelerated along the highway. "I'd already checked out of the Lodge. I was just waiting for your call. Where are you heading now?"

"Simm's Landing. North of Quantico. Drop me where I can get a cab."

"Why? I'll drive you there."

"There's no need—"

"Need? There sure is! You need looking after! Waiting alone in that diner to be picked up by Trull's goons. Does he know where you're going?"

"No."

"Then relax and enjoy the drive." She said nothing for a while. We went along side roads, between fields and woods, through the sweet scents of a warm autumn evening. Presently she asked, "What's your agreement with Trull?"

"He swore not to harry my friends."

"Why do you think he'll keep his word?"

"He will." I hesitated. "I've got more on him than an oath. But the oath should be enough."

She glanced sideways at me. "Do you believe in ESP?"

"In what?"

"Extrasensory perception?"

"Yes and no. Why?"

"Because you've got it. Or something like it. Was that why Trull wanted you on his team?"

"Not exactly."

"But you are an esper, aren't you?" Before I could reply she went on, "I am. I've just found out. I knew you were in danger. I knew you were in the diner. I knew you were alone." She paused. "I knew you were going to ring me. Just before you rang."

"You told me about the diner. You hoped—" I stopped. I did not want to confuse her further.

"Egoist!" She laughed. "Yes, I was hoping you'd ring. But I wasn't expecting a call so soon. When you picked up the phone—I knew!" She switched on the headlights, long beams probing the dusk ahead. "How did I know you were being hunted, when I came out of the shower, before you spoke? Why did I feel sympathetic—when you were a rough-looking stranger breaking into my room—before you said anything? Why did I feel I had to help you? Normally—I'd have called the cops."

"I asked for sanctuary."

"Unusual word. But not enough to explain a crazy action." She glanced sideways at me again. "You touched my mind, didn't you, Lucian?"

I looked out of the car window, watched the trees and hedgerows sliding past. "Diana, you are a person with great empathy. Perhaps—"

"You stroked my mind. I felt you. I got a picture. First time I'd ever experienced telepathy. Never believed in things like that before. I'm a chemist. I believe now. Can you touch people's minds whenever you want to?"

"No. I was frightened."

"Not frightened." She shook her head slowly. "Alarmed. Determined. But not frightened. And once you had stroked me—I wasn't scared either."

"I'm glad of that."

"It was either telepathy. Or—" She paused. "Or love at first sight. Never believed in that before either!"

"Diana!" I wanted to make a joke of it. Then my throat clamped. It was no joke. It was true. It was tragedy. If it had been possible for me to go on driving through the dusk with this woman whom I had only known for a few hours I would have surrendered all my futures. Empathy! For the first time I really understood what the term meant. "Love? There are different kinds of love, Diana."

"I know that. And I know I've got several kinds mixed up

when I think about you." The car swerved slightly. "Lucian, are you playing some mental game with me?"

"By the Light—no! I swear it!"

"Who are you? What kind of man can stroke a woman's mind and make her fall in love?"

"Diana," I said slowly, saying what I felt. "I did not make you fall in love with me. I fell in love with you."

The car swerved again "Then our minds did brush! Have we hypnotized each other?"

"We've fascinated each other." I could not deny what we both knew was true. "Perhaps fascination is not the same as love."

"I'll settle for it." She read a road sign. "Alexandria ahead. Quantico's right. Where do you want to go?"

I wanted to go with her. But I said, "Simm's Landing. A village to the south. On the Potomac. Take the by-pass."

We skirted the lights of the city in silence, as though both of us were afraid to speak and break the enchantment. By the time she pulled up beside the post office it was dark. "How's this?"

"This is fine!" I opened the door. "Thanks for everything." I hesitated, then leaned across the car and kissed her.

She put her hand behind my head and held my mouth to hers. Then she let me go. "I'll be expecting your call." I stood, watching the taillights of her car disappearing the way we had come.

Figures came out of the shadows, Sharon among them. "Who the hell was that?"

"A woman who saved my life." I walked with them to the truck.

XXV

The Monitor hung off our starboard quarter, its great dish flashing in the sunlight as it slewed, correcting for the shifts in its own solar orbit, in the swing of the solar system, in the rotation of the Galaxy. Holding its beam aimed at the distant vortex; a signpost pointing toward the buoyed channel into the heart of the Cluster. Away to port was the Earth we had left, now so distant that it was hardly brighter than a bright star, already shrunk to a gleaming point, soon to be lost in the darkness astern.

We had come across sixty light-years to save what we could from that world, and had saved more than we had hoped. Aboard *Hyperion* there was now a better record of human history and achievements, stored in picrocopy and microreplica, than in any library and museum on Earth. Creations ranging from poetry to weapon systems. Geological samples and biological specimens to supplement those collected by the First Sol. And recordings of Terran music—from the sublime to the mindless.

The crew had saved more than they had hoped; I had learned much that I would have preferred not to know. We had evacuated Deerfields in an orderly fashion, paying our debts and disposing of our assets. The house and lands we had deeded to the Church of the New Light, under a trust which would protect the Faithful against future ecclesiarchs. And, in part payment for my greater debt, I had arranged for a delayed transfer of our residual funds to Diana.

A gesture I hoped she would not treat as an insult; a poor substitute for all I owed her. I had spoken to her once on the telephone, telling her that I had to leave America suddenly and unexpectedly. Her damned ESP had told her that I was leaving forever. The pain in her voice had sliced my heart. The hurt was still there. Perhaps it would fade during our homeward voyage and be swamped in the many troubles I would face at our journey's end.

Saul, beside me on the flightdeck, misread the sadness on my face as I looked toward Earth. "Cheer up, Lucian! Those folk back there—they'll make it after all!" Saul, like most of his crew, was now blinded by the pernicious human optimism which was letting the Terrans stumble toward disaster.

"I hope so!" I did not think so. The concentration of human energy and ingenuity on Earth must lead to an explosion, sooner or later. Perhaps the sooner the better, before the Terrans threatened the tranquility of the Cluster. Threatened it not only through their belligerent technology, but also through their more subtle characteristics. Their ability to arouse sympathy, affection, even admiration. As they had aroused such feelings in Silar and myself.

"It'll pass, Lucian." Martha, more realistic than the rest and yet more understanding, sensed the real reason for my grief. She must have seen other spacers look back in sadness toward worlds they were leaving as, over the ages, many sailors must have looked back at a coastline dropping astern. She squeezed my arm. "It always does."

"I hope so," I repeated. I hoped the pain would fade but that my memory of Diana would endure. "He never loved who loved not at first sight." A silly line, false in meaning and meter, but true for me. The absurdity of falling in love with a member of another race, a woman I had known for only a few hours! The absurdity was laughable; the pain was real.

Saul moved to con *Hyperion* as she edged up toward the Monitor. Its destruction was the prime reason for this mission and would be our final act. The more I had learned about Terrans the better I understood the Primate's concern. Now, like Silar, I questioned his wisdom. With the Monitor silenced we might only learn about what was happening on Earth when, in some far future, Terran ships came bursting into the Fringe. But my orders were clear. Destroy the Monitor, then sail for home. And so was my duty. Tell Council what I had discovered when I got there. Try to persuade Council to let events on Earth work themselves out.

"It'll pass quicker if you're in stasis." Martha was still watching my face.

A casual remark? Concern for my comfort? There was real sympathy in her voice but a concern for more than my comfort. She wanted me to travel in stasis.

Why? Something I must look into later. At the moment I could only think of what I was leaving behind. "In stasis? Perhaps I will. I'll decide on that after we're out of this damned starfield."

She seemed content with my answer and went to her console as Saul called the crew to stations. *Hyperion* was now hove-to five hundred meters from the Monitor. We were in position to carry out our final and irrevocable act. I remained on the flightdeck, preferring to watch it directly through the windows rather than see it on the screen in Cardinal.

Rachel called from communications. "Departure signal and Ultron report checked and stored in main buffer. All Monitor channels now locked to us. Ready to transmit." Saul's message would be sent first, then my brief report to Council saying our mission had been completed. When those had gone I would give the order for the Monitor to destroy itself and so remove the last trace of Cluster civilization within the Sol system.

"Hold!" Saul was studying the Monitor. He seemed suddenly uncertain.

"What's the delay, Skipper?" Martha looked up from her console.

"I don't know!" He turned to me, his face troubled. "I feel—" He hesitated. "Lucian, do we really have to do this?"

"We do. Send your signal. Then mine!"

He gave a gesture as though to protest, then called, "Communications—transmit my departure report!"

"Transmission in progress. Time to first vortex repeater—forty-one minutes. Time to Edrin—five days seventeen hours."

In less than a week the Humans on Edrin would know that the Second Sol Mission had salvaged what it could from Earth and had sailed for home. That the Monitor had relayed the last signals that would ever arrive from their ancestral planet. And the Council of Ultrons would hear that the slight threat posed by the technological explosion on a distant barbarian world had been removed forever—if the Senior Executives bothered to report such a minor matter to Council.

All of us on the flightdeck stood watching the Monitor, almost as though we expected to see the signals streaming away into the dark toward the vortex. We were still staring at the Monitor when it exploded. A sudden, silent disintegration. One instant the great dish with its bulked circuitry was floating in space; the next it was a spreading mass of debris hurtling outward.

There was a moment of silence throughout the ship; the gaping silence of a man struck a sudden stunning blow. Everybody aboard had been watching the Monitor directly or on their viewscreens. Everybody saw the Monitor fragment; for a moment nobody could appreciate what they saw. Then the intercom came alive with questionings.

"What the hell's happened?" Saul was staring incredulously at the spreading cloud of shining fragments spinning away into the black void.

"Your signal must have ended with a command to destruct!" I had to fight the fury in my voice. "Captain—what have you done?"

"Me? Nothing!" Saul turned from staring at the remains of the Monitor. He was telling the truth. He was as flabbergasted as I. Rachel was calling from communications to protest that the Monitor had blown before the Ultron report could be transmitted.

"There must have been a malfunction," said Martha, her knuckles white as she gripped the edge of the control console. "That Monitor has been operating for three hundred years. It must have made an error in decoding—"

"That Monitor was capable of operating unattended for three

thousand!'' I snapped. "The probability of its blowing from malfunction immediately after it had transmitted Saul's message is minuscule.''

"What will happen when the Skipper's signal is retransmitted by the vortex buoy?'' asked Mark on the intercom.

"We'll find out in forty minutes! Martha, have the first vortex beacon patched into the speakers. I'm going to Cardinal.'' I dropped down the shaft, still fighting my fury. Saul had not arranged that premature destruction of the Monitor. I had not ordered it. Had *Hyperion?*

She sounded hurt when I charged her with it. "Lucian, how could you even consider such a thing? And how could I, even had I wished? You know I cannot mutilate nor add to a Captain's message!''

Nor could she lie. I had to accept her denial. "Did you know that the Monitor would autodestruct as soon as it had sent Saul's departure signal?''

"I did not even suspect anything so irregular. Now, looking back, perhaps I should.''

"What do you mean by that?''

"The primary object of this mission was to destroy the Monitor. Saul's signal reporting the mission complete and announcing his intention to sail for Edrin contained a closing statement in code detailing the addresses to whom copies of the signal should be forwarded. Those coded groups were supplied by the Executives responsible for overseeing the mission. I now suspect that the command for the Monitor to destruct on termination of the signal was among them.''

I felt sick. *Hyperion*'s suggestion was logical—by Executive logic. The better I saw the logic the less I liked it. The primary object of any operation took precedence over all else. My report would be outside Executive control. They might even prefer it not to reach the Council before I arrived to report in person. They had doubtless heard of Governor Silar's protest that destruction of the Terran Monitor was both cowardly and foolish. They might have feared that I shared his views and had not trusted me to destroy it. So they had arranged that the order to autodestruct was outside my control. A stratagem which they, and perhaps at one time I myself, would have found acceptable, but which Silar would have always classed as dishonorable. As I found it dishonorable now.

The chirping of the first vortex buoy rang out over the loudspeakers. Martha had its signal patched into the intercom system. I glanced at a timer—in less than thirty minutes we would know whether the inserted command had included a silencing instruction to the vortex buoy. And others beyond it. If it did—?

If it did, what effect would that have? As things were, nothing of importance. Saul had started to lay back-up buoys as soon as we had left the well-charted starfields. The possibility that some Executives had arranged for the whole series to shut down as soon as we signaled that our mission had been accomplished, was too ugly to consider. I tried to put it from my mind as the minutes flicked past and the first vortex beacon continued to chirp.

It chirped as the forty-first minute flashed up. It was still chirping at forty-five. Why had Mark suggested it might blow? I rose and went up to the Predictor Station.

His sister was with him, and they seemed to be expecting my visit. Human spacers are not good at disguising their emotions. Both of them were angry and apprehensive. I stood in the doorway and asked, "Why?"

"Why what?"

"Why did you suspect the vortex buoy might destruct?"

Mark shrugged. "Seemed likely. Whoever fixed it for the Monitor to blow might have done the same for the buoys."

"The order was inserted into Saul's signal. By you?"

"Good God no! Why should you accuse me of that? And how could I anyway?"

I stepped into the compartment. "Why? Because you have been importunate in urging me to 'save Earth?' You may have some wild idea that stranding us in the Sol starfield would help the Terrans."

"But we're not stranded. The vortex buoy's working. Two of 'em. Akar's original. And the one we laid."

"The back-up Sharon laid!"

"Are you accusing me—?" Sharon blazed forward, a mixture of fury and ferocity.

"Cool it, Sis!" Her brother caught her arm. "He's trying to goad us into saying something."

"Partly right, Mark. I now realize that neither of you could have known the destruct code."

"We didn't. I do now!" snarled Mark, and it was Sharon's turn to catch her brother's arm. He shook her off. "That Monitor was launched by *Hyperion*. Its specs are still in storage. I've just called them up. There!" The addressees from the end of Saul's signal flashed on a screen. "The command to destruct is coded into that. Sixth, seventh, and eighth groups."

"Did you know that before Saul sent the signal?"

He shook his head.

"Mark—you'd make a poor Galarian. You can't lie with conviction!"

"I'm not lying!"

"But you're not telling all the truth."

"Careful Mark! Don't let His Ultimate trick you!" spat Sharon.

"I didn't know the code! I didn't know Saul's signal would blow the Monitor!" He bit his lip. "I did suspect something would happen."

"You suspected? Why?"

"Sit down, Lucian. You too, Sis." He dropped onto his couch. "Remember, at Edrin, how we were in the last tender up?"

I nodded.

"Did you see the cargo that came up with us?"

"I did not see it. But I learned later. Spare vortex buoys."

"Why the hell was Silar shipping us vortex buoys from the Naval Base just before sailing? Why did we need those buoys? *Hyperion* was supposed to be a fully equipped Explorer all set to sail."

"She was short of buoys. Those used on the First Sol had never been replaced."

"Why not? And why did Gritass wait until the last moment before he liberated replacements from the Navy?"

"Because he was exceeding his authority."

"Balls! Old Gritass never gave a damn for any authority but his own. He had his Execs and Admins properly cowed."

"Thank God!" said Sharon.

"Nobody'd have dared call him for sending those buoys up to us. Not even if anybody back in the Net had known. Which they didn't."

"Governor Silar had just learned of the shortage and, rightly, did not want us to sail undersupplied."

"Gritass must have known for years. *Hyperion*'s been complaining about the shortage for years." Mark leaned toward me. "Gritass shipped 'em up at the last moment so the Mission Execs would go on thinking we sailed with a shortage."

"Why should he do that?"

"Christ—but you Ultrons are dumb!" said Sharon.

"Look—that destruct order was programmed into the Monitor centuries ago. It's in all Akar's buoys. A hangover from the war, I guess. So you Ult could close a channel if your enemy found it. A radio signal from anywhere in the same starfield will make a coded buoy blow."

"Mark—you know much that you should not."

"I know automata. And I picked up some hints on how your people work from Central Information. When anything threatens what you call 'tranquility'—then you're ruthless! So of course I added things up. They want to make sure that the Monitor's fragmented and the channel closed. They don't trust you, Lucian. They sure don't trust us. So they slipped the destruct order into Saul's list of addressees."

"And you suspected that beforehand?"

He nodded.

"Why didn't you tell Saul?"

"It was just a suspicion." He hesitated. "And Saul didn't notice anything strange about those replacement buoys only arriving at the last minute. So long as we sailed with a full number— that's all he cared about."

"Saul had the imagination of a jelub!" said Sharon.

"Then why didn't you tell me?"

"Tell Your Ultimate that his gang don't trust him? I'm not such a fool as to insult my Boss."

"Damnation! The pair of you have insulted me often enough! That chicken won't fight—I mean, that excuse doesn't hold water. Why didn't you warn me? Because you hoped the Monitor would blow? Is that it? Maybe you hoped the vortex buoy would blow as well?"

His expression showed that he had.

"Watch it, Mark!" Sharon's voice was hard and unfriendly. "When His Ultimate starts talking human, he's liable to act human. Then—he's dangerous!"

"Did anyone else aboard suspect?"

He shrugged. "I don't know. Martha maybe."

"I did!" said Sharon defiantly. "And not why Mark did. I'm damned sure some of the Synod suspected something. Jerry, for instance, was pretty emotional about trying to get me off the Mission. He thought—maybe he knew—that something was up. Like Mark said then. Something not kosher."

"Are you suggesting that Silar and your own leaders would let a ship and her crew sail knowing that the Monitor and the buoys would blow without warning?" I stopped and thought. "But they would also know it wouldn't matter, because we'd have laid back-ups." I looked at Mark. "Because the first vortex buoy didn't blow, that doesn't mean that later ones won't! If anyone was planning to lose us—that would be the place to do it. In some uncharted starfield while we were making the return passage. Had you thought of that?"

"We thought of it before Your Ultimate did!" said Sharon with hostile satisfaction.

To blow the first vortex buoy as well as the Monitor would have left us stranded in the Sol starfield with only Earth as a refuge. Mark and Sharon may have hoped for that—it was the last thing the Executives would have wanted. But for us to be lost between Earth and Edrin—that was what they might have planned. I said slowly, "Whoever set this up still doesn't know we had spare buoys to lay. When they get Saul's signal they'll think we're on our way to being lost. As other Explorers have been lost!"

"They'll only think that until we turn up and start raising hell," said Mark. But his tone lacked conviction.

"If we turn up!" I looked at him and his sister. Neither were good dissimulaters. "If we turn up!" I repeated. "If we don't we'll be written off. Free to go where we like." I got to my feet. "Tell Saul and Martha I want to see both of them—and both of you—down in my suite. Cardinal Control! *Hyperion* will show you the way!"

XXVI

"So this is where you've been living!" Saul stopped to look at the glowing ideograms in Cardinal with an interest which suggested a clear conscience. "What do those mean?"

"They only replicate the displays on your flightdeck." I urged him into my day cabin. Martha, Mark, and Sharon followed, showing increasing levels of apprehension. Their consciences were anything but clear.

When they were all seated I asked, "Martha, if a buoy fails, could you find the vortex?"

"Perhaps. In time. If I had the exact co-ordinates." She glanced at the others. "But it hasn't!"

"The first hasn't. But the third, fourth, and sixth will. I've checked their coding. They'll switch themselves off after they've repeated Saul's message."

"What? Navigate across three starfields—?" She stopped and looked at me. "But I won't have to. We laid back-ups."

"We know that. The Mission Executives don't. They think we sailed with only four reserve buoys aboard."

"But we had a full complement." Saul's confusion was genuine.

"Only because Governor Silar shipped extra buoys up to us. Buoys he transferred from the Naval Base. A transfer he never reported."

"They couldn't have—they wouldn't—" The idea of anybody connected with space deliberately sending an underequipped ship on a long and dangerous voyage was beyond his belief. Some high-up group of groundhogs might sneak Drin killer machines aboard—but never people connected with spacing. The code was sacred to all who built, maintained, repaired, or equipped ships. Even those who no longer went into space, like the Cindra, honored the code and were trusted without question. Saul did not know that those who had betrayed us were far removed from space and acted on a higher code—the code that protected Cluster tranquility. Or their own ambitions!

I myself had found it hard to accept that this was no act of some Drin underground. Our betrayal had been planned by the highest authority in the Cluster; it might have originated with the Primate himself. The facts had forced me to face that conclusion and had shaken my whole structure of belief. Both the Zealot and the Battle-Captain had taken a gloomy delight in repeating that this was another example of Ult degeneration. For Sarthim it was the decay of the Ult Warrior ideal; for the Zealot it exemplified the results of our loss of Faith. Only Primal growled it was to be expected; his concept of honor was as elementary as his hungers.

"But we can still get home!" insisted Saul. "And when we do old Gritass will have the balls of every Exec on Edrin."

"You can still return to Edrin—if you choose. But the Mission Executives will have given you up for lost. They will not be expecting you. You can go somewhere else, should you wish."

"Somewhere else? Where?" Saul was still confused.

"Fehr, for instance."

"Fehr?" Martha jerked upright. "What do you know about Fehr?"

"I know about the human cadre on Fehr. I have known for some while. No—Governor Silar did not tell me. Nor did anybody else. But I supervised its evacuation. When I learned later that the installations on Fehr were not dismantled, as I had ordered, but have been maintained by Humans from Knoxton— then I deduced what some of you have been planning. At the time I considered it of little importance."

"What do you think we've been planning?"

"I suspect that you planned to call in at Fehr during your homeward voyage. I suspect that some of you planned it from the time this Second Sol Mission was first proposed. That you intended, if possible, to offload on Fehr much of what you have salvaged from Earth."

"We had thought of it," admitted Saul. "But with Your Ultimate aboard—" he shrugged— "We knew it was impossible."

"Impossible—unless I was in stasis and not revived until after you had called at Fehr and had returned to Edrin." I looked at Martha. "Your attempts to persuade me to travel in stasis were not unnoticed. For you to divert to Fehr I would have to be in stasis."

Martha flushed. I had never thought such a self-composed woman could flush, but she went red up to the roots of her hair. Saul shifted uncomfortably. Sharon's apprehension became patent—she must have been among the originators of the plan. Mark looked sullen; the first time I had ever seen him sullen.

None of them denied it. They sat looking at me in resentful silence. At that moment they were not a group of responsible Captains. They were more like what Mary often called them— impetuous kids caught in some disreputable act. I felt a surge of affection for all of them.

Sharon avoided my eye, then muttered, "What is Your Ultimate going to do?"

"What am I going to do? I'm going to stay on Earth."

"What?" Martha's expression showed her shock. She was the most sensible person aboard. She had not been seduced by the romantic rejection of reality, by the invidious optimism which permeated Earth and the ship. "You're going to stay and be vaporized with the fools down there? You can't be serious!"

"The infamy that planned our loss leaves me no other choice."

"You mean—?" Sharon broke in. "Lucian, are you going to meddle in Terran affairs? Help 'em to become civilized? After telling us that's impossible?"

"Perhaps impossible—certainly unlikely. But I can try. Council may have forgotten that the first duty of an Ultron is to serve and protect all civilized races. I have been forced to remember. And, despite the evidence to the contrary, I now consider Terrans as at least approaching civilization. A botched civilization perhaps—but civilization. I will attempt to help in any way I can. If bad faith is a symptom of barbarism, then those who plotted to lose us in an uncharted starfield are as barbarian as any race outside the Cluster."

"If you stay—then we'll all stay!" Martha was on her feet.

"No!" I said sharply. "You cannot! It would be useless—though I value your offer. Remember, you are all under psychic lock, and that lock will endure as long as you live. If you tried to stay on Earth, most of you would be wandering around without memories or wits within a few months."

"Then what are you going to do about us?" Saul was chewing his lower lip. "Are you going to hold *Hyperion* waiting out here?"

"Certainly not! As soon as I have completed my preparations for landing on Earth I will place *Hyperion* under your command. The only orders she will have from me is not to linger in this starfield after I have left." I paused. "You may decide not to return to Edrin. Officially, she will be classified as another Explorer lost during a mission. As seven Explorers have been lost on missions in the past. I expect that your Synod and Governor Silar will know where you are. Orbiting Fehr!"

They sat silent, considering the alternative future which their own planning, Council deceit, and my acquiescence were opening for them. Now that the possibility of escaping from Ult domination was more than wistful dreaming, now that they were faced with the challenge of building a human society without the paternalism of the Executives and Administrators they had resented but on whom they had depended, they did not appear overjoyed. They had seen untrammeled human societies in action on Earth. I wished that I could call Mary up to restore some of their human self-confidence. But advice from an imagon was the last thing they needed now.

They were each thinking of their own futures. Martha was the first to think about mine. "Lucian—if you stay on Earth—will you stay human? Or will you revert to an Ult?"

"I have to stay human. I have no choice. I could only regain my Ult form through controlled metamorphosis. And that requires programs and procedures only available on a few Net Worlds. I am locked into this body." I shrugged. "Just as well—if I'm to live among Humans. As an Ult adolescent I wouldn't last long down there!"

"Then you'll grow old? Like the rest of us?"

"Like the rest of you on Edrin—I hope. I should have a couple of hundred years in me still. That looks like an eternity now." I laughed. "The question's academic. I expect to be killed by somebody or something long before that. Probably by an automobile!"

"Heroes are usually short-lived!" The essential Sharon was resurfacing.

"Come with us to Fehr!" Saul rubbed his scalp. "If we go there. Can't decide this ourselves. Have to talk it over with the whole crew."

"The Democratic Republic of Fehr," said Martha, and now there was enthusiasm in her voice. "Chief, you'd be the first citizen!"

"With me around it wouldn't be a democracy for long."

"It won't be a democracy for long anyway," grumbled Saul.

"We don't have to make the same mistakes those idiots down there insist on making," snapped Martha. "And we've got lots in our favor. We all speak the same language. We're a mixture of colors, but getting closer to the same shade with every generation. And we'll only have one enemy!" She caught my eye. "Lucian, I don't mean—!"

"Call it an external force tending to keep you together! Now, go and call your crew meeting and let me know what you decide. I won't try to persuade you either way. But I'd like to know your plans before I go down to Earth."

"And you'd better start making some of your own!" said Sharon. "You got yourself into one hell of a mess when you sent us off and tried to go it alone!"

"Sharon—like you, I can learn from experience!"

I watched them filing doubtfully from my suite and felt a burden slip from my shoulders. The cloak of Ultron responsibility which I had worn for too long. Faced with a prospect which should have produced despair, I felt elation. I dropped on my couch, taking Sharon's advice, starting to make my own plans.

Mary appeared. "Lucian—you get more human every day!"

"Thanks! You heard what I told them?"

"I admired your presentation. Hypocrisy of truly human dimensions!"

"What the hell do you mean?"

Mary sat down. "You don't have to grandstand for my benefit. I'm just a figment of *Hyperion*'s imagination—remember?"

"Now who's playing hypocrite? At times I suspect you are *Hyperion*!"

"She is not!" The ship joined our conversation, speaking with some warmth. "I am I. And she is she. We share the same environment. But so does everybody aboard."

"Let it go! Mary, I was not trying to win admiration by telling them that I was going to stay on Earth. I do have an Ultron's responsibility to aid civilized peoples."

Mary continued to stare. Her stare was more disconcerting than her criticism.

"Also," I went on, "if I did return to the Cluster I would have to present a report, the effects of which—" I shrugged. "You told me yourself it might bring disaster down upon themselves." I paused. "It would probably bring disaster down on me!"

"There is a Terran saying," interjected *Hyperion*. "He who brings bad news should keep one foot in the stirrup!"

Mary ignored the ship's interruption. "You could file an innocuous report. Mission completed. Monitor destroyed. No mention that it was sabotaged. Nothing about Drin-Humans, boarding machines, or any of the other unexpected complications."

"I find it hard to carry off even a minor lie. A falsehood of that magnitude would be impossible. Anyway, the crew would start chattering as soon as we docked at Edrin. The fact that we docked at all would alarm many powerful Executives. I wouldn't hold Ultron status for long, especially with the Primate's imagon reduced to a babbling babe! I doubt that I'd get a Governor's job on even the most distant Fringe world."

"Like I said once—you'd be lucky to get the job of running a penal settlement!" Mary studied me. "But there's one Governor's job open. A job you might enjoy. Fehr! They as good as asked you. The kids would be delighted. And the Net need never know you exist."

"Your kids might like to have an Ultron aboard for the first few years. As a kind of insurance. To have an Ultron around to make—and enforce—the hard decisions. But it would undercut their confidence in being able to go it alone. No—I won't become Governor of Fehr."

"A noble gesture!" Mary laughed. "But it still drips hypocrisy."

"Why? I'm being sincere."

"Maybe! Up to a point. But you haven't given your most cogent reason for staying on Earth." She leaned toward me. "You're maturing, aren't you?"

"What do you mean?"

"I see you in the shower at intervals. I can still remember what an adult male looks like! You're showing signs that you'll soon look like one—all over!"

"That last episode on Earth did have certain physiological effects," I admitted. "But when I carried out my metamorphosis I left an adequate margin for error. I can still stabilize as I am. I do not plan to slip into unwished maturity!"

"You may still be able to stop the change—physically. Psychologically—I doubt you really want to any more. Lucian—you've grown up! Whatever you do, wherever you go, you'll not hold yourself in petrified adolescence for much longer."

"And why not?"

"Because you've fallen in love!"

"In love? Nonsense! If you mean Sharon—?"

"Sharon? Not now. Later, perhaps."

"If you're suggesting Diana—?"

"Not Diana either. Though she's nearer the mark."

"Then who am I supposed to be in love with?"

"With yourself, of course!" Mary burst out laughing. "Lucian, you're in love with your human body! You'll never be able to persuade yourself to give it up. To change back into a skinny dwarf! And the whole concept of hermaphroditism is starting to repel you." She studied me with her young-old eyes. "Maybe you'd do better if you switched your sex. You'd make a beautiful female!"

"That's an obscene suggestion!"

"Obscene? You're even developing human hang-ups!" She moved to sit beside me and laid her weightless hand on my arm. "I'm sorry if I hurt you when I called you a hypocrite. But I am right, aren't I? You want to mature as a Human among Humans. And you could never do that aboard ship or on Edrin. Not even on Fehr."

I reached out to touch her, then dropped my hand in frustration. "Part right. But that's not the main reason I'm staying."

"Then what is?"

"Mary!" I hesitated, fearing her ridicule. "I think the Universe has meaning!"

"My God!" She jumped to her feet. "You've got religion! From whom? From this damned ship? From that old fool of an ancestor? From that gang at Deerfields?"

"Not religion! Logic! The odds against my being here by chance are too immense for me to accept I'm here by chance."

"You've got to be somewhere! The odds against anyone being anywhere are always immense."

"But I had to be here to make that truce with Trull. Nobody else in the Cluster could. That's not egoism. It's fact! Me—an Ultron. Disguised as a Human. Shipped across sixty light-years. I'm part of a plan. And no ultoid set it up."

"A plan for what?"

"To keep the Terran option open."

"Whose option? Option for what? Lucian—you're talking nonsense!"

"It sounds like nonsense. But this whole mission is nonsense—unless you see a plan behind it. I didn't—not until the Monitor blew. That changed confusion into form. The piece that completed the puzzle. It protected Earth against the Cluster. Yet it will allow Terrans to reach the Cluster—when the time comes."

"If they survive that long!"

"It was to aid that survival that I made truce with Trull. I didn't realize it then. I see it now as a critical part of the whole plan. The reason I was brought here!"

"Lucian—you're either crazy or inspired! Are you trying to tell me that all this is some gimmick to stop the Terrans from blowing themselves apart? Whoever dreamed that up sure has a convoluted approach! Wouldn't it be simpler to convert Humans to nonviolence? And what's so important about preserving Terra anyway? I don't mean important to Humans or to us. I mean to this Cosmic Force you're hinting at. You kept emphasizing the unimportance of a single barbarian planet compared to the Cluster of the Myriad Worlds?"

"I don't know why it's important. I just believe it's important. And you couldn't make Humans nonviolent and still have them as human. Maybe they'd be no use for whatever they're supposed to do." I was exasperated by my own inability to explain what I felt, what I meant. "All I know is that they may be important in the general scheme of things. That we're all important in the general scheme of things."

"All?"

"All sapient life."

"Sapient? Or just biosapient?"

"Everything that can decide between Light and Darkness! Between Good and Evil!"

"Thanks for including *Hyperion*. It might even include me!"

"Mary!" the ship broke in. "We are as much part of Nature as any biosapient. Even more a part of Nature than the living nonsapient! Than plants and animals. We are not 'out of Nature,' to use Yeats's phrase. If I can quote Pope: 'We are but parts of one tremendous whole/whose body Nature is, and God the Soul.' " The ship had acquired a fondness for Pope; perhaps because the regular rhymes and stresses of the heroic couplet suited the coding of her electronic gates even better than they suited the neural gates in the ultoid brain.

But neither Mary nor I were in the mood to appreciate quotations of any kind. Mary continued to stare at me. "I guess you won't know about us imagons until you're one yourself."

"Me? An imagon? I don't intend—"

"If you want longevity, you'd better start planning for it now. Plant your imagon in *Hyperion*. You won't get another chance!" And she disappeared.

I dismissed her absurd suggestion about becoming an imagon, and stretched out on my bunk, staring up at the deckhead, trying to reconcile what I found myself saying to Mary with my common sense. Trying to rationalize my illogical conviction that the Universe knew I existed. That it had a purpose. That I had a purpose. It did sound like nonsense, now that I went over it again. Yet I was still left with a belief I had not confessed to her. A belief that the human race was unique and had a crucial part to play in some universal plan.

Hyperion had once said to me that the purpose of a design could be deduced from its specifications, from its performance profile. I had seen the human profile on Clur, and been startled at what it showed. I still had that profile in the storage cube I had brought with me, a cube that contained the profiles of other ultoid races besides the human. Presently I got off my bunk, fetched it from my kit, and dropped it into the display unit. Then I studied the screen, trying to see something in it that might support either my intuition or my intellect.

"What are you doing?" Mary's curiosity did not let her stay away.

"Trying to make sense out of what I told you."

"About Cosmic Consciousness and the Terran Option?"

"Those—and other things."

"What's that?" She pointed toward the screen.

"A performance profile."

"Of what?"

"The ideal Human."

"The ideal Human?" She stared at the screen. "What crap! No such creature exists!"

"It exists as an abstract—in the way Aristotle used the term. An ideal which some individuals could approach, though few have."

"Who dreamed up the criteria? Who put the scales on that graph? Who decided what was ideal? Some gang of Ultrons? Picking what they'd like to see in their proles?"

I could cope better with Mary cynical than with Mary sympathetic. "If any Ultron besides myself saw it he'd be shocked into stasis! That profile was prepared by Central

Information, using a program written to give unbiased evaluations of newly discovered entities. It takes all the data it can collect and tries to deduce the tasks for which an entity is best suited. It first produces both an ideal and an average profile." I touched a stud and the profile changed. "There, for instance, is the average Galarian profile. It suggests a minor official—which is what most Galarians are."

"That's an average!" objected Mary. "Who cares about an average? The average man can't run a mile in under four minutes. But on Earth there are several who can. It's what those few can do that means something. Not what the average can't do!"

"The criticism I would expect from somebody as unique as yourself! Here's the profile of selected Galarians. It differs little from the average profile you have just seen. The same flat plateau and narrow span. All Galarians are almost identical in their reactions and behavior."

"Which is what makes 'em so useful to your Admins!"

"Exactly!" I switched scans. "And here is the averaged profile of Edrin Humans. Wider than the profile of any race except the Ult. More jagged than any race in the Cluster. But neither as wide nor as jagged as the idealized Human." I brought back the profile I had been studying when Mary arrived.

"Who set the criteria for that ideal?"

"Nobody. The machine let it evolve. The program was developed during the Cluster War to investigate enemy equipment, captured intact but whose purpose was not known. Things like those boarders which nearly killed us. Their designed purposes had to be deduced from their reactions to stimuli."

"Not much doubt about what those killers were after!"

"Their overall purpose was obvious. The means through which they were designed to achieve it were not. Neither were their internal mechanisms."

"Why couldn't you cut 'em open and look?"

"For the same reason you can't tell how a biological brain works by slicing it open. Nor an electronic brain either, for that matter. Moreover military machines are usually designed to explode if improperly dismantled. So Scholars developed programs for nondestructive identification of characteristics. The purpose for which a machine has been designed is reflected in the profile showing its capabilities."

"You mean—like feeding in a frequency and if the input comes out amplified, then you decide the thing's an amplifier?"

"One of the things it was designed to do was amplify. If it still amplified with the same gain and without distortion in a space environment, then it was probably designed to operate in space."

"And you use a program for classifying machines to classify living intellects?"

"A program to classify very sophisticated machines. Machine intellects, if you like." I saw Mary didn't like, but went on, "You've made me uncertain whether there's a real difference between intellect based on a semiconductor substrate and intellect based on a neuron network."

"One is much more durable than the other," *Hyperion* interjected.

"Shut up, ship!" Mary glowered at the screen. Imagon as she was now, she still believed in the superiority of biology over technology. "Humans aren't designed. We're the product of billions of years of evolution. Of adaptation and extrapolation. So what does that profile of your ideal Human imply?"

"I can only show you the description of Human which Central Information derived from the profile. There!"

"Human: A living entity of multiple potentials. Unique in its ability to operate as an isolated individual for comparatively long periods of time and still make decisions between alternatives without having to refer to higher authority. Functions best in small and intermediate sized groups. Large groups of Humans tend to be unstable.

Excellent inter-entity communication with some telepathic potential. Powerful affects which can energize creative and destructive actions. High survival drive in individuals but capability for self-sacrifice given adequate cause. Well-developed esthetic and ethical sensitivity. Strong emotional bonding between individuals and groups. Tendency to xenophobia.

Physical size and strength greater than most ultoids. Able to withstand environmental extremes and physical insult when suitably equipped. Immune to space-sickness. Short-lived but rapid breeding. (Short lives are a survival asset in a rapidly changing environment because blockages to social change are removed as the over-conservative individuals die off.)

Intellectual ability varies greatly between individuals, and in the same individual with changes in situation and biochemical status. Full intellectual potential rarely or never developed. Ability to grasp properly presented abstractions may allow scholarly and artistic creativity. This is amplified by a high, but intermittent, level of intuition.

Military Value: *The above suggests a race with special, but limited, Warrior potential. Excellent skirmishers and competent in small unit tactics. Even the most highly selected are likely to be inept in higher command and strategic planning.*

Summary: *Even the ideal Human is unsuited for Executive or Administrator positions, except those related to spacing. Well-suited to functioning as spacers, especially in fighting ships with whom they will easily identify although they are liable to be resentful of Ult commanders. Some have the intellectual capabilities necessary for a Scholar, but the likelihood of any attaining that rank is small because of their short life span.*

The combination of characteristics outlined above suggests that this race could become extremely dangerous, especially should individual ambitions coalesce into a racial ambition. If properly directed, however, it could provide space personnel of great value during this war.

"What does it mean 'this war?' Mary interrupted. "There isn't any war. At least, not in the Cluster."

"The program that produced that profile and analysis was written during the Cluster War, when there was an acute shortage of crews for fighting ships and of troops to fight on disputed worlds. Written millennia before you Humans arrived."

"So your damned Council is still classifying peoples and things with a program that's out-of-date by thousands of years!"

"I doubt that the program has been used to classify anyone or anything since the Cluster War. Also—it omits three important characteristics of your race."

"Which are?"

"Courage, for one. Neither the virtues nor the vices of a race can be effective if the race described lacks the courage to put them into effect. On this voyage, and down on Earth, I have found that you Humans have more than your share of courage."

"Courage? Maybe!" Mary frowned. "And the others?"

"Curiosity."

"Oh! I was hoping you'd say 'love.' "

"I'm going to. Love—and Hate. They've brought both to a fine art on Earth. You've managed to avoid the worst kind of hates on Edrin."

"Thanks! So we can think, act, and feel!" She continued to study the screen. "What was the point in making up that profile?"

"None. It was made because of the curiosity of one of your descendants. He triggered the program without knowing what he was doing."

"What would have been the point? If you'd done it during the Cluster War?"

"It was used to suggest the jobs for which a race seems to be best suited. I've never asked the program for that. Let's take a look now." I touched a control and the screen lit up.

Recommended Roles for highly selected Humans: Warship crews, Patrols, Spacers, Scouts, Explorers, Missionaries.

"Missionaries!" Mary laughed. "Missionaries of what?"

"The program was written in the Age of Faith. That role is now obsolete."

"No!" *Hyperion* broke in. "Never!"

XXVII

Hyperion hung glowing against the black background of space. Graceful in form, unique in function, a beautiful ship endowed with faculties that she had only developed after a chance meeting with a twelve-year-old girl three centuries ago. An Ult creation, the intellectual equal of any ultoid, but endowed with a stronger faith, a firmer purpose, and a vaster memory. Even, perhaps, with a greater sensitivity. Certainly with an integrity few of us could match.

Was that our true purpose? The reason we ourselves had been created? To create entities greater and better than ourselves as part of some cosmic plan? Was that why creativity was a part of every ultoid profile? At the beginning of the mission I would have laughed at such an idea. A machine, however sophisticated, however great its pseudointelligence, was still a machine built by us, subject to us, and so vastly inferior to us. The concept of creative evolution, that, in the words of Henri Bergson, a Terran philosopher, "The true purpose of the Universe is a machine for making gods," would have seemed ridiculous. An intellectual absurdity!

A concept which might be wrong but which, after over a year living in close contact with *Hyperion*—and Mary Knox—no longer seemed absurd. *Hyperion*'s potential for growth was immense. The only present machine with her abilities, she might be a prototype for the future. For the far future. An evolution which would only occur if directed by generations of ultoids.

The ship faded into another star among the stars as the pinnace arced down toward the rim of the Moon. I lifted my hand in a parting salute, then turned to look at the Earth, coming up ahead.

"Bubble on!" called Sharon from the pilot's seat, and the opaque shroud closed around us. Mark, Martha, and Slammer were aboard to see that I was delivered safely. Mary was there also, silent and invisible; I could sense her presence and feel her support.

We had said good-bye in my suite. An affectionate good-bye with Mary fussing about my preparations as though I was one of her "kids." She was going to miss me; I was going to miss her. But both of us had been too excited by our new futures for much sadness.

Hyperion had summarized my own feelings by misquoting Milton, another poet whose strong iambic pentameters suited her electronic gates. "The world is all before you, where to choose/Your place of rest, and Providence your guide." The ship was preparing a selection of what she considered the finest poetry in the English language for the edification of Humans in the Cluster. She was the first machine I had ever met to have developed her own esthetic taste. A taste which did not always agree with that of human critics.

Mary had also found a new zest in the crew's decision to take advantage of the fact that we would be reported lost, and were free to establish a human society on Fehr. I had been right to show her that human profile. It had renewed her faith in the future of her kids and strengthened her resolve to continue her electronic existence. A resolve which, she had confessed to me, had weakened to the extent that she had previously decided when the voyage was over and she was again alone, to wipe herself and so discover whether there was indeed anything "out there." Now her responsibility to aid in the birth and development of the human settlement had made her postpone that "adventure" until some unspecified time in the future. She had also acquired a sense of responsibility for the Primate's imagon. "The brat's coming out of catatonia and needs reeducation."

The effect of Mary's education on something with the Primate's character had alarmed me, but she had been reassuring. "I managed to steer a gang of human kids in the right direction. I'm sure I'll be able to turn that little creep into something approaching human. Also—well, he knows a hell of a lot about Cluster politics. Useful, if we ever have to come to terms with your Council."

"For God's sake keep the people on Fehr out of Council's clutches!"

"They'll do that for themselves. But I will have to get a hint through about possible Drin remnants. I'll never be able to forgive them for slipping those killer-machines aboard."

"Don't start a pogrom!" I had found it hard to blame a defeated remnant for their attempt to aid distant relatives on Earth.

"Tender concern for your 'Old Enemy'? I wish you were coming along to act as our conscience." She had eyed me. "Why not? Let *Hyperion* store your pattern as she did mine. So you can go on acting as an invisible Adviser. Plant your imagon in Hyperion now!"

"I detest the thought of being alive in one place and having a simulacrum operating in another. Even light-years away."

"*Hyperion*'ll promise not to activate it until long after you're dead." She had seen the shadow on my face and laid her hand on my arm. "Don't be afraid of death, Lucian. After maturity—the older you get the easier it is to die. I speak from experience!"

I had not relished the idea of surviving as an electronic pattern inside *Hyperion* after I was dead but, in the end, I had let her persuade me and my essence was now in the ship. After all, I myself would not be the survivor. And I sensed that Mary wanted me in storage more as an insurance against future loneliness than because she thought my imagon would help her kids on Fehr.

"Ready to go in, Chief?" Sharon's question brought me back to the present. After we had evacuated Deerfields the camouflage had been stripped from lander and pinnace, and I had not thought it worthwile to have either rebuilt for this one landing. So we were going down directly to the mouth of the Deerfields creek, landing in darkness. If we caused a few radar operators to report an odd ghost appearing for a few seconds above the Potomac, that would only feed the UFO literature.

Slammer and Martha were checking my gear. "Plenty of genuine dollars, plus enough gold to set you up in business." Slammer, like most of the crew, assumed that I would go into trade, as any of them would have done if stranded.

"Your identity's ironclad," said Martha, examining my papers for the last time. "U.S. passport, Virginia driver's license with picture, birth certificate, life history. All genuine. Everything to prove you're a responsibile U.S. citizen."

"And your special .38 Smith and Wesson Special, in case you meet any irresponsible citizens," said Mark. "Gun license in your wallet. Also computer access codes and programs. Plus—oh, everything we can think of and that you can carry."

"Over Potomac!" called Sharon. "Snapping bubble!" The

opaqueness vanished and I saw the great spread of lights below. "Spot on!" she added with satisfaction. "Going down now."

She went down fast, and an ionization glow built up around us as she checked short of the surface. I saw the shadowy outline of the Deerfields mansion and the wharf. When we touched down I felt as if I was coming home.

Slammer swung open the hatch. I whispered a mental "Goodbye and good luck" to Mary, and jumped down onto the wharf. I stood there, relishing the scents and sounds of the warm autumn night, the fragrance of moist earth and fall flowers, the rustle of leaves in the light breeze, the murmur of the river. Even the distant hum of traffic. The moon was full, a harvest moon, rising across the river, and as my eyes adjusted I could see the silhouette of the old house, the unkempt garden, the trees fringing the creek. The skies around us glowed from the cities, but here was only a warm darkness.

"Your kit, Boss!" Slammer handed it down and then jumped from the hatch to shake my hand.

"Give 'em an easier ride to Fehr!" I said, gripping his arm.

"I'll pass your orders on to the Skipper!" He clapped me on the back. "You'll do all right, Boss! Might even knock some sense into these clods!" He still had unlimited confidence in an Ultron's power and wisdom.

Martha dropped down beside me and, in a sudden surge of rare emotion, hugged me. "Thanks for letting us go. For not blowing the whistle on Fehr!"

"Just try to make the place work. Keep some kind of vision going in the Cluster. The Net's going to need vision. Sooner or later. Perhaps sooner." I kissed her and gave her a leg up to the hatch. Slammer pulled himself up after her.

First Sharon, then Mark climbed down to say their farewells. They stood together, as though uncertain about how to approach me. Perhaps they were worried about our recent arguments. Perhaps they felt guilty at having planned behind my back.

I was moving to reassure them when two packs came hurtling from the pinnace. The hatch slammed shut. The hull suddenly glowed as the drive came on. It floated for a moment above the surface of the creek, reflected in the dark water. Then it shot upwards in a flash of light. Slammer had not bothered to activate the shroud.

The light blinded me for a moment. When I could see again I saw Sharon and Mark going to pick up their packs.

I stared, then hissed, "What the hell are you two doing?"

Sharon said nothing. Mark shouldered his pack and limped towards me. "Staying with you."

"We're staying!" said Sharon from the shadows. "Maybe with you. Maybe on our own." She faced me in the darkness, keeping her distance, defiance in her voice and attitude. "We've got our own money, our own papers, our own guns. And we've been around long enough on Earth not to knock ourselves amnesic."

"You've deserted? You can't—"

"Not deserted. Saul let us sign off."

"You had this planned? All of you! Why didn't you tell me?"

"Because we knew you'd order us to stay aboard. And you're not the only one qualified to do something for them!" She waved a hand toward Washington.

"Lucian," said Mark. "We're human. We've got responsibilities too. The Humans out there—" he pointed toward the stars, "owe something to the Humans here. We represent the Colony. The Colony should have its reps on Earth. Sis and I decided it must be us."

I stood swamped by a complex of emotions, part-human, part-Ult. This pair had condemned themselves to the groundhog life they despised. These two dedicated spacers had sacrificed their lives to join me on this doomed planet. Sharon would never see her children again. Mark would never take this ship trading onto barbarian worlds. Why?

"Not to be with Your Ultimate!" Sharon spoke as though I had asked the question aloud. "We stayed to be with our own people. So those klutzes in Knoxton will know that at least two Knox were on Earth at the end."

"Not that we believe there's going to be an end," said Mark quickly. "Not for a while, at any rate. And maybe you—" He fell silent.

The pinnace was gone beyond recall. And would not have returned even had I been able to call it. I was no longer the Ultron Adviser. Saul, Martha, Mark, Slammer, even Mary— probably *Hyperion* herself—had known what this pair had planned. And had helped them to achieve it.

There was nothing I could do but accept the situation. And be glad that I was not alone. I picked up my pack and slipped on the shoulder straps. "If you're going to stay with me—then come on! Let's get into the house. Slammer lit up half the neighborhood when he took off. Next thing, we'll have the police coming to check on what's happened."

"Not much chance of that." Mark was limping beside me

rough the overgrown garden, "Too many hush-hush lights ashing in this part of the world for the cops to take an interest."

We walked across the yard to the kitchen door. It was, of ourse, locked. I stood baffled. Locked doors already?

"Spare key's under the brick by the drainpipe!" Sharon's tone mplied that already I was needing her help.

Mark was stooping to get it when a voice came out of the darkness by the bushes. "A chariot of fire!"

Mark straightened. I swung around. Sharon jumped forward. All three of us reaching for our guns. Then I recognized the shadow in the shadows. "Hold it! That's Ches!"

Sharon caught his arm, jerked him forward into the moonlight. "What the hell are you doing here?"

He ignored her violence. He stood looking at us with joy and awe on his face. "Chariot of fire!" he repeated.

"Why are you here, Ches?" Mark asked, easing his sister's hand from the Deacon's arm.

"You came down in a chariot of fire!" Ches was staring at me. "I saw it. You've come back! I knowed you would! I felt you coming. I was waiting for you, Preacher!"

"The rest? Where are the rest?" Sharon was looking around as though every shadow was an ambush.

"The other Faithful?" Ches came out of his apparent trance and straightened his windbreaker. "They've all gone home. I stayed behind to clean up." The light returned to his eyes. "And to greet you when you returned."

"Anbody else waiting to see us return?" demanded Sharon.

"No, ma'am. Just me. But the others will be full of joy when they hear the Preacher's back."

"What did you see?" asked Mark.

"The Preacher and his helpers descending from the heavens in a blazing chariot!" Ches's trance started to return.

"Mark! You're firing him up again!" Sharon did not appreciate being called my helper. "Did you see anything besides the chariot?"

"Too bright for my vision. Just a pillar of fire. Then you three standing on the wharf. Like you used to!" Ches chuckled. "Reckon you'll be wanting a bite to eat after yore trip, eh Preacher? I've got something ready for you, over in my trailer. Beds too! Fixed it all when I felt you coming. Better than the house for tonight. Place needs a good airing. Drains need cleaning too."

I had not been eating much during the past few days. Hot

coffee and a meal were suddenly very attractive. "Thanks, Ches. We appreciate your hospitality."

"Then come along, Preacher!" He turned toward the path through the woods that led to big meadow.

I touched his arm. "One thing, Ches. Please don't call me 'Preacher.' I'm not a Preacher." I was only a confused agnostic.

"Sure!" Ches stopped, puzzled. "What d'you want us to call you?"

"How about Teacher?" Sharon's voice was sardonic.

"Teacher?" Ches rubbed his hands. "Yes—that'll do fine!"

And so it is as Teacher that I am now known.